DRAGONFLY DREAMS

Franki deMerle

Katmoran Publications
www.katmoranpublications.com
www.reincarnationbooks.com

ISBN: 978-1-939484-12-3

Second edition 2013
First edition 2010
Copyright 2010 by Franki deMerle

This is a work of fiction.

Reviews of Dragonfly Dreams

'Shortly before 2:30 AM, Daphne awoke from a vivid dream. She dreamt she was in Scotland and had just been widowed. Her husband had been murdered. It was some distant time in the past, and she was dressed in a long black gown with a stiff white headdress She could feel the tightness of her corset contrast the softness of her gown's material on her skin. Richard was there, but other people in the dream were saying he was responsible for her late husband's murder. She was confused and didn't know what to believe. She had thought she could trust Richard, but a voice in the dream announced, "During the Protestant Reformation, these sides were divided." As she wondered what that meant, Richard captured her and took her against her will to a castle, where he raped her. Then, when he left her alone with a woman companion to look after her, the two women escaped. They disguised themselves as men and used bed linens to climb through a window and down the castle wall. She was terrified. She and her companion rode across the nearby border to England, where they thought they would be safe. At first, when they told their story of what had happened, they were given sanctuary by kind people. But after about a week or so, word came to the household from the authorities that she was to be held as a prisoner again. She did not understand why. Then she was told that Richard had also fled Scotland and was also imprisoned, but in another country.'

"Daphne Robin and her sister Deandra were both accustomed to strange dreams. Deandra has dreamed, since childhood, that she was a soldier with lots of brothers. In her dream she was a man and someone was beating her face in. Daphne's dream about Scotland came shortly after her marriage to Richard Gatorman, owner of a construction company as well as Daphne's boss. Scotland was a place Daphne had always wanted to go to so when the dream coincided with Richard announcing that they would be honeymooning in Scotland, she let her excitement override the possibility of a warning. But, Richard had always been the perfect mate. He was loving, caring and offered her everything she could ever want…so she thought. The honeymoon would turn out to be the beginning of her seeing the true Richard she had married. A marriage that she soon realized had been a big mistake. The only out for Daphne becomes sleep in which her dreams have her flying the skies with a handsome man. If it weren't for her dream time she would probably give up on life itself.

"Deandra, being an officer in the Army, enlists the help of her friend Major Ursa-Barrios to help Daphne escape the abuse being inflicted by Richard. Major, as he likes to be called, has had his own dreams over the years. In his dreams he helps a young lady and falls in love with her. Could Daphne possibly be the woman in his dream? Could Major possibly be the man in Daphne's dreams?

"As Deandra, Daphne and Major come together, they start searching for the answers to their dreams. Deandra wanting to know who the person getting their face bashed in is and who are the brothers. Daphne wants to know who the woman in Scotland could be as well as who she soars the skies with. And Major wants to meet the lady from his dreams.

"Franki deMerle has done it again with a book of mystery, love and a certain air of suspense. The more I read, the more I wanted answers to the character's dreams but I wasn't really expecting what the dreams actually turned out to be. - Martha A. Cheves, Author of Stir, Laugh, Repeat

Franki deMerle is a compelling writer...a bewitching voice ... an enchanted 'take' on reality. – Billy Kravitz, blogger, TV & film writer

Dedication

For dreamers everywhere

DRAGONFLY DREAMS

Franki deMerle

PART I, Daphne
SATIN ISLAND

PART II, The Major
MAJOR PROGRESS

DRAGONFLY DREAMS

Franki deMerle

PART I

Daphne
SATIN ISLAND

Lady Rainbow Goddess
Traveling the sky's night of love
Rabbit dreams of you
Though you're married to the Sun

Your companions skim the lakes
While you control the tides
And in your circling motions
You set the cycle of life

Was it you who hired Ophiucus
To stifle the snake's ego
For boasting to all the other gods
After you gave birth to this world?

Did the Sun know?
Your ever changing form
Silvery wings of light in the night
He slept as it was done

You are a gentle tigress
Prowling the night sky
A sensitive and kind mistress
For the faithful dragonfly

Is it any harder to believe
Than the creation of six days
All we behold born of nothing
From a male having his way

Which is easier to prefer
Which is more likely
For the act of giving birth—
Man or womankind?

Between the archer and the sting
The snake lies penned between
He dares not speak but knows the truth
Not the Sun but the Moon

Dancing above the ocean crests
Flying among the stars
Light reflected in rainbow wings
Of your singing avatars

The surf beats out the rhythm
The wings keep perfect time
And sing the tales of your glory
As you dance across the sky

Chapter 1

Snake in the Pool

There are places we can reach only in our dreams while our bodies sleep. Daphne Robin liked to imagine that these were the places of heaven and hell, the places where one went when one was free of a physical body. Being in a body was more like purgatory. In her dreams she was free to fly. Sometimes she found she could "consciously" control events in her dreams in ways she never could in waking life. She read that this was called lucid dreaming, and that some came by it naturally, while others could be taught to do it. For Daphne it was a natural gift, and it was total freedom.

She had been raised in San Antonio, Texas, in a Catholic family, even though she no longer considered herself Catholic. Her younger sister Deandra, who was now an officer in the United States Army, still attended church, but both of them had begun to explore the more metaphysical side of spirituality while they were still in high school. They had read books from the library, and spent many nights staying up late discussing what they read.

Since early childhood, Deandra had been plagued by nightmares of being a United States Cavalry officer in a fight to the death with Native Americans. The dream always ended the same way—with her own death as she worried about the fate of her brothers. After being startled awake by Deandra's screams, Daphne spent many nights holding her sister, as Deandra cried herself to sleep.

Many times Deandra would ask in her childlike manner, "Where are my brothers? Are they safe?"

Daphne would always answer, "We don't have any brothers. Now shush. It was just a dream."

Sometimes the response came, "My God, they've bashed my face in." Daphne would do her best to reassure her sobbing sister.

Their parents were convinced that bad dreams simply meant the dreamer had eaten food they shouldn't have or watched too much TV. But Daphne and Deandra shared a bedroom, and even little Daphne knew that, to her little sister, there was something very real about her dreams.

The Robin sisters grew up in a poor family, and both couldn't wait to get away from their roots. Both sisters were short and slender. Daphne was an introverted brunette, while Deandra was an extroverted, petite blonde. Deandra was ambitious, but Daphne was content to accept life as it came to her. Deandra joined the Army, got her college degree, and then her commission as an officer. Daphne simply graduated high school and then found jobs doing clerical work—first in Albuquerque, New Mexico, and then in Flagstaff, Arizona.

By 1994, Daphne's latest job was working in the office of a construction company in Corvallis, Oregon, south of Salem. Her job was mundane, but it paid the rent for her one-bedroom room apartment. Corvallis was far enough away from her parents, who still lived in San Antonio, for her to feel independent. They kept asking her how far she was going to run to get away from them, and she kept reassuring them that her moves were about her freedom and seeing other places—not about them at all. Still, every time she moved, she used up what savings she had to make the move and pay for apartment and utilities deposits. It hadn't been easy. When her parents offered to pay for her to come home to visit, she couldn't in good conscience take what little they had. She also couldn't afford to take off from work. She kept promising to visit, but she didn't know how she'd ever manage it. Still, she had enjoyed living in Albuquerque and Flagstaff, and she cherished her independence.

But so far, western Oregon was her favorite place to live. Corvallis wasn't very big, so she could get around easily, and it was an easy drive down Highway 20 to Newport, on the Pacific coast, if she felt like spending a day off at the beach. Meanwhile her sister, Deandra, was stationed in Vancouver, Washington, just across the Columbia River from Portland. Portland wasn't that far from Corvallis. The two sisters took turns visiting each other every other month and talked on the phone a lot in between visits. Deandra got to visit their parents occasionally, as she sometimes had to attend military conferences in San Antonio. She had also offered to pay Daphne's plane fare, so they could travel together to visit their parents, but Daphne needed to work. She didn't get paid for time off, and she was aware that she could be easily replaced.

Daphne's boss, the owner of the construction company where she worked, was anything but mundane. Richard Gatorman was tall, blond, handsome, and rugged. His skin was well-tanned from years of working outdoors, and he had piercing green eyes that seemed to look right into her soul. Daphne liked to fantasize that he was her knight in shining armor, but she wasn't about to ask him for time off. Still, he was easy on the eyes, and she'd never had a steady boyfriend in her life. She'd been shy as a teenager. Dating had always been Deandra's purview.

Daphne had been working for Richard for over six months when he finally asked her to join him for lunch one day. She jumped at the offer. He took her to Ping's, a Chinese restaurant in Albany. Albany was a small town between Corvallis and Interstate 5. In the restaurant's entryway, a poster displayed the Chinese astrological signs with the years ruled by the signs.

"It says here I was born in the year of the snake," she commented.

"Snake, huh?" he responded. "Is that like the biblical snake in the Garden of Eden? You gonna try to seduce me?"

"You want me to?" she flirted.

"Maybe you're more of a snake charmer," he continued without answering her question. "You certainly are a charmer."

Daphne blushed, and just then, the receptionist came to show them to their booth. Once seated, Daphne asked him, "So how do you know about this place?"

"I live just across the highway," he answered pointing north. When the waitress returned to take their orders, he didn't wait for Daphne to respond. "We'll have two egg drop soups and two of my favorite special," he told the waitress.

Daphne raised her eyebrows. "You didn't even ask me," she laughed in surprise.

"I know what's good here," he said, looking straight at her. "Don't worry—you'll like it—it has pork, shrimp, and chicken. It's a chef specialty.

"That poster back there said snakes are clever, intelligent, and make good financial managers and guardians of buried treasure. I guess I hired the right person to mind my shop."

"Glad you did," she smiled back. "So which year were you born in?"

"Huh? Oh, sorry," he answered, "I got distracted looking at those pretty eyes of yours. I was born in the year of the horse."

"I like horses," she replied.

"Horses are social, competitive, and opinionated," he told her. "In other words, I know what I like." The waitress brought the soup.

Daphne enjoyed the meal, the company, and Richard taking care of the check. She was relieved that things were going so well, especially since he was her boss. But she was also very much aware of her inexperience with dating, so she was glad he took the lead. He left a big tip. She took that as a sign of generosity. They began having lunch together whenever he wasn't tied up at a construction site or meeting with clients or suppliers. One morning, several weeks later, he showed up early at her apartment on a work day as she was just getting dressed.

"I thought I'd take you to breakfast," he offered.

She liked the surprise. "I won't be a minute," she said as she grabbed her shoes and purse. Going out with Richard made her feel special. It made her feel feminine and appreciated.

That evening, as she went to leave work, she realized she didn't have her car. She went into Richard's office, held up her keys, and smiled as she shook her head. He understood.

"No problem," he assured her. "We'll grab some dinner on the way home."

She suspected then that he was becoming as serious about her as she was about him. After dinner she invited him in. She was hoping for romance. The first kiss progressed quickly into discarding of clothes and making love. He was her first. Daphne was pleased he stayed the night. She made breakfast the next morning.

As they ate, he said, "We'd better take separate cars today."

"Good idea," she agreed. She didn't mind. It was only practical.

When he mentioned he had errands to run and couldn't have lunch with her, she took advantage of his absence, and called her sister, Deandra, when she went out to grab a sandwich.

"Guess what," Daphne told Deandra, and continued without waiting for her sister to try to guess, "I'm in love. He's tall and handsome and owns his own successful business, and he treats me like a princess."

"Wait a minute," Deandra responded. "This isn't your boss, is it?"

"Yes, it is," Daphne confirmed. "What of it?"

"That's never a good idea," Deandra counseled. "What happens when you two break up?"

"That's not going to happen," Daphne countered. "I just know it. You're jealous."

"How can I be jealous? I've never even met him."

"You know what I mean," Daphne shot back defensively. "You're just jealous because I'm in love and you're not—because I finally found someone. Anyway, I just called to share my good news. Don't be such a wet blanket. I have to get back to work. Bye."

She was disappointed with her sister's reaction, but took comfort in knowing it was just jealousy. Besides, what did logic have to do with love? She took her sandwich back to work and ate at her desk. She was disappointed when she didn't see Richard the rest of the afternoon. She even stayed a little longer than usual, just in case he showed up, but finally locked up the shop and went home.

That evening, he showed up at her door unannounced. She was delighted when he knelt down in front of her open door, held up a beautiful diamond ring in a gift box, and said, "Will you marry me?"

"Yes!" came out of her mouth before she could even comprehend what was happening.

He stood up, put the ring on her finger, and then took her in his arms for a deep, prolonged kiss. "You plan the wedding, and I'll plan the honeymoon," he told her.

"Oh, let's just have a small ceremony with family and any friends you want to invite," she said, as she pulled him inside her apartment and closed the door.

"Works for me," he agreed. "It's just me and my mother. I'll ask Bill, the foreman at work, to be my best man."

"And I'll get my sister to be my bridesmaid," she said, "but I don't want a fancy gown I'll only wear once. I'll buy a pretty dress I can keep and wear again."

"I like the sound of that. There's that charming snake protecting my treasure." He smiled. He couldn't take his eyes off her glowing face.

Richard's mother lived in nearby Philomath, a little town just west of Corvallis, so they arranged a weekend when Deandra and all three of their parents could be there for the wedding. Deandra paid for their mother and father to fly round trip from San Antonio and for the three of them to stay in the Days Inn Motel in Corvallis. The happy couple was married in a civil ceremony in Albany. The family left after the wedding reception, and the couple spent their honeymoon night in their new home, Richard's house, just a few blocks east of the courthouse.

Shortly before 2:30 AM, Daphne awoke from a vivid dream. She dreamt she was in Scotland and had just been widowed. Her husband had been murdered. It was some distant time in the past, and she was dressed in a long black gown with a stiff white headdress. She could feel the tightness of her corset contrast the softness of her gown's material on her skin. Richard was there, but other people in the dream were saying he was responsible for her late husband's murder. She was confused and didn't know what to believe. She had thought she could trust Richard, but a voice in the dream announced, "During the Protestant Reformation, these sides were divided."

As she wondered what that meant, Richard captured her and took her against her will to a castle, where he raped her. Then, when he left her alone with a woman companion to look after her, the two women escaped. They disguised themselves as men and used bed linens to climb through a window and down the castle wall. She was terrified. She and her companion rode across the nearby border to England, where they thought they would be safe. At first, when they told their story of what had happened, they were given sanctuary by kind people. But after about a week or so, word came to the household from the authorities that she was to be held as a prisoner again. She did not understand why. Then she was told that Richard had also fled Scotland and was also imprisoned, but in another country.

She woke up in a sweat. Richard was sleeping deeply beside her. It had been a most disturbing dream, but she knew the only one she could talk to about it was Deandra. Then she realized that Deandra would just tell her the dream meant that she had made a mistake by marrying Richard, and that Deandra had told her so. Daphne lay there thinking about the dream until she drifted back off to sleep.

When she awoke again, Richard was no longer in bed, and she still felt haunted by the previous dream. She wondered how abnormal it was to have a nightmare on her wedding night. She considered that it might be an omen. She wondered if her sister had been right, and if she had made a mistake marrying him.

Just then Richard entered the room with breakfast for both of them on a tray. She was delighted and quickly brushed the dream aside. When she picked up her napkin, she discovered an envelope with plane tickets underneath.

"What's this?" she asked as a big smile spread across her face.

"You didn't think we weren't going to have a honeymoon, did you?" he replied, waiting in anticipation for her reaction.

"Well, I thought we might wait and choose together," she offered.

"No," he corrected her. "The deal was that you handle the wedding, and I handle the honeymoon. Remember?"

But Daphne only heard part of what he was saying as she opened the envelope that held the tickets. "SCOTLAND!" she exclaimed as she read the destination with delight.

"I knew you'd like it," he said confidently. "Castles, the highlands, and far away from here."

Daphne had always wanted to visit Scotland, but now, after having just had a bad dream about it, it was a bit eerie. Still, she was truly delighted, and she let him know it. Maybe she'd find time later to discuss the dream with Deandra—or maybe not. Maybe it was just a dream. She tried to convince herself that's all it was, but deep down inside she suspected otherwise. Richard made her happy. What could go wrong?

Meanwhile she had a trip to get ready for. They were leaving in just two days. They would fly to Boston's Logan airport, where they would change planes for Glasgow. Richard had thought of everything, including a bus and rail pass so they could travel as they pleased. He'd made reservations at an inn called the Auchrannie House in Brodick, a little town on a bay on the Isle of Arran. Later that day, while Daphne packed, Richard drove to a bank in Salem to change some US dollars into British currency.

Chapter 2

Horse Makes a Journey

The layover in Boston was extended due to a delay of the incoming flight that Daphne and Richard were to board for Glasgow. Richard lost himself in the spy novel he was reading, while Daphne restlessly walked around. She'd been sitting on a plane all day and hoped she'd be able to sleep while they crossed the Atlantic Ocean. At one point, she went into the ladies' lavatory and discovered a couple of Scottish women, who were laughing so hysterically that tears were running down their cheeks.

"What's so funny?" she asked them. Her question only prompted more howls of laughter.

Finally one of the women caught her breath and said with a heavy brogue, "Whenever you yanks want somethin' ta work, you give i' a kick." The two of them started laughing heartily again and kept on laughing as they left the lavatory.

Daphne didn't get what the joke was, but she was glad to see that Scots had a hearty sense of humor. But as soon as she entered the toilet stall, she understood. Instead of a handle to flush the toilet, there was a button low down on the wall to push with your foot. Then she laughed too.

The plane finally arrived several hours late. Once on board, Daphne realized she had never been on a plane this size. She was relieved to find their seats were by a window and not in the center of the plane. Richard had no problem going right to sleep, but with children running up and down the aisles while a movie being shown, Daphne couldn't manage to doze off. As they approached their destination, the flight attendant brought warm, wet cloths to help the passengers wake up and wash the sleep from their eyes. There were also customs forms to fill out.

Once on the ground, Daphne found herself having to adjust to being greeted by friendly, soft-spoken people in a different accent. She and Richard went through customs with no problem. Daphne was disappointed when the customs agent didn't even bother to stamp her passport. It was her first time overseas. As he handed it back to her, she asked him if he would please stamp it.

"Oh, it's not necessary, ma'am," he said with a smile and motioned her to move on.

Richard found a taxi to take them to the train station. The train took them west to the coast, where they would meet the ferry to the Isle of Arran.

When they got off the train, the rain was coming down at a forty-five degree angle, due to the strong sea breeze. Richard carried his own luggage, so Daphne thought nothing of him not offering to help with hers. It wasn't far to the ferry station, but by the time they made it, she felt chilled to the bone. Even though it was the middle of June, it felt more like February back home. She wasn't prepared for that, and she found herself thinking about how she could layer the clothes she'd packed to stay warm if this weather turned out to be normal on the island. Fortunately, there was hot chocolate for sale while they waited for the ferry.

The ferry itself was very comfortable. They sat at a booth with a table, and Daphne realized how exhausted she was. She put her head down on the table and dozed off. As she woke up, she heard a woman's voice saying, "Would ya gi' to the lifeboats?"

She awoke with a start, instantly alert and alarmed. Richard was sitting across from her laughing. There was a woman standing next to the booth holding a can labeled "Lifeboat Fund." Daphne was so grateful to realize the ferry wasn't sinking and there was no need to get to the lifeboats, she stuffed a five pound note into the can.

Once they landed on the Isle of Arran, they found there were no taxis or buses on hand to take them to the inn. It all seemed very informal. Richard phoned the Auchrannie House from the ferry station, and about twenty minutes later, a car arrived to pick them up. Daphne's first impression of Scotland was that it was very grey overall, but there were colorful foxgloves and other wildflowers blooming everywhere. Brodick was a delightful little town. The houses they passed had colorful gardens, and some even had palm trees. That was most unexpected. The palm trees were all short and stout—Daphne thought of them as Shetland palms, much like Shetland ponies. Their driver was a very friendly lady, who worked at the inn and talked about how she'd just come back from a holiday in Portugal, where it was sunny.

"So is this weather normal for this time of year then?" Daphne asked her.

"Oh yes, of course," she answered.

"So summer is always this chilly?" Daphne responded in surprise.

"Oh no," the driver shook her head. "Summer doesn't begin here until July."

"We're a bit further north here," Richard explained as if he wasn't also surprised by the weather. Daphne noted to herself that he had also packed summer clothes.

The Auchrannie House was lovely. It was like a very large house with a homelike atmosphere and hallways and stairs that twisted and turned until Daphne was convinced she'd never find her way out again. Once they were inside their very comfortable room, she collapsed on top of the featherbed, sinking down deep and warm.

"It's just as well I have no idea how to get back to the front door," she told Richard, "I don't think I want to get out of this bed until it's time to go home."

"You just stay there," he agreed. "I'm going to wash up." He disappeared into the bathroom. Daphne's eyes closed.

He woke her in time for dinner. She dressed and they went to the casual dining room together. Over fish and hot tea, he told her, "There's a castle not far from here. It's appropriately called Brodick Castle, and you can take a bus to get there." He handed her a brochure.

"Oh, this looks wonderful," she responded as she glanced over the brochure. "The castle has been added onto over the centuries, so it will be like taking a trip through time. And the grounds are full of botanical specimens from all over the world. Maybe that's how they came to have palm trees here. And if you follow the walking trail, there's a waterfall in one direction and some standing stones in another."

"Good," Richard commented. "Glad you're interested."

After dinner, they went back to their room. Richard kicked off his shoes and laid down on the featherbed while Daphne slowly and purposefully unbuttoned and removed her blouse and then her bra. Seeing she had his undivided attention, she slipped off her shoes, jeans and panties.

"Is this leading somewhere?" he asked, as she began to undress him. She just smiled. Once all his clothes were off, she climbed onto the bed and straddled his groin…

The next morning Daphne awoke to find herself alone in the bed. She wandered into the bathroom expecting to find her husband there, but it was empty. She turned on the tub faucet to take a bath, but she was surprised when the water came out green. She turned off the tap, and had just gone back into the bedroom to use the phone, when she found a note from Richard next to the phone that read,

"I thought you'd want to see Brodick Castle, so I took the ferry to the big island. Then I plan to take the train into the highlands. Be back in time for dinner.

"Love,
Richard"

Now she was fully awake. *Why did he pick up the brochure if he didn't want to see the castle?* She thought. *Isn't this supposed to be our honeymoon?*

Then she remembered the green bath water and why she had intended to use the phone. The pleasant voice at the front desk assured her that green was the normal color of the water on the island, and that it was perfectly safe to bathe in.

"Thank you," Daphne said and hung up the phone. *Ok. Green baths and a single honeymoon in a foreign country. Well, at least they speak English.* She went back to the bath, ran the tub full, and then noticed there were no washcloths. *Whatever. I'll ask at the desk when I leave to visit the castle BY MYSELF.* She slipped into the tub. She was pleasantly surprised to discover the green water was very soft. As she splashed it onto her already wet face, it merged with her tears.

She dressed in layers for warmth, and then stopped at the front desk, once she managed to find it again, after getting completely turned around in the maze of hallways. There the sweetly smiling desk clerk softly informed her, "Wash cloths are personal items, and so they're not provided by the inn. But they can be purchased at numerous shops in town."

"How odd," Daphne responded.

"Oh, not at all," the lady told her, still smiling pleasantly, "That's how it's done here."

Daphne went to the breakfast room and ate alone. She took a bite of what she thought was ham, only to discover she had no idea what it was by taste. She asked a server if it was meant to be ham and learned that it was bacon. Daphne realized bacon must be cut and cured differently on this side of the Atlantic. *Ok, this is closer to Canadian bacon,* she realized. She wished she had Richard with her to discuss all these cultural differences. Instead, she left her breakfast unfinished before the tears came pouring down again.

As she walked through the little town of Brodick, the fresh, brisk air helped her compose herself. She stopped in a pastry story and bought herself something sweet to fill her empty stomach. Then she stopped in a gift shop and bought two washcloths. She briefly considered only buying one, but quickly rejected the idea. It was, after all, her honeymoon.

Back out on the street, Daphne noticed as she walked down the sidewalk that many cars parked on the street had the keys left in the ignition, like they were just waiting for someone to get in and drive them away. Then she realized it was just part of life on this island, where the only access was by ferry, and the people who worked on the ferries lived on the island. The ferry workers probably knew which cars belonged on their island, as well as to whom they belonged. Brodick was the biggest town on Arran and the only ferry port, and it was a very small town. The cars were perfectly safe left unlocked with their keys in them in plain view. *How nice to have that freedom*, she thought.

She managed on her own to find the bus to the castle. After a short bus ride, she walked up the long drive to the castle itself and paid for the tour. The cell where Robert the Bruce had once been chained to the wall was dark and creepy, but as she moved forward in time through the castle's additions, things became more cheerful. By the time she had finished the tour and was back outside, she began walking the grounds. She had forgotten the peculiarity of her situation and was actually enjoying herself and the scenery. The grounds were truly lovely. She saw trees she'd never seen nor heard of before, even though she came from a part of the world known for its trees. She especially enjoyed the Himalayan Magnolia, and all the different varieties of rhododendrons in full bloom made her feel at home.

She found and followed the path up the side of a steep hill to the waterfall. The peacefulness of the place made her forget everything else. She stayed a while, enjoying the view and the sound of bubbling water falling down the hillside. She laughed to herself when she realized the waterfall at least wasn't green.

Then she made her way back down the hillside and followed the path and the map on the brochure to the standing stones. By this time, the path had widened into a paved driveway, and the stones were on either side of it. Daphne realized the giant stones were now standing on private property and that she was now standing on someone's private road. She could see the gates to it up ahead with the "Private" sign posted, but she was already on the inside, and no one else was around, so she took her time. The stones were massive—like sentinels standing guard throughout time. It occurred to her that, with the rain usually blowing at varying angles according to the wind from the sea, instead of falling straight down, all one had to do to stay dry was to stand on the opposite side of the stone from the direction of the wind and rain. She mused that maybe it was the true purpose of the stones. Laughing to herself about it, she headed back to the Auchrannie House.

Richard was waiting for her in the room when she returned from her day out. "Where have you been?" he asked impatiently. "I told you I'd be back for dinner. You kept me waiting, and I'm hungry."

"I had a wonderful day," she answered. "Thank you for asking." The palm of his hand slapping her face was completely unexpected.

"You're my wife, and you NEVER talk back to me," he informed her. "What's in that bag?" he demanded. "What did you waste money on?"

She meekly opened the bag to show him as tears streamed down her face. "The inn doesn't provide them," she explained. "You have to bring or buy your own." She was relieved she had bought two.

"Yeah, that's what they told me too," he admitted with a much calmer voice. "Let's get something to eat. I'm starving," he said, as if everything were completely normal. He turned around and headed out the door into the hallway.

As she rushed out the door behind him, Daphne used one of the washcloths to dry her face, hurriedly tossing it into the bathroom sink as she passed it. She would have preferred staying in the room, but she was also hungry and afraid she'd get lost in the twisting hallways again. Over dinner, they discussed their days—his on the train in the highlands and hers exploring the castle, grounds, waterfall, and standing stones.

The next morning, the couple woke up together and ate breakfast together. This time Richard explained to Daphne the different methods used in curing bacon in the United States and United Kingdom. Daphne listened politely. She realized her new husband needed to feel superior to her by sounding like an expert. She also feared saying anything that might challenge his feeling of superiority. She wasn't sure if his change of personality was due to crossing the ocean and all those time zones or their recent change of marital status, but she was frightened by it.

"There's a standing stone circle on the far side of the island I'd like to see," she told him, knowing full well he'd think it a waste of time. "There's a bus that circles the island on the road along the coast. I thought it would be a scenic ride. This is a beautiful island, and I'd like to see more of it."

"You go right ahead," he answered. "I'm going back to the big island to find a decent golf course and, hopefully, someplace I can rent a set of clubs. After all, this is Scotland, home of the sport."

"Ok," she agreed with a smile. "We'll meet for dinner, but I can't promise when I'll be back. Everything depends on the bus schedule, and apparently here on this island, the buses only run when they appear to have a need, or the drivers feel like leaving, or whatever—I haven't figured it out yet, but it's very laid back. I kind of like it. So, if you get back and get hungry, you go ahead and eat without me. I'll be back when I'm able to get back."

"I'm taking a ferry to Great Britain," he answered in a tone of voice that expressed his lack of amusement, "then a train to God knows where, maybe all the way across to Edinburgh, playing golf, and coming all the way back. You're staying here on the little island, taking a bus ride around it, and you can't meet your husband in time for dinner?"

"It's not such a small island when you go around the circumference of it," she responded defensively but cautiously. "I only wanted to be sure you didn't go hungry—just in case."

"Well, then, sweetie, I appreciate that." He smiled as he reached across the table and cupped her chin in his hand.

They finished eating and went their separate ways. Daphne enjoyed the peaceful bus ride and the beautiful scenery. She got off the bus on the west side of the island at Machrie Moor. Following the bus driver's kind directions, she made her way on foot across the moor. She was aware of all the sheep and careful of where she stepped, so it was slow going. The last thing she needed was Richard getting angry at the smell of her shoes. Not only was there sheep dung, the moor itself was uneven, full of holes and pockets in the ground. She'd never walked on a moor before. Daphne felt she was having a real adventure. Her spirits soared when she realized it was actually the summer solstice. Somehow, knowing it was a special day made it all seem magical.

She found the ring of stones with the cairn in the center. At first, she just took it in visually. Then she walked around it in reverence, thankful the drizzle of rain that had been coming down all morning had finally stopped. After walking completely around, she stood on the west side of the circle looking toward the east and up at the sky. She didn't expect anything unusual. The sun was almost at its zenith in the sky. As she looked up she saw a rainbow to the south. It was beautiful. Here she was alone on her honeymoon out on a moor, but she was perfectly happy. It was the summer solstice, she'd found a ring of standing stones in the middle of a moor, and there was a rainbow in the sky. To Daphne, this was truly a special moment worth remembering. She felt as if everything in the universe was in its proper place—including her. She marveled at how much the light of the sun and moon would have meant to the people who built this circle, and wondered what life had been like for the person or persons whose remains were buried in the cairn.

She turned around and looked out across the moor to the west toward the sea. The colors all appeared soft. The moor looked like green satin and the sea was a silky grey. Daphne savored the moment and the view. She liked the thought that this island was made of green satin. She wished for a moment that she could live on an island like this. Then she brushed the thought aside by imagining how isolated she might feel if she got her wish.

She waited for the rainbow to fade before leaving. She made her way back across the moor to the road and decided to start walking north along the road rather than wait for whenever the next bus might come along. She had a good long walk, breathing in the sea air, before a bus stopped alongside her. It was the same bus driver she'd had before, and she gladly took the lift to a teahouse on the north side of the island. Along the way, the driver pointed out some castle ruins that once housed Robert the Bruce.

The teahouse was small, but warm and welcoming. She ordered some tea and a scone. A couple of other people came in with their golf clubs and sat at another table. She listened to their conversation about how many golf balls they had each lost on the moor and in the sea. Daphne gathered from their conversation that they played golf just about anywhere. *Well, of course they do,* she thought. *These are true Scots—not Yanks, like Richard out looking for a proper course.*

After her tea and scone, she went out to the road and continued her trek back toward Brodick. Right on cue, the bus arrived. Again it was the same driver, and this time he pointed out some larger standing stones south of the road on the hillside. She felt like she had her own personal tour guide. She arrived back in Brodick in plenty of time to visit the shops, buy some postcards, and learn about the many World War II pilots that had crashed into the mountain on the island due to fog and bad weather. She arrived back at the Auchrannie House before Richard. She guessed he'd be deliberately late, so she left a note in their room for him:

"My dearest Richard,

"I'm waiting patiently for you in the casual dining room. Please, feel free to take as much time as you need to freshen up before dinner.

"Your wife,
Daphne"

By this time, Daphne had deciphered the room directions posted throughout the inn. She was able to find her own way to the dining room.

Chapter 3

Dog Opens the Door

On board the plane flying back across the ocean, Richard turned to Daphne and said, "When we get back home, you won't be working any more." When she looked surprised he added, "No wife of mine needs to work."

Daphne smiled. "Thank you," she said, thinking he was trying to make up for everything he'd done wrong so far.

When they arrived at Boston's Logan Airport, Daphne was amazed at just how noisy people were in the States compared to the soft-spoken Scots. She preferred the Scots and was very grateful she'd gotten to visit their beautiful country. It wasn't the honeymoon she'd dreamed of or expected, but she had a wonderful time when Richard had left her alone.

Once they were home, he kept his word. Daphne worked only until a new office clerk was hired. Then she settled into her new role as home-keeper. She still had her own car and bank account of what she'd managed to save, such as it was. Richard gave her an allowance for groceries and extra money for shopping, as he needed her to buy things for him.

Daphne sugar-coated the stories of her honeymoon for her parents and sister on the phone, but Deandra expressed the opinion that not working was a bad idea. "Two incomes are always better, unless you're already pregnant," Deandra suggested.

"No, I'm not pregnant," Daphne responded emphatically. "He said I didn't have to work, and I took him up on it."

"Well, as long as it's not because he told you he didn't want you to work," Deandra conceded. "But if something happens and you have to go back to work, you don't have to work for Richard."

"What difference does it make?" Daphne responded defensively.

"You're kidding, right? It's a really bad idea to work for your husband. And a man who tells you he doesn't want you to work is controlling you. That's bad news. Controlling leads to abusing. He hasn't ever hit you, has he?"

"Of course not," Daphne lied.

"Good," her sister sounded relieved. "If he ever does, you get away from him as fast as you can and report him to the police."

"Deandra, he's my husband, and we just got back from our honeymoon. Now quit worrying." After they finished talking, Daphne thought about Richard slapping her. She quickly dismissed it as the stress of having just gotten married and traveled across so many time zones, even though she was the one who wasn't able to sleep on the plane. Still, it was in the past.

A few weeks after Daphne had stopped working, Richard came home one day and told her, "Close your eyes and wait until I tell you to open them. I have to go get something out of my truck. It's a surprise."

She closed her eyes and waited patiently, wondering what sort of surprise it would be. She heard the door open and close, and then a couple of minutes later, it opened and closed again.

"Ok," Richard told her, "you can open your eyes now."

When she did, she saw he was holding a guitar case in one hand and a stack of music books in the other. "These are for you," he said.

She was ecstatic. She opened the case, which was a hard shell lined with velvet, and picked up a beautiful

Spanish guitar with nylon strings. "I've always wanted to play classical guitar!" she exclaimed. "It's beautiful!"

"And in tune," he added. "I seemed to remember you telling me something about wanting to play when you first came to work for me."

"You remembered. But where can I get lessons?" she asked.

"You won't need them," he said as he set the stack of music down in front of her, pulling a DVD from somewhere inside the stack and setting it on top. "You have everything you need right here."

"And lots of time to practice," she added. "Oh, thank you, Richard."

"Anything for you," he told her. "When you learn to play, you can play me to sleep when I'm tired."

"A captive audience," she smiled. From then on, the days, weeks, and months flew by as she struggled to learn to read the music and learn increasingly more difficult pieces. There were pictures in the beginner book showing the correct hand and finger positions, and the DVD helped her fill in the gaps. She had a natural feel for the music, and she'd always been especially fond of Spanish music. After several months, she really was able to keep her promise and play her husband to sleep when he was tired from work.

Right before Thanksgiving Day, Daphne tried to surprise her husband at work by bringing a large casserole and several pumpkin pies for the workers. Richard was out at a construction site when she arrived. She was greeted by her replacement, Judy, who helped her set a table for the workers for when they came into the office. Daphne took advantage of Richard's absence to ask about the workers she hadn't spoken to since she had quit working.

"You know about Carlos, of course," Judy began.

"No," Daphne corrected, "is he ok?"

"Oh, no," Judy told her. "His hand was crushed a few months ago in an accident on site. It happened right after you stopped working. You know he used to play guitar very well, but the accident put an end to that. How could you not know? He gave Richard his guitar and music to give to you. He remembered you'd said you wanted to learn to play. Did Richard not give you the guitar and music?"

Daphne stared at her in disbelief. "That's Carlos' guitar?" was all she could manage to say.

"Of course," Judy said. "How did you not know?" she repeated.

"So, is Carlos able to work?" Daphne asked, trying to steer the conversation away from the guitar out of embarrassment that she hadn't known it was his guitar.

"No, he's been on workman's compensation and getting some sort of training to help him work in some other area. His wife went to work at a dry cleaner shop. They take turns with the children."

"I had no idea," Daphne said, feeling ashamed of not knowing. "Just tell everybody I dropped off the food, and don't mention our conversation—especially to Richard." With that, she left quickly.

Carlos had been very courteous and helpful to her when she had first started working there. He had even taught her some phrases in Spanish, which was very helpful when talking to the other Latino workers. The thought of him being injured was bad enough, but she had to wonder what he must have thought of her never visiting, calling, or even sending flowers or a card. He must have thought her ungrateful for such a fine and precious gift. How could Richard have given her the guitar and music and let her think he had bought them for her? By the time she got home she was in tears. She loved her guitar and loved playing. She sat down on the floor of the living room, picked up the guitar, and hugged it as she cried. She felt so ashamed enjoying the instrument as a result of Carlos' personal tragedy. She wanted to call him and his wife and apologize, but she was just too ashamed. She was afraid if she told them the truth, it would get back to Richard. She just didn't know what he would do then—to her or the guitar.

By the time Richard came home from work, she had put the guitar away, washed her face, and busied herself in the kitchen making dinner. He thanked her for the surprise delivery at the office, but assured her it wasn't necessary to feed his employees.

"Well, it was just kind of spontaneous," she explained, even though she'd been planning it for over a week, "but if you don't want me to, I won't do it again."

"It's better if you don't," Richard told her. "Better not to start something they might come to expect."

"That's true," she said in a flat voice. She continued to pretend she didn't know what had happened with Carlos and the guitar. She also didn't mention to him that her period was almost three weeks late.

The following week she went to a walk-in clinic in Corvallis, where she learned she was pregnant. *Maybe this will change things,* she thought. She waited until the next morning to tell Richard.

"I have something special to tell you," she said cheerfully over breakfast. "I waited until you had a good night's sleep."

He looked up with a sudden scowl on his face. "What did you do?" he demanded.

"Relax," she told him. "This is good new—happy news. And it's more a matter of what we did. I'm pregnant." She smiled broadly. "We're going to be parents."

He stared at her in silence, his face like a blank stone she couldn't read.

"I'm going to have your baby," she told him. "Aren't you happy?"

"I let you stay home and not work, even got you a guitar to keep you happy, and this is how you repay me—with another mouth to feed?" He stood up and grabbed his jacket. "Great. This is just great," he complained angrily as he walked out of the house.

Daphne felt like the bottom had fallen out of her world, and she had fallen with it. She didn't know what to do. She wanted the baby, but without Richard she had no income. *How could he not want his own baby?* She spent the day sitting on the sofa crying.

As she sat there, she recalled the disturbing dream she'd had on her wedding night—the dream where she was in Scotland and Richard had murdered her husband. Just by thinking about it, she recalled the feel of the stiff white headdress, the tightness of her corset, and the softness of her black gown on her skin. She remembered how Richard had taken her prisoner and raped her. She recalled how he had then fled the country, and how she had been imprisoned again after escaping from him. She wondered why she had not heeded the warning of the dream and left him right then. But she couldn't possibly have understood. She still didn't understand.

She remembered the first time he took her to lunch at Ping's restaurant. He was born the year of the horse, and she was born the year of the snake. She wondered how she managed to miss the likelihood of a horse trampling a snake. She realized his rages were very much like a herd of stampeding horses running her down. When Richard came home from work, Daphne was still sitting on the sofa in a daze.

When he went into the kitchen and saw that the breakfast dishes hadn't even been removed from the table, much less dinner started, he went ballistic. Daphne heard him yelling and heard the crash of dishes being thrown across the kitchen. She was aware of him hitting her and tried to protect her abdominal area and the baby. By the end of his rage, he went to bed ordering her to clean up the mess. She did. She felt like she was watching herself go through the motions without actually feeling anything. Then she caught a couple of hours of sleep on the sofa.

After Richard left for work the next day, Daphne miscarried. She called his office and left a message on his phone that the baby had died. After her miscarriage, she managed day to day by going through the motions of pretending to be married, while finding solace playing her guitar. Eventually she started frequenting the public library. Reading was an escape that cost no money.

Daphne wanted to talk to her sister on the phone. She wanted to tell Deandra about her problems, but she was simply too ashamed of her situation to share it. And Deandra had been so judgmental of Richard. Daphne didn't want to be reminded how wrong she had been. She admired Deandra for finding a way through her army service to complete her college education. She saw her sister as successful, and she saw herself as a total failure. Deandra was a US Army officer, while Daphne couldn't even manage the one gift so precious and unique to her gender— to give birth to life. She had failed at independence, marriage, and womanhood. On top of that, she was living in constant fear with a man she no longer trusted.

Daphne hated that she had taken Richard's name. She hated the name Gatorman, because it represented him and because it was ugly and masculine compared to her maiden name, Robin. *What an irony,* she thought. *I'm a robin that's been eaten alive by an alligator.*

Then one night when she was feeling particularly lost, alone, and vulnerable, much to her surprise, something wonderful happened.

Chapter 4

Rabbit Dreams of the Moon

Daphne was sound asleep when a man arrived in her dream with a warm, orange glow about him, like a fireball of warmth and energy, and he was smiling the warmest smile she had ever encountered. To say she was attracted to this dark-haired, olive-skinned creature like a moth to a flame didn't begin to describe it. He was somehow intimately familiar to her. Before she knew what was happening, she was flying along at his side, too fast for feet to keep up, much less touch the ground, and with no effort.

They were flying fast above houses and trees, and as they left the planet further and further beneath and behind them, it seemed they were flying on the wings of pure harmonious sound. It seemed it was the vibration that was propelling them. Daphne felt like her body had turned into pure harmonic vibration, and together they flew on the same wavelength until they were soaring among the stars beyond the solar system.

Daphne found herself dreaming of this angel and flying with him almost every night. Sometimes he appeared to her in a silvery light with bright white hair, but most of the time he was dark surrounded by light. One night, he sang to her as they flew, and he truly had the voice of an angel, but somehow she sensed he was a real man. She didn't know how she knew this, but then she didn't know how any of this was happening or why. They were out among the stars, and she was weightless and totally burden-free. He flew around her in circles as he sang, and as he flew, he left a trail of shimmering, iridescent light, until finally, he himself had turned into a shining, sparkling silver dove. And then they made love out in the stars. It was as if their minds and hearts had merged, and they had joined their very souls together. He was like a dove made of pure moonlight. They shared their thoughts and beings. There were no secrets between them.

The dreams continued night after night—not every night, but often enough that she was eager to fall asleep at night just so she could meet him again, and she was extremely disappointed on the nights when she didn't dream about him. While awake, she fantasized about him. She wondered if it was possible that he was actually a real person somewhere, but then she also couldn't imagine that he couldn't be real. Somehow she just knew—or maybe it was necessary for her to believe he was real just to continue with her life. Seeing him in her dreams—being with him— gave her hope that her life wasn't a total failure. She held firmly to the belief that somehow, somewhere they would find each other in waking life. It was imperative that she believed in him, because as long as he was real, she could believe she was lovable. He and the dreams made her feel very, very special.

The dreams of him were more vivid than any she could ever remember. They felt more real than the real world when she was awake. She wondered if she had lost her mind, but all her senses seemed more alive than ever before, so she decided it was better to be crazy and in love with a dream than sane without any hope for her own future. In her mind, she lived in her dream world, while going through the motions with her body in the waking world. Mostly now she stayed home and took care of Richard's needs. When Richard wanted sex, she pretended he was her dream lover, even though Richard was only into satisfying himself. Richard, of course, didn't have a clue what was going on inside her head. But it worked for her, and he was none the wiser. The rest of the time, especially while practicing guitar, she was with her dream angel in her mind. She knew she had fallen in love with a dream. There was no way she could return to life as she had known it before, nor did she want to. She was addicted to the emotional high she experienced when she was with her dream angel. It was all she had to look forward to, and she became obsessed with her dreams and her dream lover. She told no one. She knew anyone else who hadn't experienced falling in love with someone in a dream wouldn't understand. They'd just think she was crazy. Maybe she was, but it was ok with her.

During her less emotional moments, she considered that maybe her dreams were just balancing out her miserable waking state. Maybe it was just a survival mechanism to keep her from falling so far into despair she might hurt herself, but if that were the case, it worked. And if it worked, it wasn't something she should try to change.

She also tried to analyze the dreams for symbolism. It had been years since she had dreamed of flying—so long that she had forgotten. Flying could symbolize rising above her difficulties. Music was an emotional high for her. Maybe she unconsciously wanted to be a star musician, but that wasn't likely to happen. She only played at home, had no idea how to go about finding places to play for a living—even if she believed she could make a living playing classical guitar—and Richard would kill her if she tried. She couldn't exactly appear in front of an audience with bruises. Knowing him, he'd break her fingers. Well, no wonder she was depressed before the dreams came along. And now she had hope. She also noticed there were roses and Christmas trees everywhere in the dreams, regardless of the waking season. Richard never brought her flowers. Christmas was a time of giving gifts. The dreams, and her dream lover, were a gift to her.

The beautiful dreams continued as months and years passed. Daphne began reading everything she could find in the library and online about dream symbolism, which led to the writings of Carl Jung and the collective unconscious, as well as books on lucid dreaming and other cultures around the world.

She remembered learning about lucid dreaming in her youth. She also recalled that as a young child, her sister had nightmares where she had been killed as a United States Cavalry officer. And yet, Deandra had grown up to be a successful US Army officer. Why had things not worked out for Daphne?

Her dream lover played violin sweetly for her. His violin had the voice of pure light. When Daphne heard it, she was lifted far above the ground itself until the Earth had fallen away beneath her, and she was sailing through the stars on the vibration of silver light. It was the voice of his violin that called to her, a voice that found her and singled her out—it was the sound of his violin that gave her wings, and she flew with him. She loved him with all her being. This love was nothing like anything she had ever felt for Richard when she thought she had fallen in love with him.

The continued recurrence of the dreams was extraordinary. Her dream lover wasn't a character in a movie or book. In her mind, he simply had to be real. Somewhere, she rationalized, lived a real man who had come to Daphne in her dreams and truly loved her. He was out there somewhere, and he had reached out to her when she most desperately needed to feel loved. Somehow, there was a way that transcended the known laws of physics and the perceived laws of time and space—a way by which two souls could reach out to each other and connect without being in each other's physical presence. It was lucid dreaming, the Dreamtime, the collective unconscious, or whatever, but it was real love that she had never before experienced.

Daphne probably didn't have to focus quite as hard on the sound of his voice, the sparkling silver light, the vibration of his violin, and the flying sensation as she did while falling asleep every night, because the same man was usually waiting for her when she started to dream. They made love in the stars, and she was amazed that he was pleased with her less-than-perfect body in the dreams. His was in excellent condition, strong and fit. He smiled at her, and she knew she was loved and accepted. In his presence, she knew none of her mistakes and flaws mattered. He accepted her as she really was. Before the dreams, she had come to believe that wasn't possible.

When she was awake, she began to pretend she was speaking to him instead of Richard. When her husband relentlessly criticized her, she reminded herself that the man in her dreams loved her just the way she was. She imagined she could feel his presence there protecting her, but she knew she was fantasizing. She knew he wasn't really there, nor could he protect her from Richard's occasional fits of rage. Still, it was a comforting fantasy. Daphne was fully aware of the difference between her dreams and her fantasies, but they made her life livable. She held onto the hope that love had really come to her in the night and swept her away.

She searched online for information on lucid dreaming, which she reasoned was the necessary conveyance for two-way communication in the collective unconscious. Much had been written elaborating on and muddling the practical application, but Daphne sifted through it. She was on a mission to master this new form of communication. She wanted to be able to communicate her name and location to her dream lover, so he could find her. She believed it was possible.

Her quest led her to a conversation between the late scientist, Nikola Tesla, and an Indian, Swami Vivekananda. Tesla and Vivekananda were discussing Prana, the Vedantic life force, and the Swami told Tesla that Prana was produced by the universal mind. Tesla responded that it could be "proved mathematically by demonstrating that force and matter are reducible to potential energy."

Daphne was intrigued, not only by the concept of the universal mind, but also by the scientific perspective that could back it up. She read that many scientists of the late nineteenth and early twentieth centuries had dabbled in what was called spiritualism.

The persistency and consistency of her dreams persuaded her otherwise rational mind that her dream lover was physically real, and somehow she had made a connection with a real man somewhere and in such a way that she never had known to be possible and couldn't explain—in a way that conventional society would only laugh at. But the dreams were so vivid and seemed so real, believing in them made her otherwise difficult life enjoyable again. She had given up control over her waking life, but she could fly in her dreams. It was a place where Richard couldn't find her or even find out about. She was supposed to be a snake, but she felt more like a scared rabbit in the daytime, remaining hidden, while keeping her secrets to herself, and then becoming a silver bird in flight at night—her escape. She, the snake, had found a way to safely leave her hole.

As time passed, she gradually felt less ashamed of confiding the truth about Richard to her sister. Deandra urged Daphne to leave him immediately, and offered to let Daphne stay with her, but Daphne wasn't ready. It was still her life. She had made her own mistakes, and she was determined to find a way to live with the result of her choices. Maybe she was just afraid, or maybe she wanted to find her own way out. Since the onset of her dreams, Daphne had given up dealing with her physical reality.

*

Several years passed. During that time, Deandra had been reassigned for a couple of years to an army unit in Texas, closer to their parents, before moving back to

Vancouver Barracks in Washington. Daphne took one day and one night at a time. As best she could tell, Richard was totally unaware of who she was. As best she could tell, he only paid attention to himself. As long as she was able to avoid provoking him, she was safe, but sometimes the most ordinary things unexpectedly brought out the monster in him. Still, she clung to her private dreams of someday being rescued by her dream lover.

She often thought back with regret about how much more confident she had been before marrying Richard. She remembered the independence she had once cherished but given up for what she had mistaken for love. She remembered how her former sense of independence had enabled her to salvage an otherwise disastrous honeymoon. But that was years ago. Now she was walking on eggshells with the man she had married, while longing to be rescued by a dream.

One day Deandra called her on the phone. "I have terrible news," Daphne's sister informed her.

"What's happened?" Daphne asked, suddenly paralyzed with fear of the unknown.

"It's Mom and Dad," Deandra explained. "They were in a car crash with a truck." Deandra paused. Daphne held her breath. Deandra continued, "They were both killed instantly. I need you to drive up to my place. We have to fly down to San Antonio to take care of the funeral arrangements and their possessions."

"I'll drive up tomorrow," Daphne answered, afraid to leave without Richard's permission.

"No, you need to come up now," her sister corrected her. "I've booked us on a flight that leaves tomorrow morning."

After she hung up, Daphne called Richard on his cell phone. In the past, he'd made it clear to her that she was never to interrupt him at work by calling, but this was different. When he didn't answer, she was very relieved.

She left a voice message for him explaining what had happened, and that she didn't know how long she'd be gone. She knew he'd never take off work just for her parents, but she also knew there would be hell to pay when she got back.

She called him that night from Deandra's house. Much to her surprise, he wasn't upset. "Just call me every evening, and let me know how it's going," he instructed her.

"Well, of course," Deandra said sarcastically after Daphne had ended the call, "he's not upset, because I'm paying your way, and you've just agreed to check in with him every night like he's your parole officer instead of your husband."

Daphne held her tongue. She was too emotionally drained from years of having been beaten down—literally and figuratively. She knew her sister was right, but first they needed to deal with burying their parents. Then they needed to take care of their parents' property. Daphne's mind was on how she hadn't seen her parents since the day she married Richard, and now she never would. But still, she dutifully called Richard every night on Deandra's phone until they returned home.

PART II

The Major

MAJOR PROGRESS

The soldier is confident
He has liberated the oppressed
Who are forced to welcome the armed
The working people who have no other choice
But to cater to egos to survive

The soldier projects himself
Onto his enemy
Any guilt he carries
Any harm done inadvertently
Becomes that of the enemy

To be able to learn how to kill
The soldier must truly believe
The perception others drill
Into his very being
He dares not question authority

This is a choice we all must make
Will we question or follow blindly?
Will we remain open to what our senses say
Or relinquish free will randomly?
Will we allow ourselves to project a movie
Or live each moment consciously?

Chapter 5

Breaking Ground

Major Ursa-Barrios woke from a strange dream. All the missile silos in the United States of America had been invaded by a fungus. He wondered what might happen if the fungus penetrated a nuclear warhead, and if the radiation might cause a mutation.

He stood up and stretched his brown, five-foot seven-inch frame. After a quick glance at his tousled black hair, he threw on some jeans and a sweatshirt and walked into the kitchen. He looked at the dirty dishes in the kitchen sink from last night's dinner and wondered if he had eaten too many mushrooms. They were very tasty, marinated in ginger and soy sauce and then sautéed in butter. Maybe he should have eaten earlier in the evening. Still it was a sweet thought that a lowly fungus could undermine the world's most paranoid egos. Probably, he was just dreaming about having left the military behind. That was a sweet thought too. After all, he had served in the latter part of the US Cold War with the Soviet Union and after. Or maybe his unconscious felt the continuing expansion of the military was like a fungus in his country. Ever since the terrorist attacks on New York City and Washington DC, the Department of Defense had been eating up more and more of the country's budget. Weren't there other priorities anymore—like education and the environment? He smiled as he thought of the recent inauguration of Barack Obama as President of the United States. Aside from the fact that ethnic minorities, like his own, now had someone other than a white male as president for the first time, hopefully, things would change as promised.

As he scrubbed the dishes and waited for his morning tea to brew, he smiled at the freedom of the day before him. It was the beginning of spring 2009. It was good to be retired from military service. Although he had a successful career, he had never felt like he fit in. All the other soldiers acted like the military was their life, but for Major Ursa-Barrios it was just something he had done to survive. He never defined himself as military. If anything, the job seemed to always stand in the way of being himself. Deep inside he knew he was more a teddy bear than a wild grizzly.

He did, however, have a very strong desire to protect others. The motto "protect and serve" had sustained him during his years in the uniform, and he had been proud to wear it. It was like he had a natural instinct that raised the black hairs on the back of his brown neck whenever he saw injustice or someone unable to defend themselves in a threatening position. The conflict he felt was that he had found his instinct riled in defense of others wearing the same uniform as much as in defense of his country. Soldiers would always suffer from ethnic bias as long as so many of their superiors failed to recognize it in themselves, in spite of all the training to the contrary. It was natural to feel camaraderie with others in the same service, but he had found that many soldiers went to the extreme of looking down on any one not in uniform, including the very civilians they were meant to serve and protect. Many openly resented having a civilian commander-in-chief. Maybe the Major felt at odds just because he knew deep inside the military wasn't really his calling. He had longed the whole time to be one of those civilians. Even though he'd made many friends during his career, he still felt somewhat isolated. He felt like a loner in the crowd. He knew his feelings made him focus more on the differences and difficulties of wearing the uniform.

It felt good to be retired. He liked his solitude. He appreciated this opportunity for introspection. His garden was his retreat. It was a constant reminder of Nature's amazing ability to renew and regenerate herself. It was a chance to reconnect with Nature in a nurturing way. He found it inspirational and hoped to renew and regenerate himself after a career in an organization that achieved its means through destruction.

He was born in 1956, the grandson of immigrants from Central America. His grandparents worked hard, and his parents had learned their parents' values and work ethic. His father had been fortunate to work as a gardener for a wealthy and generous man, who upon his death had left him part of his estate. Meanwhile, the Major had earned his college degree and military commission by way of a Reserve Officer Training Corps (ROTC) scholarship. His parents had been adamant that he get a college degree, and that was just how he managed to do it. He felt very fortunate to have such a good life, but still the military was not a natural fit for him. He believed in serving his country, but there was a lot about the military system that was harmful to a creative personality. His true loves were flower gardening and playing violin. He was basically a gentle soul, and many times had wished he could have followed in his father's footsteps as a gardener, but his parents did not want that for their children. Still, a military career came with a high price, even for those fortunate as he was not to be injured, wounded, or killed in the line of duty. For some, the price of giving up their own free will— and sometimes beliefs—when they came into conflict with orders from the chain of command could be just as damaging as bullets or shrapnel. The Major was exceedingly grateful that he had come through the experience with his body, mind, and integrity intact. It was his soul that had suffered. Now that he was retired, he intended to spend time with his true loves, and hopefully heal the unseen damage.

As he left the clean dishes to dry themselves in the drainer, he smiled to himself while he stared out the window at the garden taking form in his backyard. He thought about the irony that if you bought into the abundant propaganda that said criticizing the service in any way was anti-American, you had crossed the boundary into the land of paranoia. It was part of the American heritage to practice freedom of speech and question all manner of authority. Each and every service member and Federal Government employee took an oath to protect and defend that very right guaranteed by the United States Constitution, but the military also spent a considerable sum of taxpayers' dollars in advertising campaigns, both for the outside public and within the service, also part of the exercise of free speech. Unfortunately, those political sound bites had come to replace sound, specific guidance from the top ranks. He wondered if it had always been so, or if it was a modern development, but he suspected the former. Wherever people were in charge, things were bound to go awry. It was just the nature of the human experience.

The concept of leadership had degenerated to creating slogans and positive labels and mantras, as if thinking happy thoughts could get the work done or solve real problems. Everything being positive was nice, but not necessarily real. He believed when you had an organization in possession of lethal weapons, it was better to be realistic. In short, he had retired when he realized he had come to perceive the highest levels of the US Army as airheads. He didn't know how much of that change in perception was due to his own personal flaws, growth, or natural personality that just didn't fit in, but he recognized it as counterproductive, and he had decided it was time for him to leave.

Funny, he noted to himself as he stepped out the backdoor onto his patio, that he'd never had a problem with an enlisted member of any magnitude that he could recall. If there was a misunderstanding, all he'd had to do was communicate, and they would get the job done. If you needed a problem solved, just ask a noncommissioned officer, or NCO. No, the problem, as he perceived it, definitely came down from the top. Maybe that was just a matter of perspective. Enlisted personnel had their feet, or boots, on the ground. When the people above you were so far above you, up in the air so to speak, it was easy to see them as airheads. He'd never been up there himself, and had never wanted to be.

He sat down on the ground by one of the flower beds and began pulling up the ever-persistent weeds— weeds that seemed to have the same sense of entitlement as general officers. Upon their own retirements, many generals and colonels made fortunes they probably didn't need from hard-working taxpayers by becoming motivational speakers. The field was created in an alternate reality to help managers avoid facing their shortcomings by making the workers feel inadequate or responsible when there were problems that couldn't be solved by positive thinking. *Ah, there it is in a nutshell*, he thought to himself. *The higher-ups don't take responsibility. They just blame the people under them.* He hoped he hadn't become like that. Nature's animal kingdom was always a food chain. He preferred plants.

His personal experience was that supervisors and higher-ranking officers often seemed to be full of praise and totally lacking in instructions—until you asked a legitimate question that inexplicably rubbed them the wrong way. After all, if things weren't running smoothly, something was wrong. And if an underling was pointing it out, they must be pointing a finger at the higher up, which of course was ridiculous, except in the world of "think happy thoughts" and "I can never be wrong." Reality never seemed to be in great demand.

Since his mind didn't seem to want to let go of his memories any time soon, he decided to take a walk around the neighborhood. He knew he had to let himself process all these thoughts before he could effectively move on, and he needed to stretch his legs. He went back inside to put on some socks and sneakers, grab a jacket and hat, and yell to the cat that he'd be back soon.

The Major's military experience had taught him that if there was a problem, you'd better cover it up fast before you were blamed for noticing—only the Major didn't believe in cover-ups. In the plant kingdom, Nature proudly displayed its "mistakes" as glorious diversity. There was no cover-up in Nature. But in the Army, once you surfaced a problem to your superiors, all of a sudden you found yourself on their hit list. It made no sense to anyone just trying to do their job and complete their mission. He had come to believe that it was a credit to the true character of the enlisted soldiers in combat zones that they didn't just turn their weapons on their commanders. There certainly was enough repressed resentment and anger for that to happen if someone snapped. There was always danger in not understanding that there was always more than one enemy.

He turned right onto a major street and walked south toward a strip mall, while recalling a phrase from one of those many required seminars, The Bullet Proof Boss. The phrase had stuck in his mind, and he had spent the rest of his career searching for one—to no avail. He had hoped for the best, but he knew he wasn't perfect either. *Give angry people access to firearms and ammunition, and sooner or later someone's bound to shoot somebody.*

He remembered one colonel in particular, Mac Muschatt, a six-foot tall, fair-skinned man with red hair, who walked with an overconfident swagger and a constant smirk on his face. The Major could never tell if Muschatt was talking down to him due to rank, height, or disdain. He was in charge of the supply office at the Major's last assignment. Colonel Muschatt was handsome by any standards, but had the sourest personality the Major had ever encountered when it came to social interactions. And, as usual, there were power issues. Colonel Mac always treated his supplies as if they actually were *his* supplies instead of the army's. It was damn near impossible to get anything out of him. He reminded the Major of a musk ox—always on the defensive, the corners of his mouth drooped like the horns of a musk ox, and he seemed more closely related to the past than the present. Like most military men, his social and civil flaws were probably his greatest strength in combat. As much as the Major didn't like him, he sensed that Muschatt would be a commander who would protect his men's lives when in danger and leave no one behind.

The Major looked up in time to see a city bus just start to pull away from the street corner, but then stop to wait for a young man running to catch it. The Major smiled at the kindness as he crossed the street.

On the other hand, he recalled that he did have some wonderful supervisors and commanders during his career. The one exception he knew to his general rule about generals was a big one. Brigadier General Raúl Gato was always available to listen to any problem, no matter how small it might seem, and to anyone of any rank. He was a genuine "people person" and, in the Major's humble opinion, that was a definite asset for any leader. They were both Latino, though the Major's ancestry was Guatemalan, while General Gato was from Puerto Rico. The Major questioned if he was culturally biased that he found it so easy to relate to General Gato and so difficult to relate to so many others. After all, hindsight was only truly useful if one applied it to oneself. Still, he had never heard anything unkind or derogatory said about Raúl Gato.

Brigadier General Gato had a sense of humor. He liked to have fun, and he liked to see his troops having fun. He didn't believe in the traditional "mandatory fun" where the commander decided on an event of his choosing, and then ordered the troops to participate and have fun. But it was, after all, the army. It was difficult to get commanders to see their subordinates as individuals. It went against the organizational grain. It was like Gato had night vision and could see all the lotus flowers that could bloom from the muddy, murky social environment that was the military. Somehow he'd maintained his independence and awareness of the very freedom the service was created to protect. The Major had been reassured to see that someone with a sense of individuality could rise to the top in a world of conformity.

As much as the Major believed in serving his country, he knew at the same time that he wasn't the right person to make the decisions at the top. It never ceased to amaze him how self-unaware many people and organizations were. Maybe looking in a mirror was too painful for most people if their expectations were too high from too many silly slogans. Maybe he had survived his experience by not looking too closely into his own mirror. For all the endless attempts at "lessons learned," as an organization, the army never seemed to really learn from mistakes when it came to dealing with people. Denial was incredibly easy for human beings, but the Major considered it a positive trait to know one's limitations and when not to push too far. He wondered what limitations of his own he had been denying.

Soldiers were no different from anyone else. He recalled with a smile a time when everyone in the entire section was buried in paperwork, and a certain Sergeant Major Bill Macroo, who had, for reasons unfathomable to everyone else in the unit, unexpectedly ordered the enlisted soldiers under him to wax the floors. One didn't normally interfere with a Sergeant Major, but this was one time the Major had to persuade the man to postpone his mysterious need for having the floors waxed. The floors were normally waxed on a schedule anyway, and this wasn't the scheduled time.

Sergeant Major Macroo had his eccentricities. He was an unusually short man, about five-foot four-inches, whose hair had been grey ever since the Major met him, and was very suspicious that his underlings joked about his lack of height behind his back, even though they rarely did. It turned out he had added extra rubber to his boots as lifts for his otherwise missing height. The end result was that when he walked down the hall, there was a distinctive and very noticeable "boing" that accompanied each step. Maybe he'd hoped to distract attention away from himself with an extra coat of wax so that everyone's boots would at least squeak. The Major laughed to himself. He'd liked Macroo as a person. He was a good man, but the Major still enjoyed an occasional joke about the Sergeant Major "Kanga."

Sergeant First Class Abejorro, however, wasn't amused with Macroo's unexplained need for extra floor wax. Jose Abejorro, who was within a couple of years of retirement, didn't appreciate being treated like a buck private when there was so much productive work to be done. Soldiers were deploying at the time, and there were records to be screened and inspections to be done and reported to make sure that all soldiers scheduled to deploy met requirements. Jose was always quick to point out the obvious priorities to everyone else, regardless of how much time was lost doing so. And even more precious time was lost by Macroo and Abejorro arguing over the obvious, but they'd still managed to get the work done, and the soldiers shipped out on time. It was Jose who renamed "Kanga" Macroo "Sergeant Major Boing-Boing."

The Major, still smiling at the memory, just shook his head. He'd been fond of both men—and many others. Jose could deliver quite a sting when he perceived an injustice. He was a righteous and relentless man. The Major saw him as a survivor. He also saw the parking lot at the strip mall was full today. *Somebody must be having a sale.* He decided to turn around and head back toward home.

Still, in spite of the many friends he'd made and the service he'd given his country, the Major had grown tired of being told it was wrong to question an order or the standard operating procedure when even he could see there were more efficient ways to get things done without damaging people. Maybe it was his age. Since he'd turned fifty, he felt he no longer had anything left to prove to anyone. He would never understand why the military was so against creative thinking. It certainly spent enough on creative, though ridiculous, slogans. He would never understand how an organization created to defend and protect a country whose greatest strength was its diversity was built on total conformity and elimination of individuality. Contrary to his military training, it was healthy to reflect, introspect, and identify problems. Maybe he was just getting tired and cranky in his middle age. He was glad he'd made the decision to move on.

After he had inherited modestly from his own parents, he had invested his money conservatively, which had turned out to be the wise thing for him to do. He had no desire to be wealthy—just comfortable. He felt very lucky to have benefited from good advice along the way, which allowed him to retire from service when he turned fifty-one years old, a year ago, without having to find another job. That left him free to pursue his long-neglected interests. Now was his time of life to live the way he wanted to. *Fifty-two already*, he thought to himself. There was a time when fifty-two was the average lifespan of his ancestors. In that sense, he had lived one life and now was starting a new one.

The military had trained Major Ursa-Barrios in all of the qualities he had to pretend to be (toughness, courage, repression of emotions, and aggression) as well as the qualities in himself he wasn't supposed to express (childlike happiness, joy in the moment, dreaming, humor not expressed at someone else's expense, creativity, self-motivated innovation, spontaneity without permission, and enjoyment of beauty for its own sake). Now he was free to experience the random kindness of the universe at his leisure.

He arrived back at his house, but crossed the street to his mailbox and collected his mail before going back inside. His black and white cat was waiting for him in the window. After dividing his mail into junk and bills, he put the junk into his pile in the pantry for the recycle bin and set the bills on his desk in front of his computer. He went into the kitchen, followed by his loyal feline, poured his first cup of tea of the day, and spread cream cheese on a poppyseed bagel. As the cat came up onto the kitchen counter to sniff the cream cheese on his plate, he petted her while gently pushing her away from his bagel.

"Here's yours," he told her, offering a fingertip of cream cheese, which she licked thoroughly. Appearing contented, she laid down on the counter.

"You know," he told her, "I thought when I retired I'd leave all those people and incidents behind, but I can't seem to get it all out of my head. I guess this is what Rose meant when she warned me to give myself plenty of time to process."

Rose was also former military and had retired before him. She was special, and he made every effort to heed her advice in all matters. He now understood she meant that he had to give himself time to just let the thoughts flow.

He had learned from his experiences in uniform to always question fear. This had served him well many times over. When he felt under attack, he'd learned to assess the real situation from reason rather than fear and determine if he or someone else was in physical danger, and if so, if it was an immediate danger or just pending. Reacting based on an initial blind feeling was bound to lead to error, and errors could cause as much harm as a potential threat. The fearful feeling of being under attack could be a verbal assault, or even just a perceived assault, based on experience in different situations. The key to reacting intelligently was to think first. He wondered how many other careers could teach that besides the obvious law enforcement and fire fighting occupations.

Adrenaline was powerful and could overcome a person faster than any external enemy. He had also learned that some were powerless to overcome it and would always react without thinking. One more thing he had learned was that he couldn't change others. That was a very unrealistic expectation, a delusion, held onto by many, especially those who refused to accept evolution. The Major didn't understand it, but denial was a human trait equal in its power to fear, and both probably shared a common origin. *You simply can't make someone see that what they pour their energy into denying is actually there.* It certainly didn't take a physical battleground for human beings to hurt and damage each other inadvertently.

The Major smiled as he finished his bagel. He picked up the phone to call his friend Rose, but there was no answer. She didn't have an answering machine, and it was just as well. He could mull through his thoughts on his own. *I guess there's really no sense dragging her back through it all again,* he thought. Although he had retired as a full colonel, he preferred to go by the reduced rank. There was no rule against a retired colonel calling himself "Major." He knew esteem didn't come from titles, and that those who promoted themselves were less likely in the long run to be held in esteem by others. It no longer mattered to him who had what rank. Unfortunately, most military and former military, Rose included, still called him "Colonel" anyway.

"Major" had a positive connotation to it, and he had spent a major part of his life in the military. Besides, there was just something not right about the vast majority of colonels he had known. For the most part, it seemed to him that colonels were more interested in self-advancement through politics than in taking good care of the soldiers entrusted to them. Major Ursa-Barrios figured they had stars in their eyes. He had retired when he realized he was becoming afflicted. Colonels always talked about taking care of soldiers, but in reality they expected the soldiers to do nothing but take care of them. A while back the service had issued an order that the word "soldier" was to be written "Soldier" with a capital "S." This was the sort of nonsense that diverted energy away from actually taking care of the people who were serving. Maybe there really was a fungus in the service, only it was the egos of the colonels and generals. He was very grateful that he had never been assigned to the Pentagon. While so many officers were anxious to get such an enviable position, he had managed to pass, much to his relief.

He'd learned that all many colonels and generals knew about management and supervision was to give regular pep talks and try to boost morale, while occasionally blindsiding a few conscientious individuals with excessive criticism for not covering others' mistakes to protect the perception of the team. *Why couldn't they just tell people straight out what was expected of them instead of always being vague and leaving instructions to the individuals' imaginations?* Maybe it was because they didn't know themselves. Not all officers were trained as instructors. *Maybe they should be.* Too much energy was spent protecting and defending oneself and one's position, and not enough energy was invested in constructive communication. At least that was the Major's perception. He had looked in the mirror and seen how he was becoming like those around him. He didn't like what he saw. To keep his self-respect, it was necessary to not lose respect for others, regardless of rank.

But then he thought about his last immediate supervisor, Colonel Jimmie Bass. Colonel Bass was a large-boned man with a thick neck and a square-shaped face that usually sported a broad, welcoming smile. He was the exact opposite of the negative stereotype the Major realized he had formed. Jimmie had a quiet persistence, almost inspired—and definitely inspirational. He had a gift—a natural instinct for inspiring those under him. He always managed to breathe new life into old problems, situations, units, and whatever group of people he took charge of. He never lost sight of his number one priority— his people. And appropriately for his name, he was a fisherman by hobby.

The Major considered that maybe his negative thoughts were a projection of his self-resentment for not being true to himself—for not choosing to follow the dream of his youth. If denial was a common human trait, so was stereotyping. He was just surprised to realize he was so guilty of it, but why? Was he arrogant enough to think himself above such human failings?

He sighed. Retirement was the right time for such introspection. He knew he had very strong values of his own, and he simply was not willing to compromise those values for political career bartering. He had noticed that the officers who were most willing to sacrifice their own identities to please their higher-ups were also the ones most likely to bully, verbally abuse, and alienate the soldiers under them. And that often resulted in imitation, which perpetuated the behavior. It was most unfortunate, but very human, and no doubt occurred in all walks of life as well. Everyone had their own experiences and had known their own share of characters. It was foolish to try to deny his memories.

Major Ursa-Barrios thought about a man who had once been his friend, Colonel Porker, an ironically thin, but otherwise ordinary looking fellow with pale skin, white hair, and big brown eyes. He was generous, kind, and thoughtful of others, but once in command, his ambitious cunning revealed itself. He had always been quietly available to anyone who wanted or needed to talk, but once in command, he was no longer accessible, even though he openly publicized that he was. He had protected himself with layers of staff quick to turn personnel away from the commander's door.

Colonel Porker was in charge of a unit on an isolated post, and so everyone there was under his command. Normally one could be brought up on charges for impersonating a general, but Colonel Porker knew he could get away with it. So everyone was intimidated into calling him General, even though he wasn't one. *The blind side of power manifests when the person in charge believes the rules he expects everyone else to follow no longer apply to him.*

The Major sat down at his computer to play a game of solitaire, but mostly he stared blankly at the cards on the screen as the memories kept coming. Some of his fondest memories of his career were of other Majors. One that came to mind was Major Leon Manx, an intelligence officer and former school teacher. Major Manx was gruff, loud, and very macho on the job, but around his wife and three daughters he was the kindest, gentlest husband and father imaginable. He was tall with dark hair, brown eyes, and dark-rimmed eyeglasses. He may have lost his temper at the office frequently, but he had a sense of humor and fairness that more than made up for it. Nothing escaped his notice, and he was extremely intelligent and well-respected.

The Major fondly recalled the December he had hung a battery-operated moose head with a motion sensor above his own office door. Whenever anyone walked by the Major's office, the Christmas lights on the antlers would flash as the moose sang out, "Ho, ho, ho! Merry Christmas!" Then it would sing a Christmas carol, and then it would repeat the routine. Just a couple of hours into the work day, Major Manx had appeared in Major Ursa-Barrios' doorway with a baseball bat and uttered the threat, "The moose is a piñata." The Major couldn't stop laughing as he silenced the moose.

The Major got up from the computer, took his hat and jacket from the back of his desk chair, and put them back in the foyer closet, being careful not to close the closet door all the way so his cat could come and go as she pleased. Just then the phone rang. It was his old friend Sergeant Ali Akbar. Sarge was a Saudi Arabian who had joined the United States forces during Desert Storm. He had a special dispensation that allowed him to wear his beard long, and for that he had been the subject of many jokes and derogatory remarks. The Major had met Sarge after the September 2001 attacks when they were both stationed at a training facility. After a good-natured dispute between them about the differences in their covers, or headgear, they had become good friends. Still, the Major never missed a chance to remind Sarge that his favorite gutrah, or head scarf, was made in Korea.

Sarge had been applying for jobs without much success. The United States military was advertised as an equal opportunity employer, but "mophead" was still a commonly used derogatory term for Arab or Islamic. The Major suggested that Sarge branch out and look for jobs further removed from the security field, where people were instinctively suspicious of everyone. Sarge was, after all, very talented in interviewing and dealing with people from all walks of life and ethnic backgrounds. The Major was sorry to hear that Sarge was still dealing with such rigid, in-the-box thinkers. *Surely Sarge's linguistic skills should be in demand?* After the call ended, the Major sighed with relief that he had made the right choice to retire.

He put on his hat and jacket again and went out the back door. As he strolled through his garden, the Major thought about how prejudice was just a way of scapegoating to get back at demons over which people felt they had no control. Spanish-speaking people were mostly good people with family values, who worked hard and knew how to enjoy life, but the Major had learned over the years that Protestant gringos resented predominantly Roman Catholic Latinos, because many American Protestants had demonized the Roman Catholic Pope as the Antichrist simply because he was a powerful dictator they could do nothing about, and also because Latinos tended to be of darker skin. That, unfortunately, was still a jealousy deeply imbedded in the white subconscious—or maybe there was also an envy of being bilingual. Anyone of darker skin tended to be a scapegoat in the infamous war on drugs, even though the demand for illegal drugs came from all levels of society—especially the rich. Sarge's people had been scapegoats long before the attacks on New York City and the Pentagon, because most gringos had never read the Koran and didn't even know that the burqa, or long dress and veil, many Muslim women wear came from the Christians long ago. Muslims and Arabs had to be scapegoats because Arab countries controlled most of the oil, and American oil companies didn't want competition from other energy sources. *People everywhere always blame other people for everything they don't like.*

He noticed that the bamboo was spreading outside its container, and he would have to do something about that. He loved the taste of the fresh shoots sautéed in butter. He appreciated having the garden to quiet his memories. He had, after all, retired to move on to his gardening. Even just looking at it and seeing all the work to be done brought him a sense of peace and belonging. And the new roses he had planted last month had survived the late freeze. Rose petals were pleasant in a salad. He had planted fragrant roses to bring the sweet smell indoors when he picked them. Then the wilted petals would go into the cat's litter box for odor control. He knew that rose petals free from pesticides were safe for his kitty, so he used a homemade mix of cooking oil and dish soap to safely control the aphids. *This spring, he promised himself, I'll bring in ladybugs.*

Chapter 6

Planting Seeds

When the Major retired from service, the first project he had taken on was to finish off one of the attic storage spaces behind the closet of an upstairs bedroom. There was a larger space on the opposite side of the room that was already set up for computer access, but the one he finished first was his hidden room. Ever since he visited Nathaniel Hawthorne's house in Salem, Massachusetts, in 1992, he'd always wanted to live in a house with a hidden room. There was no current need for an underground railroad, but given human history, one never knew what might happen next. On one hand, it was good to be prepared for all contingencies, but on the other hand, having a hidden room in his home was just a cool idea. *Now, I live in a cool house.*

This particular space that he finished off had its entrance in the closet, which made it very easy to conceal. Once he'd finished that, he completed the other room that already had shelving, electricity, and computer lines. The second, larger room also had a lock on its door. It was just the Major and his cat in the house, but he recognized the possibility that a relative could need to move in with him someday, in which case it would be nice to have a private place. He figured it was just an idea that wasn't likely to ever be used, but knowing the option was there gave him a satisfying sense of coolness. That in itself justified the effort.

One evening right about dusk, he stepped out the back door onto the patio. He looked across the yard and saw a grey and white possum-like animal moving slowly through the flower bed along the back fence. When it reached the far corner, it turned so that it was facing him. *It looks like a possum,* the Major thought, *but it has little round, brown ears set high and back on its head.* All the possums the Major had seen before had white ears that blended with the hair on their heads and faces, so their ears weren't very noticeable. And their ears had been more pointed than round. This one had a pink pig-like snout, white face and head, and very noticeable round, brown ears on top of its head. Most of its body was white, turning grey toward its rear, with a long grey tail.

"What are you?" the Major asked out loud.

It stuck its long snout down into a clump of pansies and came up munching. It looked at him again as it continued to munch. It was kind of cute with those round, brown ears.

"Are you a possum?" he asked again. It proceeded to find another tasty something in the flowers and munched some more.

The Major went back inside and looked up possums online. He found that the Washington possum indeed had round, brown ears. It tended to waddle along fence lines around dusk—just like this one. Its diet included slugs, which the Major was all too happy to share. He found it interesting to learn that Washington possums tended to be immune from rabies, and they would not attack unless provoked or cornered.

He learned that even though possums were endowed with claws and more teeth than most animals, their preferred reaction to confrontation was to drop into an apparent catatonic state. They even defecated when they did it and emitted a foul odor to fool any predator into thinking they were already dead. He very much admired any battle strategy that altogether avoided having a battle. They also had opposable thumbs, which put humans in good company. The possum, or more properly, the opossum, was the only native marsupial in North America. *This possum is welcome in my yard anytime.*

Just to be on the safe side, he went around to his neighbors and mentioned to them how delighted he was to have been visited, and that he hoped he was on the possum's habitual route. He instructed the neighbors not to hurt the animal should they see it. It wasn't likely, since possums were nocturnal.

The Major decided not to deal with the bamboo today. Instead he planted all the bulbs he had bought that had been waiting in his garage for the first pleasant, sunny April day. He planted drifts of columbine, astilbe, acidanthera, foxgloves, and trilliums with ferns scattered throughout for his naturalized garden. And he added the ever-popular periwinkle vine that bloomed in the spring as a ground cover underneath. He had already planted four beds of roses and daylilies in various places. His daffodils and hyacinths were blooming, and the tulips were up with big fat buds. The irises were showing their leaves, but they would bloom later. The cherry and maple trees were in bloom.

He planted hostas along the fence beneath the trees. Then he filled the raised bed circling the fir tree with red and pink peonies interspersed with fragrant lilies. There were many left over after that bed was full, so he put the rest in front of the daylilies, and then planted calla lilies in among the daffodils and tulips. His garden would be filled with colors.

After a light lunch, he rosined his bow and practiced the *Rondeau* by Mouret on his violin, the theme from Masterpiece Theater. After only a year of relearning, he was very pleased with his progress. He'd played off and on throughout his military career, but there had been times when he was overseas that he left his cherished instrument behind in storage. The last few years of his service had been especially stressful and time-consuming, and left him too tired to deal with much of anything else when he came home. So he'd spent the past year picking up the pieces he used to know well. He had learned well during his career how to relearn to play—he'd had to do it many times.

He read through the theme from Schindler's List and then James Horner's theme song from The Titanic. After playing a Gaelic air, a Japanese nursery song, and *Ricordo Ancor* by Warbeck, he loosened his bow strings, wiped down the violin, and put it away feeling quite satisfied.

He noticed the room and the foyer were filled with rainbows. He loved the way the sun came in through the skylight above stairs over the foyer and filtered through the beveled glass chandelier, splattering rainbows everywhere. It made him appreciate these rare sunny days all the more. On days like these, this part of his house was filled with bright, beautiful colors. It made him feel all the more fortunate to have a nice home and a good life.

He sang the Mexican folk song *De Colores* out loud in his rich tenor voice to the rainbows. It was a happy song, and it felt good to use his voice. He mused about the importance of color to the human eye and spirit and thought about the symbol of the rainbow in various cultures around the planet. He recalled nights when there was a rainbow halo around a full moon and marveled at how simple it was to refract light into a rainbow, yet the combination of colors still held their ancient mystery, joy, and hope. *It's good for a soul*, he thought, *to live in a house with rainbows inside.* To have them in the foyer was a welcome all its own, and to have them in his music room was even better.

Just as he was thinking a hot bath would feel really good and had decided to go take one, the phone rang. It was the hardware store saying that the hatchet he had left just the day before had been sharpened. He decided the bath could wait. After he picked up the hatchet, he headed down the street to the Backyard Bird Store, just because it seemed like a nice thing to do to complete the day. He didn't need to buy anything, but he always liked to look.

The store was filled with pretty and amusing things. While he was browsing, a wren flew into the store and landed on the wall full of bird houses. *Must be house hunting,* the Major thought.

Just then he looked down and saw a small garden statue of a cat in a meditative pose wearing a prayer shawl. He didn't need it, but it made him smile, so he bought it. When he got home he sat it on one of the bricks ringing the fir tree where the peonies and lilies were planted. He turned it so that it faced the rose beds. Then he went inside to take his hot bath that had been temporarily postponed. He realized that for the first time in very, very, very long time, he was happy.

As he soaked in a pikaki, or Hawaiian jasmine, scented bath, he realized a jasmine vine would cover up the stalks of the yucca trees in the front of the house that had been killed by the unusual winter. His cat was fond of the pikaki scent, and she made herself comfortable on the rim of the tub. She was half black, mostly on top, and half white. Her legs, tummy, and paws were snow white while her tail and most of her back were black. She had medium length hair, and her face looked like she was wearing a black mask. He had adopted her as a kitten from a no-kill animal shelter. She was now his roommate and companion. He had discovered her preference for flower scents quite by accident, and now she'd trained him to use them himself. Of course, he'd never admit that to anyone. Sometimes she'd join him and they would play in the water like a couple of kids. He'd decided it didn't matter if he came out smelling like flowers, because women seemed to actually like it. Besides, he'd sweat it off in the garden soon enough.

As he relaxed in the soothing water, he reminisced about when he had first arrived at his last duty assignment. It was Major Martin Fox who had been so kind and efficient introducing him to the rest of the staff and giving him the charts and information he needed to get started doing his job. Major Fox had found him a desk in the basement next to his own office, and even made a sign, "Major Ursa-Barrios's Burrow" so others could find him easily. The Major was also able to find the offices of others easily thanks to the many signs Fox had made for everyone—each unique.

Martin was a cheerful man and extremely knowledgeable. He was also young, very tall—six-foot five-inches, lanky, handsome, and happily married. Unlike so many, Martin had great people sense. In spite of the long hours he put in at the office, Martin was a family man. His wife was equally sensible, independent, and great with their well-adjusted daughter and son. Major Ursa-Barrios respected the way Martin stayed focused on his mission and, unlike so many others, never strayed outside his lane. It was fortunate Martin understood that doing one's own duty was more important than trying to do that of others. An organization worked better when its members understood this, and the Major respected Martin for it.

After Major Ursa Barrios had been there about a year, Major Fox was reassigned to the Pentagon, where Major Ursa-Barrios knew Martin would be a great asset. It was only after he was gone that the Major had come to fully appreciate how adept Fox had been at dealing with the many dysfunctional characters at that post. The Major admired him greatly and once again, as he had done so many times over the years, silently wished the best for the man and his family.

After his bath, the Major sat down in front of the TV. He checked the news and weather and then turned it off. As he leaned back and rested his head on the back of the sofa, he stretched out his legs and recalled Colonel Desmodon, who had been deputy commander at the Major's last duty assignment. George Desmodon, five-foot eleven-inches tall, slender, blond, and fair-skinned with piercing blue eyes and a prominent, straight nose, was the son of Romanian immigrants. He had grown up with his younger siblings in Greensboro, North Carolina, where his father repaired home appliances, often late into the evening, and his mother worked selling clothing and cosmetics from 2 PM until closing in a department store. George had spoken of how he had relished being left in charge of his brother and two sisters. He saw it as an opportunity to be in control and have fun. He took the initiative, did as he pleased, and became adept at coercing his younger siblings into getting into trouble without their parents finding out. To hear George tell it, the Desmodon kids became ardent pranksters and juvenile delinquents, but they didn't get caught, and their parents were unaware. George loved to talk about his childhood pranks at the office. His eyes would twinkle as he told his stories.

Like his mother, George was a natural salesperson. He was a charmer who could talk his way into or out of whatever situation as needed. When it came time for college, he got his bachelors degree in business on student loans. He wasn't a very good student, but he knew how to get by. He still bragged about it. He managed to cut classes often and turn his assignments in at the last minute, but he always passed the tests. He was bright, likeable, and fearless. Once he had his commission as an army officer, he got a deferment on his student loans. Then he managed to stay continuously enrolled in whatever college was convenient in order to indefinitely delay having to pay back what he owed, all the while incurring more loans he hoped to never repay. He racked up more and more debt, while living on the principle that the day of reckoning would never arrive. Over time he accumulated numerous degrees in a variety of subjects. To George, getting around the system was a game he very much enjoyed playing. And he loved to talk about it to anyone who would listen. The Major had found him very entertaining.

George was popular, except with Colonel Mac, who was in charge of supplies. For some reason, those two seemed to be natural enemies from the start. The Major wondered if they had a rivalry in the past that would explain the hard feelings. Both liked to be in control. Desmodon was very likeable, while Mac Muschatt seemed to like only himself. The two of them were like sugar and vinegar.

Desmodon was obsessive about the oddest details, such as always having a clean desk and books being stacked in perfect order of height. And he definitely had a dark side. He paid attention to other people's cues so he could always play himself off as an expert in whatever was their particular field of interest. He was always willing to do special favors for others, especially if it meant bending or breaking a rule, but unlike his college student loans, he expected his favors paid back. Where he didn't care about rules and regulations, he very much expected others to be loyal to him. In return, he would be loyal to them and, if necessary, break rules to keep them out of trouble.

He considered anyone who questioned his methods or actions to be disloyal and unworthy of his protection. Anyone he thought of as disloyal was an enemy who didn't deserve fair treatment or respect. Any enemy was his prey, and it was open hunting season all year long.

He also bragged about how his parents thought the world of him. *And they should,* the Major often thought. He was their first born, their darling son, and they were very proud of his great success as he relayed it to them. He worked hard to stay on top of what information others had about him by directly feeding them what he wanted them to know. He was quite talented in many regards.

George Desmodon's army bosses loved him. They loved to hear how well their units were doing, and they made sure to reward his accomplishments with awards and promotions. He told them exactly what they wanted to hear and that he had everything under control. He was best at not allowing problems to make it to their attention. With George, the world was black and white. One was always for him or against him, and he was a formidable opponent, simply because he had made many friends within the higher ranks. By the time Major Ursa-Barrios first served under him, Colonel Desmodon had been promoted to his rank without having ever seen combat, and they were on the opposite side of the country from where Desmodon had grown up.

Colonel Desmodon had chosen Lieutenant Colonel Crockodell as his assistant. Crockodell was always fighting a personal battle of the bulge and had one of the biggest beer bellies in service the Major had ever seen. There was much talk behind Crockodell's back, especially by the enlisted soldiers, of how he was able to maintain the army's physical fitness standards or whether he had a physical condition that exempted him. The Major was amazed the man was able to find uniforms to fit his unusually large waist size.

The Lieutenant Colonel actually had a job as a section chief, and there was no position for a deputy commander to have an assistant, or a deputy's deputy, but Colonel Desmodon bragged that he was really the person running everything. He felt he should have an aide of his own. Desmodon was very aware that the unit was somewhat isolated and rarely inspected, and he made the most of it. Crockodell was patient and had a keen sense of survival. He thought that by cozying up to the overly confident deputy commander, he'd be able to take care of his own greed and get away with it.

After Major Fox had left, Colonel Desmodon and his assistant Lieutenant Colonel Crockodell had many loud and immature laughing sessions at Major Fox's expense. They made jokes about excavating what had been Martin's office. They said Martin had kept his office such a mess to hide that he didn't know what he was doing and scare others from going into it. *Well, they were partly right.* Major Ursa-Barrios smiled to himself at how Martin had confided in him that Colonel Desmodon was obsessive-compulsive. Martin had always kept his work covered with a mess of charts and maps just to annoy Colonel Desmodon, and also to keep him from messing around in his work. The Major didn't come to understand until after Martin had left that the Colonel was also inclined to manipulate whomever and whatever he could for his own personal advantage, often at the expense of other individuals. As near as the Major could tell, Martin had successfully avoided becoming one of Colonel Desmodon's victims.

Martin had also liked to wait until Colonel Desmodon was out of the office. Then he would go in and rearrange the books on George's bookshelf so that they were no longer in perfect order by height. Martin was well-suited for missions requiring stealth. Major Ursa-Barrios appreciated Major Fox's sense of humor and friendship. He knew Martin would be successful at whatever he did, because he was focused, clever, confident, and sneaky when necessary, but most importantly he was a nice person with his priorities straight. The Major knew that Martin was the type of officer who wouldn't stop to think about rank if another soldier was in need of help, and would probably be promoted soon at his new assignment. He truly wished him and his family the best.

Colonel Desmodon, on the other hand, had issues. Everyone did, but Major Ursa-Barrios had difficulty understanding this particular Colonel. He had appeared supportive of the Major most of the time, but he always seemed to have hidden agendas. Come to think of it, the Colonel always presented himself publicly as supportive of everyone, as did all politically motivated officers looking for promotion. But it really bothered the Major the way he kept encountering the attitude, "Those rules or regulations don't apply to me." He was figuratively slapped in the face with it by Colonels Desmodon, Porker, and Crockodell as well as Chief Warrant Officer Jellie. The latter was an exceptionally sad case, as she had been promoted to be the head of a section for which she was clearly not qualified. In return, of course, she had to tow the party line and do whatever the Colonels wanted, which usually went against the regulations. But then to those with their own personal agendas, incompetence was the best qualification.

Maybe the Major didn't understand the obsessive-compulsive problem, but he didn't think a colonel wrestling on the floor of the hallway, in plain view of all the staff, with Sergeant Leach was appropriate. Sergeant Leach was a very attractive, if not-so-bright, tall brunette, in excellent physical condition who was in the process of getting her second divorce. It was an ugly mess. The husband she was divorcing worked in the same section. One of them should have been moved elsewhere, but the section chief had more than enough to oversee just to accomplish the mission. The husband was clearly unhappy, but had little to say about the situation, except that he wanted custody of his son. She had two older sons from her first marriage, and she had plenty to say to smear his reputation, but nothing to back up her stories. The judge apparently didn't find much to support those stories either. She didn't wait for the divorce before becoming involved with more than one officer. Where Colonel Desmodon should have at least kept up the appearance of remaining professional and impartial, he didn't. And when everyone standing around watching had cell phones capable of taking pictures, the Major knew it was a mistake that could come back to haunt George. On the other hand, Sergeant Leach was just a sad case that never seemed to learn from her many mistakes.

And Colonel Desmodon's prior relationship with Chief Jellie was curious as well. Chief Jellie was a beautiful woman with a curvy figure whose hair color changed at least from month to month. She appeared on the surface to be friends with everyone. The Chief had been promoted shortly after the Major had settled in. He took her to lunch to congratulate her, and of course hoping to befriend her. During the course of the conversation, she had mentioned her unpleasant childhood and violent father. She had commented that there was nothing nice about her family or upbringing. While he respected that she had appeared to turn that around and make a success of herself in the service, he noticed her body language was extremely defensive. There was an invisible barrier he suspected he would never breach and quickly decided it was best not to try. He eventually became accustomed to the lies that she would tell about various people behind their backs. It was his impression that she sincerely believed them, though there was usually evidence to contradict her. He decided she was just another person who lacked personal insight and steered clear of her.

After the wrestling matches with Sergeant Leach had started, Warrant Officer Jellie had come to work with both wrists bandaged. She said she had cut them while climbing her own fence, because she had locked herself out of her house. She told the story like it was a joke, and the other officers had a good laugh. The Major had held back, wondering what was funny and what part of her story was supposed to make sense. Whether or not there were actual cuts underneath the bandages, to the Major this was a cry for help. But she wouldn't talk to him about it, and none of the other officers would take his concern for her seriously. Instead, they should have made sure she got adequate counseling. Life was hard enough for everyone, but deception only made it worse, and it was a way of life for those whose only goal in life was promotion. In an environment where they were expected to follow orders without question, it was easy for the higher ranks to suborn all manner of deceit and dishonesty, sometimes with the best of intentions. Still the system was all the service had, because it was created by human beings, and humans were full of good intentions, blind spots, and delusions.

The Major had not appreciated Lieutenant Colonel Crockodell's derisive remarks in his presence about Latin American music, although he was confident that Crockodell was merely clueless about both music and cultural differences after tuning out all of the army's equal opportunity training. Or maybe after so many unreal slogans shoved down his throat, Crockodell just couldn't swallow anymore. So he didn't hesitate to show his true prejudice.

Crockodell was one of those country boys who thought the only image of a true American was himself, and that all people who lived in cities were exactly like him. It always amazed the Major that some officers could travel to other countries in the line of duty and never even realize they didn't understand their own country. Crockodell was a nice guy when he wasn't trying to scam money from the enlisted soldiers. It particularly angered the Major when Crockodell staged a free cookout for the General and invited only officers, while making the enlisted do all the work. Then he tried to sell the leftovers to those who hadn't been allowed to join in. The Major had refused to attend on principle. All he could do was vent to his friend, the Inspector General, off the record. Shortly before the Major retired, Crockodell had been arrested for submitting false travel and housing receipts to steal money from the government he was under oath to serve. Not long after he had confessed, Crockodell was arrested for drunk driving and leaving the scene of an accident without rendering aid to the pedestrian he had struck with his car. The last the Major heard of him was that he had joined Alcoholics Anonymous. He hoped AA helped, even if it was just a ploy for mercy from the courts.

The Major certainly had known a lot of interesting characters. He suspected it was just human nature. If television sitcoms were any indication, crazy people were in every profession and walk of life. He wondered if he had pursued a different career whether he would have met the same characters with different names and faces, but he suspected he wouldn't have met as many. Still, he reflected on how different the situation would have played out if Colonel Gary Shepherd, Colonel Desmodon's predecessor, had remained in charge. Colonel Shepherd was of average height and weight with an unremarkable face. Physically he just didn't stand out in a crowd, but he was naturally curious about people, so he went out of his way to get to know his soldiers. He was all about taking care of soldiers, and since he took the time to know them, he was very good at it. The Major had always respected and admired him for it.

Enough was enough. He went to bed. Soon after, a warm, furry body curled up next to him and began to purr.

The next morning the Major's girlfriend picked him up for their date. Rose was a lady of charm, wit, exceptional beauty, and refinement. For retired military, she was very creative. Blonde and petite, now she had a green thumb instead of a green uniform. They had many interests in common. He relied on her guidance and trusted her implicitly.

Rose had made reservations for the two of them at the Lavender Tea House in Sherwood, Oregon. The Major had met Rose Biegel when he had first arrived at his last duty assignment. Lieutenant Colonel Biegel had been in the process of retiring. The two of them enjoyed a pleasant drive down to Sherwood. The cloud cover was back, which cooled the temperature down just enough, but the rain hadn't come in from the coast yet. Everywhere cherry, pear, and apple trees were in full bloom.

At the Lavender Tea House, they were served a pot of lavender Earl Grey, butternut squash soup, tea sandwiches, red grapes, orange slices, strawberries, and freshly made scones with jam and clotted cream. It was a heavenly meal, after which they each bought a package of the lavender Earl Grey tea to take home. After lunch they stopped by Al's Garden Center, where Rose bought a couple of lobelias and the Major bought some creeping phlox to plant along side his new pond. He and Rose discussed where the rosemary, which was in full bloom, might fit in his yard, but he decided to wait on trying that.

Before heading home, Rose took the Major to another tea and gift shop called The Stash, in nearby Tigard. The store had a great variety of teas from around the world as well as pots, cups, and accessories. The Major took advantage of the available treasures to do some early Christmas shopping.

When they got back to his house, Rose was greeted by the Major's cat. She was quite fond of Rose. Rose, who played viola, often discussed duets with the Major, but they just never seemed to get around to actually playing together. He played a couple of pieces for her, and she seemed pleased with his progress. He mentioned that he had never actually heard her play.

"I gave it up a long time ago," she admitted. "I just never seemed to find the time to practice."

He gave her a small gift of lip balm made from Oregon roses, and she gave him a gift of aromatic bath salts. They walked through the yard together and looked at the rose beds. He showed her all the other plants he had planted since she'd last visited. She pointed out a potential spot for rosemary. She seemed especially taken with his meditating kitty statue.

When Rose left, the Major realized it had been yet another idyllic day. Retirement wasn't so bad after all. He also realized he needed to exercise and practice his violin.

Chapter 7

Choosing Flowers from Weeds

The next morning, shortly after a breakfast of oatmeal with fresh blueberries and a cup of hot chocolate, the phone rang. It was Captain Roan. Captain Roan was now on active duty in the US Army Reserves, and the Major was very fond of her. She had worked her way up through the enlisted ranks, completed her college degree, and earned her commission. Unlike most Captains and Lieutenants, she was older, experienced, and focused on the mission instead of trying to prove herself while looking for that next promotion.

Rebecca, or Becky, Roan had a sense of graceful dignity. She was tall and slender with light brown, slightly graying hair and a huge smile. She could endure the most oppressive situations and come out standing straight up with both feet on the ground. The Major very much admired her strength of personality and her stamina. In spite of the uniform, she was a free spirit.

The first time he had ever seen her, she was dancing sideways down the hallway past his open office door with a big, beautiful smile on her face. It was her way of maximizing her exercise by not wasting any available opportunity. She was a Lieutenant then, and she had learned the hard way that many enlisted soldiers resented her for having earned her commission, while many officers looked down on her for having started out as enlisted. But it never seemed to dampen her effervescent spirit. She also had a very sensitive, empathetic side that made her stand out like a sore thumb in the military. She and the Major had continued to cross paths at various assignments after that. He very much admired her ability to maintain a positive outlook on life though surrounded by narrow-minded, judgmental people with tunnel vision.

Becky enjoyed Nature, hiking, camping, and the great outdoors. The Major believed she had never met a bird or animal she didn't love. It was obvious to him that this love of outdoor life was a strong factor in her joining the army.

Somewhere along the way, he had learned Becky Roan was partial to dragonflies, hummingbirds, and rainbows. They had laughed about how dragonflies spent most of their lives as nymphs. He noticed that wherever she was assigned, a hummingbird feeder would appear outside her office window, and hummingbirds would follow, if there were any in the area. The dragonflies and rainbows were more in her choice of decorations. Once he knew this, he made an effort to buy a nice card at the store when he came across one with dragonflies and rainbows. He would send the card to her for no special occasion including a note of encouragement and support. It was his way of acknowledging her individuality in spite of the common uniform.

He thought about Becky's hummingbirds. He believed that the colorful birds of the world, especially the tropical birds of his grandparents' native Guatemala, were the inspiration for the mythology of angels. Captain Roan just liked to surround herself with angels. To his thinking, that made her indisputably good company.

He had always enjoyed their discussions about dreams, symbolism, and mythology. She was very knowledgeable about Nordic mythology as well as the myths and cultures of Australian aborigines and several Native American tribes from the Great Plains. He recalled her telling him that the Lakota counted time by the moon, so they had thirteen months in their year. It really made more sense to him, since the moon was far more consistent than mythology usually gave it credit for. The Major never tired of being reminded of the common thread of symbols that connected all humans worldwide regardless of belief systems or geographic origins. Maybe it was because his own grandparents were from Central America that he felt the more mixing of genetics from various parts of the globe, the more likely the human world was to admit to common ground, work together, and get along in the long run. He had to admit that initial contact between different cultures and races never seemed to work out well for those with the weaker weapons. Still he refused to give up hope. The rainbows in his foyer and music room were a constant reminder of that hope—one light made up of all the colors of the rainbow.

Becky Roan had once reminded him that hummingbirds reflected the colors of the rainbow. "They show us how to use flowers for medicine," she had explained. He remembered their conversation of all their favorite edible flowers: roses, pansies, nasturtiums, lilacs, lavender, and of course peppery marigolds. "Hummingbirds bring us the message to explore the past and extract only sweet joy from it," she had told him. She certainly had learned from that message. Her hummingbirds had taught her well.

During the Major's final assignment, then-Lieutenant Roan had been working with Warrant Officer Jellie, who was out of the office because she travelled quite a bit. While Chief Jellie was elsewhere, Lieutenant Roan worked long hours to get the job done, only to have Jellie take the credit for all the work when she returned. Jellie was insecure, jealous, and felt threatened by anyone she thought might show her up on the job. She made her inadequacies more obvious to others by working so hard to conceal them. She worked especially hard to impress Colonel Desmodon, but he could see right through her and used that to manipulate her as he usually did with other peoples' flaws. When Jellie felt threatened, she was vicious. The Chief had a record of lying behind others' backs, and those lies could sting like poison. If it hadn't been for their Inspector General intervening and setting the record straight, things would have gotten out-of-hand.

Major Ursa-Barrios respected the fact that Lieutenant Roan never quibbled about who got the kudos from the boss. But when a soldier on leave died in an accident, and Chief Jellie failed to process his leave paperwork, his family was in danger of being cheated out of some of the money that was due them. Chief Jellie's solution was to lie and say that the soldier was absent without leave. But Lieutenant Roan knew that was wrong, so she brought the matter to Colonel Desmodon's attention. Big mistake. Especially since the Colonel had put the Chief in her position to cover for him and frequently referred to Jellie as his "little sister." But unfortunately for Lieutenant Roan, she was honest, followed the regulations, and trusted her chain of command. That was a fatal combination. She had empathized with the grieving family instead of covering up for the team. In the army, doing the right thing was frequently about protecting careers instead of taking care of people. Colonel Desmodon was not interested in hearing anything that didn't fit his preconceived idea of what he thought he should be hearing. Roan got blindsided.

Again, if Colonel Shepherd or Colonel Bass had been in charge it would have been a completely different outcome. Colonel Desmodon never appreciated being given pertinent information. Whenever Colonel Ursa-Barrios had tried to bring problems to his attention along with suggestions for solutions to those problems, Colonel Desmodon accused Colonel Ursa-Barrios of lecturing him. Colonel Ursa-Barrios could never understand why any commander would not want problems with potential solutions brought to his attention. But Colonel Desmodon preferred to believe he knew everything that went on in his unit, and being told something he hadn't been aware of threatened that delusion of total control. Besides, this was the army, an alternate reality unto itself. The upside was that everyone in uniform changed duty assignments on a regular basis, and if there was a rotten apple over you, all you had to do was wait it out. Change was the natural state of matter and of the military.

Chief Jellie, who was covering her own mistakes as well as the Colonel's and had her own personal reasons for wanting to stay in favor with her commander, of course contradicted Lieutenant Roan when Colonel Desmodon inquired about the matter. Colonel Desmodon then fired Lieutenant Roan two days before Thanksgiving Day and just a month before Christmas.

What were they thinking? Surely they must have realized Lieutenant Roan would stand up for the family. After all, her boyfriend had been killed in Iraq just a few months earlier. Colonel Ursa-Barrios was appalled, but he very much admired the way Lieutenant Roan chose to view her misfortune as an opportunity to find a better job with nicer people. She immediately transferred to another unit, where she was quickly promoted to Captain and made commander of a company. He was proud of her. And it was a good thing she moved on so quickly, because as expected, Chief Jellie immediately began her untruthful gossip campaign, which spread throughout the post like wildfire, and successfully deflected any suspicion from herself or her commander. *Yep, that's how the system really worked.* The Major felt dirty just remembering it.

When Colonel Desmodon moved on to his next assignment, no one had any doubt that he would soon be wearing a star instead of an eagle. Colonel Ursa-Barrios had vainly hoped that Colonel Porker would be a big improvement. White-haired with big brown eyes and several small, unobtrusive scars on his face, he had always been a thoughtful, considerate, and positive person, but all too soon his innate lack of leadership skills and obvious political ambitions had become apparent. He quickly lost sight of all the many hard-working soldiers supporting him. He was a great disappointment when, like so many before him, he made it clear that everything was all about him. And it was an even bigger surprise to Colonel Ursa-Barrios when Colonel Porker demonstrated his belief that the regulations and United States Constitution didn't apply to him. As soon as he took command, he started using his new office to preach his evangelical version of Christianity. Even chaplains were trained to respect other belief systems, but maybe that was his problem—he wasn't a chaplain. No matter though, since the Inspector General straightened him out.

The Major was delighted to talk to Captain Roan. Even though she was working full-time, she was back in school studying abnormal psychology. She mentioned she needed to find some more sources for a paper she was writing. The Major didn't know much about the subject, but he had talked to Doctor Albert Bernstein, a clinical psychologist, as a patient, so he mentioned Dr. Bernstein's books to her.

She also mentioned she was looking forward to learning to play the uilleann pipes, a soulful musical instrument related to Irish bagpipes. She was her usual optimistic self, and he always found talking to her very inspiring and uplifting. They both hoped someday to play a duet. He reminded her how similar she was to her hummingbirds.

"In what way?" she asked.

"The way they can take the time to stop and hover with a friend, and then shoot straight up in the air and take off," he explained.

"You're comparing me to a helicopter!" she laughed.

"Helicopters don't have wings," he chided, "but you're right. Hummingbirds are the helicopters of the bird world. They just make a more pleasant sound and reflect rainbows."

After their conversation, the Major went outside and hacked off the top of the dead yucca. Then he planted a jasmine vine next to the remaining dead stalk and a dwarf Korean lilac bush nearby. He did some weeding and then finished off his little pond, now surrounded by lithodora, forget-me-nots, creeping phlox, lavender, and daylilies. Satisfied with how his garden was turning out, he started to go back inside when he noticed his empty flagpole. He had a brand new United States flag in his garage, but he hadn't yet run it up the flagpole as he had intended when he first moved into his house.

He thought about his procrastination for a moment and realized it was just part of the natural reaction to being retired. He'd spent his time doing all the things he hadn't had time for before. Raising the flag was just a reminder of being in uniform. Most retired military wouldn't see it that way, but he was glad to be a civilian now and free to not go through the ritual if he chose not to. He enjoyed his freedom. He also had been seriously reconsidering which flag to raise. Of course he had proudly bought the standard US flag, but then lately he had been thinking about getting one of those US rainbow flags from years before when Jesse Jackson had run for President. He really liked the symbolism, felt it better represented the diversity of his country, and it really was prettier. The US liked to see itself as the hope of the world for democracy and freedom, regardless that most of the rest of the world would like to be left alone, but the Major felt the old Rainbow Coalition flag better symbolized hope. Someday he might look into getting one, but these days most would take it to mean he was gay, which he wasn't.

He went inside and poured himself a glass of iced green tea, reminding himself not to let the cat, who was fond of cold green tea, have any because it wasn't decaffeinated. Then he tightened his bow and practiced his scales and a few Irish airs on the violin. When he was done, he picked up a book he was reading by Karen Armstrong about fundamentalism in Judaism, Christianity, and Islam. He headed upstairs to the room where he kept his exercise equipment. He would read while he had a brisk walk on his treadmill.

The walk seemed to have cleared his head. As he worked through his yoga routine, he realized he hadn't heard from Captain Deandra Robin in a while. Maybe it was the yoga that made him think of her, as she avidly practiced it. She was sixteen years younger than he was, and he thought of her as a kid sister. She was petite, agile, and naturally bubbly and cheerful.

He knew Deandra grew up in San Antonio, Texas, and her family was poor. Like many impoverished young people, military service was an opportunity to pursue the American dream and rise up out of poverty. While Deandra had never married, she had often spoken about her older sister, who had chosen marriage to a man who didn't want his wife to have a career. Deandra's brother-in-law finished high school with barely passing grades. He had no hopes for college, even if his family had been able to afford it. He worked hard in the construction business. In western Oregon, lumber was plentiful. The brother-in-law knew the area and how to work and network with people. Eventually, he applied for and received a small business loan to start his own company. He had apparently prospered.

Deandra finished her graduate degree in occupational safety and was pursuing another degree in physical therapy. She was a perky, optimistic, hard worker, but she was also very sensitive, which was a quality the Major very much liked. Unfortunately but understandably, sensitivity was considered a detriment in the military. The Major wondered how she was managing the emotional stress. He felt she'd be much happier in the civilian world,

but then maybe, like some people, she thrived on the stress
of working full-time while working on another degree.
Many of the service members he had known were, to their
credit, perpetual students. But he also knew that personal
success in life depended on putting yourself in situations
for which you were best suited and finding the options to
do that for yourself. Sometimes it was easier to tell yourself
you'd be a quitter if you sought a change to an environment
that better suited you. He knew that scenario very well in
himself. Still, Deandra had told him many times she
believed she had been a soldier in past lives. Who was he to
argue with someone's beliefs? He decided to give Deandra
a call.

Chapter 8

Dragonfly Visits the Garden

Captain Robin answered her home phone, which was unusual for a work day. The Major knew immediately from the tension in her voice that something was wrong. "I'm waiting for my sister," she explained. "She's on her way up from Albany. She finally couldn't take it anymore. She's afraid for her life, and I'm afraid he's following her."

The Major understood. There was a very real possibility of a physical threat to Deandra's sister. He and Deandra had had many conversations over dinners at the Old Spaghetti Factory and McMenamin's about her older sister Daphne, who was a source of constant worry for the Captain.

Daphne was just two years older than the Captain and married to a man named Richard Gatorman. Richard owned his own construction firm and was a good provider, but he preferred Daphne to have no outside interests or activities. He wanted her literally at home. Whenever he caught her going out for the day, even just to window shop, he got violent. According to Deandra, Daphne was his punching bag. The Captain had been trying to get Daphne to leave him, but Daphne had no money and nowhere to go but to her sister. Richard would surely find her there.

"It's the economy," Deandra continued. "The housing construction crash has put his business on the brink of bankruptcy. She told me he blamed it on her and was constantly taking it out on her. He said she was spending too much shopping online. Colonel, he doesn't even want her leaving the house now, so she has to order groceries online for Pete's sake." The Captain still called the Major by his properly earned rank. She was sounding even more exasperated and agitated.

The Major tried to calm her down. "I understand completely," he reassured her. "Men who have no control over themselves are driven to try to control others, especially when under unusual stress. And when he's under stress, he has no control over his adrenaline, which makes him feel the need to fight with someone. Only control freaks are basically cowards, so they take it out on someone who can't fight back. Have you persuaded her to leave him yet?"

"Finally. I've been wiring her money from time to time that she's kept hidden from him. I got her a cell phone a while back so he wouldn't know she was calling me. He doesn't like her to call. He doesn't like me, and the feeling is mutual."

"Of course he doesn't like you," the Major interjected. "You're a successful, independent woman. Control freaks don't like anyone they can't control. He's a coward, and he knows that you, being a soldier and an officer, would fight back. He sees you as a direct threat because of that and an indirect threat since you may influence Daphne, in which case he would lose the total control he has over her."

"Well, she called me a few hours ago. He was drunk, so of course he beat up on her, but this time she was smart. She kept fixing him drinks until he passed out. Then she grabbed some things, took a taxi to the train station, and called me from there, while she was waiting to get on the train to Portland. She could have come to the station here in Vancouver, but that would have been too obvious. Of course, when he wakes up and finds her gone, he'll know exactly where she went. He could drive up here and get here before her train arrives. But he'll come to Vancouver first. She can blend in better in Portland if he finds her there and she has to run from him."

"Ok, call the police or sheriff or whatever law enforcement applies where he lives. Tell them his wife called you because he got drunk and they had a fight. Tell them she left him, but that you're concerned he may still be drinking or, at the very least, still over the legal limit for driving, and that you don't want him to cause an accident if he tries to go looking for her. Tell them she went to stay with an old boyfriend or relative or girlfriend in Redding, California, since that's in the opposite direction—make up something he's likely to believe when he sobers up. Ask the officer to make sure Richard's ok by making a courtesy check at his house—don't sound angry with him—and get his car keys if possible. At the very least, it will delay him from starting out. Does Richard know your truck?"

"Yes, of course he does. I was just down for a visit last month."

"Then I'll meet her train and bring her to my house or to the women's shelter, whichever she prefers. There's no way she can go to your place for both your sakes."

The Captain gave him the expected arrival time of the train, agreed to call the Albany police department, and they hung up. The Major was glad he had called. He was also glad he had finished off the hidden room behind the spare bedroom closet upstairs. That bedroom had only one window, which was protected by two very tall arborvitae when looking directly at it from the street, and there were maple trees on either side when looking at the window from an angle. He put clean sheets on the bed just in case, cleaned the upstairs bathroom and put out clean towels and a washcloth. Of course, he would try to persuade her to go to the women's shelter first, where there would be counselors to help her and where she would be able to get medical attention if needed. But Daphne was Deandra's sister. He reasoned there must be a repressed independent streak in her somewhere, so he felt he needed to be prepared for that. Plus she would be frightened out of her wits. He had to be prepared for anything from total depression to hysteria.

He drove across the river to the train station in Portland to wait, just in case the train should actually arrive early. While he was waiting, the Captain called him on his cell phone. She had called the Albany police and told them Daphne had called her from a girlfriend's in Redding, just as the Major had suggested. The officer promised to check on Richard and call her back.

Daphne wasn't difficult to spot when the bus arrived. She was brunette, where the Captain was blonde, but the Major knew better than to trust women's hair color anyway. She was small in stature just like Deandra, and there was enough of a family resemblance to recognize. There was also something else vaguely familiar about her. He couldn't quite put his finger on it, but it was there—like something from a dream. And she was the only one wearing sunglasses at night. She was constantly glancing around nervously. The Major called the Captain back on his cell phone, told her to hold on, and then approached Daphne.

"Excuse me, ma'am, but your sister, Deandra, wants to talk to you," he said, smiling as he handed her the phone. She hesitated, but then took the phone, and the relief was obvious when she put it up to her ear. The Captain apparently explained to Daphne what was happening.

Daphne ended the call and gave the phone back to the Major. "Thank you so much," she said wiping away tears of relief.

"My car's right over there," he said, pointing out his little blue Saturn coupe.

"Oh dear," she said dismayed. "I hope my baggage fits into it. I was expecting my sister's truck."

Chapter 9

Weeds Might Be Wildflowers

The Major kept his silence as he crammed three large, over-stuffed, cloth suitcases, and an equally large, over-stuffed duffle bag, a hard shell guitar case, and an overnight bag into his car. He was grateful that the back seats folded down and that he only had one passenger to transport, since only the passenger seat was now available for use. He was thinking that either Daphne had been planning her getaway for some time, or she had packed at lightning speed, grabbing everything in sight. Nonetheless, he kept his thoughts to himself. He was actually more concerned with the fact that she was wearing those sunglasses.

"Welcome to the City of Roses," he said once they were in the car headed back across the river. "By the way, even though Deandra calls me 'Colonel,' I prefer to be called 'Major.'"

She was silent and appeared to be staring straight ahead.

The Major allowed her the silence, but as soon as they were across the river he said, "Welcome to the Evergreen State. Do you need to see a doctor?"

"Roses and Christmas trees," she said with a smile, remembering her beautiful dreams.

"Yes, we have plenty of both here," he agreed, relieved to see her smile. "Do you need to see a doctor?"

She felt her rib cage with both hands, wincing a bit. Then she shook her head and looked away. "Nothing's broken. I just couldn't take anymore. If Deandra hadn't sent me money, I would have just walked away with nothing and kept walking. Who knows where I would have ended up?"

"I'm just glad you ended up safe," the Major answered. He wasn't sure if the sunglasses were hiding black eyes, red eyes, or both, but then maybe Richard was smart or experienced enough at wife beating to know to hit her where it wouldn't show. "But you know that it's not safe for me to take you to Deandra's place, don't you? There's a battered women's shelter in Vancouver. I don't know where it is, but I know how to get you there. I'm sure they'll be supportive. They probably have counselors available. You've been through a lot and could probably use someone to talk to about it."

She continued to look away and shook her head again. "Sounds too institutional. Do I have any other choice?"

"Well," he answered slightly hesitating, "I have a hidden room at my house. You'd be safe. Only you, Deandra, and I would know where you were. But I have a cat, and if you're allergic, that would be a problem for you. After all, it's my cat's home."

She turned back toward him. "You'd do that for me?"

"Of course. What good would it be to have a hidden room and never get to use it?" As soon as they had crossed the I-5 Bridge, he took the exit for Highway 14 and headed east toward his home. "So do you want to go to the shelter?"

She shook her head again. "I thought those places were for women who had no place else to go. I can't take someone else's place and put a total stranger in danger."

The Major smiled. He surprised himself by realizing he was actually glad she wanted to come home with him. There was that feeling of familiarity again, and it was somehow comforting. He just wasn't sure where the feeling came from. "So does that mean you're not?" he asked her, continuing the conversation.

"In danger?" she asked incredulously. "Why else would I be here?"

"No, of course you're here because you're in danger. You prefer to use my hidden room—does this mean you're not allergic to cats?" He definitely felt comfortable with her.

Finally she smiled. "I love cats. That's why I'm here."

"I'm sorry," the Major responded, "but I don't understand."

"You must," she contradicted. "You just said that your home is your cat's home."

He laughed at the communication glitch. "What does loving cats have to do with you being here, por favor?"

"Oh, of course, I'm not exactly thinking clearly right now," she admitted. "Richard, my husband, wouldn't let me keep her. I tried to take in a stray—she was adorable, but clearly hungry. I picked her up and she actually hugged me back. She had longish hair, so even though she was skinny, she was still cuddly. She hung onto me like she was just as starved for love and affection as food. So I brought her inside and fed her. I needed her too. I needed someone to love me back. It felt so good. I used my own hairbrush to brush her. Then he came home. All I wanted was to take her to a vet to make sure she was ok, get her some cat food and a flea collar. He went through the roof. How could a grown man feel so threatened by a helpless little cat? I feel so guilty for having taken her in and put her in danger like that. He hit me a few times, and then when she hissed at him for hitting me, he grabbed her none too gently. I remember screaming when he threw her into the cab of his truck with no protection—cats don't understand how to ride in vehicles. It broke what was left of my heart for him to hurt her. I felt so helpless and broken. I couldn't even get off the floor. I should have fought him back for her. I should have stopped him." Her voice was rising in pitch and becoming hysterical. Tears rolled down her face from under the sunglasses.

"No," he interjected. "He would have probably killed both you and the cat. You couldn't stop him without further violence."

"But there was further violence," she objected. "When he came home he said he had taken her to the 'Humane Society shelter' and had her euthanized. There's nothing humane about that, but I don't even know if he really took her there or if he just murdered her or threw her out of his truck and left her injured and helpless." She sobbed violently for a while before continuing.

"Then I poured him a large drink, went to the back of the house, and gathered the things I had left that were important to me for fear he would destroy them, too, like my guitar. Only the most important thing, the cat, was already gone. I kept pouring him drinks and just kept refilling his glass until he passed out. I called a taxi and got my stuff out to the street. I called Deandra from the train station.

Before the Major could comment, she continued. "With Richard, everything is always about Richard. It's like nothing else exists or should exist unless it serves him. I know I'm making him sound like a spoiled brat—I chose to marry him, and I stayed married to him all these years. He can be very charming when he wants to be, but he just doesn't know or care about other living creatures having needs or feelings. To him, that precious kitty was just a thing to throw away. I think that's how he sees me, except he's kept me all these years. I don't know why. If he'd only thrown me away first, the kitty wouldn't have been hurt. I just don't understand him. But after he took the little cat away, I just couldn't stay with him anymore. I feel like I was an accomplice. I feel so awful. Now I know what they mean by the phrase 'under duress,' but it doesn't make me feel any less guilty for being so afraid of him."

"You must have been terrified."

"Just numb. By that time, I was past being scared, finally. The poor little cat was far braver than I've ever been. I wasn't afraid of him killing me anymore. Part of me wished he had. Does Deandra know about this hidden room?" she asked.

"No. It's just something I've kept to myself for no particular reason other than ever since I visited Hawthorne's House of Seven Gables, I'd always wanted to live in house with a hidden room. It wouldn't be a hidden room if I told people about it."

"Could we please not tell Deandra? It's not that I don't trust her. I'd just feel she'd be a whole lot safer if she thought I'd gone to a shelter and didn't really know where I was. If she doesn't know where I am, she's less likely to try to get between Richard and me to defend me, like I should have done with that sweet little cat. I hadn't even picked a name for her yet. I know I'm not making a whole lot of sense right now, but could we please tell Deandra I went on to Seattle to a shelter there?"

"Whatever makes you feel safer," he acquiesced. "Actually it makes sense. If she doesn't know, she can't inadvertently give it away to anyone. I already told her I was going to take you to the women's shelter, so she'll have no reason to doubt me. Just try to relax. You're safe now. Besides, I had Deandra call the authorities down in Albany. She told them you and Richard had a fight, that he had been drinking heavily, and that you had left him and gone to stay with a girlfriend in Redding, California. The police officer promised to go by your place and check on him to make sure he was ok and didn't try to drive under the influence."

Daphne let out a very long, slow exhale as she sank back against the seat of the car. The Major turned onto his exit off the highway. He thought to caution Daphne to slide down in the seat below the window level before he reached his neighborhood. When he got to the house, he pulled into the garage and closed the garage door behind them.

"We're home," he told her. "You just catch your breath a moment while I unload the car. I'll come back and get you." He started to get out of the car and then turned back to face her and added, "That cat chose to adopt you. She was protecting you. She chose to come between you and your no-good husband to save you. She did what was her nature to do. She gave herself willingly to show you it was time to stand up for yourself. Stop beating yourself up about what happened. Richard already did that. Start being grateful to the cat for her courage and for saving you. Her example was her gift to you in exchange for your kindness to her. Don't belittle it—honor it. Please."

She nodded silently, taking it all in. This was an officer, albeit retired, and a gentleman. He liked cats. He was considerate. Yes, she definitely trusted him. This was a man she could easily like.

He got out of the car and unloaded it. After he'd brought all her baggage into the house and upstairs to the bedroom that was to be hers, he closed the blinds on all the windows they would have to pass on the way. Then he went back to the garage, got her out of the car, and led her into his house. Once inside, she finally took off her sunglasses. The Major saw her eyes were red and very puffy from a whole lot of crying, but no bruises. He was relieved by that. She had every right to cry. They were greeted at the foot of the stairs by the Major's feline housemate.

Daphne smiled, knelt down, and offered her hand to the black and white long hair. "What's her name?" she asked.

"Purvati, this is Daphne," the Major introduced. "And Daphne, this is Purvati. She's named for the Hindu goddess of dance, Shiva's consort. Purvati, or Parvati, is the rhythm of time and the seasons. She understands that all is change, and that all change is now. She not only lives in the moment, she is the moment. And she's always reminding me of this. Always she's telling me, 'mow, mow.'"

After sniffing Daphne's hand, Purvati let Daphne pet her. "She's so soft—like satin," Daphne observed.

"She could pass for a Turkish Van," the Major explained, "but she's a shelter cat, so she's what we call a 'Van-alike.' Just be sure you keep the toilet lids closed when not in use or she'll jump in. She's been known to join me in the bathtub. Turkish Vans are also known as 'swimming cats' because they like the water, unlike most other cats."

"I'll think we're going to get along just fine," Daphne commented.

"Well, don't get jealous," he cautioned. "Vans tend to bond closely with one person, and in her case, that's me. We've been together since the day she was weaned from her mother. Also, don't ever let her outside. She's an indoor cat, and she has one of those chips in her shoulder, but I wouldn't want to risk her getting lost or having a bad experience with another animal or worse—a car. Sometimes I carry her outside for fresh air, but that's not very often, and I never let her run loose."

"Thank you for explaining," she replied. "I wouldn't dream of doing anything that might hurt her. She's precious."

He smiled and showed his new guest up the stairs to the spare bedroom. "I put all your things in the closet," he said as he opened the closet door. "And back here," he said as he slid a panel in the back wall on the far side of the closet, "is your safe hole." He reached in and flipped the light switch so she could see inside. "It's small, but secure. There's a larger room over here," he continued as he moved to the opposite side of the bedroom and unlocked a door to what appeared to be another closet. He turned the light on and stepped over the sill, inviting her inside. "You can use the shelves for storage if you don't want to risk your things being seen in the closet, should anyone come looking." He handed her the key. "Of course the other space is the only one that's actually hidden."

She nodded her understanding as she took it all in. Daphne wasn't sure if she was more overwhelmed by the sudden unfamiliar feeling of safety, the freedom of so much safe space and privacy, or her amazement that a total stranger had just handed her the key to this good fortune.

"Take your time settling in. I live downstairs, but there's a bath up here on the other side of the stairs. We'll work out a way to communicate so you can know when it's safe to come down. If you want your privacy, just close the door to the bedroom. There are clean sheets on the bed and clean towels in the bathroom. I'll bring up some food for you. If your door is closed, I'll just leave it outside and knock, but don't let it sit there for long. Purvati will think I left it for her. Oh, and speaking of Purvati, anytime you open a closet door, please pay close attention. If she goes in, and you come out and close the door behind you, she'll be trapped. And you won't know it for hours, because she'll explore and then have a nap before wanting back out."

"I'll try very hard to remember," Daphne promised. She smiled as she watched the cat, her tail straight up in the air, follow the Major back down the stairs.

He phoned Deandra and told her he had met Daphne as planned, but that she feared for Deandra's safety if she stayed in the Vancouver-Portland area. So, at Daphne's request, he had put her on the train to Seattle, given her a little more cash, and made her promise to find and go straight to a women's shelter as soon as she arrived. He told Deandra that her sister had been noticeably crying a lot, but there were no visible bruises on her face, and that she was carrying a guitar and one suitcase.

"That's the classical guitar Richard gave her. And then she found out it had been a gift to her from someone who worked for Richard. The man had been hurt on the job, so he could no longer play. He asked Richard to give it to her for him, but Richard made her think it was a gift from Richard. She found out anyway. She plays beautifully, but Richard wouldn't let her play for anyone but him, the selfish bastard.

"Anyway, I got a call back from the police officer in Albany. When he went to Richard's house, he could see through the window that Richard was passed out on the floor of the living room, so he broke in. An ambulance took Richard to the hospital. He's being treated for alcohol poisoning. Even if there are no complications, they're going to make sure he gets into some sort of rehab program. I just hope Daphne calls me when she gets to the shelter to let me know she's ok."

"You know, they may have rules about that for the protection of all the women. So don't be alarmed if it takes a day or two before you hear from her," he advised, covering for his guest.

"I'm just so relieved she's away from him finally."

That night, Daphne dreamed she was flying above the trees, across the Columbia River, and over the lights of the bridges and city of Portland, when her dream lover joined her in the night sky. He took her hand and led her back down to the bed in which her body was sleeping, where he tucked her in and kissed her good night.

"We're home," he said, just as he had earlier when she was awake and they had arrived. She had finally come home. And she knew he would never hurt a defenseless kitty.

Chapter 10

Routine Maintenance

The next morning, the Major awoke from a very pleasant dream. He dreamt he brought Daphne home with him, but instead of driving his car across the I-5 Bridge, they had flown through the air like angels across the Columbia River to his house. Once home, he tucked her into bed.

"What a sweet dream," he told Purvati, who was purring on top of his chest, their hearts perfectly aligned. The Major had dreamt of flying throughout his adult life, and often he dreamt he was with a wonderful woman, whom he took to be an angel.

"I wonder why I never dream about Rose?" he said as he gently ruffled the scruff of the cat's neck.

Then he remembered what his mother had told him when he was a child, "Pay attention to your dreams. When the conscious babble is silent, you can hear your true inner voice." He pondered her advice for a moment, before deciding it was time to get out of bed. As he stirred, the kitty jumped off the bed, trotted to the bathroom, and waited for him to go through his routine.

He knew he had taken a leap of faith bringing a stranger with so much baggage into his home, but Purvati trusted her and was at ease, which was most unusual for any first encounter with his kitty. Had there been drugs or anything suspicious somewhere in all that baggage, surely Purvati would have noticed. The Major knew Deandra Robin, and this was the sister she had spoken about so much over the years.

And then there was that comfortable familiarity he kept feeling when he was with her that put him at ease. Still, he had to wonder what was in all those over-stuffed bags.

*

Daphne moved all her belongings into the room with the key and sat on the floor among her bags. She wondered if she was being unwise trusting yet another man, but her own sister had sent him to rescue her and told her to trust him, so she had. After all, he was owned by a sweet and beautiful cat, and he was kind. His cat was clearly well cared for, and that spoke volumes about the man. Still, she had to question if she'd made herself a prisoner all over again. But she felt safe. He had given her the key. If she was a prisoner, then she was her own jailer.

For the first time in her adult life she felt safe and free enough to try to decide what she, and no one else, wanted to do. She knew she hadn't been exactly rational staying with Richard all those years, and she'd just been through a difficult emotional ordeal. It was time to rest before making any more decisions. *I'm safe for the first time in years. This is amazing.*

Then she thought about what the Major had said about the cat she had tried to rescue—how the cat had given her a gift of its example. She decided to learn to trust again. This time she was the stray, and this kind man and his cat had taken her in and adopted her.

*

Once he was dressed, the Major took a breakfast tray of grape juice, jasmine tea, toast with butter and huckleberry jam, a bowl of sliced bananas and strawberries, and a freshly picked daffodil in a vase up to the door of

Daphne's bedroom. When he knocked lightly, she opened it immediately. "Room service," he joked with a big smile. "How did you sleep?"

"Best sleep I've had in years." She was positively glowing, and the puffiness around her eyes had diminished. "That's the most comfortable bed I've ever slept on. But looking at all of this," she indicated the breakfast tray, "I think I must still be dreaming."

"It's an air mattress," he explained. "Sorry I forgot to show you the controls, but we can do that after you eat."

"Oh no, I wouldn't change a thing about it."

"Well, when the temperature rises or drops, the air in the mattress naturally expands or contracts, but I'll show you later. Buen provecho. Bon appétit!" He excused himself and went out to check the mail.

When he came in from collecting his mail and pulling a few weeds along his way back up the walk, the phone answering machine was beeping, so he played back the message. "Hola! It's me, Mad Dog. I'm back on the ground with some leave time. Let's hook up for something kinky. The mile high club just isn't the same when you're alone in the cockpit."

The Major called him right back. After they ended the call, the Major smiled to himself. Mad Dog Hawkins was a pilot and one of the Major's most shameless friends. He had blond hair, green eyes, and was a couple of inches shorter than the Major. Mad Dog was an attractive man, but he was not beneath embarrassing anyone at any time. However, for whatever reason, the Major liked him anyway. The Major liked Mad Dog's brazen sense of humor. Unfortunately Mad Dog also had a condescending way of insulting people and could launch into an argumentative rant at any time. He questioned everything except his own opinions and mannerisms, was an avowed atheist and socialist, and completely socially inept. Still the Major was glad to hear from him. He enjoyed his company both for his intellect and his spontaneity. Mad Dog's atheism and socialism didn't bother the Major at all—except when Mad Dog was out to convert people that weren't interested.

Mad Dog grew up as a racist, red neck, Louisiana Republican. He was gung-ho about serving his country all through his high school and college years. After becoming an army officer and a pilot, he had gradually outgrown the racism and narrow-mindedness of his youth and had begun to tolerate diversity and eventually even came to embrace it. Flying helicopters while serving in Iraq was the tipping point for him. As he had described it to the Major, he had an epiphany. He realized that he had spent over two years in combat zones, but had never actually fought for freedom or democracy. He had been fighting instead for the Fortune 500. His epiphany was that "United States interests overseas" actually meant "United States business interests overseas," and he had begun to feel like a mercenary. He described the first half of his career and life as having been "young and dumb." The transition had been painful for him. *Unfortunately his intolerant upbringing simply reversed itself instead of getting lost in the process, as so often happens when people reverse their own duality.*

By the time the Major met him, Mad Dog had some serious issues with authority. After he'd known him a while, he realized Mad Dog had actually developed those issues while growing up, and they had only been made worse by his experience in Iraq. According to Mad Dog, military authority was vertical, while equality was horizontal. In Mad Dog's own words, "We're all human beings. 'All men are created equal.' Authority of any kind, if it's truly American, should be more horizontal." Mad Dog accepted no compromises.

He left the service soon after that. He didn't have trouble finding employment with his flying skills. The Major didn't take offense with Mad Dog. Instead, he found he was never short on laughter whenever Mad Dog was around, but Rose Biegel didn't care for Mad Dog's company. She said he was crass and out of control. She was right on both counts, but the Major liked Mad Dog for the same reasons Rose didn't. Maybe it was a guy thing. Whatever, he thought it might not be a good idea to let him know about Daphne, unless of course an immediate need should arise to fly her somewhere. At any rate, today was not the day to go out and leave her alone in a strange place.

Just then his cell phone rang. Much to his surprise, it was Daphne. "Deandra had given me your number as a back-up when I called her from the train station in Albany, just in case I couldn't reach her and she wasn't there when the train arrived. You said we needed a way to communicate?"

He looked up and saw her leaning over the banister. He had to laugh. He'd been so caught up in the intrigue he had missed the obvious.

"Room service?" she queried, holding up the tray with the empty dishes. He was pleased to see she had kept the vase with the daffodil. He went up the stairs. "Thank you so much for everything, Colonel," she said as she handed him the tray. He set the tray on the floor and explained why he preferred "Major" to "Colonel." He also realized Deandra still called him Colonel, but he had long since stopped noticing.

Then she asked the obvious, "Don't you have a first name?"

"It's Alfonso, which was my father's name, so I was always called Junior or Alf when growing up. It was cool to be Alf when I was a teenager because of the television sitcom—alien life form. And I have to admit that's a good description of most teenagers, but after a while it got old. And then there was the song, *What's It All About, Alfie?* I didn't like being called Alfie. So once I became an officer, I just went by my rank. That's the way it is in the service anyway—everybody's first name is their rank.

"Now if you'll please excuse me, I need to do the dishes, and I'm sure you have a lot of unpacking to do," he said with a smile, as he picked up the tray.

Daphne laughed. "No, no, let me show you. Please," she added as he hesitated. He set the tray down once more and followed her into the extra room, as he called the extra attic closet that had been converted. Inside he saw that one lower shelf held a couple of pairs of blue jeans, sweatshirts, T-shirts, socks, and underwear. A music stand had been set up in front of the folding chair that had been there, and the guitar case was on the floor next to it. To his amazement, all three large suitcases were sitting open along the top shelves, and they were crammed full of all kinds, colors, and textures of yarn. On top of the yarn in one of the suitcases was the largest pair of knitting needles he had ever laid eyes on.

"You knit, I presume?" he asked.

"It's a very important part of who I am, and it gives me a creative outlet—as well as a sense of accomplishment," she explained. He was delighted she felt comfortable enough to open up to him and share with him. "Knitting is basically yin and yang, feminine and masculine, two fundamental stitches called 'knit' and 'purl'. There are also occasional twists and turns, doubling and dropping stitches, but knit and purl are the basics. They're the foundation of the fabric woven by the process, sort of like an expression of the duality of the universe. You can do all of one without the other, or all of the other without the one, but either way comes out looking the same."

"Huh?" He was lost, but she was too enthusiastic to stop. He noticed the same bubbly personality coming to the surface in Daphne that he had always liked in Deandra.

"Just knitting is the same as just purling, even though they're opposites, because whatever you knit always has two sides. The only way to change the pattern," she continued, "is to mix the two stitches in some way, and how you mix them determines the finished look. So you can change the pattern by some balance of the stitches, but you can also add to that with color and texture. You can see the difference in colors; that's obvious. But here—feel the difference in the textures." She took his hand and moved it over the different types of yarn. Some were soft and some were very soft, but she was right—they felt different.

"And, of course," she added, "then there are the fun yarns, like with glitter."

The Major was pleased both by the contents of her baggage as well as her enthusiasm in revealing them to him. "I have a little footstool you can use for your guitar," he offered, remembering that Deandra had said Daphne played classical, and he knew that classical guitarists always used a footstool. Daphne was impressed that he was so observant and considerate.

"Now unfortunately I really do need to do the dishes," he excused himself as he picked up the tray and went back downstairs. "Remind me to show you the controls on the air mattress," he called back over his shoulder.

Chapter 11

The Waxing Moon

Feeling comfortable that Daphne was safely ensconced upstairs and not an emotional basket case as he had originally feared, the Major met Mad Dog Hawkins and their mutual friend Danny O'Hare at Who Song and Larry's. It was a Mexican restaurant on the Columbia River across the street from the Old Apple Tree, a local landmark, and the land bridge that crossed Highway 14 and led to the old Fort Vancouver, a National Historic Site. The three men were seated at a table with a relaxing view of the river.

Danny was also of Hispanic origin, but when he married a blonde of Irish descent, he chose to take her surname instead of her taking his. He officially changed his name. It was an odd marriage as far as appearances went. Irene was a warrant officer in the Army Reserves with a grown son still living with her. Danny never moved in with her. He kept his own apartment. When she opted to mobilize, they ended up on opposite coasts, with her on the Atlantic and him on the Pacific. As far as the Major and Mad Dog were concerned, that was nobody's business but the O'Hares's. Danny didn't talk about it, so they didn't ask.

Danny was the only one of the three of them that was still in uniform. He was bright, but judgmental, and sometimes he had difficulty understanding other points of view. They were both younger than the Major. The year before the Major's retirement, Mad Dog had suddenly resigned his commission, and Danny had never quite forgiven Mad Dog for that. Danny thought Mad Dog had made a stupid mistake, since he was more than half-way to retirement, but the Major had agreed it was the right thing for him to do. After Mad Dog's epiphany of sorts while stationed in Iraq, he had since viewed the military in a very negative context.

Mad Dog had simply realized he no longer believed in what he was doing in uniform, and it was time for him to move on. One of his best qualities was his ability to see his own big picture. Otherwise, he never noticed the big picture, because it wasn't about him, but he could see his own. Once he had identified a problem in his life, it just wasn't in his nature to leave it alone. If he saw a problem, he had to solve it, and so he had. Actually the Major admired his decision, as he himself at the time was counting the days until he could retire and be free to do things that brought him happiness.

"I understand congratulations are in order," the Major began as the server brought them chips and salsa.

"Man, word travels fast!" Mad Dog seemed surprised. "Who did she tell, or does my reputation precede me? No, don't tell me you know her, too."

The Major was used to unexpected comments from Mad Dog, so he kept a straight face, but now he was very puzzled. "As I was saying," he continued nonplussed, "I understand Captain O'Hare is now Major O'Hare. Congratulations!"

Danny smiled. "Thank you, Colonel. I very much like my new job and the people I'm working with."

"And I truly enjoyed that concert we went to last month. Thank you again for that. I wouldn't have known about it if you hadn't told me," the Major answered.

"Well, thank you for going with me. You know I hate to go to things like that alone," Danny responded.

"Enough with the mutual admiration society," Mad Dog interjected. "Or was there more to this date than you're telling me?"

"Oh yes," Danny said sarcastically. "We're dating now—a hot item. Didn't you know?"

"That's better," Mad Dog said. "I just didn't see how you two could dip into salsa and not think of other things, that's all."

"Well, most people don't discuss them in public," the Major mentioned.

"It also reminds me of how much damage our country has done over the past century by overthrowing legitimate democracies in Latin American countries," Mad Dog continued.

"Here we go," Danny sighed.

Knowing that any conversation with Mad Dog could literally lead anywhere, and wishing to avoid another argument between the other two over Zionism and Palestine, the Major decided to change the subject. "So, Mad Dog, what did you do with her that you didn't want her to tell anyone?"

"Are you talking about me?" Danny interjected. "Who are we talking about anyway?"

Just then the server brought a plate of enchiladas for Danny, quesadillas for Mad Dog, and queso y flautas for the Major, with extra guacamole and sour cream for all. After the server left, Mad Dog, with exaggerated drama, dabbed his mouth with his cloth napkin, cleared his throat, stood, and raised his rum and coke. Then, of course, he paused again for emphasis before announcing, "I'm getting married."

After another genuinely stunned pause, the Major offered an exuberant, "Felicitación!" as he stood up and raised his ice tea glass at the same time that Danny exclaimed, "Again?"

"This will be the last time," Mad Dog answered confidently.

"Permita que le de enhorabuena," the Major continued, still standing.

"Taking bets!" Danny mocked. The Major sat down.

"No, really," Mad Dog insisted. "She's Bolivian. If I cross her, she'll take me out."

"Seriously," the Major asked, "what's her name, and how did you meet her?"

"Mercedes Águila. We met at the gym. We were running on neighboring treadmills, and I couldn't keep up with her. So, I had to stop to ask her out, so I could save face," Mad Dog explained. "At dinner I told her I have this thing about redheads, and the next time I saw her, she'd dyed her hair auburn. Ooo-la-la. So I proposed before she got away."

"Well then, we have a double celebration here," the Major said. "Dessert is on me."

"None for me, thanks," Danny declined. "I still have to fit in the uniform."

"Me neither," Mad Dog added. "I have to be able to defend myself. Mercedes is in great shape. Besides, if I lose my girlish figure she might leave me."

The Major decided to skip dessert himself and gave the server extra on the tip instead. He said adios to his friends in the parking lot, congratulating each one more time, and headed home to see how his new housemate was getting along with Purvati. Then he laughed at himself for the thought. His cat had taken to Daphne like catnip and was obviously exactly what Daphne needed. So much for Purvati being a one-person cat, but he didn't mind at all. Animals frequently demonstrated a natural ability to sense and provide nurturing to species other than their own. Humans often did as well. *Well, not all humans, but then the world is built on duality.* Maybe it was true that opposites attract. Daphne and Richard were definitely opposites. But then based on his own experiences, the Major was sure Richard hadn't presented an honest representation of himself to Daphne when he lured her into the trap of his emotionally diseased world. And maybe

Daphne had been too unsure of herself to just be herself instead of trying so hard to please him.

"The hazards of being young," the Major mumbled to himself as he drove. He was grateful to have reached the age he now was. His mind wandered to all the emotional perils kids growing up today must face. No matter what time period one grew up in, the species imperative was always impressed upon you at a young age: marry and have children. *The problem with that,* the Major thought, *is that it only allows for the happiness of those cut out for it who are lucky enough to pair up with the right mate. Marriage just isn't for everyone. Having children certainly isn't. But then the evolution of the species hasn't kept up with technological and lifestyle changes.*

Then he thought about Mad Dog getting remarried. Mercedes would have to be an extremely strong personality to handle marriage with Mad Dog, who had already proven to be impossible for two other women to live with. He hoped she didn't want children, because he knew Mad Dog would never go for that, having been physically abused as a child himself. The Major wondered what Daphne's thoughts were on the subject, but decided that now was definitely not the time to ask. Personally he felt there were enough children in the world and felt no imperative to reproduce his particular combination of genes. He was more than satisfied with Purvati's companionship.

Chapter 12

The Song of the Dragonfly

When the Major walked into his house, he was greeted by the sounds of beautiful Spanish music being played on guitar. He tread silently up the stairs to get closer to the music without disturbing the guitarist. He saw through the open bedroom door that the bed had been made. There was a noticeable lump in the center of it under the covers. He knew if he patted the lump it would purr.

The door to the former computer room, now Daphne's new studio, was also open. Her back was to him as she played. There was no music on the stand. She was playing from memory. When she'd finished it, he whispered so as not to startle her, "That was beautiful. What was it?"

"Danza en E minor by Jorge Morel," she replied. "I wish I could have taken lessons or a master class from him, but that's not likely to happen. He must be getting well on in age by now. He's my favorite classical guitarist, and I love that Danza."

"It was beautiful," the Major complimented. "I've heard him play on public radio, but I'd never heard that particular piece."

"It's my favorite of his. The man's a genius both as a performer and a composer—a truly rare talent."

"I should warn you that I play violin," the Major added. "There's no way you won't hear me. We can work it out so that it doesn't interfere with your practice."

Again she was impressed with his thoughtfulness. "I have doors I can close," she reassured him, smiling.

"Good. And maybe a duet someday?" he said as he turned to leave.

"Please wait," she pleaded. "There's something I need to tell you."

He turned back around, came into the room, and sat down on the floor to give her his undivided attention.

She put the guitar back in its case and turned to face him fully, taking a deep breath and letting it out before she began. "I was terrified of becoming homeless. That's partly what kept me with Richard for so long. I know Deandra would never let that happen, but I felt I would be intruding on her lifestyle if I moved in with her." She hesitated slightly and then continued, "No, that's not really true. Deandra would tell me what to do, and I would feel obligated to do whatever she said, because she would be supporting me. I just didn't want to go from the frying pan into the fire so to speak."

"Deandra would never hurt you, but you want to be free to make your own choices and live your own life for a change," the Major affirmed.

"Exactly. I knew that no matter where I ended up, in a shelter, with my sister, or even with my parents, I'd be living under someone else's roof and subject to someone else's rules. I know that's just life, but frankly, I've had enough. I'd actually rather be homeless, and I'm terrified of that. I'd almost rather be dead than homeless, but I feel I have a life to live, and I've been waiting my whole life to start. If I were homeless, it would just be one foot in the grave with the other to follow soon after. I want to live my life before that happens. So the whole point of me telling you this is just to say thank you. But that sounds so inadequate. I'm so grateful to you for giving me the space to breathe and be myself and be safe, but I can't be obligated to you, if that makes any sense at all. I have to break free of feeling that I have to be what other people want me to be."

The Major understood clearly everything she was saying. His response surprised himself as much as it did her. "I want you to be free to be yourself, to be comfortable, and to be safe, because, and I know this is sudden, but I love you. I care about you. I feel like we've already known each other somehow, and I feel very comfortable with you. Even Purvati cares about you. I know you can't and shouldn't respond to that until you're ready, even if it takes years, because right now the best thing for you is to do whatever makes you happy. Meanwhile, if I've made you uncomfortable, I didn't mean to. I didn't even know I was going to say any of this. But trust me when I say you are under no obligation. You have a home here."

"This is amazing," she responded. "I was young when I married Richard. I didn't have any confidence, so I let him bully me to the point where I was afraid to even question him or anything he told me."

"I had suspected as much," the Major commented without explaining further. He was satisfied to have his own suspicion confirmed.

After a few moments, when it became obvious that was all he had to say, she continued, "It took years for me to realize even that he was just a big bully. I was terrified of him. I let my fear get in the way of my ability to think my way out of the situation. But once it became about someone else, a helpless kitty cat, I guess my maternal instinct should have kicked in and taken over. No, please let me finish," she put her hand up to stop him from interrupting. "I understand what you said about the cat protecting me and showing me the way out. And she was just so adorable. She had long hair—what you'd call a tortoise shell—almost black with big green eyes. When I'd pick her up, she'd rub her precious little head against my neck and hold tight to me. She trusted me, and I loved her. I trusted Richard, but he didn't know what love was. I don't know why I couldn't admit that for so long. I don't know why or how I let myself collapse into that helpless state to begin with, but it happened. I let it happen. I trusted the wrong person, and I unwittingly allowed myself to be enslaved by him. I actually thought I was being a good wife, and that I had to take it—you know, for better or for worse. Then the kitty woke me up and showed me what love was really about and that I had to get away from him. She trusted me, and she lost her life because of it."

She paused. She was sobbing heavily by now, so the Major handed her a box of tissues. "The part that really hurts," she continued, "is that I couldn't find a way out that included saving the kitty. I didn't stand up to him when he took her, because I was afraid he'd kill her right in front of me. I don't even know for sure that he took her to the pound, but even if he had, and I'd been able to rescue her, I couldn't take a cat on the train. Besides, I had to sneak out at night to catch the train, and the 'shelter'—there's an oxymoron—was closed. I feel like I'm just rationalizing. I only brought her home because I wanted to love her and give her a good home. I feel so selfish that I ran away without trying to save her too, but as you said, I need to honor her sacrifice."

"There's always the chance that someone else rescued the cat," the Major offered. "She may be alive. She may even have found a good home. She certainly rescued you. Did you know Purvati is sleeping in your bed as we speak? She accepts you as you are—as do I."

"I don't know what to say, but are you sure it's not the other way around?" she asked.

"How so?"

"Maybe I'm the one who slept in Purvati's bed?"

The Major smiled. "Touché. About being homeless—no one wants to be homeless."

"The kitty didn't deserve to be homeless," she interjected.

He continued, "The human race has spent its existence searching for better forms of shelter. It's self-protection. When I was in service, I had a conversation once with a Lieutenant Colonel. Larry Bullock was his name. I don't know much of anything about his past or his upbringing, but he was very elitist. Money was everything to him. According to Larry, it was the only reason to choose a career. To him, all decisions were about money. He seemed to actually believe that poor people had consciously chosen to be poor. He refused to see that different options were available to different people. For those reasons, I thought he just wasn't very smart. He certainly had minimal insight when it came to people."

"People with little insight about others usually have little insight into themselves," Daphne observed.

"Probably so," he agreed. "Larry and I were talking about the economy one day. His lack of perception was astounding. This was back when George W. Bush was president. I expressed concern about the growing numbers of homeless people as an indication that this 'free market' aka 'Reaganomics' didn't work very well. His actual response, if you can believe it, and I swear I'm not making this up, was, 'People are only homeless because they want to be.' I told him he was incredibly naïve, to which he responded, 'Naïve? You're calling me naïve? I'll have you know that I have six college degrees!' He was quite indignant, and before I could stop myself, I blurted out, 'Well they didn't do you any good, did they?'"

Daphne laughed. "Good comeback. That's very sad that he actually believed that."

"I don't know that I believe he really had six college degrees," the Major added. "He may have, but over time, I had heard him lie or exaggerate about himself so many times, I quit believing anything he had to say. I once heard him say that he was working in law enforcement when he wasn't. I would imagine his degree or original degree was probably in economics, but he obviously only understood the dollar signs as they pertained to him and no one else. Very sad."

"You're absolutely right," she added. "There may be a few free spirits out there who choose to wander and not have any roots, but they're few and far between. And there are the mentally ill who have no one to care for them who are probably living in a world of their own, but the vast majority of homeless are homeless simply because they have no where to go for shelter. If I didn't have Deandra to call for help, I would be homeless right now. I'd be lost, and not because I'd want to be. People make bad choices that they don't know are mistakes at the time or they would choose differently. It's probably easy for someone with a good income to deny the needs and pain of others. They think it can't happen to them, and I hope for their sakes they're right. But I've learned to appreciate having shelter for the moment, because I don't know what will happen tomorrow."

"And how many college degrees do you have, little wise one?" the Major asked.

"None," Daphne responded.

"No, you have the highest degree of education," he corrected her. "You have a degree of life."

She smiled and picked her guitar back up to continue practicing, but then she said, "I want to at least honor my kitty with a name. I want to give her a worthy name to remember her by. I know I'll never forget her. I just want to give her a name she might have liked. Any suggestions?"

"Let me think," the Major paused. "She followed you like a little shadow. She tried to protect you. She had her own maternal instinct toward you—very feminine, like the moon. Moonshadow?"

Daphne smiled. "I always loved that song by Cat Stevens. It would be most appropriate to name the kitty after another Cat."

"Except he's Yusuf Islam now," he corrected.

"Yes, you're right about that too. Not too many men change their names. I had to change mine when I got married, but Cat chose to change his. That's different."

"Actually he'd changed his name before," the Major added. "His original name was Steve something, a Greek name I believe."

"But he was Cat Stevens when he wrote and recorded that song. Moonshadow it is. I need to learn that one on the guitar. Then every time I play it, I'll remember her, my very own little Moonshadow. Thank you." She not only was safe and protected, but this kind gentleman had given her a way to honor the memory of the cat who saved her.

"Just remember," he added, "her sacrifice was the one that won the war for you. It woke you up and got you out of there. Little Moonshadow beat Richard. He'll never get you back, will he?"

"Absolutely not," she affirmed. "You're right. Little Moonshadow will always be remembered."

"And she's still following you in spirit watching out for you," he explained. "Think about the words."

She laughed again and started to pick out the tune. She knew she had finally begun a new life.

Chapter 13

Wildflowers versus Cultivated

The next day after breakfast, the Major told Daphne he needed to run some errands and asked if she needed anything. It was actually a cover for the fact that he had promised to take Rose Biegel to the tulip festival up at Woodland, on the Lewis River. He picked up Rose, and as they chatted during the drive north on I-5, he was careful not to mention Daphne or Deandra. Rose asked about Purvati and his garden, and the Major asked about her rose garden. "And I have some news," he added. "Remember Mad Dog Hawkins?"

"Who could forget him?" she responded.

"Well, he's getting married again," the Major informed her. "He's engaged to a Bolivian lady named Mercedes Águila."

"I certainly hope this Mercedes knows what she's getting into with Mad Dog," Rose said. "Maybe Mercedes will be a civilizing influence on him—or at least a taming influence."

The Major smiled.

Before going to see the tulips, they stopped at a family restaurant on the east side of I-5, appropriately called Rosie's, for a pleasant lunch. The Major had met Rose, the owner, before, and introduced the two Roses to each other. He also pointed out the owner's original paintings, which decorated the walls of the restaurant. His Rose was appropriately impressed with the artwork. She had a bowl of chili, while the Major ordered clam strips, green beans, and mashed potatoes off the senior menu.

The tulips at the festival were, of course, blazing with color. There was also a garden with other bulbs, including varieties of anemones the Major hadn't seen before. For the most part, the heavenly fragrance of the hyacinths did a good job covering the smell of manure. In the gift shop, the Major bought two packages of five bulbs each of fragrant Asiatic lilies, one red and one white. Rose was used to him doing his Christmas shopping at odd times of the year, so even though he told her the vase he picked out was for his niece, he felt no need to explain the jigsaw puzzle of beautiful flowers, and Rose didn't ask. He was thinking Daphne might enjoy it while she was in hiding. They could work the puzzle together, or she might like the time alone to think about what to do next with her life.

The Major felt conflicted when he reminded Rose that he had promised her a surprise for Sunday night and would be at her house around 6 PM. He had tickets for the Oregon Symphony and had already asked Rose to reserve Sunday evening for him without telling her where he was taking her. He had asked her before he even met Daphne, and he certainly hadn't expected someone else to enter the picture. *Life has a way of throwing curves into my path when I least expect it.* he reminded himself. *If it didn't, I'd just keep going in the same direction and miss the curves in the path I'm meant to follow. I guess if life came with a road map, there'd be no need for surprises. That would probably get boring. But is a sense of stability too much to ask? Yes, the natural state of matter is change. Just go with it.*

Rose was special, and he valued her friendship above all others. Daphne, on the other hand, was a big unknown in the middle of a transitory crisis, and yet there was chemistry there. He already felt the bond and attraction. He couldn't explain it, and he couldn't deny it, but he already had a relationship with Rose that was very important to him. He loved them both in different ways. He decided to wait and see how things played out at home, while not risking his relationship with Rose. It wasn't exactly honest, but experience told him that when it came to relationships, sometimes honesty could cause hurt without solving problems. At least that's how he rationalized it to himself for the moment. Things had happened quickly, and without adequate intelligence, it was not his nature to rush anything.

As they drove back through town, Rose reminded him that she wanted to see the lilacs in a couple of weeks at the Hulda Klager house. He readily agreed. He loved the smell of lilacs, and Purvati couldn't resist a lilac-scented bubble bath. The last time he had been in the Klager house gift shop a couple of years ago, they had sold it there, and he decided all three ladies in his life would get a bottle. Maybe by then, he'd be able to take Daphne to see the lilacs as well.

After seeing the tulips, Rose and the Major had planned to stop by Horseshoe Lake. It was such a beautiful day, but since neither was feeling very energetic, they made a spontaneous decision to stop in the Visitor Center right before the freeway entrance instead of continuing the short way down to the lake. They picked up some free maps, had a lovely chat about Woodland and Mount St. Helens with two ladies who worked there, and the Major bought a cap for his brother.

It was a pleasant drive back to Vancouver. They talked about all the different flower festivals—tulips, lilacs, fruit trees, rhododendrons, dahlias, and of course the roses. Rose was excited to learn that Pink Martini, one of her favorite music groups, would be doing a live recording with the Oregon Symphony. The Major also told her that the Pearson Air Museum had scheduled an exhibit of Snoopy, World War I Flying Ace, cartoons. Rose collected Snoopy memorabilia, most appropriate for her surname, Biegel.

He dropped her off at her house and headed home. He came inside where Purvati was waiting for him. He picked her up, and they had a prolonged hug, as was their custom whenever he'd been out of the house. Sounds of

Daphne's guitar came from upstairs. He didn't want to interrupt, but as soon as she'd finished the piece, he was waiting at the top of the stairs to ask her what it was.

"Oleander Etude by Ralph Towner," she beamed. "It's another one of my favorites."

"I brought you a little something," the Major offered, handing her the bag with the puzzle he'd bought. "I didn't know if you liked jigsaw puzzles, but I thought the picture was pretty."

"It's beautiful, and I love puzzles."

"I can bring a card table up. You can work it wherever the light is best for you up here. Then if anyone happens to come up here and sees it, I can say I'm doing it."

"That's great. Maybe it will help me sort things out—you know, literally put the pieces together."

The Major went back downstairs and brought up a folding card table. "I hope it won't disturb you, but I need to practice my violin."

"No, not at all. It would be lovely to have some music while I work on this beautiful puzzle. Thank you so much." It was a peaceful evening.

The next morning, the Major went out into his backyard. Ignoring the bamboo while noting its latest advance, he cleaned and weeded the three beds of roses, carefully leaving the volunteer pansies. Then he sprinkled a bit of Epsom salts around each of the four roses in each of the beds, and spread mulch in them to help keep down the weeds. He did the same for the fourth bed of four roses in the front yard.

Along the way, he distracted himself by pulling up dandelions and duckweed. He didn't mind the dandelions so much—he just didn't want them taking over and ruining his otherwise attractive lawn. But he absolutely detested duckweed. He wasn't really sure if what he called duckweed was the real thing. It certainly resembled it, but he didn't know exactly what the overzealous weed was. He just knew he hated it, so he called it duckweed anyway. Rose had agreed that it definitely looked like duckweed. Whatever it was, he didn't want it. He mentally declared war on the duckweed, but since he refused to use chemical weed killers, it would be hand-to-hand combat all the way. He knew it was a war that could last years, but felt his cause was just, because duckweed was just plain ugly in his eyes. *Feo,* he thought to himself every time he saw it. *Feo.*

His original intention that morning, besides taking care of the roses, had been to make a new bed for his new fragrant Asiatic lilies. All in good time. In the process of attacking the duckweed, he discovered a cluster of volunteer wild geraniums. His bleeding heart bed was only half full and starting to bloom, so he filled in the rest of the space by transplanting his newly found treasures. He also had several more forget-me-nots that needed homes. They were already blooming bright blue flowers. He loved them. In walking the backyard, he discovered he'd been robbed. The squirrels had stolen all the trilliums he had planted. He sighed and resentfully hoped they had been tasty or at least replanted elsewhere, and then he proceeded to replace them with the forget-me-nots.

The cell phone in his hip pocket rang. It was Daphne. "If the coast is clear, I could sneak downstairs and make you lunch. Are you ready for a break?"

No one was around but them, he wasn't expecting anyone, and the last he'd heard was that her husband Richard was still in the hospital. "Go for it," he responded. "I could definitely use a break."

Lunch was made of reheated leftovers from his refrigerator. They had a pleasant meal together without any surprises. He very much enjoyed Daphne's company, but he was also aware that she was still married. He would put his feelings on hold while he waited to see what she decided to do for herself.

After lunch, he went back out and made a bed for the new lilies next to the rose bed that wasn't in a raised planter. After the bulbs were all planted and covered with mulch, he spread chili powder and crushed red pepper over all the bulb beds as a deterrent to future theft. He was out of cayenne pepper at the time, which he knew would solve the problem. He made a mental note to himself to buy a larger quantity of cayenne pepper next time he was at the store, so he could spread it over the beds.

Chapter 14

Embodiment of a Rainbow

After he'd showered, shaved, and cleaned himself up, the Major decided to call Rose. She was home and had been working in her own garden. "Have any plans tonight?" he asked.

"You asked me to keep tonight open, so I did," she replied. "Maybe dinner might be included? I'm famished."

"Then you'd better grab something to eat before I pick you up. I have something all set up, but unfortunately the timing doesn't allow for a dinner stop. We would have had to have started earlier. Sorry, but you'll like it. So be sure to eat before I get there."

"Definitely. Not a problem. See you soon," she said, hanging up.

He was grateful that Rose was so flexible like that. He knew he didn't have to tell her how to dress—Rose was always tasteful, even at her most casual. After they'd hung up, he decided to level with Daphne.

He went upstairs. The door was open and she was sitting on the floor leaning up against the bed knitting with those oversized needles she'd brought. Instead of one strand of yarn, she was using three.

When she saw him, she smiled and said, "Knitting is a lot like putting the pieces of a puzzle together. You weave the yarn into stitches, and then hopefully, you end up with something useful. I thought the least I could do was to make you a blanket. I hope you like lots of colors. Since I wasn't sure, I decided to make it a rainbow of colors. Rainbows are not only beautiful, but they symbolize hope, and you've given that back to me—you and Deandra."

"Well, I certainly didn't expect you to make me something, but I love the concept," he responded and decided he could spend a little more time with her before leaving her alone yet again. There was something about her that put him deeply at ease with himself. "Thank you," he said after he'd settled himself on the floor and crossed his legs.

They both fell silent watching the cat as she meandered into the room, but after a few moments Daphne began to feel awkward. "So tell me about Purvati," she asked to get the conversation started again. She put the knitting aside.

"Well, she was a shelter kitten," he explained. "Someone brought her mother and litter of four to the shelter. I met her and her feline family before she was weaned. The first time I picked her up, I held her up to my face to see if her fur would make me sneeze, as some cats do, and she sucked my nose, the little charmer. And I didn't sneeze. We'd already bonded." He beamed with pride as he spoke. It was obvious to Daphne that the Major was in love with his kitty.

They both smiled. "I bet she was precious. I'm glad you shared that. Truthfully though, what I meant to ask was about her namesake."

"At the shelter," he responded obtusely, "the whole litter was named after Star Trek characters, and she was named after some Vulcan woman…"

"No, no," she interrupted him, chuckling. "I meant the goddess you named her after."

"Oh, you mean Parvati," he finally realized. "Parvati, the Hindu goddess of dance. She was Shiva's consort. Of the Hindu trinity, Shiva was the god of destruction, but much like native Central and South American cultures, destruction is just part of the cycle of life. It's more like in physics where nothing is ever really destroyed—it's just transformed. It's more like that. Native American culture didn't have the fear of death the Europeans brought across the ocean with them."

"So, if he was the god of death, then she was the goddess of life?" she reasoned. "That's appropriate—males as warriors while females give birth."

"Not as I perceive it," he offered, "although I was a warrior, or soldier, myself. I see opposites as more like being flip sides of the same coin."

"How is that any different?" she questioned.

"Shiva was the god of destruction and transformation or the constant changing of the universe. Parvati, as the goddess of dance, set the rhythm, or the pace of that change."

They lapsed into silence for a few more moments while Daphne thought about what he'd just said. "So you keep the household running, but Purvati sets the pace," she deduced.

"That just about sums it up pretty well," he smiled. He liked her response.

Daphne thought, *What a contrast there is between a man who would leave a kitten to be killed and one who would let it suck his nose and fall in love with it.* She definitely preferred the latter.

"I guess consorts of any culture," he continued, "are always comparable to the sun and the moon. It's sort of inevitable, since the sun is pretty much universally associated with male attributes and the moon with female attributes."

"And the moon sets the rhythm of the tides. The heart beats in rhythm. So Parvati is the goddess of rhythm and life, which is a dance. The sun and the moon—day and night—with the common ground, or merging, at dawn and dusk," she concluded his thought with her own.

"Ah, there's a poet in you," he observed.

"Sort of goes with the instrument," she agreed.

"And a Spanish one at that," he said approvingly.

"True," she admitted, "and in my humble opinion, Spanish is the most musical language on the planet, except for Hawaiian."

He smiled broadly. There was much common ground here to explore and upon which to build a lasting relationship. Then he realized the time—he had almost forgotten about Rose and the symphony. He really wanted to stay with Daphne, but he'd already made a commitment to Rose, and he didn't believe in breaking promises.

"I wanted to tell you I'm going to the symphony tonight with a friend," he explained. "I always leave a light on in the living room to make it look like someone's home, so I will again tonight. The blinds in the front will be closed, but be aware of creating a shadow if you need to go down to the kitchen." *Well*, he rationalized to himself, *that wasn't exactly leveling, but it was a start*. He started to leave and then turned around and added, "Savik—that was what they called Purvati at the shelter. I'd almost forgotten. It was six and a half years ago."

"Don't worry about us," Daphne said, stroking the cat. She smiled as he left.

He picked Rose up about 6:20. They got back on I-5 and headed south.

"Ok, I'm looking forward to being surprised, but the suspense is killing me," Rose told him. "We're either going to downtown Vancouver or to Portland," she surmised.

"You'll like it," was all he told her. He smiled and said nothing else. They passed downtown Vancouver and were crossing the I-5 Bridge.

"Ok, so we're going to Portland. Something restful but not dinner. So, we're going to a movie?"

He smiled and said nothing.

When they turned onto the Morrison Bridge toward downtown Portland, she guessed, "A play?" And then they turned south onto Broadway toward the Arlene Schnitzer Concert Hall. Before long, the flashing lights of the marquee came into view, and then she knew. "The pianist Garrick Ohlsson! Oh, this is a wonderful surprise. I do believe I'm up for this." And now they were both all smiles.

"The tickets were kind of last minute, so we won't be able to see his hands because we'll be off to the other side in the fifth row." He didn't tell her the seats were only fifteen dollars each, just because they were in the first five rows. They both loved the Schnitzer Hall and the Oregon Symphony. Sound-wise, there wasn't a bad seat in the house, and symphony-wise, the musicians were all above first class.

After they were seated and perused the program, Rose saw that James DePriest, who had been the conductor of the Oregon Symphony for many years until 2003, was conducting, and she was delighted. They read in the program that he was now the director of conducting and orchestral studies at The Juilliard School in New York City. The Major saw that the first piece on the program was The Rainbow Body. He thought about the rainbow blanket Daphne was making him and the rainbows that appeared in his foyer and music room whenever the sun was out.

This particular piece, The Rainbow Body, was composed by Christopher Theofanidis and inspired in part by the Tibetan Buddhist concept of an enlightened soul being absorbed back into the universe in the form of energy or light after the death of the physical body. The piece itself was spectacular, and the performance was superb. Conductor and symphony were as one entity. The Major found himself aware of a sense of serenity—that everything was just as it should be—as well as realizing there was much more to Daphne than met the eye. In a very personal way the piece hit home for him. The music made him feel like he was flying out in space through the stars like a bird of spiritual light. He found himself thinking how serene his own home was, and how Daphne fit right in, even belonged there. He felt everything was just as it should be, because she was there. He was sure now that she must be the woman he had flown with and made love with in the stars in his dreams. The universe had found a very strange way of finally bringing her to him. But it had at last. He realized that he was going to have to tell Rose about Daphne, and that he was going to wait for Daphne to deal with her broken marriage. But he knew now that the lady he wanted in his life was Daphne Robin.

The rest of the performance was equal to its beginning. Rose was right (she usually was—she wasn't one to offer an uninformed opinion) about both Garrick Ohlsson and James DePriest. On the Sibelius Symphony Number 1, the conductor and the entire symphony excelled.

When they arrived back at Rose's house, she invited the Major in for a cup of tea. He readily accepted, thinking it might offer an opportunity to find a way to confide in Rose about Daphne. He also needed a shot of caffeine before driving back home across town, as he was starting to feel sleepy. He told her about the fragrant Asiatic lily bed he had made, how the squirrels had stolen his trilliums, and his security measures of chili powder and red pepper. He told her about his war on duckweed and how he'd been putting off attacking the bamboo and dandelions. He told her about transplanting the wild geraniums and forget-me-nots. What he forgot to tell her about was Daphne. On the way home, he rationalized to himself that it was because he was tired.

Chapter 15

Shadow Falls across the Moon

The Major awoke from a nightmare. Purvati was standing over him looking concerned. He had been dreaming of funerals—going to each funeral in succession of every soldier he had ever known who had died, whether he had actually attended their funeral in real life or not. There were a lot of funerals. One officer had drowned in the Gulf of Mexico while on leave with his family. They were on the beach, and he went out for a swim, only to be caught in the undertow and pulled out to sea. He was a strong swimmer and made it back to shore, but it was too late. His lungs had already filled with water, and his heart gave out. He died on the beach.

A couple of privates had been killed in a tragic automobile accident. They were so young. Only the driver had worn a seatbelt. The Major remembered the one survivor, who was on crutches when he got out of the hospital. He had been the driver. He admitted he had been speeding and driving recklessly. The Major remembered the very young man telling him, "I have to go to prison. I have to live with knowing that I killed my friends."

There were several motorcycle accidents. The most vivid in his memory was the one rider who slammed into the back of an eighteen wheeler truck at a high rate of speed. There wasn't much left of him.

And then there were the suicides—so many that he wasn't sure anymore exactly how many there had actually been. One soldier had hung himself because his marriage had ended. There were others, but only one he still questioned. That soldier had allegedly been stealing supplies and was about to get caught, but the Major remembered that, at the time, he thought the evidence didn't add up. The Major himself had just inspected the soldier's inventory on Thursday. The next day, he had written his report saying that everything was in order and no discrepancies were found. The soldier had seemed in good spirits. Then that weekend, while his wife was out of the house at work, and the soldier was alone with his toddler son, he allegedly shot himself in the head. Stranger things had surely happened in this world, but the Major never figured him for a man who would intentionally leave the boy unsupervised, much less permanently traumatize the child with being in the same house when he committed the act. That soldier had been a responsible, doting father up until his sudden death. And why, the Major still wondered after all these years, would he have killed himself after being exonerated? But the Criminal Investigations Division had insisted on ruling it suicide. The Major had no authority to say otherwise. He wondered how the widow and child had managed over the years. He wondered how all the other families had coped as well. He figured that when a person reached a breaking point that led to suicide, they were no longer capable of considering the consequences created for those they were leaving behind. But he still didn't believe that particular one was a suicide.

There were two natural deaths he remembered. One sergeant was in his thirties and the other in his forties. Both had died in their sleep. The official cause for both was heart attack. He wondered now if sleep apnea was involved.

But of course, the vast majority of the funerals in his dream were for all those in Desert Storm, Afghanistan, and the second Iraq war. He wondered why his country had such a difficult time learning lessons from its own history. The contrast between Viet Nam and Desert Storm and the parallel between Viet Nam and Afghanistan surely should have prevented the ill-fated invasion of Iraq by the second President Bush—except that it hadn't. He thought about all the civilian Iraqi families with lives and daily routines that were normal for them until suddenly disrupted by the invasion. They had been left without the basic modern services of electricity and running water for years, and just as suddenly, their private homes were subject to being invaded and searched by foreign soldiers. Many civilians were arrested and torn from their loved ones, and sometimes they were killed in the crossfire of urban warfare. The American politicians kept denying that the United States was occupying Iraq, but to the Major, it was obvious that the United States was occupying Iraq. And the American news media regularly reported US military fatalities, but only rarely did they mention Iraqi civilian casualties. *It doesn't take a genius to figure out you make enemies by killing people's loved ones.*

The Major sighed as he fixed himself a cup of jasmine tea. He was grateful that everything from the dream was in his past. He hoped this would be the last of the nightmares, but he knew the unconscious wouldn't forget traumas so easily. He remembered the last time it had gotten to him. He had called Mad Dog Hawkins to talk about it. "Don't feed the emotion," was Mad Dog's advice. *Good advice.*

More advice came to him from past conversations with Becky Roan. "Explore the past, and extract only the sweet joy." That was a harder one to apply here. Hummingbirds live in the present. He should be happy just to be alive. He looked out at his garden. He actually was happy with his life. *Thank you, Becky,* he thought. And now he had the woman of his happier dreams in his own house, under this very roof.

Still the heaviness of the more recent dream hung over him. He pondered the attraction of joining the military for so many young people. There was the obvious package of incentives—the monetary bonus for signing up, the education benefits that anyone from a less than wealthy family had trouble getting otherwise, the call to serve for some, and the superficial prestige of wearing a uniform. He refused to speculate on the women's reasons, but he knew all too well that most of the young men attracted to the military were the type that loved to cross boundaries, challenge limits, and push the envelope. Unfortunately, they had grown up with the false impression from video games and Hollywood hype that this was the macho way to go, when in fact, a good army was a well-disciplined one, where everyone followed legal orders and only legal orders were given. He sighed again and sipped his tea. If only that were really the case. Those disinclined to respect boundaries were also disinclined to respect the law and rights of other people, cultures, and societies. He knew this from experience. He took another sip of tea. Those eager to please for self-advancement and because they craved recognition would usually do anything, right or wrong, if they thought it would make them appear heroic or great.

He truly admired the young people who entered the service because they wanted to serve. He wished that had been his own motivation, but it honestly wasn't. His parents had seen it as a way for him to get an education and honorably rise above the social stigma of being Latino. Maybe they were also proud of being part of their country and saw no other way to give back to it, but he had simply taken the easy way out. He wanted to please his parents and have a secure paycheck. He had to admit to himself that he honestly had not pursued his career for the sake of serving. That was something he had learned along the way. At least he had no regrets about having learned it.

He sipped his tea as he looked out the back window at all the work he had done in his garden. He decided that if it was successful and produced an abundance of blooms, he could share them with some of the local nursing homes for those patients without flowers in their rooms. Then he laughed at his assumption of grandiosity, knowing Nature, and her squirrels, had her way of delivering unexpected and unwanted surprises. Still, it was a nice idea. With all the suffering people, and all the indignities inflicted on the poor, one didn't need to be a military hero to serve. He sighed again and took another sip of tea. He had come to see the military as being made up of a majority of emotionally immature people all the way to the top levels, propagating false advertising to other emotionally immature people, and creating a self-perpetuating organization. He knew he was truly conflicted, which was another motivation for retiring when he did. He wished he was wrong, but all he had to go on was his own experience, and this was what it told him. *Maybe I'm projecting myself onto others? Or maybe I'm just processing these memories so I can move on.*

He wished there was a way to warn anyone with creative talents not to be lured into the trap as he had been. It wasn't that service didn't provide a good career for someone suited to it, and it truly had provided him an honorable way of making a good living with benefits for which he was grateful, but at the same time, it had required him to use all of his natural creative energy to suppress his creative talent. As he had learned from Dr. Bernstein, that just wasn't mentally healthy. Nor had it been healthy to be in an environment with others who not only were not naturally creative, but scoffed at sensitivity, while needing constant direction because they lacked any inner moral compass of their own. Not all of them were that way of course, but all it took was a few close at hand to make him feel uncomfortable, like he didn't belong, and, well, dirty. At least now he was free to grow flowers and play his violin. He counted at least four times he'd had to start over with the violin because his job had kept him away from it for so long. Sacrifice was the nature of service, but at least if you died in the line of duty, it was only once. Being cut off from an integral part of oneself was, after all, a form of spiritual or emotional death.

But enough about him. Daphne was a sensitive, compassionate, intelligent woman, and they had a lot in common. They both loved music and had similar tastes in music. They were both interested in other cultures and liked to read. And they both liked animals. She was creative with her knitting, while he had his gardening. *There's nothing more intimate than sharing dreams with each other.* And now, he was free to tell this woman of his dreams how he felt about her. Hopefully, he could persuade her to consider spending the rest of her life with him. They could enjoy the garden together, no matter what actually bloomed. They could enjoy all of life together. With Purvati, they would be a family.

He fixed a tray with jasmine tea, a blueberry bagel, cream cheese, and a copy of the program from last night's concert with The Rainbow Body circled, and carried it upstairs. It was still early, and her bedroom door was closed, so he left it outside the door. He hoped the tea didn't cool off too much before she found it. Still, he had found jasmine tea was just as pleasant cold as hot, so maybe it wouldn't matter. He knocked softly, conflicted about waking her if she was sleeping, but also not wanting Purvati to get into the cream cheese. As he turned to go back downstairs, he saw the kitty coming up the stairs— probably expecting to get in between him and Daphne as she had last night before he had gone to the concert. She seemed to enjoy having twice as much attention.

He picked her up and carried her down the stairs. "Let's let Daphne have her sleep," he told her, "and let's not get into her breakfast. I'm going to have to keep an eye on you, aren't I?" She purred.

He thought about The Rainbow Body and Lady Rainbow, the Mayan moon goddess, who had been protected by the singing of dragonflies. He thought it was interesting that the Tibetan Buddhist chants could be easily compared to the drone of dragonflies. He made a mental note to discuss this with Daphne. He was sure she would also find it interesting.

About a half hour later the phone rang. Deandra Robin sounded like she was hyperventilating. She was talking so fast that the Major had to tell her, "Just calm down. Take a deep breath and let it out slowly." He could hear her inhale and exhale. "Now please start over so I can understand you."

"Richard Gatorman is HERE. He's in my house," she said. "He checked himself out of the hospital against doctor's orders and came up here. I told him Daphne had gone to Redding, but he said he knew that was bullshit. He knew she had taken a train to Portland. So I told him she had gone on to Seattle, but he doesn't believe me. Why should he? I already lied to him once. Colonel, I don't want him in my house, but he says he's not leaving."

"Are you free to call the police?" the Major asked, very concerned.

"No, he's not going to let me do that."

"Pretend to keep talking to me. Act like you're trying to find out from me exactly where Daphne was going in Seattle. I'm hanging up now to call the police," he explained. He called the police and reported the situation, giving them Deandra's home address, but leaving out the part about Daphne being in his house. It didn't feel right to not tell the police everything, but what they didn't know, they couldn't let slip when they confronted Mr. Gatorman. He simply told them Deandra had called him, said she couldn't get the man out of her house, and that she was very much afraid. The Major told the police he thought it best they handle the situation, and of course, they agreed.

Chapter 16

The Seed Germinates

When the Major went back upstairs, he found Daphne's bedroom door open. She was sitting on the bed eating her breakfast.

"Your husband is in town," he told her. "He's at your sister's house."

"But I thought he was in the hospital. Isn't he still in the hospital?" she questioned, just catching a piece of bagel that almost fell out of her mouth.

"Apparently he checked himself out," he explained. "He somehow found out you had come to Portland. How did you pay for the train ticket?"

"I used my debit card," she answered.

"Well, that's probably how he found out," the Major reasoned. "I'd recommend you sever all joint accounts with him as quickly as possible."

"Oh, I've already done that," she rebutted, "not that he let me have access to his money anyway. When Deandra set up my cell phone, she also set up a bank account for me here in Vancouver, so she could make deposits if I needed money, and also so Richard wouldn't know. The bank sent me a debit card. He doesn't even know I have it."

The Major studied her face and body language for a few minutes while neither of them said anything. *Deandra said he knew she'd taken the train,* he thought. Then it dawned on him what had happened. "You called him on your cell phone?" he asked incredulously.

"No, of course not. But I did call the hospital to find out how he was doing." Another long silence followed as the Major tried to follow her reasoning. Finally, when it became obvious he wasn't going to say anything, she explained, "I am his wife. I've been thinking I need to do something soon to change that, except I don't have money for a lawyer. Please, try to understand. I was the one who encouraged him to keep drinking so he would get drunk enough to pass out, so I could leave without his knowing. He's in the hospital because of me. I feel responsible."

"And the person you spoke to at the hospital was...?"

"His nurse. I called the nurse's station. I wasn't going to call him," she answered defensively. She was starting to feel like he was interrogating her. "I never intended to put him in the hospital," she emphasized.

The Major paused another moment taking this all in. He could see her concern, and he understood she was in a terribly conflicted position. But until this moment, he just hadn't realized exactly how isolated and alone she felt. He wished he had spent more time with her and spoken more with her, so she might have discussed her concerns with him first. But he realized that from her perspective, he was barely past being a stranger who was just being kind to her. "Did the nurse you spoke to ask how to reach you in case of emergency?" he asked her, deliberately softening his voice, trying to keep from upsetting her further.

"Well, yes," she answered, "I gave her my cell phone number."

"And until then, Richard hadn't known that you even had a cell phone?"

Daphne gasped and covered her mouth with both hands at the same time as she realized what she had done. "The area code is 360 for Vancouver. The nurse must have told him I called, and he must have asked her for the number."

"He probably told her he couldn't remember it, which would be credible for an alcoholic. Or maybe he said he just didn't have it with him, and the nurse wouldn't have known you didn't want him to know where you were, unless you had thought to tell her," he added.

"And I didn't think to. I just wanted to know if he was going to be ok."

"And that would sound like normal spousal concern. The nurse had no way of knowing you were a wife in hiding," he finished the thought for her.

"Can I impose on you one more time, please?" she begged.

"Depends," he answered cautiously, not knowing what might be coming next.

"Can you please give me a ride to the train station? I need to leave as quickly as possible."

"Why? He doesn't know where to find you. He doesn't know me or where I live. Deandra and the police don't even know you're in town. You're actually safest right here. He came up here thinking you were with Deandra. He knows now that you're not. I think you should just stay put."

He could see the relief in her face, and her shoulders noticeably relaxed. "What would I do without you, Major?" she smiled.

"Ditch the cell phone?" he suggested. She gladly handed it over to him. He turned to leave the room.

"I was thinking about our conversation before you went to the symphony," she started. She was relieved when he politely turned back around to listen, something Richard would never have done without an angry, explosive reaction. "We were talking about the Hindu god and goddess, Shiva and Parvati," she reminded him.

"Yes, I remember," he smiled and the tension in his face disappeared.

"The Hindus believe in seven spiritual centers in the physical body," she continued, "and there are seven notes in the scale. In Hindi music, the first and fifth notes of the scale, corresponding to the genitals and the throat, are never altered, while only the fourth, corresponding to the heart, is ever raised a half step. And the other notes can only be lowered a half step. All that determines the scale for the raga, and time of day traditionally determines which scale or raga could be played."

When she saw his surprise, she explained, "I love the sitar. After all, it's a cousin of the guitar. I guess I've read a lot to understand its music. I even tried to learn Hindi once, but just the different alphabet and all the different ways to pronounce letters that we only hear one sound for was complicated enough, without the sentence structure being reversed from ours. It was too much for me. Before that, I used to think English was a difficult language, but the Indian people seem to have mastered it."

"That explains why Indians speaking English are so precise in their pronunciation, and why their music is so intricate," he reasoned. "Makes sense that such an ancient culture would have such a well-developed ear for subtleties that English speaking cultures tend to miss."

"Maybe that's why many Americans have difficulty understanding them speak English," Daphne laughed. "We're just not used to that kind of precision in speaking. And along the same line of thinking," she added, "it follows that Spanish-speaking people would be more fluent with their feelings, since it's such a musical language."

"I never thought of Hindi and Spanish as consorts before," he mused, "but they are opposites in many ways. The concept fits with Hindi being intellectual, or the masculine and Spanish being the emotional, or feminine."

"The Indian civilization is older," she continued the analogy, "and the moon reflects the light back. One is the eastern hemisphere, and the other is the western."

"It's nice having someone intelligent to talk to," he complimented her. "You know Shiva's transformation requires sacrifice. There's a whole lot about sacrifice in the native Mesoamerican culture."

"Change and sacrifice are part of the transformation of life," she summarized.

"And you've made quite a sacrifice to be here with us. Thank you for having the courage to take that step."

She blushed and lowered her head slightly, smiling. Then she looked up at him. "I appreciated the program you gave me from the symphony. I would have loved to have heard The Rainbow Body. Could you tell me about it, please?"

"I was hoping to discuss it with you," he began. "And I wish you could have been there with me. It was quite the experience. I suspect you're familiar with Tibetan Buddhist chanting."

She nodded that she was.

He continued. "In Central America, where my grandparents came from, there was a moon goddess known as Lady Rainbow. When she was ill, she was healed by the singing of dragonflies. That's how The Rainbow Body felt when I heard it—like thousands of dragonflies singing— and the symphony and conductor and audience were all woven together into one being by the music, much like your rainbow of yarns being woven into one blanket."

"Wow," she responded. "That must have been really something."

"It was, and even though that was the best composition of the evening, in my personal opinion, the performance just continued to get better after that. I think they sort of wove themselves together with the first piece. Then the rest of the concert was nothing short of magical."

She leaned back and closed her eyes, obviously trying to imagine it.

"Someday, I'd like very much to take you to a symphony," he offered.

"And I would like very much to go with you," she agreed, and then added, "You know Richard isn't likely to ever show up at one."

The Major thought about that for a minute. "If you hid in the trunk of the car, like Prince Charles used to when he was sneaking out for a visit with Camilla, and I parked in an underground parking garage—and there's one a few blocks south of the concert hall—it might work, unless Richard just happened to be on Broadway at that time of evening."

"Hmm. There's always that." Her shoulders dropped in disappointment.

"All in good time," he added. "I promise we'll go to a symphony together someday."

"That would be nice," she said unconvinced. "So, how does a moon goddess become ill?" she asked him. He looked puzzled, and then she realized she had changed the subject back and he hadn't caught on. "The dragonflies' singing healed her," she prompted him. "How does a moon goddess become ill?"

"Oh, that. She fell in love with the sun," he explained.

"So she was like me? She only reflected his light and not her own?" she asked.

"No, actually her grandfather cursed her, I think," he answered.

"Why would he do that?" she questioned.

"I'm not sure. I don't remember. My guess would be that either he had someone else in mind for her or he had a history with the sun. Anyway he objected to her falling in love with the sun."

"That's sad, but good that the dragonflies were on her side. It's good to have friends to support you," she observed.

"Elder generations like parents and grandparents may want the best for their children and grandchildren, but they don't always know what that is," he commented.

"Why do you suppose that is?" she asked.

"Hindsight's a marvelous thing," he answered, "and I'm really into it a lot myself these days. But looking at the past can't help you see what's going to change in the future, unless you realize something you missed before. Although examining the past with the benefit of hindsight usually does exactly that. Take myself, for example. I was the obedient son. I trusted my parents' judgment that getting a college education and a military commission was the best way to go for me. They wanted to be sure I was financially secure. They were also keenly aware of the prejudice against Latinos. They felt that being a military officer would put me above such reproach—that it would even the playing field against bigotry, so to speak."

"And did it?"

"Well, yes, in a lot of ways they were right. And yes, I'm financially secure and had an honorable career. But I wasn't true to myself."

"How so?" She liked that he was opening up to her.

"I had to repress my true personality to fit into the uniform. It was a lifestyle uncomfortably alien to my nature. I was laughed at by other officers far more for playing violin and for my violin being so important to me than because of my ethnic background. I told myself that the bigotry and stereotyping I might have encountered outside the military would have been far worse. I told myself a lot of lies just to get along from day to day, but in hindsight, being judged, criticized, or laughed at for being who you really are is just as damaging.

"When I was young, I was innocent and naïve—like most young people. I didn't know when to keep my mouth shut. I didn't know there was something wrong in their eyes with letting them see me for who I was, but I learned the hard way. And then I made the mistake of letting on how their verbal abuse hurt me, which was another source of criticism. In the Army, you're not supposed to be an individual, and you're definitely not supposed to have feelings. In any branch of the military, you're only supposed to conform to what they need you to be. It's considered unprofessional to ever express your feelings. I gradually learned to associate 'professional' with inhuman."

"Well, no wonder the Army has so many suicides," she interjected.

"True," he agreed. "I've known too many myself. As a matter of coincidence, I dreamt about a lot of them just last night."

"I don't believe in coincidences," she commented. "I believe everything happens for a reason. We just perceive coincidence, because our conscious minds can't put all the pieces together all at once to understand. At least, that's how I see it."

"That's a valid point, and it may be so. But anyway, I learned to spend most of my life keeping myself to myself and telling myself that it was ok to pretend to be something I wasn't. I can only imagine how much damage was done to young people not cut out for military service back during the days of the draft. I'm proud that I survived it all honorably, and I'm proud that I served my country and honored my parents. But I'm also proud that I really am a sensitive, creative individual. I had to spend time with a psychologist to learn to accept that. I actually had to go to a doctor to learn how to be myself again."

"I'm glad you did," she responded. "It sounds painful, but I can relate, because for so many years, I didn't allow myself to be myself either, but for different reasons. I guess it's a good thing we're adaptable. But it's even better to realize that there are always better options, and it's ok to choose one. If you'd realized that when your parents were pushing you to become an officer, what do you think now that you might have done then?"

"Well," he said, "I picked up the violin on my own and was never a virtuoso or prodigy, so I wouldn't have been able to get a scholarship to study music, and I'm not sure I would have wanted a performing or teaching career anyway. But I always wanted to follow in my father's footsteps and be a gardener. I love flowers. It would have been hard work, and it would have been much harder to break out of the ethnic stereotyping, but who cares? I think I would have been happy. And I might have worked my way through college anyway. If not, I simply wouldn't have had a lot of the luxuries I have now. My brother worked his own way through college and became an engineer. I don't know what I might have studied other than ornamental horticulture or landscaping—maybe botany—but I think it would have been a better fit for me, and I wouldn't have had to deny my own true nature for so long."

"So did the dragonflies represent Nature in the Lady Rainbow story?" Daphne wondered.

"Maybe so," he mused. "I've often wondered about that myself—what they were meant to symbolize. There's the obvious iridescence of their wings that refracts the sunlight like rainbows, which I'm sure is why they were associated with her name, Lady Rainbow. Or maybe they were an ally of the sun? I had thought once that maybe they represented time, since that's supposed to heal, but it never fit the story. I think maybe they were supposed to be like her animal self, another manifestation of her that was there to protect her. And that would mean that part of her came forward to heal herself. We all have a part of ourselves that can be symbolized by another species from the animal kingdom, and it's important for us to be in touch with that part of ourselves to stay healthy—at least that's what my grandparents believed. Either that, or maybe the dragonflies were psychologists who help people see what should be painfully obvious if they aren't busy denying who they are to themselves just to survive day to day. Funny, I'd never compared myself to a goddess before—that's a new one for me. Please don't tell anyone."

"No worries there," she reassured him. "Does your psychologist know you've compared him to a dragonfly?" They both laughed.

"I wonder what he'd make of that," the Major answered.

"Well, now you have my cell phone, so I can't call anyone in touch with Richard again," she said. "But, as for the sun and the moon, we all have male and female natures in our personalities, just different balances of each."

"Balance is the key," he replied. "Living's definitely a balancing act. Don't get me wrong, though. I'm truly grateful for my status in life. I'm just a whole lot more grateful that I'm retired and free to be myself. I've had to relearn not to accept invalid criticism. The military has a tradition of destroying a person's self-esteem the same way and for the same reason that kidnappers do it to their victims—to get the person to identify solely with them as the authority so the individual will lose their true sense of identity. That part I resent and will never allow to happen again. I suspect that's why there was such a backlash of veterans against the Viet Nam War—they were subjected to that kind of treatment against their will, and quite naturally, they were angry about it. It feels like being violated."

"That sounds like some powerful feelings you have there," she commented. "I can relate. Maybe you should write about your experiences and ideas. Sharing your thoughts might be good therapy, and you might give others some insight as well."

"I'll give that idea some thought," he said. "I'm pretty good at putting words on paper, but everybody publishes these days. I doubt an unknown like me would have a very wide audience. And on top of that, as a country, the United States is still dealing with accepting its diversity. It hasn't even gotten close to the looking-for-insight stage yet."

"Oh, I disagree," she objected. "Maybe not on the whole society's level, but lots of individuals are searching for insight. Many people find themselves in situations where they feel trapped and not able to express or defend themselves. And a whole lot of them don't have the financial resources to see a psychologist. That's why self-help books are such big sellers. It's unfortunate, but it's not unusual to feel you're alone in your predicament. I know I did. Self-help books have helped to keep me sane."

"Well, maybe if I could figure out the dragonfly thing I could start with that," he said. He was still wondering about those dragonflies. He had for a long time whenever he'd thought about it, which actually hadn't been that often. His interest was piqued now, and he resolved to contemplate it further.

"The beating of their wings is like the beating of the heart," she suggested. "Maybe Lady Rainbow was healed by acknowledging the true feelings of her heart and following them."

"That certainly rings true," he admitted.

"Then dragonflies, as well as birds, are angels," she added.

"I have another friend who likes to decorate with rainbows and dragonflies," he went on. "She's especially fond of hummingbirds, who also sing with their wings."

Daphne picked up her guitar, sat down in the folding chair, and played a beautiful piece of music for him. When she was done, she explained, "That was El Colibrí."

He smiled. The Hummingbird.

Chapter 17

Fruit and Peanuts

The next morning, the Major sliced and mixed two bowls of apples, bananas, and strawberries with red grapes and fat-free Cool Whip. Then he poured two glasses of iced green tea, put it all on a tray with silverware and napkins, and took it upstairs. Daphne's door was closed, but instead of leaving it this time, he knocked and waited patiently. When the door opened, she was looking down at where he usually left the tray, but when she saw his feet instead, she looked up in surprise and smiled.

"I thought we might have breakfast together this morning," he offered.

"I'd like that very much," she replied as she stepped aside to let him into the room. He moved toward the card table, and she quickly grabbed the half-empty jigsaw puzzle box sitting on it so he could set the tray on top of the partially worked puzzle. He pulled up the rocking chair, while she got the folding chair she had been using to practice guitar.

After they sat down and began to eat, he commented, "I thought you might be getting lonely up here, and it's always nice to have someone to talk to. I usually have breakfast with Purvati, but the conversation's always a bit one-sided."

"And what do you and Purvati usually discuss?" she deflected.

"Well, I tell her what I'm planning to do in the garden, or if I have to go out to run errands or meet someone, but she usually wanders off if I'm not eating anything worth waiting for. If it's something she likes, she has to wait until I've finished, and she will, but otherwise, what's the point? I'd like to ask her how she slept or if she had any interesting dreams, but she plays most of the night, and I know how she's slept in the early morning hours because it's on top of me."

"Well, it just so happens I've been sleeping very well here," Daphne answered, eagerly taking the bait. "I think I'm catching up on a lot of lost rest. Before, with Richard, it was more like sleeping with one eye open, so to speak, only I don't think I was consciously aware that it had come to that. At least it was that way until I started lucid dreaming about flying." She paused, waiting for him to comment.

"I can't imagine having to share a bed with someone you knew you couldn't trust," he said thoughtfully.

When she realized he wasn't going to comment on the dreams about flying, she continued, "I think trust was destroyed in that relationship a long time ago, but I didn't know what else to do or where else to go. I wouldn't let myself admit that I had become trapped—it was too humiliating. I actually believed that I was what was wrong. The truth is that it takes two to make a relationship and two to destroy it, but I took all the blame on myself, because that's what he kept telling me. I don't know why I believed him.

"Anyway, when I did dream at night when I was with him, at first it was usually an unpleasant dream, like my subconscious was trying to wake me up to what was really going on. But I worked very hard mentally to forget those dreams. Come to think of it, doing that took a lot of energy out of me. Then I started having nice dreams, and they were truly amazing. I would dream I could fly and walk through walls like I had superhuman powers. Then I would spend a lot of energy during the day fantasizing about being able to just fly away. All of that took a lot of energy out of me."

She waited for the Major to say something to confirm her suspicion that he was her dream companion. When he didn't say anything, she added, "There was always someone else in those dreams with me—someone who sang beautifully and played violin." She paused again and waited for the Major to say something, but he just broadened his smile knowingly. So she continued.

"Anyway, I had this great dream last night, only it wasn't about flying. I dreamt I was in one of those multiple-cinema movie theaters, and there were three rooms to choose from. In the first one were all of Richard's friends, everyone we've known since we first started dating. They were having some sort of buffet with picnic or barbeque-type foods. I didn't want to be around any of those people anymore, so I went into the second room. It was an actual movie theater showing nothing but war movies. I sat down and watched for a few minutes, but I was tired of Richard's war, so I left and went to the third room. It was the smallest of the three, and it was filled with knots and tangles of yarn—huge balls of tangled and knotted yarn." She stretched her arms out as far as they could go to try to demonstrate the enormity of the tangled balls of yarn.

"Somehow I knew that the way to undo the war that was going on in the next theater was to undo all the knots and tangles in the yarn. So, I sat down on the floor and began to do just that. I knew that when I freed all that yarn, it would be available to make something beautiful and useful."

The Major paused to swallow his bite of fruit and take a sip of tea before responding. "Well, that certainly makes my dream pale by comparison. While you were dreaming about how to change the world, I dreamed I needed to eat peanuts." They both laughed.

"Now that I think about it," she said thoughtfully, "I think the yarn was all the knotted nerves and tangled emotions inside me. I think I'm on the right path to freeing myself from all of that and finding peace."

The Major looked at her in admiration. "That's a truly wonderful thing."

"So what do peanuts represent to you?" she asked him.

"Probably something I'm not getting in my diet." He noticed her sudden skeptical look. "Or it could be paying attention to the little things, the details that are so important, like the detail I had missed until yesterday—that we needed to spend time just talking and getting to know each other. After all, we are living under the same roof."

"That's better. After all, you come from a part of the world with a rich history of dream interpretation. And I'd like that very much—getting to know each other," she agreed. "I know I've imposed myself on your home, your personal space, your routine, your life. I'm well aware that you had a life before I showed up, and I must be an interruption."

"No, not really," he contradicted. "I prefer to think of you as more of a special addition rather than an interruption. I think this is as good a time as any to tell you that I already had a girlfriend before you arrived. Rose Biegel is the friend I went to the symphony with."

"I kind of figured out there was someone," Daphne lied to reassure him, even though she suddenly felt crushed inside. She felt like she should have seen this coming, since she only just came into his life. "I mean it was possible you were going with just a friend, but the day you brought me the puzzle, you had been gone quite a long time as well. And any man as sweet, considerate, and nice-looking as you is bound to have someone. But thank you for telling me. I don't want to cause any problems between you and Rose. What a lovely name, by the way."

As soon as she'd said it all, she realized she was doing the same thing she always did, in spite of the conversation they'd just had the day before about repressing one's true feelings. She didn't know whether she was blindsided more by his admission or by her own wishful thinking. *Why can't I just tell him I think he's the man in my dreams? What if I'm delusional and he decided I should leave? Who would want to hide a crazy woman with a violent husband—especially since the Major already has a girlfriend?*

"Then I'm glad we talked about it. I should clarify that, even though we've been seeing each other for a couple of years, we've never even discussed seeing each other exclusively," he said, trying to leave the door open. "We're not engaged or anything."

"But silence is often inferred as consent, even though it rarely actually means that. Maybe you should talk to Rose about it," she counseled, even though she really just wanted to run away and cry. But she had intruded on his world. She wanted to find hope in him saying that since he and Rose weren't officially committed to each other, maybe there was room for her. But then maybe she wasn't good enough for him, she told herself. She certainly had no right to come between him and this woman for whom he obviously had strong feelings.

The Major was genuinely surprised. He felt blindsided. It had never occurred to him to discuss their relationship with Rose. The obvious had once again eluded him, but his appreciation of Daphne's depth of perception only grew. He decided he was going to spend more time with her. He felt her input could be enlightening. Maybe he had been living alone too long. After all, communication was the key to successful human relationships of all types.

After they had finished eating, he took the tray of dishes down to the kitchen. He resolved to ask Daphne to critique his violin practice. He knew in his heart she was right that he needed to talk to Rose about their relationship. Instead, he called Deandra to find out what had happened with Richard. He silently scolded himself, *I should have called back sooner to make sure she was alright*, especially since she hadn't called him back to tell him what had happened.

"Oh, I'm so sorry I didn't call you back," she opened the conversation. "You were a lifesaver, and I feel like a jerk."

"No, not at all," he assured her. "I should have followed up to make sure you were ok."

"I'm fine. The police arrived less than ten minutes after you'd hung up. Unfortunately, just before that, Richard had grabbed the phone from me to see who I was talking to but discovered there was no one on the line. I told him that I had faked the call just to avoid talking to him. And then the police arrived before he had a chance to hit redial. I told them that I wanted him out of my house, but he'd refused to leave. He told them he was just trying to find his missing wife and suspected me of foul play. I told them that was ridiculous, and that Daphne had left him because he was abusive. He said he knew she was here with me, because she had called on her cell phone, and the number was from this area code. So I explained that the number was from here, because I was the one who bought her the cell phone and account, since he wouldn't let her have her own phone or access to any of his money. The police told him he had to leave. He demanded that they search my home for his wife. I told them to please feel free to look through the whole house if that would satisfy Richard that she wasn't here. I just didn't want him in my home. I told them that when I opened the door, he had forced his way in.

"So they looked through the house, assured him no one else was here, and told him to leave, which he did. But as he was leaving, he told me he knew Daphne had plenty of time to sneak out the back while I was stalling him. The police advised me to get a restraining order, and they told me how to go about it. So that's what I've been doing. That's why I haven't called you back before now. I have no doubt Richard's still in Vancouver, probably hanging out in my neighborhood waiting to catch her, but fortunately she's nowhere around. The minute I see him, I'm calling the police to have him arrested for violating the restraining order. Meanwhile, even with the economic downturn in the construction business, he can't stay away from his company forever."

"Maybe he's running things by phone," the Major suggested. "At any rate, you don't open that door again without looking to see who's there first."

"Got it. Lesson learned," she agreed. "And I'm keeping my cell phone in my hand whenever I go out the door just in case."

"On the other hand," the Major considered, "maybe he's had time to think about what you said about having bought her the cell phone and realized she could actually be anywhere."

"Let's hope. He's not stupid when he's not drinking. Maybe he'll figure it out. When he realizes Daphne escaped his control, I feel sorry for whoever he takes it out on."

"Maybe he'll take it out on the people that work for him," the Major offered, "or better yet, on himself. Has anyone told him he needs therapy?"

"I've been telling him that for years," Deandra answered. "That's why he hates me so much."

"From what Daphne told me about him, he probably doesn't hate you. He just hates what you say to him. There's no point in trying to reason with him. From what she told me, he doesn't really consider anybody but himself, unless he needs something from them, or unless he sees them as getting in his way. I would imagine that talking to him is like talking to an angry toddler—no way he understands anything more than what it is he wants.

From what she said, he expects everybody else to either give him what he wants or get out of his way. Still, whatever he chooses to do is his choice and his responsibility," the Major concluded. "I'm just glad you're ok and no one was hurt."

Chapter 18

Size of the Blossom versus the Entire Plant

Major Ursa-Barrios went back upstairs and apprised Daphne of his conversation with Deandra. Her immediate reaction was to want to call and talk to her sister, but now she had no cell phone. The Major reassured her that was a good thing, because Deandra did not need to know Daphne's whereabouts for the safety of them both. At least, not yet.

Then after closing the blinds in the living room, he brought her downstairs. After giving her strict instructions not to use any form of communication with anyone, he showed her his computer, so she could go online to find out what sort of legal assistance was available in Portland for women of no means who needed out of a bad marriage. They agreed her search needed to be limited to Portland, as she and her husband were legally residents of Oregon, and the divorce laws differed between Washington and Oregon.

The Major was also adamant that she not pick up his phone under any circumstances, even though it sat right next to his computer screen. She agreed, admitting that the last thing she wanted to do was put anyone else in danger or help Richard find her. She was just relieved that Deandra was alright. So he left her on his computer.

He went out to his garage, got a bucket and hand spade, and began the endless job of digging dandelions out of his front yard. He'd decided to start with the front, so that if anyone should happen to stop by, he could catch them outside. Then Daphne wouldn't be in danger of being discovered. As it happened, a neighbor did come by.

"I just had to tell you that I've seen you working so hard on your yard," she greeted him, "and I just love what you've done with it. All the flowers are so colorful. I've been enjoying the view from my windows. You work so hard at it."

The Major thanked her, more than a little grateful for the break, and gave her a brief tour of his back garden and all the changes he had made. She hadn't yet seen the pond he had put in, and together they made a wonderful discovery—the first rosebud had appeared. He was amazed at how large it was. He felt like a proud, new parent. He and his neighbor walked back out to the front yard, said their good-byes, and he went back to digging dandelions. When he'd finished about a two foot row down one side of the yard, he stood up and stretched his back. He laughed out loud when he looked across the rest of his yard covered with big yellow blooms that weren't supposed to be there. In spite of the bucket full he had dug up, he had actually accomplished very little.

He quickly gave up on his approach and decided to just get out the old gas-powered lawn mower he had nicknamed Gillette. It had a grass catcher attached and always gave the grass a good, close shave. Later in the summer, when the annual drought and higher temperatures set in, using Gillette would only kill the grass. He could just raise the height setting on the mower, but he also had an electric mower, which he used as a mulcher. He had nicknamed that one Munchkin. He knew it was excessive to have two mowers, but he already had Gillette when Mad Dog gave him Munchkin as a gift. And he also knew it was both silly and eccentric to name lawn mowers, but life would be boring if you didn't have eccentricities so you could laugh at yourself. Sometimes silliness was good. That was his perspective, and he was sticking to it. The world needed more laughter. But the mower needed both oil and gas, of which he had none on hand, and he'd need to clean the air filter and check the spark plug before using it. So he decided to ditch his plan to catch the dandelions in the grass catcher in favor of expediency. Gillette went back into the shed, and Munchkin came out of the garage. He'd just kept the old gas guzzler as a backup anyway, but he hadn't bothered doing any maintenance on it. It was simple enough to change the settings on the electric mower and attach the smaller grass catcher bag.

While he was mowing, he thought about how his distant Native American ancestors had referred to most everything that was now considered inanimate as if it were a living being. He mused that maybe personification was in his genetic make up somewhere. At any rate, he got the yard mowed with the dandelion flowers and seeds safely collected. He decided to tackle the rest of the dandelions another day.

He went back inside to see how Daphne was doing in her quest for legal divorce assistance, but she was no longer at the computer. Before he could find her to ask her, he noticed there was a message on the answering machine. He listened to the message. It was from Rose. She needed to make a trip down to Heirloom Roses, which was south of Sherwood, Oregon, and was inviting him to go along with her. Before calling back, he went upstairs and found Daphne sitting on the floor knitting.

She looked up and smiled when she saw him. "I have an appointment in Portland tomorrow," she announced proudly. "Is there a way for me to get there without imposing on you?"

"There sure is. I'll draw you a little map of the neighborhood and show you how to get to the bus stop," he explained. "You can catch a bus to downtown Portland, or go to downtown Vancouver and catch a bus across the river, where you can then catch a train. Portland has buses and trains. Making connections are no problem. And congratulations! But can we please talk about this later? I need to get over to Rose's house. We'll probably be gone the rest of the day."

"No problem," she echoed. "I need to mentally rehearse for tomorrow anyway."

He turned to leave, but then turned back to face her. She sensed something important and put down the knitting needles. "I think of Rose as a special friend," he explained, "and you're right that I need to talk to her about how she feels about our relationship. I'd like your permission to tell Rose about you. She's as trustworthy as they come. She's also a retired officer. Deandra has met her, but I don't think they really know each other very well. When Rose was in service, she was an Inspector General, which required her to keep secrets. I know she won't tell anyone."

"I'm trusting you with my very existence," Daphne responded. "You knew enough not to tell Deandra, which was the right choice for her sake. If Deandra knew where I was, she wouldn't be able to resist calling me and coming to see me. She unintentionally could have led Richard straight to me. So if you trust Rose with our secret, so do I. Thanks for asking me first. I love how considerate you are."

"Ok, thanks," he said, turning away before she could see that he was blushing. There really was something about Daphne that he had already come to love deeply. *She really belongs here with me. I hope she doesn't have any problems getting that divorce.* He went downstairs, called Rose, and told her he was on his way over. He also missed seeing the despair in Daphne's eyes.

She'd done it again. She agreed with him because she wanted him to like her. *Hell,* she admitted to herself, *I want him to love me.* She didn't know Rose, and she certainly didn't want to be an intruder in someone else's life or relationship. She felt heartsick. If only she had dragonflies, birds, or angels around her now to somehow guide or help her. Then she realized she actually did. She had the beating of her own heart, and she should listen to it. She promised herself that this time she would. She would stand on her own two feet, take matters into her own hands, and follow the beating of her own heart. This time she would get it right. *I won't let you down again, Moonshadow. This time, I'll do the right thing.*

Chapter 19

Picking the Flower

Rose and the Major had a pleasant drive down to Heirloom Roses. It was a beautiful day. First they stopped for lunch in Jantzen Beach, just across the I-5 Bridge in Portland. The Major took the opportunity to tell Rose, "There's something I need to talk to you about when we get back in the car, but not here. I don't feel comfortable discussing it in such a public place."

That clearly puzzled her, but they had a very enjoyable lunch anyway.

Back in the car and headed south, he asked her, "How do you feel about our relationship?"

Her immediate response was laughter, which he took as a good sign. Then she said slowly and thoughtfully, "Well, I cherish your friendship," as she gently put her left hand on his right shoulder as he drove. "Words can't begin to explain how much your friendship means to me." She hesitated before adding, "Of course, since it's been strictly platonic, it's only fair to tell you that I've been seeing someone else." She looked at him intently watching for his reaction and trying to read his body language.

He did his usual pause as he gathered his thoughts. Her admission of seeing someone else totally surprised him. He wondered why that possibility had never occurred to him before. *That's what I get for taking her for granted and waiting for the relationship to unfold naturally. Maybe it's a good thing, since now I have Daphne in my life.*

It wasn't easy for him to be verbally open about his feelings, even with Rose, but somehow the conversations he'd been having with Daphne had really helped him. *I haven't had any difficulty talking to Daphne. That's a good sign.*

He decided to go for it and spill it all. "Ok. We have a very special friendship, and I didn't want to ruin it. I'm actually glad you're seeing someone else, and that it hasn't come between us, because as much as I care about you, and you're a beautiful woman." He hesitated slightly, as he quickly glanced at her and then back at the road. He was relieved to see she was still smiling, so he continued, "I've met someone else too, much to my surprise. I actually thought you and I were just taking our time getting to know each other, but it has been over three years now. I didn't want to make a mistake by making a play for this new lady, and ruining our friendship in the process, if you were just being patient with me and expecting the relationship to become more intimate."

It felt a little awkward to verbalize his feelings. He'd surprised himself by being able to so easily. He now realized he had been holding back from talking to Rose about their relationship, because he had liked it just the way it was. He didn't want it to go any further.

Rose laughed again. "I'm very flattered, but it takes two people to feel that way to make it work, in which case we would have become more intimate long before now. I knew you weren't gay, and I knew I wasn't unattractive. I also figured out the chemistry just isn't there between us. But it's good to talk about it. So please, tell me about this other lady."

"It's actually a very complicated situation," he began. "You remember Captain Robin?" She looked puzzled, so he added, "Deandra Robin?"

"Oh, yes, of course. She's some sort of safety specialist," she acknowledged.

"Yes, that's her. No, I mean that's not her," he stumbled over his own words. "No, I mean, yes, that's Captain Robin, but she's not the lady in question. It's her sister," he explained.

"I thought her sister was married. Did she get divorced?" Rose asked.

"No, and that's a big part of the complication," he answered.

"That's not like you at all, seeing a married woman," she interjected. Her facial expression told him she clearly did not approve.

"They're separated, and she's seeing a lawyer about getting divorced. But as you so aptly phrase it, the chemistry is there, and I can't help how I feel about her." *No*, he thought to himself, *I want to feel this way about her*, but he didn't tell Rose that. He was going to explain about hiding her in his house and then thought better of it. He wanted to share with Rose about Daphne starting to make him a rainbow blanket to symbolize the hope and new life she was entering as well as the synchronicity with the symphony playing The Rainbow Body, but decided it was one of those personal things where the experience didn't translate well into words. At least he wasn't sure how to put it all into words. He could have added the cliché, *You had to have been there*, except Rose had been, at least for the symphony and The Rainbow Body part. But to explain the rest would have required the entire story of Daphne hiding in his house. *Damn, this is complicated.* He let it go for now, and instead, he asked Rose, "So who is this man you're seeing?"

That brought the smile back to Rose's face.

The other man turned out to be another retired officer, in fact a retired Lieutenant Colonel, but no one the Major had ever encountered. His name was Stephen Steed, and Rose was clearly in love with him. She explained, "I've been looking for the right opportunity to tell you about Stephen, but I was concerned that it might jeopardize our friendship. So, I've been procrastinating. I think you and I are too much alike in that respect. Stephen and I have known each other for years. We met when we both worked back in the other Washington, and we actually dated a few times back then. Then duty assignments separated us, but he recently retired and chose to settle in this area. He's been living in Portland. We ran into each other in Powell's Bookstore the day after you and I went to the Lavender Tea House. Let's get together with the four of us for dinner sometime soon," she suggested.

"Sounds great," he answered with a lump in his throat, "but I'll have to ask Daphne. She's shy about meeting new people. She can be very... withdrawn," he tried to cover. "She might not want to be seen out with someone else until her divorce is final."

"The turn's coming up soon," Rose interrupted. "And I can certainly respect her waiting until she's divorced."

The Major was relieved that she didn't seem to pick up on his hesitation. He'd made it safely through the conversation that he'd been putting off. He and Rose were still friends, and Daphne was still safe.

They arrived at Heirloom Roses and were delighted to discover a sales table outside. Rose, as usual, browsed the gift shop first before heading back into the greenhouse, which was full of small rose plants of every variety. The Major always enjoyed going down every aisle as if he were seeing old friends again. Some roses had started to bloom. He was pleased to find a grandiflora with a full flower that smelled heavenly. He had considered buying it back when he bought the roses he had planted, but he didn't have a place in his garden for a grandiflora. Still there was something satisfying in knowing he had good taste.

Meanwhile, Rose was busy picking out rose after rose after rose. When the Major realized how many she was buying, he made himself useful by getting carts and loading the roses.

"Is Steve into roses or gardening?" he asked.

"He prefers 'Stephen'," she corrected, "and no, he's not into either." She stood up from leaning over the roses, put her hand on his shoulder, and added reassuringly, "Don't worry. You're not being replaced. You're still my friend and gardening buddy."

The Major was greatly relieved. "Just as long as we still hang out together and do fun stuff like this," he asserted. Then he added, "I'm sure you'll like Daphne. She knits, and I bet the two of you have interests in common." He knew Rose liked to sew and kept up with where all the sales in the area were for fabrics and crafts. He figured that eventually Daphne would need to resupply her yarn, and Rose would be the one to help her find what she needed. Then he thought about the three suitcases stuffed full of yarn and wondered how long it would take her to knit it all up.

After Rose had chosen all her roses and a vase from the gift shop, the sales lady told her she could choose five more roses from the sales table for one dollar each. And she could also pick out one of the free mystery roses that weren't labeled. She had no problem picking her free mystery rose, but outside at the sales table, she only found two that she wanted. She told the Major he was welcome to pick the other three, if there were any he wanted and could use. He chose three of The English Lady, a Harkness rose, which would be perfect for the front of his house. He had planned to replace the bushes in front of the living room windows next year with roses, but for three dollars total, next year had just become this year.

After they loaded the trunk of the car with the new roses, they went to Al's Garden Center in Sherwood. Rose had a few more plants she was looking for, and the Major always felt it made good sense to stop at both places in the same trip, since they were relatively so close to each other. He hadn't planned to buy anything there, but found three tiger lilies, one yellow, one pink, and one red, that would complete his lily garden. Then he smelled something sweet and familiar and followed his nose to a blooming, creeping Daphnis. He couldn't resist. Rose smiled knowingly at his selection. He had one variegated Daphnis bush in his backyard, but it was an early bloomer—February to March. This one was obviously a later bloomer, and the smell was heavenly, even better than lilac he felt. To the Major, better than lilac meant it had to be really sweet.

After all the shopping, they were both tired. So they stopped, appropriately enough, at Rose's restaurant in Sherwood for dinner. They needed a break, and they wanted to let the Friday afternoon traffic clear out a bit before heading back through Portland. The Major had the chicken Florentine, and Rose had quiche. Then they headed back through Portland and across the river.

Chapter 20

New Moon

The Major came home with Rose's revelation about
Lieutenant Colonel Stephen Steed, three new roses to plant,
and a new Daphnis. He unloaded his car, leaving the new
plants in the garage for the moment, and headed upstairs to
see Daphne. Her bedroom door was closed. He knocked
gently, but there was no response and all was quiet. He
decided she must be asleep, so he went downstairs. He
resolved that tomorrow at breakfast he would tell her how
he felt about her and introduce her to the heavenly scented
bush with her name.

That night he dreamed the doorbell rang, and as he
opened the front door, a large dog charged into his house
before he could stop it. Purvati was hissing and growling,
the dog was barking, and as the Major was trying to get
between them, a young boy was there trying to tell him
something. But with all the racket and distraction, he
couldn't make sense of the child's poor pronunciation. He
woke up to silence in the house. Purvati was sleeping
peacefully on his bed. It was easy to deduce that the dog
invading his home symbolized his fear of Richard
Gatorman finding out where Daphne was hiding, but the
child was trying to tell him something. As he was getting
dressed, he wondered what it was his unconscious was
trying to tell him—something he had somehow missed.

He went to the kitchen where he fixed two bowls of
oatmeal with fresh blueberries and two cups of hot
chocolate, loaded a tray, and carried it upstairs. The
bedroom door was still closed, even though he had slept
late. He set the tray down and knocked. When there was no
response, he called her name. When again there was no

response he announced, "Daphne, I'm coming in," and opened the door.

The bed was made. On the card table was the rainbow blanket neatly folded with a note that read:

"Dear Major,

"As safe as I feel here, as fond as I've become of you, I can no longer impose on your generosity. Please remember me every time you use this blanket (machine wash delicate on cold, machine dry on lowest setting). I hope it makes you feel as safe and warm as you've made me feel. You are the kindest, gentlest man I've ever known, but I'm just a messed up intrusion who can only cause you trouble. Please cuddle Purvati for me, and tell her I hope she can forgive me for leaving so suddenly. I wish you and Rose all the happiness in the universe. I'm going to a shelter where I can get some counseling, get some help with the divorce, and figure out who I really am. I will call you soon.

"All my love,
Daphne"

He stared at note in disbelief for a moment. Then, he reread the way the note was signed, "All my love, Daphne."

The Major reached for the door to the computer room and saw the key was in it. Knowing it would be empty, he opened it anyway. It was. He opened the closet. None of her things were there. He went into the hidden room and switched on the light. It was also empty. He sat down on the floor and wept until he heard the sound of slurping coming from the hall. Remembering he had set the tray on the floor, he got up in a hurry, banging his head on the low door frame to the hidden room, and rushed out to stop Purvati from drinking the hot chocolate or eating the blueberries, only to find it was just the oatmeal she was slurping. The caffeine in the chocolate and the blueberries weren't good for cats, but if she ate too much oatmeal, he knew she'd throw up. He took the tray away from her and set it on the card table next to the beautiful rainbow blanket.

He looked around. Something was missing. "Well of course something's missing, you dunce," he scolded himself out loud. But something was nagging at him. He sighed as he sat down and began to eat breakfast alone. He reread the note, which only brought more tears, until he reread the closing.

"I will call you soon.

"All my love,"

Then he realized what was missing. It was the jigsaw puzzle he had bought her. She had taken it with her. She kept his gift. He smiled.

Chapter 21

Making a Bed

The Major spent a restless night, but Purvati was by his side, and he took comfort in her soft cuddles. He latched onto the last line of Daphne's note, "I will call you soon." Finally around eight in the morning, Purvati began meowing insistently for him to get up. He didn't want to and stalled for another fifteen minutes before getting out of bed. He and the cat had breakfast together, with him sitting on the floor by her food dish. Then he let her lick his empty oatmeal bowl, after which she threw up four times, but he was right behind her with a roll of paper towels each time and managed to catch it all in four different paper towels, saving himself from having to clean the carpet.

While he was brushing his teeth, he realized he had to put hope aside, not throw it away, but just put it aside, and get back into the present. He should change the sheets on both beds and do the laundry, but he wasn't ready to do that just yet. Then he remembered the three English Lady roses and the Daphnis plant in his garage that needed to be planted. It was a cloudy day but not raining, so he went down to the garage and smelled the sweet, divine smell of the Daphnis, which he hadn't been able to share with Daphne. He remembered he'd had the thought of taking it up to her room for a day to fill her space with the beautiful scent. He chuckled to himself when he lifted it and remembered how heavy it was. Maybe it was just as well he didn't have to carry it up the stairs. Besides, there probably would have been a dirt trail to clean up.

He assessed his tools and what was needed for the job. After a quick drive up to his favorite outdoor supply store, he came back with manure, top soil, and mulch. He unloaded the trunk of the car in the driveway. Then he grabbed his landscape cloth, shovel, loppers, the precious Daphnis, and the roses and hauled everything he needed out to the front of the house. It took several trips for him to move it all.

In front of his living room windows was a row of thirteen-year-old, over pruned nandina bushes. He knew the age, because the house was thirteen years old, and they were old enough to have been part of the original landscaping. He loved nandinas when they were allowed to grow tall and willowy, and were graceful enough to show off their red berries. But these had been pruned over and over again to prevent them from doing what came natural to them. Their natural form would have grown to obscure the living room windows and become a potential hiding place for a prowler, but they would have looked so much more beautiful compared to the artificial box shapes they'd been pruned into. So instead, he had used them for draping nets of multicolored lights across at Christmas.

The Christmas lights reminded him of his father, who while the Major and his brother were growing up, had always taken the family throughout the town to see all the beautiful Christmas lights. His father had died right before Christmas one year. Before his father's death, the Major had always thought it must be especially hard on family members to lose a loved one right before that particular holiday of family get-togethers and gift giving. But then when it happened to him, he realized it was a blessing. Every Christmas, he saw his father and felt his father's presence in the Christmas lights. Life was full of losses, but always followed by renewals.

So he mumbled to the nandinas that he had appreciated all they had given him, but it was time for them to go. He would find another way to display his nets of lights next Christmas. He smiled to himself remembering his father was a gardener and how much he had wanted to follow in his father's footsteps. As he lopped off branch by branch, he saw that the centers of the bushes were dead and rotted. He'd never dug up a nandina before and hoped the roots were shallow, but he knew from the size that wasn't likely. After he'd chopped them down, he began digging the dirt out from around them. They were well entrenched. It was after lunchtime when he finally broke the last one free.

Lunch would just have to wait. He had another hole to dig and four plants to get into the ground first. He saw no point in cleaning up and then getting filthy again. And he would be eating alone again. Eating alone had never bothered him before. He had never felt alone with Purvati, but now it just wasn't the same. At least his most recent loss was about to result in renewal through roses and an appropriately named Daphnis.

There was a large landscape rock, more like a small boulder, that sat between two of the former nandinas. He decided it would make a good accent and background for the Daphnis, so that determined where he dug his hole. After lining the edges with a double row of landscape cloth, he put the manure into the holes first and then filled them with topsoil, mixing in a bag of time-release pellets of rose food. He planted a rose where each of the nandinas had been and the Daphnis was centered in front of the rock. Then he spread the mulch around the new residents. As an afterthought, he got out some "safe for pets and wildlife" slug poison and sprinkled that all around them. He'd nicknamed the possum, who around twilight routinely patrolled his backyard for slugs, Posey, but he'd never seen Posey in the front yard. He wasn't taking any chances with slugs eating his English Ladies and Daphnis.

After he'd put the tools away and cleaned up, he admired his work. Something was missing. He added a rock border to protect the roses from the lawn mower and show them off, and decided that was much better. The view from inside was an improvement as well. He hoped Daphne would come back to see it someday. He realized she'd never seen the view through the living room windows. For that matter, the only time she had ever seen the front of his house was as she was leaving. He was sure she had looked back. He hoped she'd call soon.

He was exhausted, but there was one more project he needed to get done, besides the bamboo. And he was in no mood to deal with the bamboo today. He got his tools back out of the garage. He had already dug the hole in the back yard next to the sidewalk and put in a pond, but it was just sitting there in the hole waiting for him to finish the project. He had the pump and a spherical blue bubbler set up so that his little fountain in the pond was gentle, aesthetic, and effective It was a soothing sound, and very satisfying. However, it needed a flower bed around it to give it a more finished look. While he was dirty and had his tools out, he prepared the dirt around the rim of the pond. It looked good, or at least it would once he added flowers. He felt he had accomplished enough for one day, so he put away his tools, went back inside, and cleaned himself up.

Just as he came out of his bathroom, the phone rang, but it was Deandra. She'd seen and heard nothing further from Richard Gatorman, which was a relief, but she also hadn't heard from Daphne.

"Shouldn't I call the police and report her as a missing person?" Deandra asked.

The Major had been relieved that she hadn't thought to do that before now. "No, there's no need," he reassured her. "I got at note from her."

"WHAT?" Deandra went from anxiety to anger in an instant. The Major knew simple jealousy when he heard it. "She wrote you and not me? How did she have your address?" she demanded.

"I gave it to her, of course. Calm down. I only just got the letter." *Well, close enough to the truth,* he thought. "She sent it to me in case Richard was somehow watching your place or meddling with your mail. I know we both have locked mailboxes, but she's understandably cautious right now. She says she's ok, at a shelter, getting counseling, and getting help filing for divorce."

"Can she do that from a state she's not a resident of?" Deandra asked.

"Well, I don't know anything about that. You'd have to ask a lawyer, but it doesn't matter," he answered.

"How could it not matter?" Deandra was sounding both anxious and exasperated. The Major realized she must have been out of her mind with worry about her sister's well being. He decided to reassure her.

"It was from Portland," he confided.

Chapter 22

Rain

The Major's neighbor knocked on the door with the two flats of annual flowers he had ordered a couple of months ago from her child's school fundraiser. As much as he needed to practice his violin and work out, he was grateful for yet another beautiful distraction. It was spring after all.

He filled in the bare spots around his backyard pond with white sweet alyssum, and they did smell sweet. He planted a long curving row of impatiens to mark the border of his columbine, astilbe, acidanthera, and fern bed where it wasn't already bordered by the outer hostas. Then it started to rain, so he set the other flat in the driveway to water it, while he took some of the petunias to the front yard rock garden with the red rose bed behind it and put the petunias between the lavender, perennial salvia, and veronica. By the time he'd finished, he was soaking wet from the gentle rain, so he put the unplanted petunias and cosmos back in the garage and went inside to change clothes. He was surprised to find he was soaked down to his boxers.

He cleaned up and put on dry clothes. He realized he felt he'd been left out by the two women he cared most about. He felt cheated by his own honesty, gentleness, and laid-back personality. He felt unappreciated by everyone but Purvati. He was glad it had started to rain. It fit his mood. The sky itself felt wounded and was crying. It was good to let troubles drown and wait for regeneration. He knew in his heart he was a good and generous person and had a lot to share. Daphne had told him as much. He would share with Purvati, since no one else was available.

He picked up a book he hadn't read yet by the artist Brian D'Amato, *In the Courts of the Sun*, and got on the treadmill, but after about only four minutes, he had to admit to himself that the hardback book was just too big and unwieldy to comfortably manage while working up any speed. The book was just too big for the book rack or for him to hold onto. By that time he was hooked, and the book won out over the treadmill. He went back downstairs and got comfortable in his easy chair to continue reading, fully expecting Purvati to come and curl up in the chair with him as she always did. But that didn't happen.

He called her several times, but she didn't come. For most cats that would be normal, but not Purvati. Then he heard a plaintive meow in the distance. His first thought was to question if he had accidentally shut her in the closet again, but the next meow told him that was not the case. He followed the sound upstairs to Daphne's room, where he found Purvati. She looked up at him and meowed again as if to say, *Where did she go? Why isn't she here? I miss her.*

He knelt down, petted her softly, and tried to console her. "I know, sweet girl. I miss her too."

The next morning he decided he needed to take his frustrations out on something. The bamboo was getting out of control, but at least it was graceful and tasted good. It earned another temporary reprieve. He walked outside, and the first thing he saw were dandelion flowers everywhere in the lawn. *Dandelions it is,* he decided. He grabbed an empty bucket and systematically policed the lawn, picking all the flowers and buds he could find. He'd work on digging them out later. First he did the front yard and then the back.

As he headed back to the garage to dump his pickings into the lawn debris bin, his focus zeroed in on the duckweed. He hated duckweed. How could a living, growing plant be so horrendously ugly? "Feo, feo, feo*",* he sighed as he began pulling it up. He had a lot of emotion to take out on it.

Feo is in the eye of the beholder, he thought to himself. "This beholder finds you feo and wants you GONE from this property," he said out loud as he pulled it up. One thing led to another, and before he knew it he was weeding flower beds. "Desapareces," he ordered each one, trying to will them not to come back.

Having dumped several bucketsful into the lawn debris bin, he was tired of bending over. Maybe he just needed to talk to someone. Not Deandra—that would only feed the emotions. He called Rose. "I just realized we're missing the lilac festival," he told her.

"We're not missing it," she delightfully corrected him. "We just haven't been yet. Let's go sometime soon."

"How's Sunday?" he suggested.

"Mmmm. Looks like rain. That shouldn't stop us. It's just the Great North Wet. How about Monday?"

"Nope. I have a doctor's appointment midday. Tuesday or Wednesday?" he bartered.

"No, I have plans, but Thursday is free," she negotiated.

"Great! Will Stephen be coming?" he asked.

"No, he doesn't really enjoy that sort of thing. He had surgery on his knee a few months ago, and he's still having problems with it. That would probably be too much for him. How about Daphne? Would she like to join us?"

"I'm sure she'd love to, but she's out of town working on that divorce," he answered.

"I'm sorry I won't get to meet her yet, but it's a good thing she's getting the divorce. Guess it's just us." He could hear the smile in her voice.

I'll pick you up around eleven and we can have lunch at Rosie's in Woodland before we see the lilacs."

"Ok," she agreed. "See you then."

He hung up the phone. He loved the smell of lilacs, and he loved Rose's company. He was relieved Stephen wasn't coming and felt a twang of guilt at the thought, but it was the truth. He wasn't quite ready to meet the man so soon after finding out he'd lost his unrealized chance for a future with Rose. Why did that bother him so much since he knew he was in love with Daphne? He decided it was normal to feel rejected. He may not be in love with Rose, but he still loved her very deeply as a friend. And of course it all reminded him of Daphne's absence. There would be one less bottle of lilac bubble bath to buy at the gift shop, or was it two? *Is it still appropriate to buy Rose little gifts?* He didn't want to push Stephen's open-mindedness too far. And Daphne had promised to call—but when?

He turned around to see Purvati sitting there watching him. "I did this to myself," he explained to the cat. "I used to think falling in love was a form of mental illness, so I was afraid to encourage the process with Rose. I thought if it was really love, it would happen in its own time. And now I know it wasn't meant to be.

"What is it about Daphne that swept me off my feet so unexpectedly? Is it that my guard was down because I was protecting her? I know she's really the woman of my dreams, because she talked about her dreams." He sat down on the floor with Purvati and rubbed her chin. "I didn't tell her about mine. When she told me I should talk to Rose about our relationship, I should have realized that I should talk to Daphne about my dreams and feelings. I should have told her I wanted to have a relationship with her. If only I'd told her. Somehow, I just expected her to know, but how could she? I left her alone to go out with Rose, when Daphne was in such a vulnerable state. I gave her all the wrong signals. I did this to both of us." Purvati looked up at him, and he added, "I know, girl. I did this to all three of us. Our family.

"When she fell for Richard, she was young and gullible enough to marry the jerk and stay with him. I've never met him, but I bet he's good-looking and talks a good line. How could anyone be so callous and hateful as to deny a beautiful animal like a cat a home or a life?"

Purvati rolled over on her back for him to pet her tummy. "Of course you agree with me," he continued. "And Daphne's feelings for Moonshadow are enough reason to fall in love with her, but I really believe she's the angel in my dreams. Why could I not talk to her about that? Why are there so many things women expect me to talk about and it just never occurs to me to talk about them? And of course, she'd be cautious with me since I didn't tell her. She doesn't want to interfere in someone else's relationship after getting out of such a bad one herself. She's an honest and trustworthy person. I let my angel get away."

Purvati purred and squinted her eyes. "You love me whether I talk to you out loud or not, but then you know me better than anyone. For not having what humans think of as language skills, animals certainly seem better at reading our thoughts and intentions. Guess I'm really in love with you first, huh, girl? You're my first love and my one true constant. And here we are sitting in Daphne's room because we both fell in love with her, didn't we?"

Chapter 23

Rest and Renewal

The Major carried Purvati in her pink pet-a-roo pouch that he wore against his chest as he strolled around the yard and the garden to give her some fresh air and let her smell the spring flowers, especially the jasmine and Daphnis. The bluebells in the front bed were in full bloom, and two big fat poppy buds had made their first appearance. They walked to the mailbox and got the mail, and then they went inside. It had started to rain again.

The Major gave himself permission to take a vacation from everything, including having to go somewhere on vacation. It was time to shut out the outside world in favor of introspection. *Without introspection, one could lose their sense of identity in this busy world.* It was time to slowly exhale before starting anything else.

He knew Daphne had his cell phone number as well as his home phone, but he needed some quiet time to think. He took a day off from his violin practice and got out a jigsaw puzzle of his own. He hadn't worked one in years. He moved the card table down to the empty dining nook next to the kitchen counter, and set it up there. There was something quieting about sifting through the pieces looking first for the frame, and then the colors of whichever section he chose to work on. This time he just chose the colors he found appealing at the time—first reds, then blues, then bright orange and yellows. It was time to put some pieces together.

Of course he had to remind Purvati that the box with all the pieces was neither a litter box nor her scratchy box for sharpening her nails. A couple of times she jumped up on the table and lay down on part of the puzzle in progress. That was fine except for the swishing tail that would sweep the pieces away, but the Major would diplomatically put an arm or the puzzle lid in the way of the tail for protection. He hoped he had found all of the pieces on the floor and reminded himself not to vacuum that area until the puzzle was finished—just in case.

He thought about the people he had known over the years, most of whom were military, of course. He thought about their personalities and how he had learned from Dr. Bernstein to watch out for and deal with the less emotionally mature types by not letting them put their emotional issues on his shoulders. Whatever they'd been up to was not only a total distraction, but took all his energy just to deal with. He had used Dr. Bernstein's book *Emotional Vampires* and its descriptions of various personality disorders as a valuable reference toward the end of his career.

He knew Deandra tended toward being a drama queen when she was upset, but not to the extreme like Chief Jellie and Sergeant Leach. They were two women who didn't know the words "I was wrong" or "I made a mistake," and of course when they were, it meant someone else had to be blamed or framed, like then-Lieutenant Roan or Sergeant Leach's ex-husband. Very childish, but that's how they operated. For that matter, many adults could be very childish in many ways, and he knew he wasn't exempt. He apparently had a problem communicating with women. Deandra was only dramatic when she was the victim, but she kept getting blindsided. He made a mental note to get her a copy of *Emotional Vampires* for Christmas. Maybe something in it would help her learn to avoid getting blindsided at least some of the time. *Not that it helped me with Daphne and Rose, and neither one of them have a personality disorder. Neither do I, but the fault is still mine.*

As he put a few more pieces of the puzzle together, his thoughts continued on about Daphne. He was finding it impossible not to think about her. She had married a self-centered control freak, who no doubt was quite the charmer at first. When you're young, in love, and still believe in fairy tales, you're apt to go along with your partner and adapt. After all, marriage was about compromise. Somewhere along the way, she must have realized that she was the only one doing the compromising. *It's a tough choice to leave someone you once cared about.* She must have thought, "For better or worse," and decided to take on the burden as part of her commitment, while more and more of her slipped away into the shadows of his domination. With no children to threaten him as the center of attention, and her trapped at home where all she had to focus on was him, that poor stray kitty must have seemed very threatening to him—and a life-saver to her. *That's what's so sad about people who were all about control— they're just scared little children still trying to get their parents' attention, or at least that's my opinion. It's simply impossible for anybody to be in full control of events and people in their lives, and yet no one likes feeling completely out-of-control.*

"What a complicated species we are," he said to Purvati. He wondered if she agreed or thought he was thinking about it too much. Cats didn't question—they just accepted themselves for who they were. Maybe that's why it didn't occur to him to talk to Rose or Daphne about what mattered most. He'd been living alone with Purvati long enough to adapt to her lack of need for verbal communication.

He thought about Colonel Desmodon's desperate need to be popular and to be the center of attention at parties and get-togethers—very much like a teenager trying to fit in. He remembered Desmodon talking about having been a latch-key kid and wondered how much that figured into it. The Major liked the guy who worked so hard to be likeable. Desmodon was simply likeable. He'd made sure the Major got promoted. Still, when the Major knew him, the man was on his second wife and Sergeant Leach in the same timeframe—much more like a teenage boy than a mature Colonel. Meanwhile, Chief Jellie had been desperately trying to get Colonel Desmodon's attention. The Major sighed.

He remembered the Colonel's "Be Nice" campaign, which he had thought was a good thing at the time. Then he remembered Dr. Bernstein's warning about how some people will take advantage of you giving them a nice, polite response to manipulate you into taking part in their web of deception. Of course, once you had compromised your own values, it was easy for people like that to get you in over your head breaking rules. And after a short while, you would tend to forget what the rules were to start with. *People like that are very good at reading other people and sensing when they are most vulnerable.* He had watched Colonel Desmodon use that very tactic on both Chief Jellie and Sergeant Leach. It almost destroyed Chief Jellie—or at least she had seemed close to some sort of breakdown by the time the Major retired. The whole thing had reminded him of the way some religious denominations insisted that women be sweet, subservient, and obedient to men to keep the women from ever voicing dissent, especially if it made sense, just to protect the delicate male ego. The Major much preferred for women, and any one under him in rank, to speak up when they spotted potential problems or perceived a better way of doing things. The way the Major saw it, if his mother had the good sense to raise him, there was nothing inferior about her gender.

He remembered the quick back-pedaling the Colonel did when the Major simply said, "No, that's not right." It was the time Colonel Desmodon had tried to require the troops to pay admission for a required briefing. The fee was actually for a cookout afterwards that the Colonel had personally invited the troops to in appreciation for their hard work, with no mention of cost. The Major knew the Colonel was expecting the General, who was giving the briefing and had asked the Colonel to arrange the picnic, to provide the money for it, but the General didn't. He should have asked up-front about the funding, but when your whole approach to people involves "being nice" for the sake of deception, you're not likely to be up-front or direct about anything.

When the General didn't offer to pay for the cookout, having expected the Colonel to arrange that as well, the Colonel was stuck with a tab he didn't want. The Major supposed it never occurred to George to take up a collection among the officers, which is what the Major felt was the honorable thing to do. He knew if he hadn't spoken up, he would have been complicit in the appearance of charging admission for a required briefing, but what really appalled him was the Colonel's choice to stick the enlisted personnel, the ones with families and lower incomes, with the cost of rewarding their own hard work. Any service member knew better than to charge admission for a briefing. Officers were expected to lead by example, and in that regard appearances were very important. However, as the Major had seen during his career, promotions were too often political, and those willing to go against regulations usually charmed their way into friendships with higher ranks, who were too busy admiring themselves to look into how things were actually being done by those under them. Naturally, the Major was labeled a troublemaker for his efforts. He sighed again. It was human nature with all its flaws in all walks of life. He was glad he was retired. He made a mental note to himself to let go of such memories. He decided he was dwelling on the negative, because he was depressed about finding and losing Daphne so quickly. Mad Dog had found Mercedes and Rose had found Stephen. He was just jealous and trying not to think about it. He told himself he had to learn to stop projecting his own problems onto his memories of others.

He turned to Purvati. "So here I am, a grown man working a jigsaw puzzle, pining over a woman I've just met, having just lost my chance with the woman I had thought of as my future, and all because I was afraid to speak my feelings. How juvenile is that?" he asked her.

She gracefully jumped from the card table to kitchen counter and began drinking his decaffeinated iced green tea. "Well, I was thinking 'that's why I have you to take care of me,' but I guess we take care of each other," he answered himself and went back to working on his puzzle.

Chapter 24

Playing Possum

The next morning after breakfast, the Major admired both the puzzle he had finished and the flowers blooming in his garden that he saw through the back window. The white azaleas and some of the purple iris were open now, and the neighbor's dogwood tree was blooming above the privacy fence. Some acidanthera had poked up through the soil, as had a ranunculus he had planted last year and thought had been lost in the harsh winter. The lithodora and forget-me-nots were in full bloom and spreading. He admired the way the cosmos stood up and gracefully blew in the wind. Four of his roses had buds. and he knew the poppies did as well.

"Lluvia," he sighed pleasantly while watching the rain through the window. All his plantings were being watered. He was pleased. Even the dandelion flowers sticking up in the lawn didn't bother him. "It's just their nature and they know it's spring," he said out loud to Purvati, who was also looking out the window with him. He knew the dandelions would win no matter what, but it was another excuse to putter in his yard, which he loved to do.

A cell phone started ringing, but it wasn't his ring. It took him by surprise. He walked to the kitchen cabinet above the refrigerator, where he had stashed Daphne's cell phone to keep her from using it again. It rang again. He had forgotten he had turned it back on after he'd found that she'd left, just in case she called him on that number, which he knew was not at all likely. But she knew he had it, and it was a number she would know.

As it rang a third time, he answered, "Hola." There was silence at the other end, so he switched to, "Hello? Is anyone there?"

"Where's my wife?" a male voice demanded.

Ah, Richard Gatorman, we meet at last, the Major thought. "I'm sorry you've lost your wife, señor," he answered. "Maybe if you had paid her phone bill, you would be able to find her. I only got this number yesterday, and you are my first caller. I'm sorry for your troubles. Please do not call again." He clicked off. He wondered how many years would pass before the phrase "hung up" would no longer be used with phones that now only required the push of a button to disconnect. His mind was wandering through a list of all the other meanings of the phrase when, true to form, the phone in his hand rang again.

This time he checked the screen and got Richard's phone number before answering with, "The Mahabharata says that the greatest wonder of the world is that no man, though seeing all those around him die, believes that he will die."

"Are you threatening me?" Gatorman asked angrily.

"Not at all," the Major responded calmly. "I'm just commenting on the amazing human potential for denial and disbelief. You called back, because you didn't believe I now have this number, which I assure you I do. Please let me also assure you again that I don't have your wife."

"I want to speak to Daphne NOW!"

"Apparently you do, and I'm very sorry," the Major answered truthfully and politely, "but there's no one here by that name." He ended the call. There were many things he would have liked to have said to Mr. Richard Gatorman, but he knew they would fall on deaf ears and just exacerbate the situation. He put the cell phone down on the kitchen counter.

"Disbelief is a pernicious condition," he explained to Purvati as they walked to the front window to look out at the lawn he had carefully policed for dandelion flowers late yesterday afternoon. "Humans are so very susceptible to denial." The roses looked healthy. No buds here yet, but in good time. He saw that one of the petunias he'd planted in the rock garden at the front corner of the yard had turned out to be white. It was a nice balance to the white jasmine vine he'd planted on the far side of the rock garden and a compliment to the candytuft by the front porch in front of the bluebells and poppies. *Balance is achieved naturally in Nature,* he thought. Purvati climbed up onto her cat tree in front of the window and looked out. The little dwarf lilac he'd planted was full of buds. Daphnis, jasmine, and lilac— all were heavenly smells to be followed by fragrant roses.

He stroked Purvati's soft coat and confessed, "I'm having difficulty believing Rose has found someone else, and it's even harder to believe that I've found someone else, and already she's gone."

Just then the phone on the kitchen counter rang again. He sighed and went back to the kitchen. "Hola," the Major answered wearily.

"Who is this?" Richard Gatorman demanded.

The Major sighed loudly and then responded, "If you don't know, why did you call me?"

"How do I know you didn't steal this phone from my wife?" Gatorman continued his interrogation. "What have you done with her? I have a right to know. She's MY wife."

"If you thought the phone was stolen or that something had happened to your wife," the Major answered, "you would be talking to the police. If the police were investigating, they would be talking to me, and probably in person, since they can track the location of cell phones. So obviously your wife has left you. And I'm talking to you on the phone instead of the police in person. But if you really believe your wife may be in danger, please go waste the time of the police instead of mine. Muchas gracias, señor." He clicked "end" on the phone to end the call. He set the phone back on the counter and waited a few minutes. As he waited, he wondered about people who seem to live for confrontation. They were usually full of hot air, but air had the good sense to go around obstacles instead of stopping and beating itself against them, when there was nothing to gain from it but bruises. Maybe these were people who suppressed or denied their feelings to the point that all they could do was spew them out, not realizing those feelings had to go somewhere.

He thought about the innate wisdom of the opossum. It had more natural defenses for fighting than its predators, but chose to avoid confrontation. That way, no animal got hurt. The Major smiled. *There's so much we can learn from Nature, but so much of the time we focus on the violent parts.*

When the phone didn't ring again, he left the kitchen and went into his music room. He walked over to his violin, got out the bow, tightened and rosined it. Then he put the shoulder rest on the back of the violin and went to work on the James Horner piece, *My Heart Will Go On*. Purvati stayed on her cat tree and looked out the window at the rain.

When he finished playing, he took off the shoulder rest, wiped down the violin, loosened the bow, and put both the instrument and the bow back into their case. Then he sat down on the end of the sofa closest to Purvati's cat tree and the window, wrapped the rainbow blanket Daphne had made him around himself, and cried himself to sleep.

Chapter 25

A Good Hearth

When the Major woke up on the sofa with the rainbow blanket, Purvati was curled up next to him. He felt safe and protected. The two of them had a nice, very comfortable home. At least he had slept peacefully and was well rested, but he remembered he had forgotten to check the mail. That was negligent of him, especially when he was so desperately waiting for word from Daphne.

He put Purvati in her pet-a-roo pouch, and together they walked across the street to the mailbox. It was stuffed full. He waited until he'd gotten back inside the house and Purvati jumped down out of the pouch before daring to look through his mail. Just as Purvati was getting out of the pouch, his phone rang. He managed to get to the phone and answer it just as the answering machine started to pick up. "Hola," he said distractedly.

"Feliz Cinco de Mayo," Mad Dog wished him.

"Que pasa?" the Major responded. Hearing from Mad Dog always cheered him up.

"Just me and Mercedes," he answered, "making wedding plans, or at least practicing the consummating part."

"Well, that shouldn't take long," the Major joked. "When are you legalizing it?"

"That's what I called to tell you. Probably next month. She wants to do it on the second, and she's calling the shots. There's no point arguing with her. She's Bolivian, you know," he kidded.

"So will I meet her before then?" the Major asked.

"I'm not into that kind of threesome, so maybe not. Actually, I've got a pretty hectic flight schedule the rest of the month, or I'd find some time to introduce you. She's a knockout in more ways than one—did I mention she's Bolivian?"

"You may have," the Major laughed. "So this will be a major part of the Rose Festival this year?"

"Isn't that why they're having it? At least that's what I told her. 'There will be a big festival in honor of our marriage, and then one every year after that for our anniversary.'"

"Oh, I get it. No way are you going to ever forget your wedding anniversary," the Major acknowledged.

"Now you're catching on," Mad Dog confirmed. "I do learn from my mistakes—after I've made them a few times."

"Ok," the Major agreed. "I'll keep the second of June free. I'm marking it on my calendar as we speak."

"Great. Got to fly. Don't do anything you won't tell me about in sordid detail." Mad Dog hung up.

The Major smiled. He was happy for Mad Dog and Mercedes and Rose and Stephen, but it only made him miss Daphne all the more. He brushed Purvati, and then went out to the garage, picked up a bucket and hand spade, and then went out into the front lawn, where he started poking holes in his lawn by removing dandelions. The ground was wet, and they came up easily—for dandelions.

When he got tired of fighting the dandelion war, he walked around back to check on his garden. The first thing he noticed was silence. The pond wasn't bubbling. He discovered the electrical cord to his pond pump was strung out across the yard. The pump, still turned on, was out on the lawn. That wasn't good. It was only supposed to run while immersed in water. He wondered what had happened as he walked around to the electrical socket next to the back door and unplugged the pump. That's when he looked up at the pond and saw that the bubbler ball and the rock it had been sitting on had both been knocked over. He looked around for footprints or evidence of what culprit had done this. Nothing else had been disturbed, except for a telltale deposit of possum poop near where he'd found the pump at the end of the cord out on the lawn.

He imagined Posey trying to use the bubbling fountain as a water fountain, falling in, knocking things over trying to get out, and getting tangled in the cord before making his or her escape. He thoughtfully reset the pump and fountain so that it bubbled close to the side of the pond rather than in the center.

After he came back inside and washed up, he saw the stack of mail he had not even bothered to look through yet. Mad Dog's call had distracted him, and he'd totally forgotten about the mail. A rush of anxiety passed through him as he wondered if there was something from Daphne that had been waiting for him since yesterday, and he hadn't even managed to read it yet. He realized he didn't even know if Daphne knew his address. *Did she take time to write it down before she left?*

Most of the mail was advertisements and catalogs he didn't want, which he quickly discarded to put in the recycling bin. There was one bill, which he set in front of his computer. That left one envelope, which actually looked like a personal letter.

He took the letter, sat down on the sofa, closed his eyes, and took a long, deep breath, letting it out slowly. Then he opened his eyes and examined the envelope. The return address and postmark were from Wisconsin. He was disappointed when he saw it wasn't from Daphne, but smiled when he realized it was from Master Sergeants Christian and Sunny Drake. They were originally from North Carolina, but Army couples had to be flexible and always ready to move, sometimes overseas. They were a delightfully positive couple with a beautiful orange tabby cat. He remembered fondly that the tabby was terrified of cockroaches and water bugs, but loved to eat mosquito hawks. Christian had worked as a recruiter, and Sunny was assigned to the Major when they were last stationed here in Vancouver. Sunny lived up to her name in every respect, and even when conditions were less than ideal, she would always smile and say, "It's all good." The Drakes were good for everyone's morale, and he was glad to hear from them.

He opened the envelope, and inside was a picture of their new baby boy. The child was, of course, adorable, and the Major knew the child was most fortunate to have Sunny and Christian as parents. The letter explained that the tabby had adapted well to the new arrival, and announced that both Sunny and Christian were being promoted to Sergeants Major. The Major was very pleased with the news. If ever anyone deserved the rank, those two did. The news and the picture lifted his spirits immensely. Sunny always had that effect. It was a rare gift, and the Major was very grateful for it.

He got up off the sofa, went over to the computer and emailed Sunny back to thank her for the picture, tell her how cute her precious little darling was, and ask how that tabby was doing. He briefly filled her in on Rose's new beau, even though he was sure Rose had already told her all about Stephen. He gave Sunny an update on his gardening ventures and mentioned that he and Purvati had a new friend. He remembered Sunny and Christian were all about positive thinking, so he thought maybe he'd try practicing a little of it himself and see if it helped. He sent the email. Then he turned to Purvati, still on her cat tree, and quoted Sunny, "It's all good."

On Thursday, he drove over to Rose's house. Both she and Stephen answered the door. *He's a living cliché,* the Major thought when he saw the man for the first time, *tall, dark, and handsome.* They exchanged greetings and small talk. The Major had been fully prepared to despise the man, but much to his utter disappointment, he really liked him. Stephen was casual, cheerful, very friendly, easy to like, and amazingly enough, a perfect compliment for Rose. The Major found himself trying to talk Stephen into driving to Woodland with them, but to no avail. Stephen admitted to having other plans and to not really being interested in the lilacs. So the Major and Rose drove off in high spirits and great relief that the introduction had gone so well.

While driving north on I-5, the Major confided in Rose how much he missed Daphne and the actual circumstances under which they had met and she had left. He told Rose the whole story. She was very supportive and encouraging that it would all work out for the best.

They had lunch at Rosie's in Woodland again, while it rained, and by the time they came out of the restaurant, the rain had stopped. They headed west to the other side of the little town and the Hulda Klager home and lilac gardens. Their timing was good. The lilacs were in full bloom. This was the one time of the year he allowed himself to stick his nose in everything that didn't belong to him—especially on this occasion. Rose reminded him to watch out for bees, as he was allergic, but the smells were so enticing he didn't care. "If one stings me, just get me to the doctor," he directed and continued his smelling spree.

As they explored the gardens, they could hear someone inside playing the old piano. At one point, it started to rain lightly again, but it just didn't seem to matter. The Major only noticed when he saw other people opening their umbrellas. Ironically, he had not used an umbrella since he had moved to the Great North Wet. He had decided that if he was going to live in rainforest country, he was just going to get wet. His ancestors hadn't bothered with umbrellas, so why should he? Now he thought of umbrellas as sun screens for use in the summer, when it wasn't raining.

The gardens naturally led to the gift shop. He was as dismayed as he was relieved to find there was no lilac bubble bath for sale. Purvati loved it, and he loved to pamper her, but he knew she wouldn't be disappointed. Cats had that wonderful way of never expecting anything except the routine necessities and whatever happened in the present. Such was the essence of unconditional love humans aspired to attain but rarely succeeded in achieving. Still, if they had the bubble bath for sale he would have had to decide whether to buy some for Daphne and save it for her as an affirmation of her pending return. And then there was Rose. He was no longer certain of what sort of gift was appropriate for him to give her. He suddenly was strongly feeling Stephen's invisible presence.

Rose bought some lilac cuttings to give her stepmother for Mothers Day, which was just a few days away. She also bought the Major a lilac bookmark in thanks for him paying her admittance to the Gardens.

After they came out of the gift shop, they strolled back through part of the garden. The Major continued to put his nose into every cluster of blossoms as they went. Finally they agreed they'd had enough, and it was time to go. "One more for the road," he said, and went to stick his nose in one last cluster of pink lilac, when he stopped short. There, right in front of his nose, resting on one of the florets, was a dragonfly. He smiled, and then said to Rose, "Ok, la vida es buena. Vamos."

They drove down to La Center, where a friend had told Rose about an interesting gift shop called The Trellis. It was jam-packed with beautiful treasures. In the back was an indoor garden area full of water fountains, bells, wind chimes, and garden statues. They found an interesting door knocker for a mutual military friend, who was planning to build her own home on some land she owned in the desert east of Las Vegas, Nevada, when she retired from service in four or five years. He also found a music box for his sister-in-law that played a piece the family associated with her talented twenty-year-old son, who played piano exceptionally well. The Major and Rose both considered the store to be a worthy discovery, counted the day a success, and headed back south to Vancouver and home.

Chapter 26

Sun versus Moon

The next day, Rose came over to the Major's house and picked him up for a shopping trip in northeast Portland. She had some things she needed to look for. His house was on the way, and after what he had told her about missing Daphne so badly, she thought it might be best to get him out of the house again. It seemed to do some good. They stopped at a nearby restaurant for lunch and headed down across the river to the Cascade Station shopping strip. The Major bought more than she did. They called it retail therapy. By the time they were done, he had Christmas presents pretty well covered, even though it wasn't even summer yet. They stopped at Starbuck's for iced green Tazo tea and pumpkin bread.

Once back across the river, after they'd unloaded his purchases, they walked his garden so he could show Rose what he'd been doing. She hadn't seen The English Lady roses and Daphnis planted yet, and she agreed that the front of the house looked much improved. They discovered the dwarf Korean lilac buds were just opening, which further cheered him up. In the back yard, one of his fragrant Asiatic lilies had survived the squirrel scavengers and was poking its head up. A peony in the tree bed had also shown itself. Several acidanthera and a new astilbe were standing tall and proud as well. His little white azaleas were in full bloom and several deep purple irises were in bloom. They found two buds on the mystery rose he was given at Heirloom Roses when he bought eight others. Rose was impressed at how well the three other roses he had transplanted were doing.

She left soon after, and he went back inside. He sorted through the presents he had bought, arranged them by their intended recipients, and put them in the computer room Daphne had used to practice her guitar. He had difficulty convincing Purvati to come back out of it so he could close the door, but eventually she paused to sniff one of the shelves where Daphne's things had been, so he picked her up and carried her back into the bedroom. Then he closed the door securely behind them.

He lay down on the bed Daphne had slept in and remembered he still needed to wash the sheets. He thought about her music, her knitting, and their conversations. He thought about the rainbow blanket and The Rainbow Body he had heard at the symphony. He considered how a little cat had been the catalyst for her leaving her husband after years of emotional and physical cruelty. Then he thought about how she had used Purvati to lead him into a discussion of consorts, opposites, and the sun and the moon. He'd always thought of cats as wise creatures. There was really nothing mysterious about them. They never held back their true feelings, and they always seemed to perceive what should be obvious to people, if only people weren't so caught up in thoughts and feelings of their pasts and worries and plans for the future.

He thought about the moon goddess, Ix Chel, in Mayan mythology, known as Lady Rainbow. He recalled that she also protected weavers. Somehow, he knew she would protect a knitter of rainbows as well, but he could use some of that hope signified by the rainbow itself. Then he remembered the dragonfly on the lilac up at Woodland. It seemed to him an omen just as good as a rainbow. He wondered if there was a way to learn to sing like a dragonfly. He looked around the room and noticed he had never hung anything on the walls in this particular room that he had come to think of as Daphne's bedroom. Maybe he should find a painting of a dragonfly and hang it on the wall.

Then he remembered Daphne's suggestion that he write about his experiences, thoughts, and feelings. Maybe somehow in writing, he could "sing" her back to him. Or even better, maybe he could write music for her. He thought about all the metaphors he had ever heard for singing, including the Australian aborigine version of singing one into the dreamtime. He thought about Lady Rainbow being the moon goddess. The moon presided over the night when dreaming was usually done, but that didn't help him much. Or did it? Maybe they would find each other in their dreams as they had been doing for years. But he didn't know how to make it happen. He just didn't know how to either sing or dream her back to him.

Then he realized what had happened. He was pathetically, unabashedly lovesick. He thought about calling Dr. Bernstein, but this was not an illness he wanted to be cured of. As much as it hurt that she was gone, he loved her and trusted her, and he wasn't about to change a bit of that. As she had honored the memory of Moonshadow, he would honor Daphne.

When Daphne arrived in his life, she waxed to a full moon and then vanished, but wasn't that natural for the moon to go through phases? Maybe he was just experiencing the darkness of the new moon? If so, it was just a matter of time before she came back into his life. Cats and possums were nocturnal, and women followed the timing of the moon, which is why all cultures depicted the moon as feminine. He remembered the note Daphne left. He had memorized it:

"As safe as I feel here, as fond as I've become of you, I can no longer impose on your generosity. Please remember me every time you use this blanket (machine wash delicate on cold, machine dry on lowest setting). I hope it makes you feel as safe and warm as you've made me. You are the kindest, gentlest man I've ever known, but I'm just a messed up intrusion that can only cause you trouble. Please cuddle Purvati for me, and tell her I hope she can forgive me for leaving so suddenly. I wish you and Rose all the happiness in the universe. I'm going to a shelter where I can get some counseling, get some help with the divorce, and figure out who I really am. I will call you soon.

"All my love,

"Daphne"

She said she would call soon. Soon was a relative term. He just needed to be patient. He believed she would keep her word. Time was perceived differently by those who lived closer to Nature than those living fully in the manmade world. Humans tended to become trapped in the daily sun cycle and the manmade hours and minutes within it, but the natural cycle of time, especially for women, was lunar. The moon would wax again as it always did. And she didn't have to close the note with, "All my love," but she had.

It was already dusk, but he decided to go outside and mow his yard. He got Munchkin out of the garage. He always started with the backyard. The backyard was bigger, and once he'd done it, it was just easier to face doing the smaller front yard. Just as he turned on the mower, he caught a glimpse of motion from the far corner of the yard. He looked up to see what appeared to be a dead possum lying on its side. He immediately turned off the mower and walked around to the front yard. He felt badly for scaring Posey. He puttered around and then sat on his front porch for about fifteen minutes before venturing back near where he'd left the mower.

The possum was gone. It had left behind a deposit of fertilizer in the flower bed where it had dropped when startled by the sound of the lawn mower. The Major mowed his lawn and hoped he hadn't scared the animal away for good.

After he went back inside, he went to the kitchen and made himself an ice cream float with frozen yogurt and Diet Rite. He had to keep reassuring Purvati that it wasn't a proper kitty treat, but she clearly wasn't convinced. It was a challenge to get it from the glass to his mouth with her face constantly appearing in between, but he was grateful for the company. And it was such a cute face. He truly loved this cat. When he'd finally finished the float, he went upstairs and got on the treadmill, while Purvati kept watch out the window.

Chapter 27

Piercing the Clouds

The moon had gone missing, and it was the Major's solo mission to find it again to restore the rhythm to the tides that pulsated the waters of life. He saw a glow softly reflecting off the water and pointed his kayak in its direction. As he paddled toward it, he recognized the color spectrum of a rainbow on the water. It was coming from above rather than below the surface. He looked up, following the arc of colors into the dark sky, and there was Daphne surrounded by a soft glow of white light. She was sitting in the night sky on the far end of the rainbow, and she was reading a book.

A soft purring and a paw on the back of his neck woke him up. He instinctively reacted by returning the favor and stroking the back of Purvati's neck. It had been one of those vivid dreams that demanded his full attention—even after he awoke. Purvati got up, jumped off the bed, and led the way to the bathroom, as was their routine. He dutifully followed, as he always did. When he splashed water in his face, he thought of the mission in the dream to restore the force of the moon to the waters of life. It was his mission alone. That meant he needed to restore the balance in his own life. He looked in the mirror at his unshaven face and realized it was up to him to find his Lady Rainbow moon goddess and bring her back into his life. He couldn't just wait around for her to call as he had been doing. Maybe Lady Rainbow was somehow using his own dreamtime to sing him to Daphne. He was absolutely sure now, beyond any doubt, that Daphne Robin Gatorman was the woman of his dreams.

He called Deandra Robin and asked if she had heard from Daphne. The answer was an expected but disappointing no. Then he realized, while Deandra was talking, that he still had the cell phone Deandra had given Daphne. *Of course she hasn't called Deandra.* His thinking was clouded and confused. He decided not to tell Deandra he had Daphne's phone or that Richard had been calling it. Even as Deandra was talking to him about her concerns for her sister, all he could think of clearly was the vivid dream he'd just had.

After he finished talking with Deandra, he looked out the window and wondered how battered women's shelters were run and about the fact that Daphne had no cell phone, no computer, and very little money. He pictured her knitting his rainbow blanket and remembered the sound of her guitar. He knew that all that yarn she had with her would only make a finite number of blankets to earn her stay wherever, and then she would be out of resources. She was very intelligent and capable of finding resources, but still he worried. He didn't want to think of his beloved Daphne playing her guitar for tips on the street or in a park. He worried about her well-being, and he worried about his own inertia in waiting for her instead of trying to find her. He rationalized that he simply trusted the message she had left him, but now he realized deep inside that he was making the same mistake he had made with Rose. And Daphne didn't even know that he had lost Rose to Stephen out of his own lack of personal insight. It was Daphne who had to tell him to talk to Rose about their relationship, or he never would have, even though by then it was too late. Only Daphne didn't know that. Somehow, he'd managed to make a complete mess of things. And he'd done it all by procrastinating.

He'd failed to take the initiative to determine his own career and path in life, and instead, he'd ended up in the military, where he'd known for years he really didn't belong. And he'd stayed there for years knowing he didn't belong. He'd had a special friendship with Rose that he'd assumed was more than friendship, and she'd found someone else. Now all he had was her friendship, and it would never be more than that. But the very woman of his dreams had come into his life, and he'd let her slip away. *No,* he thought, *I must get this right—this time of all times. I must find her. But how?*

He simply couldn't afford to make his usual mistake with Daphne. She was more than special. This was some sort of crucial crossroads in life, where he felt he had to get the lesson right this time. Where he and Rose were good friends and had much in common, Daphne somehow supplied the pieces of himself he was missing; or at least she could see where to look to find them, when he couldn't even see what was missing. He felt he needed her with him before he could continue with whatever the next phase of his life was meant to be. They were somehow meant to help each other. They were meant to be together. Why else would Rose have not told him about Stephen until Daphne had come into his life?

So where would he start looking for her? All he knew was that she had gone to Portland, and Portland was a big city. Where did he look in his dream? Across the water was obvious—he had to cross the Columbia River to go to Portland. Somehow the rainbow was the key. It was the path that led to his finding her. *There must be some other clue. What am I missing? What else was in the dream? She was sitting on a rainbow across the water…*

In the dream she was reading a book. He mentally inventoried all the possessions he knew she took with her, but she didn't have any books. And yet she was clearly well-read. She liked to read. She would be inclined to seek answers from books. Maybe there were books at the women's shelter, but he didn't know how to find any women's shelters in Portland. They were there, but their locations were always kept secret to protect the women needing shelter.

She said she was going to "get some counseling, get some help with the divorce, and figure out who I really am." He was sure a women's shelter would help her to get counseling and connect her with Legal Aid, so that meant she was figuring out who she really was. She would call him after that. Figuring out oneself could take a really long time. After all, that was the journey of life. *We're supposed to be helping each other figure these things out. That's why we're supposed to be together.* He felt a momentary flutter of panic in his stomach, fearing that he had lost her for good. He was determined not to let hope slip through his fingers this time. *How can I find her? Think, man. Recuerde.*

He knew she didn't have the money to leave Portland, unless she found another kind stranger to help her, and there were lots of kind strangers in Portland. There were also those not so kind, and that frightened him. He had to figure this out. He thought about her in the dream sitting on the rainbow reading a book. When she was interested in sitar music, she didn't just listen to it, she read about it. When she was interested in anything, she read about it.

It wasn't until he was washing the breakfast dishes, as Purvati paced the kitchen counter, that it came to him in a flash. It was right in front of him all along. The clues were all there—Portland across the water, rainbow, and books. He knew exactly where she would go for whatever information she needed to help her sort out the puzzle pieces of her life—to help her figure out who she really was. He turned off the water, dried his hands, and gave the cat a quick pat on the head and rub of the chin. He grabbed his car keys and headed south across the I-5 Bridge to Portland.

After crossing the Willamette River, he headed west on Burnside. He turned right onto 10th Avenue, went around the block to 11th and parked in the Powell's garage.

201

After leaving his car key with the parking attendant, he went into Powell's City of Books, a city block divided and organized into sections by all the colors of the rainbow. He reasoned that she would have connected with Legal Aid for help getting divorced. That left only one section where he might find her trying to find herself. She would be looking for insight into how to avoid the mistakes of her past with Richard. After checking the store directory, rather than trusting his memory, he headed straight to the red room, where he was sure, based on his conversation with Daphne, the dragonflies would be waiting. On the far side of the eastern religion shelves, he began searching the rows of the psychology and self-help books.

And there she was. She was sitting on the floor, much as he expected, reading a book intently. She didn't even look up when he approached. He sat down on the floor next to her without saying a word. When she did glance over at him, she dropped the book on the floor, threw her arms around his neck and gave him a joyful hug. He hugged her back and didn't want to let go.

"We need to talk about our relationship," he said. He was determined not to let her get away from him again.

She pulled away from him and looked into his eyes. "I thought you were seeing Rose?" she questioned. "Did you two talk?"

"Yes, and she had already found someone else. I met him, and I like him. He's right for her. I've realized Rose and I are best friends. That's all—just best friends. I love her, but I'm not in love with her."

Daphne's heart felt like it was in synch with the wings of ten thousand dragonflies all beating in unison, and for once in her life, she made no attempt to hide how she felt.

"How have you been?" he changed the subject back to Daphne. He could clearly see she looked positively radiant in spite of all she'd been through. "How are you holding up?"

"I was feeling kind of shattered," she admitted, "but being here with you is like being sung to by thousands of dragonflies." She paused for a couple of seconds and then added, "And talking to the psychologist has helped a lot too. He told me that going back to Richard would be harmful to my mental health. Legal aid is helping me file for divorce, with the stipulation that I do not want anything from him that I didn't already take with me, not even his name. I now have a restraining order to keep him away from me."

"Deandra has one of those as well," the Major mentioned. "As long as he respects it, or you call the police as soon as he breaks it—which reminds me, take my cell phone since I have yours. When he was at Deandra's house and the police arrived, he seemed motivated not to be arrested and left. He kept calling your cell phone, but I kept telling him I had only just gotten the number, and that there was no one there by your name, which was true at the time. He seems to have stopped calling. I told Deandra you went to a shelter in Portland. With both restraining orders, it should be safe for you to see her now."

"Let's hope he's gone back to Albany," she said. "If he has, he'll have to deal with knowing I have a restraining order and have filed for divorce. Maybe that's why he was trying to call. So, how in the world did you find me? I mean, I'm really glad you did, but do you come here often, to Powell's I mean?" she asked him. "This is simply an amazing place—a whole city block of multiple floors of books! I could be wrong, but you don't seem to me like the type to browse the self-help section."

"Yes, I come to Powell's, but I only came to this section because I thought you would be here," he explained.

"De veras?" she smiled, and he smiled back broadly as he nodded his head.

"Still, I have been known to read a self-help book from time to time," he admitted. "Anyone that thinks they can't learn from others or that they're perfect has a serious problem."

"Anyone like that would probably need more than self-help anyway," she commented. "I have so much to tell you—that is, if you're interested in hearing it."

"Yes! I definitely want to hear all about it. Did I mention Ix Chel?" he asked her. She waited patiently, knowing they were thinking on the same wavelength. He continued, "She was not only the moon goddess known as Lady Rainbow, but she also protected weavers. First she led you to me, and now she's led me to you. I think she's woven a web around us."

She studied his face as she thought about that for a prolonged moment. "A web of light," she added, followed by another prolonged silence as they looked into each other's eyes. Both their lives had changed in such a major way, and yet she couldn't remember exactly when she had realized they were now on the same path. This time neither of them felt awkward with the silence.

Finally he said, "If we buy that book, my parking is free. I can take you to collect your things, and then I can take you home—or to Deandra's if you prefer."

"I only have one bag of clothes, my knitting needles, my guitar, and a beautiful jigsaw puzzle I was hoping we could someday put together—together," she explained, "and a lady at the front information counter was kind enough to hold them there for me behind the counter. I donated the rest of the yarn to one of the ladies at the shelter. She had a toddler about two-and-a-half years old and another little one only eleven months old, both boys. When she found out she was pregnant again, that was when she got the courage to leave her bastard husband. She was terrified of going through another pregnancy not knowing if he was going to kill or hurt the baby before it was even born, and the children she already had were already terrorized by their father. She was afraid they would be irreversibly emotionally damaged if she didn't get them away from him, so she finally left. He was a pharmacist. Can you believe that?"

"Maybe he was using some of his products," he suggested. "So was she ok?"

"She will be. I felt so fortunate. At least I had my own clothes and my guitar. She only had the clothes they were wearing and a bag of diapers—no maternity clothes or toys or anything for the new baby and no home, but the shelter people are working on that with her. It turns out she had attended nursing school. Anyway, she knew how to knit better than I do, and someone had given her some regular size knitting needles, but she didn't have any yarn until I showed up. So I gave it to her, except for what I used to knit a baby blanket for her. At least she has something to work with now, and knitting is a very calming activity, at least for me. So it worked out well. Now she has yarn to knit, and I have less baggage."

She collected her things while he paid for the book. Once back in the car they both started to speak at once. "Ladies first," he offered.

"Coward," she kidded. "Ok. I've had difficulty practicing guitar since I left your place. This old Neil Diamond song keeps running through my head, 'You are the sun. I am the moon. You are the words. I am the tune. Play me.' And I can't seem to play anything else," she confessed.

The Major smiled. "Purvati and I have missed you. We want to you stay," he admitted.

"Then can we go home now, please?" she asked him. He exited I-5 onto Highway 14 East as soon as they were across the river and headed for home, while she used his cell phone to call the shelter and let them know she'd found a safe place to stay.

Chapter 28

The Rainbow Appears

After Daphne greeted Purvati with a cuddle and settled her clothes and guitar back in the upstairs bedroom, she and the Major took a stroll around the yard. The little Korean lilac was blooming and very fragrant. It was still so small, just a baby plant and a dwarf at that, they had to kneel on the ground to stick their noses in the blossoms. Maybe the Major was prejudiced, but he was sure it smelled far more heavenly than any he'd smelled at the Klager Lilac Festival. He beamed with pride and pleasure.

The Major discovered that the wild geraniums he had transplanted were blooming little pink flowers, and he was pleased. There was so much to learn about Nature's diversity. Now that he was retired, he had time to look, observe, enjoy, and learn. The jasmine vine had taken to the dead yucca stalk and was full of buds again. Daphne knelt down on the grass to smell the blooming Daphnis he had planted in front of The English Lady roses in front of the house. The look of pleasure on her face and the fact that she kept sniffing again and again made it clear how much she loved it. Most of the new daylilies he had planted along the driveway were up.

In the back yard, three fragrant Asiatic lilies had survived the squirrel feast and were up. The irises and azaleas were in bloom, as were the forget-me-nots, lithodora, and annuals. There was one peony standing tall in the tree bed and two lilies poking their heads up there as well. Astilbe and columbines were coming up, and the bleeding hearts were in full bloom. The acidantheras were standing tall. Several of the roses had buds, and he was relieved to discover the mystery rose would not be a climber after all.

But there was no fountain in the pond. "Something has trampled your sweet alyssum," Daphne observed. "Actually squashed would be a better description."

He laughed and shook his head. "Poor Posey," he said. Daphne looked confused.

"Posey's a wild possum. This yard is part of the regular path it follows foraging for food. It eats slugs, so I'm glad it visits regularly. See that blue globe on the bottom of the pond?"

Daphne looked. The water was a little murky and covered with white alyssum petals. "I see the globe. It's blue if you say so. It's kind of hard to tell."

"Yeah, well, I've had the pump and that blue globe set up so that the water bubbles out of the globe. Apparently, to Posey it looks like a possum water fountain, but as you can see, the slope of the ground up to the rim of the pond is steep, and, well, ponds are slippery. At least this time Posey didn't fall in, get tangled in the electrical cord, and pull the pump out of the water. I guess we're making progress, but it must be putting its paws on the globe to get to the bubbling water."

"And its weight pushes the globe over," Daphne finished. "Or maybe it's just going for a swim? Instead of a water fountain, maybe it sees a possum swimming pool. And then after it swims, it might dry itself off in the sweet smelling alyssum."

"Could be, but for now I think I'll just leave that globe at the bottom of the pond as long as the pump stays in the water where it belongs.

They moved on toward the back fence and the bamboo bed. Daphne marveled at the bamboo while the Major just sighed. "Don't worry," she reassured him. "If I can handle Richard Gatorman, I can handle bamboo." He was relieved to hear it, at least until she exclaimed, "Look! It's coming up in the rose bed."

"No, that won't do at all." He gave it a long hard look. "Ok, that's it for the bamboo. It's got to go now." He went into the garage and came back out with shovel, hatchet, and loppers.

"Are you sure?" she asked as they sat down to rest. It's so graceful, and—"

He cut her off. "No doubts. I'm sure. It's out of control. I've been putting off dealing with it for a long time, but I've invested a lot in my roses. They provide summer odor control in the litter box as well as beauty, serenity, and personal satisfaction. This invasion can simply not go without response. My roses have been attacked. I must do what I must."

Together they dug, hacked, and cut out stray bamboo roots in all directions. "That's a lot of work just to keep it contained," Daphne commented.

"That's why it's got to go," he explained. "We can salvage some. I have a very large decorative pot, and I've been wondering what I should plant in it. I just have to save some of the roots, and there are plenty of those."

"Ok, since you're sure." She got up, picked up the loppers and lopped it all off.

"Well, that's a relief," he said as he got up and started clearing the mess. "We can dig out the rest another day. We'll trim and save the canes. When they dry, they're very useful as stakes."

"You do know we'll have to do this again as soon as it grows back," she mentioned.

He gave her a look that she clearly understood to mean, *I don't have any explosives. We'll deal with it again another day.*

She smiled and agreed, "Mañana."

"Whenever," he corrected.

"Short war," she commented.

"Retaliatory strike," he corrected. "Not as exhausting as full-scale war."

Daphne laughed as they put away the tools. Then they went inside, and cleaned up. Daphne called her sister to explain her new circumstances.

Deandra responded, "I'll be over to see you as soon as I get off work."

"I have so much to tell you," Daphne told her sister right before she hung up the phone. Then she turned to the Major and said, "And I have so much to tell you."

He sat down on the sofa to listen. She sat down next to him and took his hand in both of hers. "When I went online on your computer to find out about legal aid, I also found the number for the National Domestic Violence Hotline, 1-800-SAFE (7233). They referred me to several women's shelters in Portland. I'm never going to tell you or anyone else which one I went to, just in case I ever have to escape again, so behave yourself."

"No worries here," he reassured her.

"I know," she laughed. "You are truly an officer and a gentleman."

"Retired officer," he corrected.

"Whatever."

"So, did you have any trouble getting to this shelter?" he asked.

"They gave me instructions on the phone where to meet them, and someone from the shelter met me where and when they said they would. Then they took me to the shelter. I explained my situation, and they were very understanding. I felt so fortunate. So many women there had children, like the one I told you about, only all different ages. So of course, there was child care. The women being sheltered took turns helping with the children. I also took part in a support group, and that made me feel lucky too. I mean, at least I had a sister to help me, and then you showed up. But I thought I was getting in the way of your relationship with Rose, and the last thing I wanted to do was to ruin a healthy relationship.

"I learned a lot about what a healthy relationship is versus an unhealthy one. And I got to speak privately to a psychologist, which really helped me to realize that I have a chance for a new life now. And I can choose to live my life so that I can be myself without having to repress my own talents, personality, and feelings. I need to stop pushing myself aside and start being honest with myself about what I really want in any situation, because unless I'm honest with myself about what I want, I'm not likely to make it happen. It's a lot of work, but it feels so liberating!"

"This I can relate to," the Major told her. She looked at him questioningly. "I put aside my dream of being a gardener, because my parents wanted me to go to college, and the only way we could afford that was with an ROTC scholarship, which led to my commission in the Army and anything but being a gardener. So now that I'm retired, I am also starting a new life based on how I want to live it."

"Then we have something incredibly important in common," she affirmed. "And here you are doing what you always wanted—being a gardener."

"That's why I spent so much time with Rose," he explained. "We had worked well together when we were in uniform, and we share an interest in flower gardening. The whole nature of flowering is about sharing. Flowers are deliberately showy and beautiful to attract attention, and not just for pollination. It's because we enjoy them and share them that we propagate and grow them. A garden is meant to be shared. Rose's family has a history of sharing flowers—giving them to friends and putting them on graves of people they don't know."

"How thoughtful and generous," Daphne commented.

"Mostly on soldiers' graves on Memorial Day," he explained. He paused a moment before finding the right words to continue, "It's not right to do all this gardening just for myself. I'd like to share it, and my life, with the right person. Daphne, I don't want to rush you into anything, especially after all you've been through, but I believe you're the right person—if you want to be. You don't have to respond to that right now. Take forever if you need to, but meanwhile my garden, home, Purvati, and I are here for you."

She gave him a prolonged hug. "I'm so glad you're part of my new life, whatever it turns out to be, and Purvati, too. I've learned so far that I want to take one day at a time and practice being myself—learning to know what I want. I hope that works for you right now. I have a lot of self-exploring to do."

"That's fine. And if you want to go back to see that psychologist any time, you're certainly free to. If you don't want me to know who or where he or she is, that's fine too. I'll give you the money for the bus or the keys to the car, once you get your Washington drivers license—if you want to be a resident here."

"Oh yes! And I'd love to meet Rose someday, if that's not too awkward," she answered.

"Well, she wants to meet you too—especially since she knows where all the shopping bargains are. I figure you might need a few things. Some more yarn, maybe?"

"We should talk about budget before I do any shopping," she suggested.

"Now there's something a man doesn't hear everyday," he joked. "I like that."

"There's more I need to tell you," she continued. "There was a woman at the shelter in the support group, and she had a dragonfly tattoo. She knew a lot about the symbolism of dragonflies. She said a lot of people take them as their totem." She looked at him with a question in her face, and he nodded his understanding.

"She explained that to the Japanese," Daphne continued, "they represent joy and light. So I was thinking that their singing healed Lady Rainbow by helping her find her joy in the sun's light."

Again he nodded, and she went on, "For some Native Americans they represent the souls of the dead, so they could also have been the voices of her ancestors—or even the voices of her own past lives. Anyway, this lady said that those who take the dragonfly as their totem tend to have very emotionally tumultuous experiences in the first part of their lives, but gain control of their lives in their later years by combining their feelings with mental clarity."

"That bodes well for both of us," he responded. He got up and walked over to his computer where he did a search for dragonfly symbolism. Then he told her, "Wiki says that dragonflies help you see through your illusions. They symbolize 'going past self-created illusions that limit our growth.' They also symbolize the 'sense of self that comes with maturity.'"

"Maybe that's how dragonflies came to symbolize hope," she suggested, "since there are rainbows in their wings."

"There are also rainbows in hummingbirds. They dig deep to find the sweetness and joy of life. Then they sing it out. They also, like the dragonflies, sing with the beating of their wings. Either way," he answered, "I think we fit the bill for having the dragonfly as our totem or whatever. Like you said once before, the beating of their wings is like the beating of the heart."

"Listen to your heart," she completed his thought. "That's where your inner light is, and its beating is the song of the dragonfly that can heal."

"As well as the rhythm of the dance of Parvati," he added as Purvati joined them.

Daphne then filled him in on the details of the restraining order and the divorce process. She explained

213

that she would get nothing from Richard, and that all she had with her was all she owned. She didn't want to be a burden, but she felt it was important to just walk away from Richard without taking anything that had been tainted by him.

"I understand, and I agree," the Major responded. "Taking anything from him would make you feel dirty." She looked surprised that he caught on so quickly. He continued, "I think we really are on the same metaphorical path, and to have you here is no burden. For me, it's fulfillment—like a dream realized at long last."

"And I get my own name back! I'm Daphne Robin again. I like my name. I never liked Richard's. As a matter of fact, I positively hated that name, but I never told him that." She laughed at herself. "That should have been a dead giveaway from the start, when I didn't even feel like I could tell him I hated his name, Gatorman, but I was young, naïve, and emotionally stupid. I should have realized something was wrong just because I hated his name. Who knew? I didn't. But I should have told him I hated his name. I should never have felt forced to change my name to start with. He would have insisted that I take his name. I wonder if that would have clued me in. What a stupid practice. Anyway, I have my name back now, and I don't ever want to change it again."

"Understood," the Major nodded. "You shouldn't have to. Changing one's name should be one's own choice. It's a matter of personal identity. Having your name forcibly changed must have felt like identity theft."

"How many men would understand that?" she laughed, delighted that he was so understanding.

"Actually, I have a friend who is still in uniform, who took his wife's name when they married. The gossip and mocking behind his back was ridiculous. I thought he did the right thing, since that's what both of them wanted. It's all about self-empowerment and choice, and we all need both. My name, for example, is Ursa-Barrios—Ursa was my father's, and Barrios was my mother's. That's my family's culture. Most men in mainstream US society have this strange sense of entitlement over women, but I hope that's passing. Society is changing. Women and minorities are finally coming into their own in what used to be a white man's world. It's a great relief to all of us, and when those who still carry that sense of entitlement realize how richer their lives can be, and how much there is to learn from being open to alternative perspectives, the world will be a better place for all of us—them too."

"So true," she agreed, "and well said. The pursuit of happiness is not the same as hoarding wealth or privileges. And liberty is not about greed or freedom to hurt others— even unintentionally. It's all about being free to make choices for your own happiness, while allowing others to do the same. That pursuit is all about following your heart and doing things to help others in their own pursuit of happiness. Maybe the pledge of allegiance should include the serenity prayer?"

The Major laughed. He was truly enjoying the conversation and her company. "It's good to feel free after having repressed myself for so many years. Lucky for both of us that others have been able to help us realize how we were making ourselves miserable, and we couldn't even see that we were doing it. We allowed others to bully and intimidate us into fear of self-expression. And my experience with my own psychologist has taught me that those very same bullies are far more repressed and damaged than I've ever been."

"Yeah, I can't really blame Richard that I was such easy prey. Now I'm free. At least I don't have others I have to take care of, like all those women at the shelter with children. They not only have to figure out their own emotional issues, but they have to try to teach their children to keep from making the same mistakes. And as if that's not enough for them to deal with, somehow, they also have to find a way to provide for themselves and their children.'

"And hope the children aren't damaged enough to end up like the fathers," he interjected.

"What a sad thought, but the mothers can only do what they learn and are able to do. So, anyway, when I went to see the lawyer, I insisted on taking my things with me. Maybe I had a feeling I wouldn't need to go back to the shelter. Or maybe it was like I told the people at the shelter—that I shouldn't be taking up a bed that someone else in more dire straits might need, since I had a sister I could go to. Anyway after seeing the lawyer and making sure the divorce was being filed and I had the restraining order, I went to Powell's Bookstore. I had heard of it before, and a couple of the women at the shelter, as well as the lawyer, gave me directions. I'd always wanted to go there ever since I'd first heard of it when I moved to Oregon. And I just felt I needed some time to myself to look through the self-help books. I'm just beginning the process of sorting myself out and trying to see who I really am, instead of who Richard told me I was all those years. So that's what I was doing when you walked up, and the first thing that came to my mind was the phrase, 'Ask and you shall receive.' And there you were."

Chapter 29

The Strength of the Eagle

Deandra showed up after she got off work as promised. While the two sisters were talking and catching up on all the details, the Major called Mad Dog.

"Hola," a female voice answered.

"Hola, Mercedes. Me llamo es Major. ¿Como esta?"

"Hello, Major," she answered. "I'm fine with English. Mick has told me about you. I'm fine, but he's away right now."

The Major had almost forgotten that Mad Dog, like himself, had another name, though rarely used. It made sense that if she only knew him as Mad Dog, she probably wouldn't be marrying him.

Mercedes seemed to be thinking along the same lines and asked, "Is Major really your name? I know Mad Dog has explained to me a thousand times that for military the rank is the first name, but you're no longer in the military, no?"

"Well, you could call me Mayor if you prefer," he joked. "Mad Dog often calls me Majara instead."

She laughed. "Whatever. It's nice to meet you. I mean it will be nice to meet you."

"Congratulations on your engagement," he offered. "Please tell me about yourself. You know Mick. He's only talked about you in relation to himself."

"I understand what you mean," she laughed. "He is truly charming and persuasive, but he has his faults, so I will tell you, as you ask. I and my family are from the estado plurinacional de Bolivia. We were very fortunate to be well off, but in the late 1970s to early 1980s, my parents sent my brother and me to the United States to attend college so we would avoid the political instability of the times. We had an uncle who had found work in California, the San Francisco area, and lived there, so that's where we lived. We both attended the university at Berkeley. I am a pharmacist. I live and work in Portland now, while my uncle and brother are still in the Bay area. My uncle, who was a landscaper and gardener, is now retired. My brother lives with him and looks after him. Now, they both do bonsai, while my brother also teaches."

"Well, we have a lot in common then," the Major responded. "My father was a gardener, and now that I'm retired, I'm enjoying my own flower gardens."

"How very nice," she answered. "I'd love to see your flowers sometime."

"Have Mick bring you by anytime," he invited. "But don't expect to come inside. You're more than welcome to, but Mick's allergic to cats, and Purvati, my cat, loves him."

She laughed. "I understand."

And now I also understood the situation much better, he thought. She was indeed intelligent. She understood what she was getting into with Mad Dog, or Mick. Mad Dog joked about never being able to leave her because she was Bolivian, but now the Major guessed at the truth. With no more union, pilots were paid very little. He had suspected Mad Dog might have been unable to support his own lifestyle and might have been getting into debt. Mercedes might be the bread winner of the couple. Or they could simply be in love—or both.

"I have also found a partner," the Major told her. "Her name is Daphne. I was wondering if there was some afternoon or evening Mick might be in town, so the two of you could join us for dinner at the Old Spaghetti Factory on Mill Plain."

She checked her calendar and replied, "Might we also invite Mick's friend, Danny O'Hare? I understand you also are friends with him."

"Of course," he said. "That's fine with me. Daphne hasn't met Danny yet either. That would be nice." Thinking back to the last time they met, he wondered what words of discouragement Danny might have for his new relationship, but then he didn't have the track record of a prior failed marriage like Mad Dog. Danny wasn't a negative person by nature—just when he suspected a pattern of mistakes that most people would have already learned from might be developing. *Well, that's certainly reasonable, except sometimes you just have to let people make their own mistakes.* The Major and Mercedes agreed on a date, and both marked their calendars. They expressed their desire to meet each other and said good-bye.

Then the Major called Rose and arranged a different meeting with Daphne and Stephen. He knew Rose wasn't comfortable in Mad Dog's company. They agreed to lunch at Beaches downtown on the river, and both marked the date on their calendars.

"I'd like to take Daphne shopping for a new supply of yarn at Fabric Depot in Portland as a gift," Rose volunteered.

The Major warned her, "That's likely to be expensive, considering the volume of yarn she first arrived with. On the other hand, I'm sure you'll be rewarded with a blanket of your own for your generosity. She does beautiful work—of course, I am prejudiced in her favor. Listen— while I have you on the phone, I was wondering where I might find a large painting or photograph of dragonflies. I thought you might have some ideas."

Rose made some suggestions, and he cautioned her not to mention it to Daphne. Since there were no pictures or hangings of any kind on the wall in the upstairs bedroom, he thought a dragonfly would be the perfect thing to hang over the bed.

After he hung up, he walked back into the living room to find Purvati stretched out on her back between

Daphne and Deandra. She apparently was equally comfortable with her new roommate and in-law. Daphne and Deandra were laughing. He hoped they would both be as happy as he and Purvati were now.

The next day, Mercedes called back to say that, regretfully, she and Mick would not be able to join Daphne and the Major for dinner before the wedding. "His schedule is just too full," she explained. "But that's a good thing. It's good for him to have so much work."

The Major, of course, had to agree. He at least introduced Mercedes to Daphne over the phone. Daphne was very interested in the bonsai that Mercedes' brother and uncle did. Mercedes promised to email the Major some pictures, as well as her brother's email address in case Daphne had any questions.

Every morning Daphne and the Major continued to find fresh evidence of possum bathing in the pond. They did everything they could to make it safe, but Posey kept pulling the electrical cord out, until finally one morning after sleeping late, they found the water pump out in the yard again. This time it was burnt out. They decided it was pointless to replace it this year.

The acidanthera bloomed white with dark red centers, and a surprise yellow gladiola showed up as well. The daylilies bloomed buttery yellow, peach, pumpkin orange, and red. But the fragrant Asiatic lilies stole the show. The red ones turned out to be dark pink and the white ones were huge. All of them smelled heavenly. In the front yard, the Major managed to win a major battle against the dandelions with Daphne's help, and the duckweed was now an endangered species on the property. Next spring would be another story. And then there was the ever-present bamboo…

Chapter 30

Time of the Dragonfly

Mad Dog and Mercedes were married by a justice of the peace in Portland with Danny, the Major, Daphne, and a few others in attendance. Mad Dog had been right when he said Mercedes was beautiful. She was not only beautiful, but very intelligent and perceptive as well.

Mad Dog managed to behave himself throughout the entire, albeit short, ceremony. There were no inappropriate wisecracks. The Major was impressed. Mercedes was good for Mad Dog, and the Major found it to be nothing short of amazing that she had managed to get her groom to behave in public. Mad Dog and Mercedes were clearly very much in love. The Major hoped the magic never wore off, and that Mad Dog would continue to avoid embarrassing his bride, although the Major suspected it took a lot to embarrass Mercedes, which was good considering whom she'd married.

Once Daphne and the Major got to know Mercedes better, they found her to be extremely knowledgeable in many subjects and very well-read. She had a law degree from her native Bolivia, and she'd had the courage to move to a new country, start a new life, go back to school in a completely different area of study, get another degree, and start over with a career as a pharmacist. She and Mad Dog were soul mates. It seemed to Daphne, after hearing stories from both the Major and Mad Dog himself, that Mercedes had rescued Mad Dog from the negative energy that had surrounded him from some of his overly critical and judgmental military friends like Danny O'Hare and Larry Bullock. She had influenced him to reeducate himself in philosophy, poetry, and literature—subjects he'd not paid much attention to when he was in college before. They had a promising new life of discovery ahead of them.

Rose and Stephen also got married later that summer at the Unity Church in West Vancouver. It was a lovely ceremony, and by that time, they and the Major and Daphne had become good friends. Sometimes the four of them went out together. Sometimes Rose and Daphne did a girl's day out, usually resulting in Daphne bringing home large bags of new yarn. And sometimes, although a lot less frequently than in the past, the Major and Rose would go somewhere in search of flowers or gardening supplies. More often now, Daphne was included in flower-related adventures.

Stephen was faithful to Rose. He made no effort to stifle her freedom. They seemed to complement each other's personalities. It made the Major feel really good to see her happy and to know he hadn't lost her friendship.

One Monday Daphne and the Major drove up to La Center, between Vancouver and Woodland, to visit The Trellis, only to find it was closed on Mondays. But on the way up, they had noticed some fields of lavender along the east side of I-5, so they decided to stop there on the way back. The place was called The Waldorf. There were dog kennels, a shed full of dried lavender bunches for sale, and then a hillside landscaped with roses and lilies. The Major was delighted at the sight and smells. At the base of the hill were the fields of lavender they had seen from the highway.

After enjoying their walk through the gardens, they came back up the hill and past the kennels to an area filled with metal sculptures and garden decorations. Daphne found a dragonfly sundial disk. "Look!" she exclaimed as she held it up for him to see.

"That's perfect, but won't it rust?" he asked.

"It's meant to," she explained, "or we could paint it. I could paint it with acrylic paints and glitter. I'd love to paint it." So of course, he bought it for her—along with one

222

of the dried lavender bunches. By the time they got home, the inside of the car was heavily scented with the lavender. Daphne put the bunch of dried flowers in a metal vase on a stand in the foyer. As soon as she was satisfied that it looked just right, Purvati jumped up onto the stand and rubbed her face in the lavender, scattering dried florets everywhere. Daphne laughed as she stroked the cat. "Just spreading the joy, aren't you, sweetie."

The Major saw more of Deandra now, but sometimes just in passing, as she and Daphne would spend time together. But they didn't see much of Mercedes and Mad Dog.

The Major accompanied Daphne to the courthouse in Portland for the divorce hearing, since Richard would be there. The Major avoided speaking, not wanting to give away the fact that he had been on the receiving end of Richard's calls to Daphne's cell phone, since Richard had the number. Daphne also avoided addressing Richard and spoke only to the judge. She and the Major were careful to keep their physical distance in the courtroom and not let body language give away their relationship. Even though Daphne's divorce went through with no problem, and the judge advised Richard to seek counseling, marriage was something neither Daphne nor the Major felt compelled to rush into.

Daphne continued to use the upstairs bedroom as her own, but as the romance blossomed, she began sleeping downstairs with her Major and Purvati. The upstairs bedroom became her music room, and the knitting took up residence in the living room in front of the television. She no longer felt she had to be the housekeeper, cook, or slave as she had with Richard. If one of them felt the need to dust, vacuum, or whatever, they did.

With Daphne's encouragement, the Major tried his hand at writing short poems for her, and much to his surprise, found he enjoyed it. She was pleased, but suggested from time to time that he try short stories. And when she expressed an interest in bonsai, the Major encouraged her to try it. She turned out to be quite talented, and soon there were little trees in trays joining the Major's flowers. The beginning bonsai trees, otherwise known as potensai, had to be kept outside to keep Purvati's paws from exploring the roots.

Eventually, once Daphne and the Major got used to each other's style and level of musical playing, they explored violin and guitar duets. The challenge was to keep from always using the violin for the melody and the guitar for just accompaniment. Daphne was perfectly willing to accompany, as that was actually easier, but the Major felt they should give the guitar's versatility and Daphne's talent their due.

Purvati, of course, got twice the attention and enjoyed going for short walks with the two of them in her pink pet-a-roo pouch. She always rode with the Major, since he was her first love. And it took a while before Daphne was allowed to brush her. Turkish Van-alikes often preferred to bond with just one person, so some things were simply just between Purvati and the Major. Daphne understood. But she was surprised and delighted one night when Purvati suddenly joined her in her bubble bath. Even though the Major had warned her that Turkish Vans and Van-alikes liked to play in water, it still took her by surprise to have a cat jump into the tub with her. Purvati liked to try to catch the bubbles and, of course, burst them. Following their bath, Daphne discovered the cat really had lived a pampered life. The kitty clearly enjoyed the warm blow dryer. Sometimes after that, when Daphne took a bath, Purvati would either join her or lay on the rim of the tub, occasionally reaching a paw down to play with the bubbles or just dangle in the water.

When the Major, Daphne, and Rose visited the Rhododendron Gardens south of east Portland, Rose dropped the hint that the gardens were often used for weddings.

"All in good time," the Major answered. "There's no rush. We're fine as we are. She's just gotten out of a bad marriage, so I'm not about to push her. And there's no financial reason to, since she has no income, and I'm not worried about the taxes. Don't worry. If we decide to get married, you and Stephen will definitely be invited."

Daphne never even responded. She looked around at the flowers, as if she hadn't heard the conversation, and then she just wandered off. So, they left it at that. The Major knew that they would get married only when Daphne was ready.

From time to time at home, the couple would sit on the landing at the top of the stairs and watch the moon through the skylight. Sometimes, they tried to visualize Lady Rainbow in the craters of its surface. Sometimes, they would see a dragonfly in the daytime on one of their outings and pretend to listen for its silent song inside themselves. And sometimes they would see a cat and sing the song *Moonshadow* together. Occasionally, Purvati would curl up between them while they were watching TV, and a night didn't go by that there weren't three in the bed—at least part of the night.

"If we ever get married," Daphne suggested one night as they gazed at the moon through the skylight, "I'd like it to be at night under a full moon."

"Well, then," the Major responded, "whenever we get married, we'll find a way to do it under a full moon, even if we have to hire a pagan priestess or a Native American shaman to do the honors. But that means that it can't be in the winter because of the constant cloud cover."

"Then whenever it works," she whispered in his ear.

"And you get to keep your name," he added, holding her close. She smiled and snuggled her left ear up against his chest. He knew she was listening to his heart beat. He also knew then that they would be getting married sometime in the next year. And he knew there was no need for anything traditional or formal. They were both happiest in casual situations. That night, they made love on the air mattress in the upstairs bedroom and fell asleep wrapped in each other's arms. When they awoke the next morning, Purvati had draped herself across both their necks and was purring loudly.

Daphne painted the dragonfly sundial herself and added glitter to the wet paint before spraying it with a clear acrylic sealer. She set it on a flat rock in the back garden between statues of the Buddha and Kwan Yin—with the dragonfly pointed toward Posey's pond, as they now called it. It just took a couple of minor adjustments to get the shadow created by the dragonfly's tail positioned for Pacific Standard Time.

"You do realize," Daphne pointed out, once the dragonfly was in place, "the only time of the year there's likely to be sunshine to make a shadow from the dragonfly's tail will be when we're on Pacific Daylight Time?"

"We'll cope," the Major answered. They both laughed, and left the dragonfly as it was.

One sunny day in August, leaving Purvati to hold down the fort at home, they crossed the river into Portland and took scenic Highway 26 west to Cannon Beach. First they stopped at Ecola State Park for the view and to watch the seagulls, cormorants, and puffins out on the rocks. Daphne was glad the Major remembered to bring his binoculars. A couple of kayaks were among the rock islands, and the Major envied them their close-up view. Daphne was grateful she wasn't out there on the water, negotiating the surf among those big rocks. When they'd had enough bird-watching, they headed south to the town of Cannon Beach. After a lazy lunch at an outside table in the shade, they browsed the shops and art galleries before heading to the beach itself. It was crowded with families and kite fliers, but the other people didn't bother them. The kites and kids were fun to watch. After a short walk, Daphne and the Major simply sat on the sand and watched and listened to the surf.

The late afternoon drive back was just as enjoyable. Before going home, they stopped at the Cold Stone Creamery across the street from the Old Spaghetti Factory for an ice cream dinner. When they finally got home, Purvati greeted them at the door with her customary cuddles.

Chapter 31

Dragonflies on the Water

To celebrate Daphne being home without being in hiding, the Major bought an inflatable boat. The first place they went to try it out was Lacamas Lake, just east of Vancouver and north of the small town of Camas. Daphne was excited about the outing.

They inflated the boat with a battery-powered air pump, carried the boat down to the water, and climbed in. The water was wonderfully cold. They took their time paddling up and down the lake. Daphne admired the houses along the west side sitting up on the crest of a hill. "They must have a beautiful view," she observed.

"I hope for their sakes there are no mudslides," he retorted. She gave him a disapproving look. "What? That's why I bought a house on flat ground. I'm just being practical."

"Of course you are," she laughed. "They still must have a beautiful view. Sometimes, beauty is worth the risk."

He had to agree with that, but he was more interested in looking for wildlife. Finally a hawk flew over. "Look!" he pointed out. "There goes Mad Dog Hawkins."

"Hope he remembers where his nest is."

"He talks a lot, but I think he's serious about Mercedes," he responded. "He's not going to mess up this time."

"I hope not. I really like her. She's smart and compassionate at the same time. I like that combination. Guess that's why I fell for you."

The Major didn't answer. Both their heads turned to watch a V formation of Canadian geese skim about a foot above the water—almost within reach of them. "Now that was beautiful," he said finally, after they were out of sight.

Daphne nodded in silent agreement. Not ten minutes later another V formation, this time mallards, flew by just overhead in the same direction. Both groups were headed north. "I'm beginning to understand what people mean when they write about communing with Nature," she finally said.

"If memory serves," he responded, "geese symbolize vigilance and fidelity. They remind us to follow our own inner compass."

"Maybe we need to be vigilant to not slip back into old, bad habits," she noted. "What about mallards?"

"Memory doesn't serve. Sorry."

"Maybe it's that beauty is enough and needs no explanation," she offered.

They had so much fun on the lake that on the way home in the car, they discussed where to boat next. He understood she needed to make up for lost years of feeling imprisoned indoors.

The next morning over breakfast, he said, "Let's just go. I'll surprise you." He drove her north on I-5 and turned east onto Highway 503 at Woodland. They quietly enjoyed the scenery until he turned right at the tiny town of Ariel and down to Lake Merwin. They got out of the car, breathed in the air, and surveyed their surroundings.

"What beautiful countryside," Daphne marveled. The lake was certainly scenic, but big enough to intimidate her. "I don't know," she hesitated.

"We both have safety vests," he reminded her, but sensing her discomfort, he added, "If you're not comfortable with it, we can just enjoy the view."

"Let's," she agreed. "We don't have that much control in an inflatable," she pointed out. They leaned against the car for a while and watched the water flow by until finally, the Major broke the spell.

"I'm thirsty, and there's a bar up the hill." The bar up the hill was home to the annual D.B. Cooper Halloween party. Cooper had been the hijacker that got away with $200,000 in 1971 by parachuting out of a plane somewhere in the general vicinity. The ceiling inside the bar was covered with a parachute.

While they drank a couple of cokes, Daphne commented, "This Halloween thing would be something Richard would enjoy. I can see him idolizing a criminal."

"Well, the stunt didn't do Cooper any good," the Major remarked. "He either didn't survive, or he didn't make it out of the woods with the money. The only part of the money that surfaced was found down on the banks of the Columbia River in 1980, before Mt. St. Helens erupted. No doubt, any missing evidence got buried under mud and ash. Maybe him too."

"Wonder what made him do it?"

"Personality disorder, most likely. Thought he was smarter than everybody else."

"Like Richard," she observed.

They finished their cokes and headed over to Horseshoe Lake at Woodland. "Now this is more my size," Daphne said with relief when she saw the lake. They inflated the boat and climbed in. The only other boats on the water were two kayaks. In the first, a man was in the kayak with his white dog sitting on the bow. Tied to the first kayak, in tow behind him and his dog, was another kayak with a white cat sitting in it. Both animals and their owner were wearing life vests.

"That cat doesn't look so comfortable," Daphne observed.

"Definitely doesn't look like it's leaving the kayak. But we are not bringing Purvati," the Major insisted.

"You don't think she'd stay in the pet-a-roo?" she asked.

"I don't think she'd fit in the pet-a-roo with a life vest on," he said.

Just then, they spotted a pair of dragonflies flitting between the water and the lake bank.

Chapter 32

The Goddess of Sacrifice

Deandra called the day after their outing in Woodland. She had accidentally locked herself out of her house. She had gone out the front door to get the mail, and had realized her mistake as soon as she closed the door behind her. Fortunately, she had her cell phone, and her truck was parked in the driveway rather than the garage. There was a remote for the garage door in the truck, but she couldn't get it to work and suspected the battery was bad.

Daphne and the Major grabbed a package of nine-volt batteries and headed over to rescue Deandra. She was waiting in her truck when they got there. "I've just been so out of it all day," she explained. "Those blasted dreams have returned again. I can't get it out of my head—being dead and looking down on Plains Indians bashing my face in."

"That same dream from childhood?" Daphne asked.

"The exact same dream," her sister answered. "Right before I was killed, I was worried about my brothers. And then after I was dead, I was watching the natives bash my face in."

"I can see how that would be distracting," the Major commented, "but shall we focus on the problem at hand?" He replaced the old batteries in the garage remote, but that didn't solve the problem. None of them could get the remote to work. The garage door wouldn't budge, and it had no handle. Deandra's phone battery had gotten low while she was calling for help, so they plugged it into the Major's car dashboard to recharge, while she called her landlord. The landlord was out of town, so they called a locksmith.

While waiting for the locksmith to arrive, the Major strolled around the property, giving the sisters a chance to chat. Deandra was clearly agitated. *She can't shake off the mood of the dream,* Daphne thought, but she couldn't seem to calm her down.

Deandra abruptly changed the subject and insisted she update Daphne on the latest news about Richard Gatorman. Daphne felt no desire to have any connection with Richard, but Deandra had apparently been keeping tabs on him and eagerly reported her findings.

"Shortly after your divorce was final," Deandra related, "Richard remarried a much younger woman named Samantha, a blonde, about the same age you were when you married him, poor thing. But with more public awareness of domestic violence today than we had back when you got married, she had to know more about the subject and what to do if he abused her."

"I really don't want to hear this," Daphne interrupted. "And you have no idea how many women don't know what to do when they're blindsided with domestic violence. I'm sorry you've felt the need to keep up with that creep, though I don't understand it. I'm trying to let go of that part of my life, hoping that some day I can forgive him. That's the only way I can heal."

"No, no," Deandra contradicted excitedly, "I haven't 'kept up with him' as you say. It was on the Portland evening news."

Daphne shook her head repeatedly. "That makes no sense. Stop."

"No, you need to hear this." Deandra was simply agitated, out of control emotionally, and couldn't hold back what she'd heard. "The first time he beat her up, she went straight to the hospital emergency room. The police were called in, and Richard was arrested."

"Well, good for her," Daphne said wearily, understanding there was no stopping Deandra when she was this wound up about something. "But I hardly see how that rates a report on the Portland news."

Deandra let out an exasperated sigh at yet another interruption. "Please, let me finish. As is sadly often the case, as we well know, Samantha dropped the charges. After all, she was still young and inexperienced. Maybe she thought she'd taught him a lesson."

This time it was Daphne who sighed loudly. "Look, we don't even know this Samantha. Just let it go. Please!"

"You need to hear this," her sister insisted, raising her voice. Tensions were rising, and Deandra was adamant that Daphne hear the whole story. "When he got out of jail, he went straight to a bar and got drunk, of course. He went home from the bar that night and bashed Samantha's head in with a tire iron."

"Oh, my God," Daphne reacted, horrified, as she instinctively put her hands over her mouth.

"He slept it off," Deandra continued. "When he woke up, he cleaned himself off, got some money from an ATM, and went back to the bar. Once he was shitfaced drunk again, he actually bragged to the bartender about what he'd done."

By now, Daphne was holding her entire face in her hands. Memories came flooding back of little Moonshadow. She closed her eyes to fight back the tears.

Deandra went on, thinking that it would somehow help her sister to hear this new information—that it would reassure Daphne that she had done the right thing by leaving Richard. "He was drunk, but he actually confessed to bashing her head in with a tire iron, saying she'd deserved it for having him humiliated by having him arrested for little more than 'keeping her in line.' Can you believe it? Of course the bartender called the police, and Richard was arrested again, only this time for first degree murder. They found the bloody tire iron with his prints on it next to her body, poor thing. The judge denied bail. Once

Richard had sobered up, there was no way he could deny it, so there's not even going to be a trial. He'd already confessed. Do you understand what this means?"

Daphne's eyes were closed, trying very hard to shut out all the feelings that were bombarding her. She felt like she was back in Richard's house, and he was roughly grabbing little Moonshadow. She didn't want her kitty taken away. She didn't know how to stop him from hurting the cat that she loved.

Deandra went on anyway. "It means he's never getting out of prison, at least not until he's a very old man, and by that time, he won't be a danger to us anymore. We're free of him for good now. We're safe, Daphne."

Deandra was all smiles, but Daphne felt anything but safe. Moonshadow wasn't safe. Samantha wasn't safe. *What about Samantha? I don't feel safe!*

Deandra continued, "Do you think maybe that's what caused me to dream that dream again? Richard bashed in Samantha's head, and I was watching Indians bash my face in. That must be what brought the dreams back."

Daphne didn't answer. She thought she heard Deandra say that Richard had bashed little Moonshadow's face in. She just sat there in the front passenger seat of the Major's Saturn. Just then, a van pulled into the driveway. Deandra got out of the backseat and went to greet the locksmith.

The locksmith got out of his van, exchanged a few pleasant words with Deandra, and proceeded to work on opening the front door. The Major, who had been walking up and down the sidewalk in front of the house, saw the van arrive and came over to watch the man work. It took about five minutes before he opened the front door, apologizing for it taking so long.

"It's pretty rusty," he explained. "Doesn't look like it gets much use."

"No, I always use the back door," Deandra told him. "That's where I park my truck." She paid with her credit card, exuberant that she could get on with her life again, then turned and thanked the Major profusely. She waved goodbye to Daphne as she went inside her home, and the van drove away. Deandra felt all was well. *Now Daphne knows she's safe.*

The Major wondered why Daphne never got out of the car, but that was her choice. Maybe she was tired or just comfortable. Or maybe Deandra had talked her ear off, as usual. Whatever the case, she was sitting back with her eyes closed when he got into the car. He assumed she was taking a nap, so he didn't disturb her during the drive home.

By the time the Major got back in the car, Daphne had wiped away the tears and was trying to get control of her emotions. She felt safe again with the Major in the car beside her. She remembered what he had told her about Moonshadow's sacrifice, but it was hard not to be upset while thinking about the pain the cat might have suffered. She remembered the Major telling her that she didn't know for sure Moonshadow had been killed—she still might be alive. Such a loving kitty may have found a nice home after all. That thought calmed her down. Then she remembered what Deandra had been saying about Richard and Samantha. She wished it hadn't happened, even though she'd never met Samantha. She had no idea who Samantha had been, but she knew full well it could easily have been her instead. She was glad Richard was locked up, but she wished she didn't know about any of it. It only brought up the guilt she felt about Moonshadow, and it left her wondering if Richard had used the same tire iron on her kitty. It was a horrible thought, and she would have to work hard to get it out of her mind. She needed get past it. She didn't want to remember little Moonshadow like that, so every time that image would come up inside her head, she focused on an image of little Moonshadow happily chasing dragonflies and being cared for by Lady Rainbow, the moon goddess. She silently asked the moon to protect all cats—especially homeless ones.

When they got home, Daphne went into their bedroom and lay down on the bed. Purvati came and curled up next to her on the Major's pillow. The Major looked in on them and smiled. *My ladies*, he thought to himself.

Daphne slept for several hours. When she woke up, she decided it was time to grow up and put her foot down. She had made her wishes clear that she didn't want to hear about Richard, but Deandra had either ignored her or just hadn't listened. Either way was unacceptable. She had a right to be heard and respected. She decided to make herself heard this time. She called Deandra on the phone and told her in no uncertain terms that she felt violated by Deandra's refusal to accept no when she had told her she didn't want to hear about Richard.

Daphne informed her sister, "You won't be welcome in our home, and no phone calls from you will be accepted for two weeks. After that, an apology will be required to reinstate our relationship."

The Major overheard Daphne's end of the conversation, which apparently was most of it. He was sad it had happened, but Daphne had calmly explained her reasons and kept to her word. In a way, he was proud of her. He also understood Deandra's reason for telling her, and that Deandra had been emotionally out of control, but he agreed that Deandra had to learn to respect Daphne's wishes on such a sensitive subject. Daphne had learned to establish and maintain boundaries that she was comfortable with. It was a healthy part of adult life. He saw it as a big step in the right direction. In support of her, he refrained from calling Deandra for the next two weeks. He was grateful Deandra knew better than to call them.

Eventually Deandra apologized and refrained from mentioning her former brother-in-law, although she clearly didn't understand Daphne's point of view. "She's just not used to me having one," Daphne explained to the Major. "She's definitely not used to me asserting myself."

"It doesn't matter what she understands. It's a good learning experience for both of you. It's necessary for your well-being, and you have every right to say no to something that makes you uncomfortable. She has to learn to respect your wishes. That's life," he responded.

But the next morning was shattered by Daphne's overwhelming sense of hopelessness. She woke up depressed after a fitful night full of dreams haunted by Richard. The Major tried to be supportive, but she no sooner got dressed than she sat down on the floor and just cried.

"The only place I have in the whole world is right here with you and Purvati," she sobbed, trying desperately to convey her appreciation for being there and knowing she was wanted.

But what the Major heard was that she didn't think she belonged in this world. He was worried. He couldn't get her to eat anything, so finally he took her out to do a little grocery shopping. She seemed better, though still a bit listless. He stopped at a fast food drive-through for a couple of milkshakes. That seemed to cheer her up.

When they got home, she practiced her guitar for about a half hour, before finishing her milkshake. He suggested they watch some TV, and she was amenable to that. By the time the program they watched had finished, she had lain down on the sofa and fallen fast asleep—this time peacefully.

While Daphne was sleeping, the Major went outside and walked around the yard. He soon discovered that two of the sprinkler heads were still going. They had failed to shut off after the morning program had run, and water had been spraying under the maple trees on the north side, outside the fence, for hours. He reset the dial to the off position, but they continued. He tried to turn off the valve but didn't have the right tool, so he went back inside. When he couldn't remember the name of the sprinkler company he used, he realized he was rattled by Daphne's earlier mood. He could remember the workers' first names, which were Pedro and Henry, but not the company name, and without that, he couldn't look up their phone number. Meanwhile the water outside continued to run. He became uncharacteristically frustrated with himself when he couldn't find the file folder where he stored all receipts from services for the house. He knew the folder was there, but he didn't realize he was passing it by every time he went through the file drawer, because it had slipped down behind the folder in front of it. Forgetting that Daphne was sleeping on the sofa just a few feet away, he slammed the file drawer shut.

Daphne woke up suddenly. She was totally disoriented. "Where am I? Where am I?" she asked.

The Major had moved to his computer desk, where the phone sat, and pulled out his checkbook to look up who the last sprinkler payment had been made out to, when he heard her stir. He looked up and saw she was awake and sitting up. "The sprinkler's broken in the on position," he explained to her. "I can't turn it off."

He was taken by surprise when she responded by running past him and up the stairs holding her head with her hands. Realizing he had woken her by slamming the file drawer, he shouted after her, "I couldn't find the file to get the phone number to call for service."

When there was no response, he continued looking through his checkbook until he at last found the name of the company. He called them and reported the problem. Henry was there in less than fifteen minutes. He turned off the errant sprinkler heads with the greatest of ease. "You need one of these keys," he explained to the Major, referring to the long handled tool he had just used. "I'll be back Tuesday morning to fix the problem, and I'll bring you one of these."

"That'll be great. I'll mark it on my calendar. Thanks for coming out so quickly."

"No problem," Henry answered. They shook hands, and Henry left. The Major went back inside.

Meanwhile, Daphne had gone upstairs to her former bedroom. She was kneeling with her head between her hands on the floor when the doorbell rang, followed by men's voices. She crawled into the far end of the closet, closing the door behind her. She leaned against the spare shelf that covered the door to the hidden attic space. All she wanted was to feel safe in a dark, quiet place. If she felt threatened, she could always crawl into the hidden attic space.

There was an afghan on the lower shelf to her right, and she felt chilled, so she covered herself with it. She still wasn't fully awake yet, and was trying to understand what was happening. Purvati pushed her way through the closet door, came up to her and huffed. "Did I take your hiding place?" Daphne asked. "We can hide in here together."

She was grateful for Purvati's company. She closed her eyes and enjoyed the warmth of the afghan. Gradually she drifted off to sleep and didn't notice when Purvati left.

The Major was relieved to have the sprinkler problem solved and out of the way. He wondered why Daphne had run upstairs, since he hadn't heard her playing her guitar. He remembered she had been holding her head and wondered if she had a headache. He went up to look for her, but she wasn't in the bedroom or the extra attic room. Maybe she had gone back downstairs while he was out with Henry. He checked all of the downstairs rooms, but she wasn't there. He flashed back to the day he had found her note and remembered how miserable he had felt to find her and her possessions gone. He felt a sense of panic rise up inside himself that he might have lost her again. He called her name over and over as he ran through the house looking for her or a note.

Daphne awoke to the sound of the Major's voice calling her name. She pushed the closet door open and answered quietly, "I'm here."

The Major went back upstairs to her former bedroom. "Daphne?" he called again.

This time he heard her soft voice answer, "I'm here."

He looked around the room, and then he saw her sitting on the closet floor wrapped in an afghan. By this time his adrenaline and sense of panic were in charge of his thoughts and emotions. "What are you doing in there?"

"I just wanted to feel safe," she answered.

Now he was alarmed, but he tried not to show it. "You're safe, Daphne," he told her as he knelt on the floor in front of her and patted her leg reassuringly. "I'm not going to let anything happen to you. What are you feeling?"

"I feel broken inside," she said. "When I woke up on the couch, I didn't know where I was, but I've figured that out now. I came in here because it was dark and quiet. I feel safe here."

The Major thought back to earlier in the day when he remembered her saying there was no place for her in this world. He decided he needed to get help, but it was the weekend. He didn't want to wait for Monday to call the office of the psychologist she had seen in Portland or his own, Dr. Bernstein, and get an appointment for her. "I think we should go to the emergency room," he said deliberately keeping his voice calm.

"But I'm not sick," she protested. "I just feel broken."

241

"They can help you feel better," he explained. "Will you go with me, or should I call an ambulance?"

"I don't need an ambulance," she insisted. "They need to save the ambulances for sick people."

"But you said you feel broken. That's a form of being sick," he persisted. "If I drive, will you ride with me to the emergency room? It would make me feel a lot better just to get you checked out. The people at the hospital can help you feel better."

"Ok," she agreed. "I need help getting up."

He helped her to her feet, put his arm around her shoulder, and helped her down the stairs. He replaced the afghan with a light jacket and found a pair of shoes she could slip on without having to tie laces. Then he led her to the car and helped her into the passenger seat.

Chapter 33

Moon, Wind, and Surf

When they arrived at the hospital, the Major parked the car in the parking garage, and they walked together to the emergency room. He had Daphne sit down in the waiting area, while he checked her in. He explained to the admitting nurse, "She was recently divorced from an abusive husband. She just learned yesterday that her ex-husband murdered his new bride, and now she's understandably depressed. I found her hiding in the closet. I'm worried about her ability to pull out of this on her own. If it wasn't a Saturday, I'd just call my doctor and take her in."

"No, it's fine," the nurse assured him. "You did the right thing." She made up an identification bracelet and took it over to Daphne, who offered her right wrist. The nurse returned to the Major, and they finished with the admissions paperwork.

The Major went back over to Daphne, sat down next to her, and put his arm around her. "It's fine. They're not very busy by the looks of it," he observed.

Daphne looked around and noticed the waiting room was empty except for another couple with a baby. "Good," was all she mumbled.

After about ten minutes, a nurse called them back to a more private area. "What seems to be the problem?" she asked Daphne.

"I'm just confused." Daphne said simply.

"Have you had thoughts about hurting yourself?" The nurse wanted to be sure.

"No, I'm not going to hurt myself. I woke up suddenly, and I didn't know where I was. I just needed to be someplace safe and quiet, so I sat in the closet. I've been feeling disoriented. I have no sense of time. I just want to feel safe."

They were sent back to the waiting room. The couple with the baby was no longer there. This time Daphne picked a different chair. Again the Major sat down next to her and put his arm protectively around her. "I'm glad we came," she told him. He was relieved to hear it. He hadn't been sure if he was overreacting.

An ambulance arrived, and a man with an injured leg was wheeled back. The man's family arrived soon after with a couple of small children and sat behind Daphne and the Major. Then another ambulance arrived with an injured woman. "Must have been an accident," the Major commented. "I'm sure they'll take care of both of them before they get to us."

"I don't mind. It's kind of nice just sitting here," Daphne answered.

"We've been here over an hour," he pointed out.

"Doesn't seem that long."

Members of the second family began arriving. It became apparent that the older man of the group was the husband of the patient. He had a sense of humor and was kidding around with the younger members of his family. At one point, Daphne actually smiled at one of his jokes. The Major noticed and commented that she seemed to be feeling better. The words were no sooner out of his mouth than one of the children behind them screamed. Daphne immediately threw her arms up over her head. The Major gave her a reassuring hug. She dropped her arms and rested her head on his shoulder.

Finally her name was called, and she was led back through a maze of hallways to a secure ward. Inside the ward, there was a uniformed security guard on duty. She was shown into the first room on the right, next to the nurses' station, given a hospital gown to put on and a bin in which to put her clothes. She told them she wanted the Major to stay with her.

Once she had changed, she discovered how uncomfortable the bed was. What passed for a mattress was only a couple of inches thick and rubber. The pillow was small and lumpy. She was glad she wouldn't be there long. The nurse came in, took the things she had put in the bin, and told her they'd be put in a locker, where they'd be safe. The nurse also explained that they would need a urine sample for a routine toxicology screening. Daphne had no objection and complied. Once that was done, the nurse explained they would be waiting on a medical doctor to come and examine Daphne to determine if there was any medical issue, and if not, she would then see a counselor. The nurse brought in a chair for the Major as the bed was the only furniture in the windowless room.

After more time had passed, he went out and asked the nurse to turn off the light, which she did. Daphne fell asleep. She was awakened suddenly by a woman screaming, "Oh my God, oh my God. Help me, God! Help me God!" over and over.

"It's another patient—detoxing I think," the Major explained. The screaming persisted. The nurses just outside the door were discussing what needed to be done. "Hang on," he continued as he reached into his jeans pocket. "Thought I might still have these with me," he said as he offered her a pair of earplugs.

"How did you manage to have those?" she asked in amazement as she gratefully took them.

"I use them when I use the chain saw," he explained. "Safety training from the military. I also use safety goggles, but they didn't fit in my pocket." He smiled as she put the plugs in and went back to sleep. She was interrupted twice by nurses taking her blood pressure and temperature. The Major left to find some vending machines and came back a little while later with a cold soda.

They had been there seven hours by the time a doctor came in to see her. He was kind enough to wake her up before turning on the light. She remembered to take out the earplugs. He listened to her lungs and heart, asked more of the same questions, and left. Not long after that someone came in and took blood from her arm. As the woman put the needle into Daphne's arm, Daphne imagined she was back at Cannon Beach watching and listening to the surf and the birds and feeling the wind on her face. Another nurse came in and explained that they would have to wait for the lab report to come back before Daphne would be cleared to see a counselor. When the nurse left, she closed the door behind her.

Once they were alone, Daphne told the Major, "I feel safe here."

"I'm glad to hear that. I was concerned about how you'd react to being back here. I had no idea they were going to put you in a ward with a guard and no windows."

"I feel safe," she repeated, and then added, "but if I ever hear anybody put down the Canadian health system again saying 'you have to wait for hours to see a doctor,' am I going to have an answer ready for them!"

"Your sense of humor is back," he noticed. "You seem to be feeling better."

"Yeah, I feel safe," she said again. "It really helped to see the guard on duty. I'm glad my room is so close to him."

After several more hours, they were told the lab work was all negative, and a counselor had been called. Once he arrived, they talked about her history, what specifically had happened in the previous forty-eight hours, and how she felt now. He was satisfied that she was no danger to herself or anyone else, so they discussed coping strategies. The Major offered to make her an appointment with Dr. Bernstein. Daphne and the counselor both agreed that was a good idea.

"I'd rather have a psychologist here in Vancouver," Daphne explained.

By the time she was given her clothes back and released from the hospital, it was early the next morning. "Is it just after sunset or almost dawn?" she asked as they walked back to the parking garage.

"Almost dawn," he answered.

"I really did lose track of time."

"Well I hope you don't mind losing some more," he responded, "because I plan to sleep most of the day when we get home."

Monday morning he called Dr. Bernstein's office to schedule an appointment for Daphne. He was relieved the doctor could see her that afternoon. Daphne was looking forward to it. The Major drove them west on Highway 14 to North I-5. When they reached the traffic light at the end of the exit ramp, there was a young man, unshaven in ragged blue jeans wearing Army boots, a battle dress uniform shirt, and an Army cap, sitting by the side of the road with a cardboard sign that read:

"Homeless Disabled Vet
Anything will help."

The Major reached into his pocket, but found he had no cash on him. He had to drive on with great regret. He knew that many of the beggars around town had drinking or drug problems and would spend anything they were given on their habit of choice, but the homeless problem had grown so much worse since the mortgage crisis had started. So many foreclosures had resulted in homeless families and more tent cities across the country. He also knew that many veterans had been coming back from the wars in Iraq and Afghanistan to veterans' services that were overwhelmed and totally unprepared, underfunded, or mismanaged. As a result of that and all the foreclosures, many vets had also found themselves homeless when they returned to the states.

"I don't have any money on me either," Daphne said, noticing the Major's gesture.

"It's ok," he answered. "The light's green anyway."

Once Daphne was safely with Dr. Bernstein, the Major drove downtown to his bank, withdrew some cash, and headed back up I-5. Taking the same exit, he was relieved to see the young man still there. He pulled his car over out of the way of traffic. As he handed the young veteran the money, he apologized for having to drive by earlier, explaining that he had to go get some cash.

The young man made an effort to stand up, with great difficulty, to take the cash. His right leg was stiff and obviously hurting. He thanked the Major profusely and added, "I just got back from Iraq with shrapnel in my leg,"

"Have you been to the Veterans' Hospital here?" the Major asked him. "Were they not able to help you?"

He made a rocking motion with his right hand as he shrugged and grimaced at the same time, signifying that he hadn't had any luck there.

"What about Veterans of Foreign Wars?"

The young man shrugged.

"The VFW will not only make sure you have a place to live, they'll cut through the red tape for you, so you can receive the disability payments you've earned. I know where they are. I'll be glad to take you," the Major offered.

"You sure?" The young man seemed hesitant. He was obviously cynical from his prior experience.

"I'm retired military myself," the Major told him. "The VFW is made up of good people. They've been there themselves." He got out of the car and helped the young man into the back seat on the driver's side. He drove east, back across town to the other side of I-205, and turned onto NE 18th Street from 112th Avenue. He was relieved to find someone there when they arrived. After making introductions, the young man explained his situation. The Major excused himself and left, heading back to the doctor's office.

He had just enough time to settle down in the waiting room with a magazine, when Daphne came out, all smiles. She naturally assumed the Major had been there the entire time she was with the doctor.

"Feeling better?" he asked her, not mentioning his prior detour.

Chapter 34

Lost Lake and Moon River

Daphne was smiling when she came out of Dr. Bernstein's office. "I'm going back to see him next week," she told the Major. He was glad to hear it. He knew this was all part of the long healing process. When they got home, she spent the rest of the day cleaning house and then playing solitaire on the computer.

The next morning was a beautiful day. The Major suggested a day trip, and she readily agreed. They packed the boat and life vests just in case.

"Where shall we go this time?" she asked him.

"I'll surprise you," he offered, and she nodded and smiled. He drove south across the I-205 Bridge and headed east on I-84.

"Waterfalls?" Daphne guessed. He shook his head. "Outlet shopping?" she guessed again.

"Rose has been teaching you well, I see," he commented with a smile. "You'll find out where we're going—all in good time. I think you're due for nice surprises at this point in your life."

"Dr. Bernstein said I've paid my dues, and now I get to be myself."

They passed Rooster Rock and the turn off for the Vista House and View Point Inn. Daphne gazed at Multnomah Falls on her right as they passed by and then at stunning views of the Columbia River Gorge to her left. Eventually, he took the exit for the town of Hood River. As they drove through the scenic little town, Daphne commented on the many shops.

"We're not here for shopping," he explained. "This is just a lunch stop. Look," he pointed to the right. "There's a perfect place." He turned the corner, found a parking place, and fed some coins into the parking meter.

They walked back around the corner to the Trillium Café and went in. They were the only the customers in the place at first, because it was just a few minutes past 11 AM. After they ordered, they admired all the original art work. The perceptive waitress/bartender gathered from their conversation that it was Daphne's first time in the Gorge and brought them a game box full of questions about the state of Oregon to help them pass the time while their meals were being prepared. Daphne, having lived in the southern part of the state for many years, of course knew more answers than the Major did. They had fun, followed by some good food. As they ate, they noticed the place had filled up with other customers.

By the time they got back to the car, the meter had expired. "Were we in there that long?" she asked. "Didn't seem like it."

"We were having fun," he said as they drove off.

"Where to now?" she asked.

"Better get some gas, just in case," he commented.

Now she was wondering how far this day trip was going to go, as she'd noticed they still had over half a tank. After the tank was full, he headed east out of town and turned south on Highway 35. They weren't on it long, when he turned right. The drive was scenic, through fruit farms and orchards. They passed the little town of Dee and turned onto Lost Lake Road. Every now and then the peak of Mount Hood appeared in the background, getting closer and closer as they drove.

"Lost Lake," she commented. "That sounds appropriate."

"That's where we're going," he told her.

"If it's lost, how are we supposed to find it?" she kidded him.

"It's there," he said, smiling.

"Well, I'll feel right at home." She was all smiles too. The road kept rising and turning. They'd left the farms behind and were now surrounded by woodland. The turns in the road became sharper and more frequent. "This is so beautiful," she remarked, "and relaxing."

"That's the whole idea, isn't it?" They only saw one other car during the entire drive, and it was going in the opposite direction. Finally they arrived at the entrance to the National Park, paid a small entrance fee, and drove in. When they reached the lake, it was a brilliant blue under a blue sky dotted with occasional, white cotton-like puffs of clouds. He parked near the boat ramp. She noted the "No Motor Boats Allowed" sign.

They inflated their little boat and put in at the boat ramp. The wind was cool, felt good, and created ripples on the surface of the lake. Daphne was quite taken by the view of Mt. Hood's peak from the center of the lake. It was peaceful and mostly quiet, except for a family picnicking on the bank who occasionally yelled for their dog, Jack, who apparently kept wandering off. Neither the Major nor Daphne felt the need to talk for the most part. They paddled around in the center of the lake with lots of resting and taking in the scenery in between. It was good to just be together and breathe deeply.

Then they both saw it at the same time and pointed without saying a word. A dragonfly went skimming across the water. They smiled at each other. No explanation was needed.

They were both exhausted but happy by the time they got home. They entered the house through the garage to discover that Purvati was not a happy kitty. She growled her discontent upon greeting them and went straight to the front door.

"I'm sorry we were out so long, girl," the Major apologized. She lay in front of the door and thumped her tail.

"No, something's wrong," Daphne said from down the hall as she scooped the litter box. "Well, that wasn't it," she said after she'd washed her hands and come into the foyer.

"What's wrong, purr-baby?" the Major asked, kneeling down and stroking the cat's fur.

"Maybe it's because we left the closet door closed," Daphne suggested as she put the life vests on hangers in the closet.

"No, that's not it," he said standing up. "Did you look at the front door as we drove up?"

"I did, but I didn't notice anything," she answered.

He reached for the door and undid the latch. Purvati got up and rubbed his legs. Now her tail was straight up.

"Aha! You seem to be onto something," Daphne observed.

He opened the front door and stepped out onto the porch. Leaning against the brick pillar, facing him so that it couldn't be seen from the street, was a small gift wrapped package. He picked it up and brought it inside.

"Good girl," he said to Purvati. "Thank you. This must have been there a while. Looks and feels like a CD. Thank you, pretty purr-girl. You're a very good kitty."

"Who's it from?" Daphne asked as she came closer to see.

"MDH," he read from the little card under the bow.

"Mad Dog Hawkins," they both said in unison. He opened it up. It was a homemade CD with a note:

"Decided not to wait for you two to get married. Consider this a 'discovery' gift.
"MDH"

"It's a compilation Mad Dog made entirely of different renditions of Moon River by Johnny Mercer and Henry Mancini," the Major observed.

253

"What a wonderful gift!" Daphne exclaimed. "How did he know? You must have told him."

The Major just smiled. "No, I haven't discussed anything of depth or symbolism with him. We should consider this a sign of approval from the moon goddess herself."

The next day the Major called Mad Dog to thank him for the gift and arranged to meet him and Mercedes for dinner the following evening at the Old Spaghetti Factory. Once they had all arrived in the waiting area, the receptionist led them back into the restaurant to be seated.

"Make sure we're not near any children," Mad Dog directed.

The receptionist looked around and then changed directions. "Ok, let's see what we can do. Follow me, please."

"What's wrong with sitting near children?" Daphne asked.

"He doesn't like to be around them because they're loud and scream a lot," Mercedes was quick to explain.

"I can understand the screaming part. That can be nerve shattering, but they don't always scream, and they can be cute too," Daphne commented as they took their seats at a table. "We were all kids once."

"Yes," Mercedes answered, "but we prefer not to be around them."

"Little brats," Mad Dog commented.

Well, the Major thought to himself, *that answers that question. They certainly seem to be compatible there.*

"Ok, then," Daphne responded out loud. "We won't discuss children."

"Or pets," the Major whispered to her. She reacted with a look of surprised disapproval, and then turned her attention to her menu.

After they had placed their orders, Mad Dog instructed the waitress that it was to be one check and to give it to him.

"No way!" the Major protested, knowing how little income Mad Dog actually had. "This dinner is to thank you for the gift of the CD, and I WILL pay for it."

Before the two men could get into an argument, Mercedes interrupted for the sake of the waitress and said, "Just make it two checks, please. Thank you."

Once the waitress had left with their orders, Mad Dog remarked, "You can't be serious. You're thanking me 'for the gift of the CD.'" His tone was clearly mocking the Major.

"It's beautiful. I love that song, and it has special significance for us," Daphne explained.

"He didn't tell you the joke?" Mad Dog laughed.

"No," the Major interrupted, "and I'm not going to."

"What joke?" Daphne asked innocently.

"It's obscene and inappropriate," Mercedes said as she shot Mad Dog a threatening look, "and no one is going to mention it again this evening."

"Muchas gracias, señora," the Major directed at Mercedes with great relief that she had taken control of the situation. He knew that Mad Dog had a favorite, but very obscene, joke he liked to tell that involved the title of the song Moon River. He clearly thought it was extremely funny, but few others that the Major knew actually enjoyed it. The Major had known when he and Daphne had received the CD that Mad Dog's intent was not serious or good-natured, but he had chosen to ignore Mad Dog's intent, and accept the gift on a higher level for the beauty and significance he and Daphne had found between them.

Throughout dinner, the conversation remained on a very shallow level, with Mercedes from time to time trying to keep Mad Dog from making comments inappropriate in a public setting where others were dining. It was obvious to Daphne that Mad Dog had a very base and debasing sense of humor. With Daphne present, the Major began to see Mad Dog in a new light. He had understood that Rose had never enjoyed Mad Dog's company. Now the Major began to realize that Mad Dog had always been argumentative, judgmental, confrontational, and unwilling or unable to understand other points of view, but the Major had always chosen to ignore it. With Mad Dog, it was always us against them. The Major had enjoyed the distraction of Mad Dog's sarcasm and oppositional nature when they were engulfed in a working environment that thrived on us versus them, because he had seen Mad Dog as an example that "us" could sometimes be "them." Now, however, he realized he was tired of it. It had gotten old and served no constructive purpose. It wasn't amusing anymore.

After that evening, the Major continued to speak to Mad Dog on the phone only occasionally, and they exchanged emails daily, but he made no further effort to get together in person. It was a shame, he thought, because he and Daphne both really liked Mercedes, but it wasn't worth the emotional strain.

Then Mad Dog went on a crusade against religion. The Major had to agree that most organized religions were about money rather than spirituality, but that didn't mean that was true of most of the people who participated in them. It was a matter of personal choice. Even though they were both no longer in service, the Major still considered his oath to defend and protect the US Constitution to be sacred, and that included freedom of religion. Mad Dog was an atheist, and he had every right to be. He had connected with other atheists speaking out about their atheism. He had resented the military having chaplains for those of different faiths, but nothing equivalent for atheists, even though, by definition, there was nothing equivalent. Now he had found a group of people where he actually fit in. Mercedes, on the other hand, had seemed to be a very spiritual person, but she had to make her own choices. The Major hoped Mercedes liked Mad Dog's new friends, and he was happy that Mad Dog had finally found a group of people he was comfortable with.

The problem for the Major's friendship with Mad Dog was that Mad Dog was against all religion. It had gotten to the point where the Major, who respected everyone's right to choose their beliefs, as long as they didn't try to force them on him, could no longer have a phone conversation with Mad Dog without him making atheism and his crusade the topic of discussion. Even every email the Major received from him, and there were many, usually several a day, was about atheism, the evils of religions, or people of whatever religion who had gotten caught doing something wrong. The Major was past being annoyed. He told Daphne he was tired of having it shoved in his face.

"Hmmm. Sounds familiar," she observed. "You need to define and enforce your boundaries," she advised.

"Perimeter check. I guess you're right," he agreed. "I don't tolerate other people forcing their beliefs on me, and I shouldn't tolerate him forcing his lack of beliefs on me either. I should be telling him I've had enough, instead of telling you. Besides, he knows I'm not an atheist and never have been. I just respect his right to be. Obviously the respect doesn't go both ways."

"That's it," she said with a big smile. "Although, I don't mind you sharing."

He sent Mad Dog back an email telling him he was getting more proselytizing from Mad Dog than from his Latter-day Saints neighbors. He used his neighbors as an example, because LDS had a reputation for proselytizing, even though his neighbors weren't like that at all—they were actually very tolerant, pleasant people. He asked Mad Dog to please stop. What he received as a response was some sort of lengthy tirade in all caps and a large font. He saw just enough to see that Mad Dog didn't take his request in context, but thought the Major was telling him to end his crusade. Mad Dog had responded emotionally to his own issues, rather than what the Major had actually said in his email. The Major scanned through it without actually reading the whole thing, decided not to waste his energy on it, and hit delete.

He didn't get any more emails from Mad Dog, and he was surprised at how relieved he was. He missed him as a friend, but he also realized Mad Dog's crusade had been a negative influence and had been draining his energy. Then he remembered Dr. Bernstein's book, *Emotional Vampires*, and realized his friend Mad Dog was one.

I guess they really are everywhere, he mused to himself. *I should have recognized all the warning signs. Maybe I didn't want to.* He also remembered the tips from the book for dealing with such personality disorders, if you chose to remain involved with them, since most people had someone in their lives like that, and you always had a choice. Sometimes it was a very important relationship, but the Major had never liked being around people who were always judging and berating other people, putting them into little pigeon holes without at least trying to see the whole person or respecting their differences. He knew that only seeing other peoples' faults, while crusading against whatever others believed that gave them hope or comfort, was a depressing way to live. He had to accept that Mad Dog was not the happy, fun person he had tried to accept him as. The Major let go.

"Diversity is the spice of life," he told himself out loud while still sitting at his computer. "People need to accept diversity to experience the full joy of living. Life is problematic enough without taking on other peoples' negativity."

"That's right," Daphne answered from the living room where she was knitting and watching TV with Purvati. "Let's just keep it simple."

"Simple is happier," he agreed. "I'm retired from wars, fighting, and crusades. It's time to enjoy life."

Chapter 35

Lady Rainbow Marries the Sun

One morning, while they were eating breakfast, Daphne informed the Major, "We have an unresolved problem."

"What's that?" he asked. She had his undivided attention.

"I've never seen you in uniform," she said. "I don't want to. I know you're a man of peace now, and you've left that life behind."

"Then what's the problem?" He had no idea where she was going with this.

"It's ok if you want your friends to call you 'The Major,' but that's not who I'm marrying. I understand about your given name. Alfonso is a mouthful. You don't want to be called Alf or Alfie or Fonzie, and 'so-so' certainly doesn't fit." They both laughed.

"Well Alfonso was my only given name," he commented. "My father's name was Ursa, and I don't want to be called that either."

"But your mother's name was Barrios," she added. "Can I just call you Barry?"

"Now, why didn't I ever think of that?" he chuckled. "Barry is so normal."

"And it's so civilian," she continued. "A wedding is a time of establishing a new identity together. I'm not marrying a military rank. I'm marrying a peaceful gardener, who appreciates Nature and its symbolism and so much more."

"Then Barry it is," he agreed.

Daphne decided the wedding would be late summer that same year, before the rains came back. It would be an outdoor, nighttime ceremony under the full moon, just as they had discussed. They decided together that it would be the last full moon before the autumn moon. The lilies Barry had planted in the spring were in full bloom and full of fragrance. Daphne chose to hold a bouquet of white lilies in a vase of water. Barry understood the significance of the water, as they had spent so much time together discussing it, and the ocean tides were ruled by the moon as well.

They had decided to have the ceremony in the backyard garden next to the statue of Kwan Yin, goddess of compassion and Moonshadow's sacrifice that had brought them together. On the other side of them was the dragonfly sundial Daphne had painted with glitter. It shimmered in the moonlight. The minister was Buddhist. The only invited guests were two of their neighbors, Deandra, Rose, and Stephen. Barry held Purvati in the pet-a-roo. They both wanted it quick, quiet, and very intimate.

After the ceremony, the small party went inside, where Purvati was set free. The vase of fragrant lilies was set in the center of an assortment of pies they had bought at the neighborhood Shari's restaurant. After everyone had sampled the pies, visited, and wished the couple well, the guests departed.

That night Barry dreamt of his past as fields of manure laid out as fertilizer to be harvested for the garden of his new life. In the dream he found himself surrounded by swarms of dragonflies in the moonlight. They glittered as they swirled around him, and the vibration of the flying swarm turned into beautiful music that elevated him into the air a few feet above the ground. With the singing of the dragonflies, he was able to fly over the fields of manure without getting any on his shoes. He drifted over the fields and into his glorious dream garden surrounded by large, old fir trees that formed protective walls. The dragonflies then left him and flew upward, where together with the moonlight, they formed a shimmering rainbow roof of pure light. He knew he was in his true home at last.

Daphne dreamed of dragonflies that swarmed around the beautiful white lilies she held. The flowers were fragrant and glowed like the light of the moon itself. The dragonflies blended into one translucent creature who shimmered in colors of the rainbow.

The rainbow being spoke to her. "You are the blossoming of your essence. You were a seed from the flower at the center of the universe, and now you have grown and bloomed. You are the adornment of the cycles of time, change, transformation, and renewal. Your physical beauty will fade with time, but your wisdom will continue to grow."

When she awoke, she saw that Purvati had curled up into her usual sleeping position with Barry. Her paw was wrapped around his neck, and her soft, furry face was resting on his. Daphne had spooned up against his back, and both of them had their hands resting on Purvati, who was softly purring.

The rains returned in the fall. Barry answered a phone survey about housing improvements, which resulted in him being contacted by a Portland company offering discounts on lifetime roofs and fences. Barry knew his roof was due to be replaced in several years and had hoped for a lifetime roof, but they were expensive. This company, which had been owned by the same family for thirty years and had an A+ rating with the Better Business Bureau, was offering a roof with a lifetime transferrable warranty as well as a fence for a price he could afford. He had observed his original wooden privacy fence was rotting and falling down from lack of maintenance. He didn't want to spend his declining years water-proofing a fence, so he talked it over with Daphne.

"The house down the street has a six foot chain link fence with white coating that looks great," she observed.

Barry looked out the front window. "It is coated with something white," he now noticed.

"It's very visible and also cheerful during the gloomy season," she pointed out.

"I wouldn't want it to be that visible," he answered.

"The fence that surrounds the former dog park down the street is coated black," she commented.

"Too dark," he said.

When they signed the contract, the company owner told them they could also choose from brown or green. They agreed on brown. The roof and fence would be replaced between Thanksgiving and Christmas, weather permitting.

During the first week of November, they saw on the news that an Army psychiatrist had opened fire in a processing center for deploying troops at Fort Hood, Texas.

"Are you angry?" Daphne asked her husband.

He looked surprised. "No, I'm not. I'm disappointed, because I know that his commander should have known this man wasn't fit for duty, but sent him anyway. How many times have I heard soldiers say to their commanding officer, 'there's a problem with this soldier,' or 'he or she doesn't meet qualifications,' only to be told by the commander, 'send him anyway; it's his turn to go; I don't care; we need bodies; send him; he's just trying to get out of it, so make him go; we need boots on the ground.' I'm sad that so many have to suffer because of stupidity, but I'm very glad I retired when I did."

The next night they heard some of the names of the fallen on the news. "I knew him," Barry said quietly. "He was a good person and a good soldier."

"Which one?" Daphne asked.

"The explosives ordnance soldier."

"Are you angry at the shooter now?"

"No, I'm very sad. That Major, the shooter, tried to get out of service when he realized he didn't belong. The Army should have discharged him for the good of the service and given him a bill for his education. Or at the very least, they could have put him into counseling and insisted on a psychiatric evaluation, but these days, all too often, they try to avoid that, because they don't have enough soldiers. With the military getting over half of the entire budget for the United States of America, the fact that they can't come up with enough soldiers means the money's being spent somewhere else. So many soldiers have had to provide their own Kevlar vests for their own protection. Makes you wonder where the money's going—weapons of mass destruction, maybe? It's such a dysfunctional organization, but then it's such a dysfunctional war. Maybe we have a dysfunctional government because we're dysfunctional people. Shooting all those people was wrong, but it took more than just his wrong to put him in the position to do what he did. He was only there because somebody didn't follow their own regulations. By focusing blame on just the shooter, so many wrongs don't get corrected."

"Are you angry at the terrorists that started all this mess?" Daphne asked.

"I'm angry with what they've done," he answered, "but they didn't start anything. They're just ignorant, emotional people, whose out-of-control anger leads them to do terrible things, but they didn't start the extreme poverty in the Arab world."

"Angry at the act, but not the person who does it," Daphne recapped. "That's a very rational attitude. It's also a very Christian attitude, as well as Moslem, Jewish, and Buddhist."

"We're all just people," he explained. "We're all capable of losing control."

They celebrated Thanksgiving a few days early with Deandra at a Mexican restaurant. "Well, what's new?" Barry asked her.

"Colonel Desmodon got Chief Jellie a job down in Houston," Deandra offered.

"Well, of course he did," he commented.

"What do you mean?" Daphne asked.

"It's still a good ol' boys club, and Chief Jellie was always one of the guys, even though she didn't have any balls."

"Could we just be nice?" Deandra protested. "I'm trying to be professional. Besides, Colonel Desmodon finally had to deploy to Afghanistan."

"I hope he comes back safely," Barry conceded. "I had an email from Danny O'Hare. He's in DC now at the Department of the Army Headquarters. That was a good move for him. I understand he's going back to school to study theology. Do you think he's planning to become a chaplain?"

"No," Deandra responded. "I think he just likes the subject. He's doing this for himself."

"Maybe he's looking forward to his next career," Daphne suggested.

Shortly after Thanksgiving, the President of the United States announced he was sending more troops to Afghanistan. "I can't believe such a brilliant man would fall for the bill of goods those narrow-minded Generals are selling him," Barry commented as they were in the kitchen putting away the clean dishes. "Look how long it's taken to get out of Iraq, and it's been 'just a training mission' for seven years. Afghans know more about fighting in their region than we do. It's all they've ever done. Outsiders just keep coming in and introducing more advanced weapons to them. I really thought this President was smarter than that. I realize he can't tell the press or the public the real reasons behind what he's doing, whatever they may be, but he promised us change. Instead we're getting more of the same. There must be something classified behind this that he can't tell the people."

"Guess he's not likely to give back the Nobel Peace Prize," Daphne commented. "Now that they're moving prisoners out of Guantanamo Bay, is this supposed to justify the prison at Bagram?"

Barry shook his head. "It's like these bright, educated people get to DC and fall into some black hole, where they can't see the rest of the country they're paid to represent, and we really have no say, because they choose not to listen."

"And we get trapped in yet another endless, unwinnable war, while supporting a corrupt government," Daphne opined.

"I'm sure he has information we don't," Barry countered hopefully, "though it's never enough to offset the killing of civilians that always happens. If we had nothing to hide, we'd have no need for secrets. If we had no secrets, it would be because we didn't have weapons of mass destruction to protect. By being the only country in the world that's ever nuked another country, we've taken the job of being the world's police force on ourselves. And yet, by being the only country in the world that's ever nuked another country, you'd think we'd be automatically disqualified for the job."

"Why don't they just arm the women in Afghanistan?" she questioned. "They have everything to lose and everything to gain. The World Health Organization said years ago that by giving assistance to women rather than men in third world countries, the cycle of poverty is more likely to be broken. It follows that it's true for the cycle of violence as well. Maybe if the women were trained with the weapons instead of the men, the country could actually be stable. I know that doesn't make a lot of sense, since the weapons would still be there."

"Not enough women Generals yet, I guess," he answered, "and the ones we have now were trained to think like the men. Besides, I'm sure the women in Afghanistan know more about fighting than the rest of us. They've seen way too much of it."

Daphne thought a moment. "It's all about the illusion of control. Lady Rainbow's grandfather thought he could control her. He thought his curse was mighty enough to defeat the sun god, but he was defeated by the lowly dragonflies he hadn't even considered."

Barry took a pair of clean glasses and filled them with cranberry juice. He handed one to his wife. "Here's to lowly dragonflies," he toasted, and they clinked their glasses.

"To dragonflies," she agreed, smiling. Then she suggested, "I think the dragonflies deserve to be recognized with an original piece of music."

"I'm interested," he answered eagerly. "What do you have in mind?"

"Something probably very difficult to play, but definitely violin," she said mischievously.

"Something that no doubt would require a guitar tremolo accompaniment," he added.

"No doubt," she agreed. "Meanwhile, let's learn Beethoven's Moonlight Sonata as a duet."

"Purvati will like that," he answered, "and so will I."

PART III

Deandra

TERRESTRIAL AWAKENINGS

The world is having a conversation
With itself
Blogs and internet communications
Thought wealth

The barriers of privacy
Come down
And all are seen
Truth found

Chapter 36

Looking Into the Mirror

Deandra stopped by the house one evening. In her usual exuberant way, she said, "Daphne, I found the most amazing store on Highway 99. They sell all sorts of metaphysical books and crystals, and all kinds of stones and jewelry—beautiful jewelry and lots of pretty things. They had a calendar of events. On the last Monday of the month, there's a lady who does past life regressions. We have to try this. It might help me find out why I've always had that recurring nightmare—the one where I was in the US cavalry, and..."

"You don't have to tell me again," Daphne interrupted. "I remember. This involves being hypnotized and regressed back past your present birth, right? How much does it cost?"

"Only twenty dollars apiece," her sister answered. "It's done as a group session. Will you go with me? I'm dying to try this, no pun intended, but I don't want to go alone."

Daphne turned to Barry. "Are you interested?"

"Not really," he shrugged. "I have everything I always wanted, but you go ahead if you want to."

"I can call and reserve our spots," Deandra offered. "I've always wanted to try something like this, but I'm afraid to do it alone. Those nightmares I have—I want to find out, but I don't want to find out what I think I'll find out and be alone afterwards. I'm afraid to do this alone, but I feel I need to do it."

"No problem," Daphne agreed. "I remember how terrifying your recurring dream is. You were dying in a massacre. I won't leave you alone to experience that again. And I'd like to find out about it too. I'm amazed that you

270

still have the same dream after all these years, and that it never changes."

That night after Deandra had left, and Daphne and Barry were getting ready to go to bed, he asked his wife, "Are you just doing this regression thing because she wants you to go with her?"

"Actually, I'd kind of like to know where my relationship with Richard came from, if it's resolved, and if I never have to deal with him again," she responded.

"Then I hope you find out," he said. "The way I see it, if you really want something, you have to find a way to make it possible. Since you always have a choice, then there's always a way to at least try. Sometimes you have to work really hard to make it real, knowing all along that there's always a chance that you'll fail, because that's life. But still you have to try. Most lessons learned in this life come from failure rather than success, but that's ok, because just by working toward your dream, you realize what's really important to you. Dreams are like that, even though they rarely come true. They show us our true selves."

"You're quite profound tonight," Daphne observed as she turned off the light. "But sometimes dreams do come true. We found each other, right?"

"Definitely," he agreed, "but you know what I mean. Life's about the journey rather than the destination. And even though knowing and understanding the past helps us make better decisions, we still can only live in the present moment."

After a few minutes, just as Barry had settled down and was ready to drift off to sleep, Daphne said in the dark, "You know, Deandra used to have a recurring nightmare as a child of being in a battle to the death with Native Americans. It was always the same dream. She kept asking about our brothers."

Barry sat up in bed. "Neither of you EVER mentioned having a brother, let alone brothers!"

"Calm down," Daphne reassured him. "That's because we don't."

He lay back down. A couple of minutes passed before he asked, "Ok, why was she asking about brothers?"

"That's the point," Daphne said. "We never had a brother."

"Ok." A few moments of silence passed. "Oh! She dreamt she had brothers," he clarified.

"That's what I said."

"Well, where were they?" he asked.

Daphne sighed. "That's what Deandra would always ask when she woke up."

"Oh," he acknowledged and decided it was time to drop what wasn't making sense to him. He fell asleep.

But the next morning, he was still confused. Over breakfast, he asked her, "So Deandra was killed by Native Americans and she had brothers in her recurring dream?"

"Yes, exactly," Daphne answered. "Sometimes she said she could see them bashing her face in, like she was watching it from above after she had died."

"Her brothers were bashing her face in?" Barry asked incredulously. "Why would they do that?"

"Not her brothers," Daphne corrected him. "The Native Americans. It sounded dreadful, but we were just children, and I didn't know what to make of it. I told our parents, and they said, 'Everyone has bad dreams from time to time,' but somehow Deandra and I both knew it was more than that. We just didn't understand it. I think she was remembering a past death."

"I've heard of that before," Barry commented.

"Native Americans bashing in faces of the dead?" Daphne asked.

"No," he corrected. "Well, actually yes—both. But I was referring to parents not understanding. I seem to remember reading a book about different children of different cultures in various parts of the world remembering living before and talking about their deaths. In cultures where belief in reincarnation is common, it wasn't so much of a problem, because the parents understood what was happening and what the children were talking about. But in cultures where belief in reincarnation is uncommon, the parents didn't understand and would tell the children it was nonsense or just dreams. Seems like there was an American woman whose child talked about a past life and death, but instead of dismissing it, she listened and investigated. She wrote a book about it."

"I think that's why Deandra wants to do this past life regression," Daphne speculated.

"You think she wants to write a book about it?" he asked.

"No, I think she's still not satisfied with our parents' explanation that her dreams were only dreams," Daphne explained.

"You think she still has the dream?" he wondered.

"I know she does. Don't you remember the day she locked herself out of her house, and we took her some batteries for her garage remote, but it still didn't work?"

"She had to call a locksmith," Barry recalled.

"She said she'd been out of it that day because she'd had that nightmare again."

"I thought she just had a bad dream," he said.

"No, she told me it was the same one. So, yes, she still has the same dream." Daphne thought for a moment and then added, "I had a strange and very vivid dream about Richard on the very night I married him. I was back in time several hundred years. Richard had murdered my husband. I think we were in Scotland. Then I woke up wondering if I'd made a mistake marrying him, only to have him bring me breakfast in bed and surprise me with airline tickets to Scotland for our honeymoon. I meant to talk to Deandra about it, but I never did. Everything went downhill from there. I wish I'd had the dream before I married him. I'm thinking maybe the reason I had it after was because marrying him was something I was meant to do in this life."

"Did I ever tell you that I like this part of the country because it reminds me of Scotland?" Barry asked. Daphne smiled. "Do you ever dream of flying?" he asked her. Her smile broadened in answer. She understood that it was his way of saying, *Dreams are real.*

"I always thought it was uncanny that I had that dream about having lived in Scotland the night before he surprised me with a honeymoon in Scotland," Daphne continued. "And then of course, we pretty much went our separate ways on the so-called honeymoon—which should have been an even bigger tip-off to me than the dream. Funny how I felt too humiliated to admit to anyone, myself included, what a tremendous mistake I'd made. It would have been so much easier to just get the marriage annulled when we got back to the states, but then I wouldn't have had a job, since I'd married my boss—Deandra was right about that too."

"But as you just pointed out, it was something you were meant to do in this life—something unresolved that needed to be resolved," Barry said. "So if this past life regression helps you resolve it, or shows you that it's been resolved, please do it for both of us. We don't need Richard Gatorman showing up in any more lives."

On the last Monday of the month, Deandra joined them for dinner. As they ate, she mentioned, "When I spoke to Elaine, the past life regressionist, she said we should think about what we want to focus on—what it is we want to learn from this session."

"Oh, I already know what that is," Daphne responded. "Are you going to focus on those nightmares you had as a child?"

"No," Deandra replied, "I want to know if I've been a soldier in my past."

"You think you were a man?" Barry asked.

"I don't have any doubt that I was," she said. "I think that's why the idea of having children always terrified me. I never wanted to ever get pregnant."

"Is there a name for that phobia?" he asked.

"A lot of women are afraid of childbirth," Daphne interjected, "but it could just as easily be from having died in childbirth."

"No," Deandra corrected her, "I think I was male and a soldier."

"That would certainly explain why the Native Americans would kill you and then bash your face in," Barry said.

Deandra shuddered. After dinner, she and Daphne left Barry at home with Purvati, and drove to the store. Once inside, they met Elaine Delphin, who introduced herself as the facilitator for the group regression. As luck would have it, they were the only two that showed up for the event. They each paid her twenty dollars, and then she led them upstairs to a very cozy room with pillows, mats on the floor, and one single bed. Daphne got comfortable on the bed, while Deandra lay down on one of the mats, and Elaine sat down in the only chair.

"This is kind of interesting for me," Elaine said. "I've never done sisters at the same time before—not that it matters." She handed them each a notepad and pen. "First, you write down what you want to focus on, or if you have a specific question you want to find the answer to. Then, just put it under your pillow, and make yourselves comfortable." Elaine had a very pleasant voice.

When they had lain back and become still, she continued, "Focus on my voice. I'm going to guide you. This is not a time for judgments, so push all judging thoughts aside. We're not going to judge or evaluate anything you experience. You're just going to let it happen. Don't force it. Just let it come, and accept whatever comes.

"I want you to see yourself at the top of a staircase. Notice the size and type of staircase, how it looks, and how steep or shallow the steps are. There are ten steps. As I count them down, I want you to go down the steps. Ten, nine, eight, seven, six, five, four…"

Chapter 37

The Dragonfly's Story

Barry fell asleep in his clothes on the sofa while watching TV. Purvati waited until he was completely still, and then curled up around his face and neck. When Daphne came home and found them cuddled together so sweetly, she covered him with a blanket, turned off the TV and the lights, and went upstairs to bed alone in her former bedroom, all the while smiling to herself.

The next morning when she awoke and came downstairs to the kitchen, Barry was up and fixing them breakfast. She waited for him to ask. She didn't have to wait long.

"Well," he said as he scrambled the eggs in the skillet, "did you regress?"

She laughed at the way he worded it. "Yes, and it was amazing. At first Elaine had us imagine we were going down a flight of stairs, and I found myself thinking, 'but I'm still wide awake—what if nothing happens?' But by the time I reached the foot of the stairs, I was really getting into it. I was in a room in a different time. It was small and dark. She had us go down more stairs. And finally I saw myself as a five-year-old girl in France in the fifteenth or sixteenth century, guessing by the women's clothes."

"Did you speak in French?" he asked.

"Well, I did then, mais, non, monsieur, I wasn't speaking at all in this body during the regression. Elaine did all the speaking. I was seeing myself as I was in a past life. I was with a family not my own, and I had no memory of my parents. I was being raised to marry some aristocrat boy who was my playmate. I liked him, but I didn't like his mother, who was in charge of my care—or maybe it was more that I felt she didn't like me. Maybe it was both, but I knew I didn't like her. I had the impression I was fair-haired. When we sat down to eat, there were servants, and plenty of good food and fancy plates. The house we lived in was big with lots of rooms—all of them filled with light from lots of windows. It was a wonderful time."

"And was Richard your little rich boy-betrothed?" Barry asked her.

"No," she responded thoughtfully, "Strangely enough, I had a very clear impression that he is now Mad Dog Hawkins."

"Mad Dog!" Barry exclaimed as he accidentally shoveled eggs out of the skillet and onto the counter in between the two plates. "Are you attracted to Mad Dog?"

"Not at all," she laughed as she helped him scrape the eggs up onto the plates. Purvati jumped onto the counter to offer assistance. "I mean, I like him, but he's your friend, and he has his own wife in this life—and that's just fine with me. I don't think I could ever tolerate his dislike of children and animals. But even in the regression, this boy, the former Mad Dog, was my childhood friend. That's all. Love or attraction had nothing to do with it. It was all pre-arranged by our elders, his parents, or somebody else. He might not like children now, but we were both children then. Besides, who knows where Mad Dog's been since then?"

"Aptly worded," he said. "So did you marry him?"

"I'm getting to that part," she said. "Just let me tell my story. After that childhood scene she brought us forward to our teen years."

"How did she 'bring you forward'?" he interrupted.

"She just told us to come forward to our teen years, and I guess I did," Daphne answered. "I wanted to, you know."

"Well, I would hope that's why you went," he commented.

"I saw myself as a young teen, taller, slender, and being attended to. I was getting married, and I was very happy to have such pretty gowns. I felt I was someone special."

"You *are* someone special," he reminded her, "but you were happy to marry Mad Dog?"

She smiled at him. "I love you, too, but please stop interrupting. He wasn't Mad Dog then, and I was more interested in the dresses. I don't even know what his name was then. The marriage was something I had no say in. I had been raised not to question—just to do as I was told."

"Ok," he said. "This explains how you were able to stay with Richard for so long. Please continue uninterrupted."

"Thank you. It was amazing how I could actually feel the clothes against my skin, and how different they felt from the clothes I wear now. Back then the corset was SO TIGHT! And women, myself included, wore this stiff headdress that surrounded the face to hold a veil of cloth. The gown just hung without a lot of fancy hoops or anything—the clothes are the only way I can date the experience. I had no sense of time or dates. But I had beautiful gowns and would be married in a beautiful gown. I was very happy. I felt very fortunate to have such beautiful clothes.

"Next Elaine took us to our early twenties. I was already widowed. My husband, Mad Dog's former incarnation, had some sort of fatal accident. There was a lord—another aristocrat—in expensive clothes on a fine horse escorting me to a boat. I guess you'd have to properly call it a ship, but it was small by today's standards—with sails. I was being sent away from France to the north to marry someone else. It was my duty to marry and have children; only I had no say in my life. I didn't want to leave France. It was the only country I'd ever known, and I'd never been aboard a ship before. I was terribly frightened. I was being sent north, not just to Britain, but all the way to Scotland, and I was terrified. I didn't want to go, but it was my duty to do as I was told. I was afraid to say how I felt. I was afraid of what would happen to me if I didn't do as I was told.

"Then Elaine took us forward to near the end of our life. I was imprisoned in England. My headdress was white, but my gown was black—almost like an old-fashioned nun's habit—but I wasn't a nun. I was in mourning. In Scotland, I had married you—your former incarnation, that is. I loved you, but others didn't like us because of our religion. We had a baby boy. And Richard was there. He was a different religion from us, like most everybody else there, and had lots of powerful friends, which made him powerful, and somehow he had you murdered."

"Humph!" Barry responded. "Whoops, sorry. That was a little personal. Please continue."

"Understandable reaction," she concurred. "Anyway, that was why I was wearing black—because you had been murdered. After he had you killed, he imprisoned me, raped me, and told everyone we were married, even though we weren't. Our son was taken from me…"

"Hold on," he interrupted. "Did you have another son from being raped by him?"

"No," she answered, "this was your child. I never learned what became of him. I escaped with a woman companion. We cut our hair, dressed like men, and climbed out the window down some bedsheets we'd tied together— just like in a movie. The woman friend and I fled to England where we thought we'd be safe. A nice well-off family took us in. We explained what happened, and they took good care of us. Then the Queen of England herself sent word that I was to be kept as a prisoner. Why would the queen even care about me, especially when I'd done nothing wrong and was seeking refuge from a murderer?"

"I don't know, love," he answered, "I was dead."

Daphne hesitated before continuing. "Are you taking any of this seriously?" she asked him.

"I have a completely open mind," he said, "but you did say I was already dead. And so was Mad Dog, but then if he hadn't died, we wouldn't have met and married. Trying to follow this could get complicated. Trust me—I'm paying attention."

"Ok. True enough,"

"One question—which queen wanted you dead?" he asked.

"I don't know. I'd never seen her. I was just amazed that that the Queen of England was making me a prisoner," she went on. "I felt I was somehow being blamed for Richard's crimes, as well as the fact that I was a different religion. In those days they probably blamed women for being raped, even though I'm sure I was too ashamed of it to tell anyone. If I had gotten pregnant by him, I probably would have tried to pass it off as yours, but he had lied and said we were married, so maybe I would have used that to save face. I'm not really sure how I handled it. I only got these intense, detailed glimpses and bursts of memories. I do know I was in a no-win situation, because I was a woman of the wrong religion. I'm sure I was Catholic, since I was raised in France, and you and I had been the same religion, so you were Catholic also. Richard wasn't. So either it was Queen Mary that didn't like me for what Richard had done and because he wasn't Catholic, or because I was French; or it was Queen Elizabeth that didn't like me, because she blamed me for what Richard had done, or because I was Catholic or French. Unless it was a queen consort of one of the earlier kings—did queen consorts ever have people kept as prisoners? Or maybe I did or said something that was perfectly natural for me as a Catholic from France that made me seem like a bad person—or even a threat to her. Maybe since she couldn't punish Richard, and she believed I was his wife, she chose to punish me instead. I don't know. I was treated well, and my keepers were all kind to me. I think they felt sorry for me. But I didn't understand. Maybe it was cultural differences, or language differences, or maybe I was just overwhelmed by my emotions. Maybe it was because I had been raped, or because the queen believed I had married Richard so soon after you were killed. If that's what the queen thought, I would have looked like Richard's accomplice. But I had run away from Richard and sought refuge in England, so I didn't understand what was happening. I felt victimized being sent away from France, and then being widowed again and losing my child—not to mention being raped. Maybe I was unable to process so much based on the way I was raised. Maybe I'd become a victim out of habit, because that was my role in life. I just didn't understand what was happening. So if I did something to deserve being kept a prisoner, I either didn't understand it or I couldn't deal with the realization of it, because so much had happened already in such a short time that I didn't know how to handle."

"Or maybe the unidentified queen thought you were a witness to something that could taint her own image, whatever that might have been," Barry suggested. "Those Tudor queens were a paranoid lot, and their paranoia was learned from necessity. And they were all involved with political intrigues all the time. Maybe it was a favor to the Scottish monarch that had little to do with you. Maybe they just needed a convenient scapegoat, and you escaped right into their hands."

"Whatever—I'm not sure the reason really matters anymore." Daphne commented. "Anyway, then Elaine told us to go to the scene of our death. I saw and felt my head on the block. They were going to chop my head off with an axe! And then she brought us forward so we didn't have to relive the actual death. So I don't know exactly why I was being executed. After I died, I felt confused that there was no Heaven as I was expecting, and Jesus wasn't there like I had expected. You were there. You told me that what we'd been taught by the church wasn't how it really worked; only I didn't understand. I just knew I didn't ever want to be a victim again. I didn't ever want to be dictated to by men or lied to by religion. I wanted to be free to speak out and be listened to. I was very relieved to be done with that life, and I was determined to make decisions for myself and learn how to say no to what I didn't want to do."

They sat quietly for a moment, and then Barry offered, "Do you realize what you've just said? About your life with Richard—I mean in this life?"

"What I don't understand," she said, "is how, after what he'd done to me in the past, I could fall in love with him at first sight in this life? That makes no sense to me at all."

Barry thought for a moment before saying, "Maybe attraction is more like gravitational attraction. When you come into the presence of someone important to you in the past, for good or bad, you fall into their gravitational field, so to speak. Maybe your unconscious recognized him, but your body did the only thing it knew to do—it reacted emotionally or with hormones or something that made you feel attraction. You interpreted that as love. Maybe you intended it that way subconsciously, so you could resolve the issue once and for all this time—make a clean get away finally, without being punished for it. We all know people who fall in love with people who turn out to be the wrong person for them, but they act it out anyway, for whatever reason. Maybe attraction just means familiarity for a purpose, and not necessarily a pleasant one."

She smiled. "Yeah. I was too submissive to men in that past life. I knew that was expected, and it was what I was taught to be, but it had the side effect of making me trust them as superiors rather than questioning or seeing them as the devils some of them really were. I guess I had to marry Richard in this life to learn to see him for what he really is, and to learn to take responsibility for my own choices. It took some time, but I finally took matters into my own hands. I finally made my own decision and got away from him. Not only that, I found you. The tables turned in this life, and we're back together."

"I'd say you're probably done with him," Barry opined, "if you can forgive, forget, and let go."

"It's a lot to forgive," Daphne reminded him.

"But if you don't, you're likely to stay tied to him," Barry pointed out.

"I guess you're right," she agreed. "I'll make a conscious effort to work on that. I had been before, but now there's even more to forgive."

"But," Barry added, "now that you know the whole story, it's even more motivation for you to forgive him and let him go."

"True," Daphne agreed and then added, "I hope for Samantha's sake, she can forgive him, too."

"That's between them," Barry pointed out. "The important thing is that we're not only back together, but we know for sure now that literally no one can keep us apart."

Daphne put her arms around his neck and kissed him deeply and passionately.

He interrupted her briefly. "Maybe there's something to names," he suggested.

"How so?"

"Well, your last name is Robin. You wanted to be able to speak out, or sing out, so that fits. Plus you're a pretty bird." They kissed again. "And Richard's a real gator-man."

Daphne giggled. "I always hated that name."

"I know. You told me," he reminded her. "Was Mad Dog killed while hawking?" he joked.

"I have no idea," she replied, still giggling.

"Did Deandra regress?"

"Yes, she did," Daphne said. "We had to wait a long, long time for her to write down her story. It was so late by the time we got out of there, I told her I was too tired to hear about it—that I wanted to hear it when I was fresh and could listen without nodding off. Besides, I didn't want to nod off while driving home. She promised to come over this evening after work and tell us all about it. She just kept saying that it was so amazing, over and over, so amazing."

"Well, then," he said, pushing the breakfast plates aside. He wrapped his arms back around her, pushed her onto the kitchen counter under him and whispered, "We have plenty of time until this evening."

Chapter 38

The Robin Sings

Deandra came over that evening and joined Barry and Daphne for dinner again. This time she brought Chinese food for the three of them. As they ate, she asked Barry, "Did Daphne tell you what an amazing night we had last night?"

"Of course I did," Daphne interjected. "I just told him about my experience though. I thought you could better tell your own."

"Purvati and I had quite the evening ourselves," Barry interjected. "But, please, do tell."

"It's ok," Daphne told her sister. "He really does take this very seriously."

Deandra swallowed her food and took a sip of tea first. Then she began, "Elaine had us focus on what we wanted to get out of the session. I wanted to know about having been a male soldier, because I was sure I had been. At least I've always felt that. Then she had us lie down and get comfortable."

"You left this part out," Barry said to Daphne.

"I started right after this with the staircases. Now, stop interrupting," she told him. "Please go on, Deandra."

Deandra continued. "Then she had us go down a ten-step staircase."

"Does anyone ever go up the down staircase?" he asked.

"Barry!" they both shouted simultaneously.

"Sorry, I couldn't resist," he apologized. "There seems to be a ten-step program for just about everything these days, but do go on. I'll keep my mouth shut. Better yet, I'll keep it full." He shoveled in another mouthful of food.

"Ok," Deandra said. "After that there was another staircase. At some point I saw myself as a little boy. My name was Tom, and I was very happy. It was the mid-nineteenth century. I had at least three brothers. One of them was younger than me—his name was Boston. I also had a younger sister, and there were some older half-siblings, but I looked up to my older brother, Autie, the most, and I wanted to be just like him."

Daphne noticed Barry suddenly lean forward with great interest.

Deandra continued, "Then Elaine took us forward to our teens, and I was a soldier in the Union Army at the beginning of the Civil War."

"Yes, you would have been," Barry commented after swallowing quickly.

Daphne was surprised. "Were you there?" she asked him.

"I don't know," Barry said. His eyes were firmly fixed on Deandra. "Please continue," he begged her.

"I can see you recognize this, or it's at least familiar to you," she said to him. "I was enlisted, but I fought under Philip Sheridan himself. Then Elaine had us go forward to our early twenties. The war was over, and I was an officer. I had been my brother Autie's aide, and I had some medals I was very proud of. Now I was west of the Mississippi River on the plains. I was under my brother as a lieutenant. I saw myself riding with him into an Indian village in the middle of winter and attacking them. My face and neck were grazed by a bullet. Any closer and I would have been killed. Others were killed, but I got out alive. Joel Elliott and his company were left behind. Autie was in charge, but he felt he had to leave them behind to save the rest of the men. I wondered if he was putting duty to family over duty to Elliott and Elliott's men. That would certainly be natural. There was a lot of criticism of him for it, especially by

Benteen, one of the other officers. Elliott had served under Benteen.

"The really amazing thing is that I recognized all these people from THIS life! Autie is George Desmodon!" Deandra could barely contain her excitement. "I'm sure of it."

"You didn't tell me this last night," Daphne interjected.

"Of course not," Deandra admitted, "because you were tired and wanted to rest before you heard it, but I told you it was amazing."

"It certainly is," Daphne agreed.

"Besides," Deandra continued, "you don't know them. You weren't there. But Barry was. I mean he wasn't at the Washita River battle, but he knew them. He was younger than me then. But anyway, Joel Elliott was Leon Manx, and Frederick Benteen was Mac Muschatt."

"That explains the animosity between Mac and George," Barry mentioned.

"But there isn't any," Deandra contradicted.

"There certainly was when I was serving with them," he insisted.

"Well, then they must have worked it out, because they seem to get along fine now," she told him.

"I'm glad to hear that," he said, "but I'm sorry to hear how Leon had died. Still, Elliott was noted for making an admirable stand with his men. It would be just like Leon to go down fighting if he could find no other way."

"So you remember this battle?" Daphne, clearly baffled, asked her husband.

"The battle on the Washita River is a famous one," Barry told her. "Although the cavalry attacked a village full of innocent women and children, Black Kettle, the chief, was willing to make peace with the white man. If I recall my studies, Major Elliott tried ahead of time to tell Generals Sherman and Sheridan, who were dictating military policy on the Great Plains at the time, as well as Custer himself, that the Indians didn't understand the treaties the same way the whites did. And that the Indians didn't even understand the concept of war the same way, but nobody listened to him."

"Custer!" Daphne exclaimed.

"Daphne," Deandra told her, "my name was Tom Custer. Autie was George Armstrong Custer's nickname. He was my brother."

Daphne looked dumbfounded.

"And it was discovered later," Barry added, "that Elliott's company, the men Custer left behind, were all killed, as was Black Kettle, the chief willing to make peace. The very sad thing was that Sherman, Sheridan, and Custer were all doing what they had learned had worked so well in the Civil War against the Confederates. The Confederates had started the Civil War, and they understood and used the same concept of war as the Union soldiers. The problem in the West was that the Indians weren't the Confederates, and it was the whites who had intruded on the Indian way of life without even bothering to learn what that was. It would be just like Leon to see the problem and point it out to his superiors. He's an extremely intelligent man. Did you know he was a middle school teacher before he joined the service? That's how he met his wife—they were both teachers."

"Ok, I get that," Daphne said, "but my sister was Custer's brother? I never expected my little sister to be someone infamous. It's just a surprise—that's all. Go on, Deandra."

"Let's see," Deandra started again, picking up her own thread. "Then Elaine took us forward to right before our deaths. It was awful. I was a Captain by now, still under my brother's command. We had ridden out to attack another Indian village—only much further north this time on the Little Bighorn River. When Autie realized the size of the village we were going to attack, he sent word to Benteen to hurry up and join us. We waited up on a ridge overlooking the village for a couple of hours to give Benteen time to catch up. We saw Reno start the attack on the village from the southern end and then retreat to higher ground. Finally, Autie said we'd given Benteen enough time. We remounted and rode north to attack the village from the other end. The plan was to trap the Indians between us and Reno's men.

"It didn't go well. We had dismounted on the high ground, and were being overwhelmed. The skirmish line to our left had been almost wiped out. The line was attacked from behind while firing at the Indians in front of them. Indians were coming at us from all directions from out of the gullies We were trying to use our shot horses for cover, but the Indians were surrounding us. Where the hell was Benteen? He was supposed to reinforce us with men and ammunition, and we had given him a couple of extra hours to catch up, but he was nowhere in sight. Keogh and Calhoun, Margaret's husband, were already overrun. Margaret was my sister. Calhoun was my brother-in-law. Keogh was a good friend and a highly respected officer.

"Then Elaine took us forward to our death. I was in hand-to-hand combat, and I wanted to know where my brothers, Boss and Autie, were, but I didn't have time to look. Did I mention our little brother, Boston, was with us as well as our nephew? It was all happening so fast.

"And then Elaine took us to after our deaths. An Indian was bashing my face in. I was watching it like I was floating above my body, only my body was dead. I couldn't even recognize myself anymore. Autie was dead near me along with George Yates and Lieutenant Smith. Smith had been clubbed as well. They didn't disfigure Autie—at least not in the same way they did me. Boss was a little way down the hill with young Autie, our nephew. They were dead too. We were all dead. What was done to most of the bodies was hideous.

"Then Elaine asked us how we felt about our lives—if we had any promises we meant to keep, or if we had any regrets. I wanted to be with my brothers, but alive again. We let the family down with all of us dying at once like that—my brothers Autie and Boston, our nephew, and our brother-in-law. Poor Margaret. We literally left her with so much grief. But we went down fighting together. We were good soldiers. I was proud of that. We fought to the end. So I wanted to be with them again as a soldier, but I regretted that we left such grief for our family."

"I have to admit it's hard to believe Colonel Desmodon was Custer," Barry commented, "but the personality fits. What are the odds of this happening?"

"I don't know," Daphne said, "but it certainly fits with the recurring nightmare she had as a child—every detail matches."

"What exactly did you mean," Barry asked Deandra, "when you said Autie wasn't disfigured in the same way? I thought it was a matter of record that he wasn't disfigured. Didn't some Indian leader order that he not be, because he had fought bravely? And the Indians weren't even sure at the time that it was him, if I recall correctly."

"Well, I did see an Indian do something horrific to the private part of his body, but I don't want to think about that. I was more focused on my own face being bashed in, and I was overwhelmed by all the deaths of people I cared about and the atrocities to their bodies. It was too much to take in. These are people I recognize and feel close to," Deandra continued. "I know you and George Desmodon didn't always see eye to eye about everything, but I have the greatest respect for George."

"And he's a very likeable guy," Barry admitted. "In fact, he's a charmer. Was Custer a born-again Christian like Desmodon?"

"Let's find out," Deandra offered. I'll go by the library tomorrow after work. I'm sure they'll have a biography on him. As a matter of fact, I recall Major Reno was stationed in the Oregon territory sometime after the Little Big Horn battle."

"I remember reading that Major Reno and Captain Benteen underwent inquiries into their conduct after the battle and were exonerated," Barry added, "but then Reno developed a drinking problem and was discharged for sleeping with another officer's wife. They took adultery seriously in those days."

"Well the drinking problem and adultery have continued to this day," Deandra confirmed, "because now we know him as Lieutenant Colonel Crockodell. I understand he was having an affair with Sergeant Leach before she got divorced from, by the way, the former Boston Custer."

"Oh my God!" Barry exclaimed. "The whole gang came together again HERE?"

"So it would seem," she confirmed.

"You said Barry was there," Daphne reminded her sister.

"No, I wasn't," Barry contradicted.

"No, he wasn't at the battle of the Little Big Horn," Deandra corrected.

"Didn't think so," Barry interjected.

"But," Deandra continued, "but he was a private in the seventh cavalry at the time. I don't know exactly who he was, but I was aware that he was a private who didn't go on the campaign with us for some reason."

"Somebody had to stay behind and hold down the fort?" Barry suggested. "Bet I was a farmer before or after I was a soldier. I don't think I would have liked being a private. I certainly wouldn't have gone in for killing Native Americans just to take their land. That was wrong."

"We were following orders," Deandra defended. "And besides, they were hostile Indians."

"White men invaded their land. The natives were willing to share, but the white men wanted it all. Next thing the natives knew, they were being told to live on reservations," Barry pointed out. "Gee, I wonder how they became hostile?"

"Isn't 'just following orders' the same argument the Nazis used after World War II to defend their slaughter of Jews?" Daphne asked.

"Ok, I wouldn't do that now," Deandra insisted. "But the point is, when Elaine had us reviewing our lives after our deaths, the words 'loyalty, duty, and service' were very strongly in my mind."

"Good Army values," Barry acknowledged. "That explains why you're back in the Army in this life."

"But what about killing innocents?" Daphne interjected.

"Well, they come back too," Deandra reminded her. "And that time THEY killed US."

"In self-defense," Daphne argued.

"Don't get me off track here," Deandra retorted. "I'm trying to remember everything."

"I think you were off track 'just following orders,'" Daphne added.

Deandra ignored Daphne's comment and closed her eyes for a moment before speaking again. "Oh, and General Gato, Sergeant Major Macroo, and Mad Dog Hawkins were part of the seventh cavalry then too," she added.

"Really?" Barry pondered. "So the whole clan really did come back together in this life."

"Group reincarnations aren't that unusual, from what I've read," Deandra explained. "The interesting thing is that General Gato now was a private then—and from

Greece. I have the impression he was a cook. He was even younger than Boston at the time, and he died in the last battle with us—well not on the hill with us, but he died somewhere in the battle. I wish I could remember everybody's names back then, but it was just too much. Last night I wrote down everything I remembered so I wouldn't forget."

"That's true," Daphne agreed. "Elaine gave us time to write it all down afterward, while it was still fresh in our minds. We had to wait a long time for Deandra to finish writing, but apparently it was worth it. Now we know where Mad Dog went after his accident."

"What accident?" Deandra asked.

"Never mind," Daphne said, regretting she'd mentioned it. The last thing she wanted was for Mad Dog to learn they'd been married in a past life. "It was a long time ago," she added.

"So General Gato was a private then, and now he gets to be a general," Barry remarked. "That's fair. What about Bill Macroo and Mad Dog? Who or where were they? I'd like to know too."

"Mad Dog was wounded at Washita like me," she explained, "only his wounds were much more serious. He almost died. He was a Captain then, and he was given a disability retirement as a result of being wounded, so he left the Army years before the battle at the Little Bighorn. I remembered his first name as being Al, but that's all."

"And the Sergeant Major?" Barry asked.

"Sergeant Ogden," she answered, "and he was at the Little Big Horn with us, or at least not with Reno or Benteen."

"So he was killed," Barry commented.

"Had to have been," she agreed, "but I didn't see it."

"Anybody else we know?" he prompted.

"I have to look at my notes," she said. She reached into her purse, took out several sheets of paper—all filled front and back with Deandra's tiny handwriting—and began to glance over them. A moment later she exclaimed while slapping her forehead, "How could I have forgotten to mention this? General Terry, who was in charge of the whole campaign—how did I forget to mention him? We had separated from him before we ever got near the Little Big Horn River, but he was in charge of the whole campaign. It crossed my mind somewhere toward the end of the battle—so many things and people went through my mind in those moments before, during, and after death."

"Well?" Daphne asked at the same time Barry prompted, "And?"

"We had been with him on the Powder River on his boat where Autie had his hair cut. He was—I mean Colonel Jimmy Bass was General Terry."

"Good man," Barry commented. "Anyone else in your notes?"

"Yes," she said emphatically. "Several actually. Let's see," she said as she ran a finger through her notes of several pages. "Ok, here we go. Autie's favorite Indian scout is a civilian I knew who worked in finance and was quite a history buff. Autie sent him away before the battle. And Becky Roan."

"Becky was there!" Barry was getting caught up in the excitement. "I would have expected her to be a Native American."

"She was," Deandra confirmed. She was another Indian scout who carried a message to Major Reno, so she wasn't with us at the end. Martin Fox was somewhere under Reno. And there was a reporter there with us. Do you remember that officer who worked in public relations—the one who was always pestering everybody over every little detail and no matter how much information you gave him, it was never enough?"

"Of course," Barry recalled. "I can't recall his name, but last I heard was he was assigned to a unit in Korea. He was very conscientious, but all his interruptions were truly annoying, even though he was just doing his job. Martin knew best how to deal with him when he got so wound up over getting all the details."

"He was there with us as a reporter, of all things," Deandra told him. "He wasn't even a soldier. It must have been terrifying for him. Anyway, there were two more people who were with us. Ben was an officer and very popular. I recognized him as Colonel Shepherd."

"Colonel Shepherd is a very popular officer," Barry affirmed, "and with good reason. He's fair, he listens to his people, and he takes care of those under him."

"Well, he was with us, so he must have died," she continued. "And last but not least, I recognized Yates, who was a good friend, and died near me and Autie. Now he's a woman, Chief Jellie."

Barry sat back and took that one in. "And are you good friends with Chief Jellie in this life?" he asked her.

"Well, I have been. And you know how close she and George Desmodon are."

"Anything else?" he asked her.

"No, that's about it. Isn't that enough?" she said with a laugh.

"You certainly remembered more details than I did," Daphne commented.

"I thought your story was pretty detailed," Barry said, "but I didn't think anyone would be able to identify as many people in one regression as Deandra did."

"Maybe it's because there were so many of us involved in my death," Deandra countered. "And we both went under with different goals. Daphne wanted to know about her relationship with Richard. I wanted to know about having been a male soldier. We both found what we were looking for."

"But is it real or a fantasy?" Barry asked. "I guess either way, the unconscious gives you your answers."

"Well, then," Daphne suggested, "since Deandra has so many names and a specific, documented, historical scenario, why don't you and I go to the library tomorrow while she's at work and see what we can find out? We could see if there was an officer gravely wounded at that first battle she mentioned."

"Washita River," Barry and Deandra said in unison.

"If we find an officer who was seriously wounded there, we can see if there are any characteristics that would correspond with Mad Dog. And what was his name then?" Daphne asked, continuing what she'd started.

"Al," Deandra answered.

"There should be some record of an officer named Al being seriously wounded there, if that actually happened."

Barry got up and went to his computer. "Ok, we have a listing of all seventh cavalry, but it's by surnames. Let me try Wikipedia and see what it has on Washita," he said as he typed. "A lot of women and children massacred—murdered might be a more appropriate word. I was right. Black Kettle was at peace with the white man, and his wife was shot in the back."

"Unfortunately," Deandra mitigated, "these things happen in war."

"But, as Barry just pointed out," Daphne corrected, "those Indians weren't at war. They thought they were at peace. So they were ambushed and murdered."

"According to this," Barry continued, "Benteen reported that Custer was deliberately inflating his kill numbers, and Benteen was right. Custer was a sicko."

"Don't be so judgmental," Deandra said.

Daphne glared at her. "We'll go to the library and research this while you're at work, ok? It's a very difficult subject to deal with. To some, Custer was a hero, but to many others, not."

"What's to research?" Deandra asked. "These are my memories. This was what I saw during the regression. Besides, I can go to the library after work. It's so close to my office."

"No one's questioning any of that," Barry reassured her, "but I, for one, want to know more. And I want to know how what you saw matches with the historical record. Since the only eye witness survivors were Native Americans, and white people, as a rule back then, didn't consider Native Americans real people due to ignorance, prejudice, and greed, the Native American accounts were discredited. Then a whole lot of speculation went on as to what the Army thought happened. Your regression may hold some bit of truth that finally explains things."

"But it wouldn't make sense for you to be the one to research it," Daphne told her, "because you'd be more subjective—looking for collaboration. So we'll do that. Who knows? Maybe when we're done, you can write a book about it. I've been trying to get Barry to write, but he's always busy."

"Besides," Barry said, "maybe we'll find out who I was."

"Ok," Deandra agreed. "I better go home and get some sleep. But at least now I understand what those nightmares as a child were about. Here's a list I made of the people we knew then and now."

Barry looked over the list:

Al, an officer, seriously wounded at Washita, Mad Dog Hawkins

Ben, popular officer, died with us, COL Shepherd

CPT Frederick Benteen, COL Mac Muschatt

Autie Custer, older brother, died next to me, COL George Desmodon

Boston Custer, younger brother, died just downhill from us, Sergeant Leach's ex-husband

CPT Tom Custer, me

MAJ Joel Elliott, killed with company at Washita, LTC Leon Manx

Greek cook, private, not on campaign, General Raul Gato

Indian scout, Autie's favorite, sent away before battle, finance civilian and history buff

Indian scout sent to Reno, CPT Becky Roan

Yates, officer and close friend who died next to me, CWO Jellie

Officer under Reno, MAJ Martin Fox

SGT Ogden, SGM Macroo

Reporter, public relations officer

General Terry, COL Jimmy Bass

"I didn't know Leon made lieutenant colonel," he commented. "Good for him. Nobody is more deserving. Well, this list will certainly help. I appreciate you being so organized that you thought to do this."

"I had trouble getting to sleep," she admitted. "I was too wound up, and now I'm exhausted. I'm going home. Good night." She gave them each a hug and left.

After she'd gone, Barry said, "Well, I wasn't prepared for all of that."

"But does it make sense with the people she said were there?" Daphne asked him. "I know they're all military, but you knew them. What do you think?"

"Actually," he answered, "my gut reaction is that is does fit. But I want to look into this more deeply and see if the pieces really match up. You go on to bed. I'm going to see what I can find on the internet first."

"Don't stay up too late," she admonished.

"You mean like you did last night?" he grinned.

The next morning after breakfast, Daphne and Barry went straight to the library.

Chapter 39

Digging up the Past

There were numerous books on the shelves of the
public library about General George Armstrong Custer and
the battles at the Washita and Little Big Horn Rivers. Barry
and Daphne checked out books on the Washita Battle, the
Battle of the Little Big Horn, a book that included
archaeological evidence from the Little Big Horn Battle as
well as Native American eye witness accounts, and a
biography of George Armstrong Custer. Daphne and Barry
spent the rest of the week reading, making and comparing
notes, and looking things up online for added comparison.
Among the first details they discovered were Custer's
family nickname, Autie, and that Custer had sent his
favorite scout away from the battle before it happened. That
scout witnessed it from a distance and was considered a
reliable source for most of the many accounts of the battle
that had been published.

Saturday morning, Barry and Daphne knocked on
the door of Deandra's house armed with books, notes, and
the list. She was excited to see them. The three of them sat
down at her dining table with their materials, including the
pages she had written right after the regression.

"You were absolutely right," Daphne opened. "It
really is amazing. Of course, the men back then all had
longer hair and facial hair, which made sifting through the
photographs in the books difficult."

"Oh, I know," Deandra answered. "None of us now
look anything like we did back then."

"That's where you're wrong," Barry informed her.
"See for yourself." He opened the Custer biography to a
page of photographs, pushed the book toward her, and

pointed to one in particular. "This was Custer as a West Point cadet before he grew the facial hair."

"Oh, my God!" Deandra exclaimed. "He looks like George."

"Just like him only a little younger," Barry confirmed. "Even in the later pictures where his hair was long and his face was covered by mustache and beard, and he was skinny, his body language in the poses for the pictures is still so George." He turned some pages and showed her.

Deandra gasped. "You're right."

"Custer didn't sit still in command," Barry continued. "He was always walking among the troops."

"Just like George wandering the halls and always visiting everybody else's office," Deandra acknowledged.

"This biography of George Armstrong Custer reads like a personality study of George Desmodon, including his natural charm, which he oozes, as well as playing pranks and having his inner circle or clique of friends, other officers, he hung out with. He was even a born-again Christian."

"In more ways than one apparently," Daphne added.

"Did you find General Porker?" Deandra asked. "They're such good friends. I know you were also friends with the General when he was Colonel Porker," she directed at Barry.

"We couldn't find a picture," Barry explained, "but there was an officer, a chaplain appropriately enough, that Custer met with in St. Louis before going west. The man's name was Thomas Holmes. He invited Custer to pray with him and got him to rededicate his life to Christ right before he went out west to massacre Native Americans. I would expect he might have attempted some religious proselytizing among the natives at some point, but he probably considered those who weren't interested in being saved as the enemy. Just a guess."

"That would be in character," Deandra agreed.

"And it would explain why Porker is more into being a chaplain than a leader of soldiers," Barry added. "I always had the utmost respect for him when we were Colonels. He truly cared about people—the soldiers and all of their families. But when he took command of the division and couldn't separate being a minister from being a commander, I couldn't understand it. He had to have known better. But if he'd been a chaplain before, it makes more sense to me now. As a military chaplain, there was no separation of church and military duties. The present must be a true learning experience for him."

"Look at this picture of Tom Custer," Daphne showed Deandra. "You may not see it, but you probably can't be objective. The fact is that he looks like you."

"I totally agree," Barry said. "And here's a picture of Boston Custer." Barry pointed to another black and white photograph in the book. "Who does he remind you of?"

"Sergeant Leach's ex-husband. Wow," Deandra said as she took it all in. "I just assumed everybody looked different each time." She went back to studying the picture of Tom Custer. "We have the same eyes, nose, and chin," she commented.

"There's a definite pattern here," Barry observed.

"We filled in some missing information on your list," Daphne mentioned. "Sergeant John Ogden, age thirty-one years at the time of the battle of the Little Big Horn, was having difficulty controlling his mount. It was shot and spooked at a very bad time. As a result, it carried him right across the Little Big Horn River and straight into the massive Indian village. Of course he was killed. He never stood a chance."

"That incident may have alerted the natives to Custer's presence, if they hadn't already noticed," Barry added. "It certainly explains the skirmish line to the left of that hill you were on, which is documented by where the men fell and the archaeological evidence. Also documented by the evidence is that you fell near Lieutenant Yates, your brother Autie, and Lieutenant Smith on what is now known as Custer's hill, and that Boston and your nephew Autie fell a little ways downhill, just like you said in your regression. Yates may well have been Chief Jellie if you look at the basic facial structure. Yates was a close friend of the Custer family and was even in Autie's wedding party. And Smith was also clubbed, just as you saw in your regression. He was found lying behind his dead mount, just as you described, probably trying to use the dead horses for cover. And after Tom Custer was killed, his face was bashed in, like you said. In fact, he was so badly mutilated, his body was only identified by a tattoo with his initials."

"Wow," was all Deandra could say. She took deep breath and then said, "I couldn't recognize myself. I was dead and looking down at what they were doing to me, and I could no longer recognize my own body."

"As for soldiers back at Fort Lincoln," Barry continued, "there were several who were privates, who listed their former occupation as farmer. They didn't stay in service for more than one enlistment, so I could have been any one of them. But there was a Greek private who was a cook, just as you described General Gato, and he was killed in the battle, just as you said. You were also right that he was younger than Boston Custer.

"Now look at this picture," he showed her.

"It looks just like my civilian finance friend who's such a history buff."

"Well," Barry explained, "this was Curley, Custer's favorite scout, and Custer did in fact send Curley away before the battle. Curley watched it from a distance. He later gave his eye witness account."

"He looks just like him, even though he's Native American in this picture and African American in this life.

What are the odds of that? Amazing! This can't possibly be coincidence—not ALL of this taken together."

"That's not all," Barry continued. "The Indian scout who was sent to Major Reno was called Bloody Knife. His picture also resembles the facial structure of Becky Roan even though there's a change of both race and gender. See the resemblance?" he pointed to yet another picture. "Turns out he was shot in the head while right next to Reno. Some say it totally unnerved Reno to have blood and brains suddenly splattered all over him, which affected his ability to command after that. Reno, by the way, did indeed become an alcoholic and eventually died of tongue cancer."

"What a horrible way to go," Daphne commented, "but maybe not as bad as in one of these battles."

"And Crockodell certainly has an alcohol problem," Deandra observed.

"And," Barry went on, "your popular officer Ben turned out to be Lieutenant Benjamin Hodgson, who died at the Little Big Horn, and no doubt put up a good fight."

"Now for the battle on the Washita," Daphne added. "The seriously wounded officer named Al would have been Captain Albert Barnitz, who didn't like Custer, and was given a disability retirement in 1870, well before the battle at the Little Big Horn. He died in 1912 at a seaside resort in New Jersey."

"Mad Dog didn't get along with Desmodon simply on the basis of religion," Barry pointed out. "Mad Dog was atheist, and Desmodon was fundamentalist Christian."

"Barry mentioned that Leon Manx was a former middle school teacher," Daphne went on. "Major Joel Elliott was a former school teacher as well as school superintendent."

"And I found a few surprises," Barry continued. "Look at this picture." He showed her another photograph.

"It's Martin Fox!" she exclaimed.

"Well, actually it was Captain Thomas Weir," he corrected, "who, under Major Reno, as you correctly placed him, disobeyed orders to stay with Reno's command, and took his company to ride out in hopes of reinforcing Custer's men. That would be just like Martin. Unfortunately, he didn't get very far. One of his men spotted some Sioux coming toward them flying Custer's colors, which had already been captured. He could see Custer's hill, the hill where you died, from where he was at that point, so he probably saw the end of the battle. At any rate, he had to turn around and return to Reno to save his own men. But he at least tried."

"Wow," Deandra repeated. "I never knew him very well, but I wish I had."

"Good man," Barry repeated. "Nice family too."

"And don't forget the last surprise," Daphne prompted Barry while showing him a photograph.

"Of course," he acknowledged and turned the picture toward Deandra.

"Sergeant First Class Jose Abejorro!" Deandra shrieked. "He's retiring this spring."

"Well," Barry said, "this picture was actually Lieutenant Charles DeRuddio, an Italian with a legitimate beef against your former older brother. DeRuddio was supposed to have command of one of Custer's companies, but Custer took it away from him and gave it to a buddy." He turned to Daphne and asked, "Was it Yates or Smith?"

"I don't know," she responded. "I'm finding it hard to keep up with all the military stuff."

"No matter," Deandra replied. "Jose has never had enough bad things to say about how Desmodon is all about awarding his buddies. It doesn't matter how many times I change the subject, or the fact that I'm an officer. He just goes on and on. He knows he can get away with it, because he's getting ready to retire."

"Well," Barry answered, "he apparently has or had a point to make. At least the switch at the time saved his life, because it put him under Reno, and as a result, DeRuddio later got his command."

"So is that it?" Deandra asked adding, "As if that's not enough."

"And Abejorro also nicknamed Sergeant Major Macroo Sergeant Major Boing-Boing," Barry said and broke out laughing. When the two women just looked at him curiously, he explained, "well, if Macroo, aka Boing-Boing, was Ogden, who couldn't control his mount…" and he burst into laughter again.

"Whatever," Deandra said as his laughing quieted down, still not getting the joke. "Was that all you found?"

"I think so," Barry started to say, but Daphne interrupted him.

"No," she contradicted. "You had this one last picture marked for some reason."

He leaned over her shoulder and said, "Oh, that's right. This doesn't mean anything to me, but I thought it might to you." He showed Deandra.

"This resembles George's brother-in-law," she said thoughtfully studying the picture.

"Which George?" Daphne asked.

"Desmodon," she answered, "but I see it's Lieutenant James Calhoun, our sister Margaret's husband who died in the last battle."

"I wondered," Barry said, "since I'd never met Desmodon's in-law. I knew you were friends. Isn't he enlisted in this life?"

Deandra sighed. "Yes, he is. A private becomes a general and an officer becomes enlisted—this is a lot to take in," she said quietly.

"We updated your list accordingly," Barry offered as he handed it to her:

CPT Albert Barnitz, seriously wounded at Washita, Mad Dog Hawkins

LT Benjamin Hodgson, popular officer, died with us, COL Shepherd

CPT Frederick Benteen, COL Mac Muschatt

LT James Calhoun, sister Margaret's husband, died in last battle, George Desmodon's current brother-in-law

Autie Custer, older brother, died next to me, COL George Desmodon

Boston Custer, younger brother, nicknamed Boss, died just downhill from us, Sergeant Leach's ex-husband

CPT Tom Custer, me

LT Charles DeRuddio, SFC Jose Abejorro

MAJ Joel Elliott, killed with company at Washita, LTC Leon Manx

Chaplain Thomas Holmes, chaplain who persuaded Custer to dedicate his life to Christ, possibly General Porker

Curley, Indian scout, Autie's favorite, sent away before battle and witnessed it, finance civilian and history buff

Bloody Knife, Indian scout sent to Reno, CPT Becky Roan

MAJ Reno, LTC Crockodell, both alcoholic

LT George Yates, close friend who died next to me, CWO Jellie

SGT John Ogden, killed in Indian village, SGM Macroo

Reporter, public relations officer

Private Alexander Stelle, born 1853 in Greece, cook, killed, General Raul Gato

General Terry, COL Jimmy Bass

CPT Thomas Weir, under Reno, disobeyed orders to try to rescue Custer but was turned back, MAJ Martin Fox

"Why don't we go out for lunch and not talk about this until we've finished eating?" Daphne suggested. Barry and Deandra agreed. She took the newly updated list with her, and they went to Rib City on Mill Plain, next door to the ice rink.

After they had finished their ribs, coleslaw, beans, corn on the cob, and applesauce, Barry finally started up the conversation. "Truthfully, at first I thought Deandra had either lost her mind or was lost in a world of fantasy. But once I saw that picture of young Autie, as he was called by his family, I had no doubts. Then after reading his biography, I learned Autie Custer's personality was a perfect match to George Desmodon's."

"Who knew?" Deandra injected.

"I never would have thought it myself," Barry went on, "but this certainly explains a lot. Custer had little respect for authority but great loyalty to individuals. He had what was known as 'the Custer Gang'—his inner circle of friends that he protected no matter what. He was very charismatic and known for his sense of humor—always playing pranks. In battle he was fearless. He presented himself to others as seriously valuing higher education, but in reality he was a poor student, lacked discipline, and was last in his class at West Point. His weakest subject was ethics."

"Go figure," Daphne commented. "That really does explain a lot. What else?"

"He valued his role as a big brother," Barry added. "How many times did I hear Desmodon refer to Chief Jellie as his little sister?"

"I thought maybe they had an affair," Deandra said. "She certainly seemed to chase after him."

"I know it looked that way, but I doubt she got her way with him," Barry corrected. "She seemed to me more like she was smitten with unrequited love. However, like Custer, he still takes care of his inner circle."

"How sad for her," Daphne commented.

"Well, no," Barry countered, "not really, since he's on his second wife."

"There must be a deeper meaning to all of this," Daphne suggested.

"Maybe so," Deandra said, "but I've got stuff I need to get done, and it's getting late, so I'm going to run." She picked up the list they had updated for her, got up from the booth, and left some money on the table to cover her meal. "Thanks for all of this. I mean that. Thanks for all your work and all this information. Bye." And she left the restaurant.

"Stay here," Daphne told Barry, as she scooted herself out of the booth and ran after her sister. Barry stayed as he was told, picked up Deandra's money, and took his credit card out of his wallet. When the waiter came over, he ordered another glass of ice tea for himself and one for Daphne.

Daphne caught up with Deandra as she was unlocking her truck. "There's something I found that I wanted to tell you," she said.

"I think you found plenty," Deandra reassured her.

"No, there's one more thing. I almost forgot. When General Sherman came up with the strategy of massacring the Native Americans—literally wiping them out—so the white settlers could take their land, he called it 'the final solution.' That's what Hitler and his henchmen called exterminating the Jews. I don't know if that's a term everyone who plots genocide uses, or if it's unique to Sherman and the Nazis. For all we know, Sherman could have reincarnated as a Nazi, or not. I doubt most of the German soldiers in World War II were cognizant of committing genocide or thought of themselves as mass murderers, and I'm sure most of the cavalrymen who died at the Washita and Little Big Horn battles never saw themselves that way. But I thought I should tell you. Like I said before, there has to be a deeper meaning to all of this."

"Ok," Deandra said soberly. She hugged her sister, climbed into the truck, and drove off.

Daphne found Barry still sitting in the booth waiting patiently. "Sorry about that," she apologized. Just then the waiter brought two fresh glasses of ice tea.

"No tu preocupes," he reassured her.

"Muchas gracias por el té frío," she thanked him, and he smiled. Then she continued, "As I was saying before, there must be a deeper meaning to all of this."

Chapter 40

Deep Roots

Barry and Daphne finished their tea and held hands as they walked outside the restaurant. Barry turned toward the west and asked her, "Do you like to fly?"

"You thinking of hitting Mad Dog up for a ride, or are we going to take a trip?" she asked.

"Just remembering some dreams I used to have when I was going through a rough patch in the Army," he said as if his mind was a million miles away. "I used to dream about this angel who would come to me in my sleep. We'd go flying without any man-made machines and make love out in space in the stars." After all this time together, he was the actually speaking out loud in public of their dreams together.

Daphne studied his face for moment before telling him, "I used to have those dreams. It helped me survive my marriage to Richard. They were so real. I didn't recognize you when I met you at the train station, but it didn't take long to figure it out. You were so kind to me."

"Why didn't you tell me?" he asked.

"Silly man," she responded. "I did, and then I waited for you to respond and tell me it was you. But you didn't. You honestly don't remember, do you?"

"No," he shook his head. "I would think I would remember something like that. My mind must have been on other things."

"Or you were thinking of taking me to the hospital and having me locked up in the psych ward—no wait, you did that anyway," she laughed.

"I love your laugh," he said, "and you are not crazy or mentally ill."

"Thanks for that," she answered. "Besides, I've gathered from comments you've made here and there that you knew and understood."

"Well, I'm telling you now," Barry continued. "You are the angel that came to me in my dreams, and then you came to me for real. Of course, you also left me, and I had to find you again, but you're here. Now, the question stands. Do you want to fly?"

"Sure," she answered, not knowing what she was getting herself into, but knowing she could trust this man.

"Come on then," he said, and still holding her hand, led her west across the parking lot and into the Mountain View Ice Arena. "It's as close to flying as you can get while keeping your feet on the ground," he explained.

"Or the water?" she corrected. They rented skates and went out onto the ice together. "You're right," she told him. "It's like flying."

*

While February 2010 dumped unusual amounts of snow on the southern and eastern United States, and while the Winter Olympics were unfolding in the other Vancouver in British Columbia, Canada, Vancouver, Washington, had more sunshine and spring-like weather than it had seen in February in decades. Barry went to work in the yard. Roses were pruned and mulched. The early blooming Daphnis bush bloomed right on schedule, filling the area around it with its heavenly fragrance. After pruning the overgrown photinias, he turned his sights on the front of the house.

Deandra had given him a natural gourd hummingbird house as a Christmas present. The seeds and insides of the gourd had been left inside for the use of the hummingbirds, who were to take up residence there. He sprayed the outside of it with a clear lacquer for protection from the weather as directed. Then he bought an iron post to hang it from, and planted the post in front of the house between the front window and the porch. He researched online which flowers attracted hummingbirds and was pleasantly surprised to find that most of the ones already growing in the yard were on the list.

"We need something in front of the front windows behind the roses that the hummingbirds will like," he told Daphne one night as they watched the Olympic Games on TV.

"Something other than those pretty white, little ball-type flowers that are there now?" she asked. "I kind of like those. I thought you did too."

"I did until they fell over onto the English Lady roses," he responded. "They were fine when we had nandinas there in front of them to keep them from falling over. Besides, they're proving to be very invasive. They're moving into the roses' space. I have to dig them out. I looked them up, by the way. They're a wildflower called field pussy toes. I think we have enough pussy toes inside. They must have come from the green belt behind the neighbors' houses where Posey, the possum, hangs out, but they belong in a field, and this isn't one."

"Yes, sir," Daphne saluted. "But I agree. Something with more color would look better there."

"Yes, ma'am," he returned the salute. "I think I'll plant a mix of delphiniums and lupines in their place about a foot and a half out from the house. They'll show up nicely behind the roses, and hummingbirds like them. I noticed the two lupines in the backyard have spawned about two dozen babies, and not all of them are coming up in flower beds. So I thought I'd rescue the strays and move them, but first I have to remove the errant field pussy toes. That's going to be quite a chore, since they've been growing there for who knows how many years."

"I saw the weather report," Daphne mentioned. "We only have two more days of sunshine, and then it's back to constant rain, like a normal winter."

"I've already started delphiniums from seeds in the planter in the garage," he said, "so I'd best start on getting those field pussy toes out tomorrow."

The next morning Daphne, Barry, and Purvati slept until after 10:00 AM. By the time Barry made it outside with his hoe, the sun had already passed overhead leaving his work area in the shade. He started hoeing and pulling up his targeted plants, only to discover the main root connecting them all was as big as a small tree trunk. He went back to the garage and fetched his shovel and hatchet. After chopping the main root out with his hatchet and pulling up smaller stalks and roots, the lawn debris bin, which he had already filled with photinia branches, was overflowing. He stopped and surveyed his work, while noticing Purvati watching from the window. He had only cleared about half the area. He decided the rest could keep until the following day when the lawn debris was due to be picked up. He went inside, washed his hands, and sat down in front of his computer.

"Now what?" Daphne asked. Usually after working in the yard, Barry liked to bathe and change clothes and then have something to eat.

"I have to write," he said.

"Finally," she sighed, glad to hear he was trying her suggestion.

"It's a novel," he explained. "You said I should write."

"Yes, I did," she agreed, "but that's quite an undertaking. A novel your first time out?"

"Well, now I have something to write about."

"You're going to write about flowers?" Daphne smiled.

315

"Science fiction," he corrected. "The title is *It Came From Inside the Earth.* I now have my villain."

"Worse than duckweed?"

"Duckweed's just ugly," he explained, "but this ... THIS is invasive. To THIS landscape cloth is no different from loose soil. We're lucky if THIS hasn't already attacked the foundation of the house and moved into the crawl space underneath."

"You're exaggerating," she commented.

He turned to look at her and asked, "Tap root the size of a tree trunk and you think I exaggerate? No, my dear, this is the stuff of science fiction."

"Or maybe a rainforest?" she laughed. "I'm glad you've found something to write about it. I'd better leave you alone." She went upstairs and left him undisturbed with his writing.

Barry chuckled as he typed:

Chapter One

Its roots ran deep. VERY deep. Slowly it rose up against the force of gravity, devouring the buried remains of other life forms along the way. Just before it broke through to the surface, it encountered something different.

"What is this?" the creature asked itself with pleasure. "This is very good. I shall spread out my roots under it and burst through it in many places all at once. Then I shall devour it, as I search for more sustenance." The creature did not know it had encountered what humans called landscape cloth, something the humans had created mistakenly thinking it would protect them from just this sort of invasion.

Meanwhile, at the Pentagon, the General concluded his briefing by instructing his staff, "Never allow your defense to be used against you by the enemy."

Chapter 41

Battle Ground

Daphne, Deandra, Barry, and Purvati were sitting around the living room one Saturday afternoon. Daphne had served decaf iced green tea for all, including Purvati, who proceeded to drink uninterrupted from Barry's glass rather than her own.

"I honestly don't know what I'm supposed to learn from this life," Deandra was saying, "or what I was supposed to learn from the past one, unless it's how to be a better soldier."

"Or how to be a better person?" Daphne suggested. "Isn't that what we're all supposed to learn?"

"Who knows?" Deandra responded.

"Personally," Daphne continued, "I think the idea is that we take on different roles, so we can learn from different perspectives. You were a man then. How did you treat women? Maybe you're a woman now to learn what it's like on the receiving end." She paused a moment before mentioning, "I looked up the date of the Little Big Horn battle in an online ephemeris. It took place just after the new moon."

"The battle was midday," Barry said. "What does the moon have to do with the battle?"

"Lady Rainbow had her back turned," Daphne said.

"What?" Deandra was confused.

"It was not long after a new moon," Daphne repeated, "and Lady Rainbow had turned her face away."

"I see what you're saying," Barry acknowledged. "She let her husband, the sun, have his vengeance."

"She was, after all," Daphne explained, "a Native American goddess."

Barry turned to Deandra, who clearly didn't understand what they were talking about. "There are myths and legends from the dream world," he told her, "that are real in the collective unconscious of humanity. Sometimes, to understand events that take place while we're awake, it helps to interpret them as dreams."

"Maybe," Daphne continued, "the soldiers in the battle back then were all nymphs, in the insect sense so to speak, and they came back together in this life to metamorphose into dragonflies. Maybe this lifetime is more important for them than the one before."

"It certainly is for me," Barry agreed. "Of course, I wasn't at the battle. And Mad Dog had his epiphany, or dragonfly moment, in this life. He certainly has his wings, as well as being sharp as a hawk—like his name. Becky Roan has learned in this life how to find the opportunity in each bad situation she encounters—unless that's a skill she brought with her from a past life. And she's as spirited as a horse—like her name. You may be right. The battle may have been a critical moment when the nymphs, or immature souls, were able to shed their bodies. And now they all have the opportunity in this life to grow their wings and fly."

Daphne turned to her sister and explained, "Dragonflies are symbolic avatars who have overcome adversity. They have the ability to heal the emotions, which are represented by the moon goddess, Lady Rainbow. When emotions heal, we see the light of the rainbow, the universal symbol of hope."

"Wow," Deandra said quietly. "That's a lot to think about. Let's hope you're right."

"Speaking of dreams," Barry added, "Before the battle, Sitting Bull had his famous dream that the soldiers would come to their camp and fall. Sitting Bull, like many people in harmony with the natural world, was clearly in touch with the collective unconscious."

Deandra added, "And both Autie's wife and I had premonitions of what was to happen; only we felt powerless to stop it."

"The power of choice is something we choose to allow or deny ourselves," Daphne said. "I speak from personal experience, both in this life and my past. The choice to take individual responsibility to choose is the most important choice we ever make. Until then, we project our issues onto others, when the real battle is inside ourselves."

Barry sat quietly for a moment and then said, "Far be it from me to side against our own troops, but in this case, I can't help but be glad the original inhabitants of the land actually won the battle."

"But these were people you know," Deandra protested, "including me. You can't possibly be glad about what happened. You might have even been there yourself if you'd drawn a different assignment."

"I seriously doubt that," he disagreed. "I wasn't there for a reason. Based on the feelings I had as a child, a young man, and even now, I seriously think I might have deserted if I been with the campaign. I know I've never liked soldiering, and I've always wanted to go back to being a farmer or gardener. Those soldiers we found in the books and online, the ones I might have been, all served their one enlistment and then returned to farming."

"Well, you might have been there, and I doubt you would have deserted," Deandra argued.

"No, I wasn't there for a reason," he insisted. "If there's a past life to this life, it makes sense that there's a past life to that life, and maybe there was even something in between. I just feel I wasn't meant to be taking part in killing innocent people, or maybe I chose not to. I was very lucky in this life with my military assignments, because if confronted with a hostile civilian, I'm sure I would choose to be killed rather than kill. According to Daphne's regression, I'd been murdered before, so it makes sense that the killing part of military duties would have been utterly distasteful to me—still is. And from experience in this life, I know that's true for most soldiers. But after thinking it over, I believe I had to go through the military experience again in this life to learn to appreciate the individuals I met—as well as to meet you, so I could meet Daphne after she'd resolved things with Richard. And I think I'm Latino in this life in this country to understand what it's like to be discriminated against, and to understand what it's like to feel other peoples' hatred and prejudice for just being different from them."

"Ok. Ok," Deandra acquiesced, "but I was there. Are you saying you're glad I died like that?"

"I'm saying you shouldn't have been there," he calmly explained. "I'm saying you should have known better than to blindly follow orders that you should have recognized as wrong. You do remember it was General Sherman who referred to killing all the Indians as a final solution? Where else in history have we heard that? You're ok with attacking civilians—men, women, and children—most of whom weren't armed—to force them off the land that had always belonged to their people? You're ok with that?"

"No, of course not," she admitted, "but it was a different time."

"Hitler lived in a different time. Time doesn't change some things," Daphne pointed out.

"What about today?" Barry went on. "You're ok with the 'collateral damage' of all the civilian lives destroyed by our own troops in Iraq and Afghanistan?"

"That's different," Deandra argued. "They attacked us first."

"WHAT?" Daphne and Barry exclaimed together.

"You know what I mean," Deandra said. "The terrorists attacked us first."

Daphne stood up and left the room.

"Iraqi civilians are not and have not been terrorists," Barry corrected quietly. "And yes, I know what you mean. It's what everyone hates about war. Innocent people get hurt. That's why war shouldn't be allowed, except when all other options have been exhausted—like in World War II and Desert Storm."

"Well, we couldn't just do nothing," Deandra insisted.

"Are you familiar with the town of Battle Ground?" Barry asked, referring to the little town just north of Vancouver.

She nodded. "Of course," she said. "As a matter of fact, that's where Elaine Delphin, the lady who did our past life regression, lives. COL Bass also lives there."

"What a coincidence," Barry continued, "or is there such a thing as a coincidence? Maybe this coincidence is pointing you in the direction of the lesson you're supposed to learn from all of this." He paused, but when she said nothing he continued, "Well, the town is named Battle Ground because it's where the US cavalry and the Native Americans met for a battle one day."

"Well, that's obvious," Deandra commented. "What's your point?"

"The point is that they met for the battle, but didn't fight," he explained.

"Let's not, and say we did?" Daphne asked as she came back into the room and sat down next to her husband. Purvati jumped up into her lap.

"Pretty much," he affirmed. "It was in 1855. Soldiers from Fort Vancouver were at war with the Yakima Indians. The post commander received orders from back east—that other Washington—to bring the Klickitat Indians to the fort to make sure they didn't rise up as well. If they wouldn't come straight to the fort, the orders for the commander were to kill them all. But the Klickitat Indians were peaceful, and he knew that. The Klickitat people weren't quite ready to come to the fort. Why would they be? It wasn't their way of living, and they weren't involved in the war with the Yakimas. So the Klickitats and the US troops from Fort Vancouver met on the battle ground. Only instead of having an unnecessary blood bath, they talked it over. The Klickitat chief told Captain Strong, the post commander, that they just weren't ready to come to the fort yet. The chief and Captain Strong agreed the Klickitats would come to Fort Vancouver when they were ready. Then the Klickitats went back to whatever they were doing, and Captain Strong took his men back to Fort Vancouver, without the Indians and without killing anyone.

"Think about it," Barry continued. "Long before Custer went west—even before the Civil War—a decade before the Washita Battle and two decades before the Battle of the Little Big Horn, a precedent was set of an Army officer treating Native Americans with respect. He did the right thing, and not only was no one killed, no one was hurt. And it happened here—out of Fort Vancouver. Maybe that's why these people came back together here. Maybe this was the lesson they were meant to learn."

"But did they?" Daphne asked.

"Who knows?" Barry answered with another question.

They were silent for a few minutes as Daphne and Deandra waited patiently for him to continue. Finally Deandra ran out of patience and prompted, "So, go on."

"That's it," he answered. "The soldiers went back to Fort Vancouver, and the Klickitat Indians went their own way. There was no battle. That's the point. There should be more Battle Grounds in the world and less actual battle grounds. It's a story worth repeating, but whoever heard of Battle Ground, Washington, unless you live in Southwest Washington? The point is that everyone has a choice. Custer was eager for a fight. He'd met with Plains Indians before and talked to them. That's why he had interpreters with him. He could have listened to Joel Elliott. He could just as easily have ridden into the village on the Washita River and talked to Chief Black Kettle. And he could have ridden into that big encampment on the Little Big Horn River and talked to Sitting Bull, but he was hell-bent on a blood bath both times. And both times he got what he wanted."

"And the soldiers that were under him—what were they supposed to do?" Deandra asked.

"Soldiers deserted from Custer's ranks all the time," Barry suggested. "That's documented. It's in all the books Daphne and I read. Benteen wasn't in any hurry to come to Custer's defense and get himself and his men massacred. Or maybe he wasn't as hell-bent on killing as your past-life brother. He made his own choice, and a lot of lives were spared because of it. Benteen was cautious, and people lived."

"That depends on how you look at it," Deandra objected. "He might have rescued Custer's men."

"That would have meant killing more Indians," Daphne pointed out. "Either way, if Benteen had reinforced Custer, more people would have died. I can see going to war to save people—like fighting the Nazis to end the Holocaust. Or in the Balkans or in Rwanda—genocide is never justified, even if you were there. You were on the wrong side."

"The military inquiry afterward cleared Captain Benteen of any wrongdoing," Barry added, "because he saved the lives of his own men as well as Major Reno's men. And if he had joined Custer, they all would have been slaughtered. They were simply outnumbered. Captain Thomas Weir tried to ride to Custer's rescue, but had to turn back to save his own men, and by doing so, didn't kill any more natives or get his own men killed."

"And what happened to the post commander who disobeyed orders with the Klickitat Indians?" Deandra asked.

"The white settlers made fun of him," Barry told her, "but I imagine he could live with humiliation, ridicule, and probably no more promotions a lot easier than with a lot of unnecessary deaths on both sides. His hands were clean—no blood on them. He lived with knowing he did the right thing. And like I said, he lived, so did his men, and so did the Klickitats he knew to be friendly."

"I never knew that about Battle Ground before," Daphne interjected. "I had always just assumed it was named for some battle. I like it a lot more now—a battle ground where there was no battle."

"¿Ellos nunca aprenden?" Barry asked.

"Huh?" Deandra grunted. "I hate it when he does that."

"Then learn," Daphne admonished her. She turned to Barry and said while laughing, "Will they never learn?"

Dragonfly Dreams

SOURCES

Special thanks to:

Dee Brown
Stephen E. Ambrose
Evan S. Connell
Brian W. Dippie
James Donovan
Adrian Finkelstein
Elizabeth Frakes
Louis Kraft
Kathryn Leedham
Paul Von Ward
Jerry D. Wert

Author's Note

This story and its characters, except for the 7th US Cavalry and the story of Battle Ground, Washington, are fiction.

Also by the Author

Ripples on the Surface, first collection of poetry, 1969-2006

Child of the Universe, second collection of poetry, 2006-2012

Deception Past, a unique novel of reincarnation and past life identity theft told through Tarot Cards, as those involved learn to resolve betrayal with forgiveness.

Five Flowers, historical reincarnation story of five Tudor queens who reincarnate as historical characters in Victorian London's Whitechapel district and again as historical characters in the US in the 1960s.

Please visit the author's website at www.reincarnationbooks.com

Please visit the author's page at www.IndependentAuthorNetwork.com

Please visit the publisher's page at www.KatmoranPublications.com

www.ingramcontent.com/pod-product-compliance
Lightning Source LLC
Chambersburg PA
CBHW070803180626
46818CB00001B/83